"*Fiona Veitch Smith has chosen a fascinating period as the background for her plot. The story opens with plenty of exciting action and the characters are lively and believable!*"

Ann Granger, author of the *Campbell & Carter* series

"*Poppy Denby, on the trail of a Fabergé egg containing dangerous secrets, encounters Russians (Red and White), theatrical types, and the police as she becomes embroiled in another adventure in 1920's London. A gripping and exciting read.*"

Elizabeth Flynn, author of *Game, Set and Murder*

THE
KILL FEE

POPPY DENBY
INVESTIGATES

BOOK 2

Fiona Veitch Smith

LION FICTION

Published by Lion Fiction
an imprint of
Lion Hudson plc
Wilkinson House, Jordan Hill Road
Oxford OX2 8DR, England
www.lionhudson.com/fiction

ISBN 978 1 78264 218 3
e-ISBN 978 1 78264 219 0

First edition 2016

A catalogue record for this book is available from the British Library

Printed and bound in the UK, August 2016, LH26

For my dad,
Dougie Veitch,
whose loyalty is an inspiration.

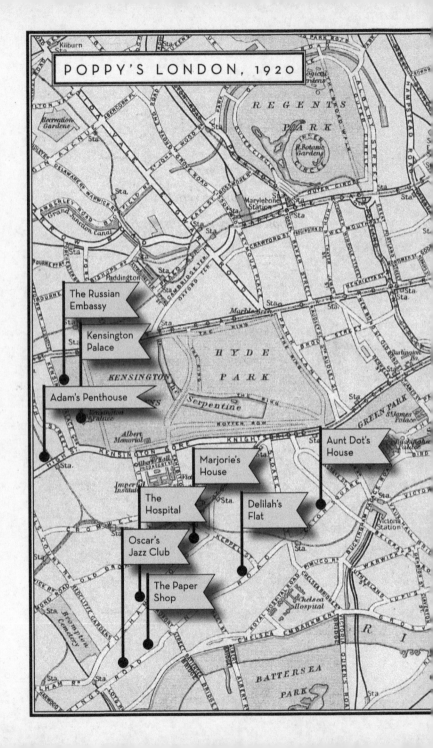

POPPY'S LONDON, 1920

The Russian Embassy

Kensington Palace

Adam's Penthouse

Aunt Dot's House

Marjorie's House

The Hospital

Delilah's Flat

Oscar's Jazz Club

The Paper Shop

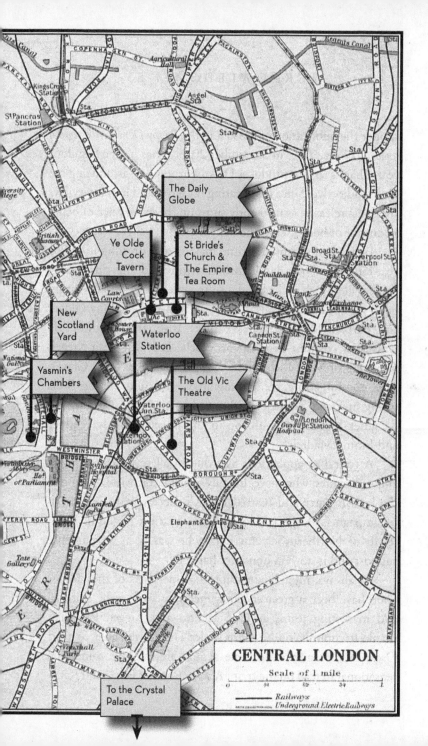

The Daily Globe

Ye Olde Cock Tavern

St Bride's Church & The Empire Tea Room

New Scotland Yard

Waterloo Station

Yasmin's Chambers

The Old Vic Theatre

CENTRAL LONDON

Scale of 1 mile

Railways
Underground Electric Railways

To the Crystal Palace

ACKNOWLEDGMENTS

Since the publication of the first in the *Poppy Denby Investigates* series, *The Jazz Files,* in September 2015, it has been a flapulous year. Thanks to film producer Dawn Furness for introducing me to that adjective. Since first hearing it I have used it in interviews and press releases, as it so aptly sums up the experience of being an author of books set in the flapper era.

I have had a flapulous time making and dressing in 1920s gear for photoshoots and launches, writing and directing a short book trailer – where I played a suffragette corpse – and visiting book groups and festivals. Thanks to film-makers Tony Glover and Barbara Keating, actress Amber Irish, the Northumbria University costume department, Noelle Pedersen from Kregel, photo editor Mark Richardson, and photographer Ruby Glover. Also not forgetting the photographic and film editing skills of my husband Rodney Smith and his beautiful assistant, our daughter Megan. Hats off too to jazz musicians Yussef Nimer and Jimmy Madrell.

A round of applause is also due to all my friends, family and colleagues who have happily spread the word, attended the launch party and toasted Poppy's success with very cheap "champagne". A special word of appreciation is due to Keith Jewitt of Northern Screenwriters, who has been an immense support and is now an honorary flapper.

As always, my fellow authors and members of the Lioness Club have been a great encouragement, as well as the editorial and marketing teams at Lion Fiction and Kregel. Particular thanks to commissioning editor Jessica Tinker, who takes to heart Oscar Wilde's advice that one should always have something sensational to read on the train. Also to Rhoda Hardie and Remy

Kinyanjui of Lion marketing, assistant editor Jess Scott, editor Julie Frederick (all the best with baby number three!) and the design team.

And finally, to all Poppy Denby's flapulous new fans: the readers and reviewers who have said they can't wait to read about her new adventures. Well, without further ado, here they are...

CHARACTERS

FICTIONAL CHARACTERS

Poppy Denby – arts and entertainment editor for *The Daily Globe*, London. Daughter of Methodist ministers from Morpeth, Northumberland. Our heroine.

Dot (Dotty/Dorothy) Denby – Poppy's aunt. A former leading lady of the West End stage; an infamous suffragette and influential benefactor of feminist and socialist causes. Crippled during a suffragette demonstration in 1910.

Miss Gertrude King – Dot's recently appointed assistant.

Grace Wilson – Dot's long-term companion and fellow suffragette, currently serving a two-year jail sentence.

Marjorie Reynolds – leading female MP, minister to the Home Office and friend of Aunt Dot.

Oscar Reynolds – son of Marjorie, owner of Oscar's Jazz Club.

Delilah Marconi – Poppy's best friend, actress at the Old Vic, daughter of deceased suffragette, jazz scene socialite and Bright Young Thing.

Victor Marconi – Delilah's father, wealthy hotelier from Malta, nephew of famous Guglielmo Marconi (Uncle Elmo).

Adam Lane – Delilah's current boyfriend, actor at the Old Vic.

Daniel Rokeby – photographer at *The Globe*, suitor of Poppy.

Rollo Rolandson – owner and chief editor at *The Globe*, American, virulent anti-prohibitionist, compulsive gambler, suffers from dwarfism.

Ivan Molanov – archivist at *The Globe*, White Russian emigré, close friend of Rollo.

Ike Garfield – political editor at *The Globe*, West Indian, new to staff.

Mavis Bradshaw – receptionist at *The Globe*, "mother" to staff.

Vicky Thompson – editorial assistant at *The Globe*, new to staff.

Lionel Saunders – arts and entertainment editor at *The Courier*; embittered rival of Poppy; ex-*Globe* journalist; snake in the grass.

Yasmin Reece-Lansdale – female solicitor hoping to become Britain's first female barrister, girlfriend of Rollo Rolandson. Daughter of British major general and Egyptian socialite.

Comrade Andrei Nogovski – security consultant at the Russian embassy; Bolshevik.

Vasili Safin – People's Commissar for Foreign Trade, Bolshevik; temporary stand-in for Russian ambassador to London, whose post is currently vacant due to civil war in Russia.

Princess Selena Romanova Yusopova – White Russian refugee, ageing actress, currently starring in *The Cherry Orchard* at the Old Vic; cousin of Tsar Nicholas II; friend of Dot Denby and Victor Marconi.

Detective Chief Inspector Jasper Martin – head of the detective division, Metropolitan Police.

Count Sergei Andreiovich – former emissary and military advisor of Tsar Nicholas II.

Countess Sofia Romanova Andreiovich – wife of Count Sergei.

Anya Andreiovich – their seven-year-old daughter; has a dachshund called Fritzie.

Nana Ruthie/Ruth Broadwood – English nanny to Anya.

Arthur Watts – barman at Oscar's Jazz Club.

The man in the bearskin coat – for me to know and you to find out.

HISTORICAL CHARACTERS

George Bernard Shaw – British playwright, founder of the Fabian Society and leading socialist.

Norman Veitch – founder of the People's Theatre in Newcastle upon Tyne, member of the Fabian Society, friend of George Bernard Shaw (distant relative of the author).

Lilian Baylis – founder of the Old Vic Theatre, the National Theatre, Ballet and Opera, champion of theatre for the people.

Constantin Stanislavski – Russian theatre director and one of the most influential drama theorists of the twentieth century.

Prince Felix Yusopov – assassin of Rasputin, son of wealthiest man in Russia, White Russian refugee.

Princess Irina Alexandrovna Yusopov – wife of Felix, cousin of Tsar Nicholas II and (in this book only) Princess Selena.

Empress Maria Federovna of Russia – Mother of Tsar Nicholas II, sister of Queen Alexandra of Great Britain, refugee. Originally Princess Dagmar of Denmark.

Queen Alexandra of Great Britain – Mother of King George V; former Danish princess.

Tsar Nicholas II and Tsarina Alexandra (Nicky and Alix) – last reigning Romanov monarchs murdered with their five children in 1918.

David Lloyd George – Prime Minister of Great Britain (1916–22); Chancellor of the Exchequer 1908–15.

WHITE OR RED?

In *The Kill Fee* you will hear a lot about White and Red Russians. To help avoid confusion, here is a short summary of the differences between them.

After the Russian Revolution of October 1917, the Russian Empire was thrust into a civil war that lasted three years. In a complex set of alliances, the warring parties were broadly divided into two groups: the Whites and the Reds. The Reds were supporters of the Bolshevik Revolution, hoping to restructure Russia along communist lines. The Whites were those opposed to it. There were many types of White Russians and associate allies, with different motivations and strategies, but they are embodied in this book by the aristocratic families and their supporters who wanted to retain the old imperial system under the rule of the tsar and his family.

However, the Whites were also split between the moderate reformers, who in the years up to October 1917 tried to get Tsar Nicholas II to implement constitutional and social reform to try to avoid wholesale revolution, and the tsarists, who resisted them. History tells us the reformers failed.

Before, during and after the civil war, tens of thousands of White Russians fled their motherland and ended up as refugees in other parts of the world. Some of them came to London – including members of the Romanov royal family – and it is against this backdrop that *The Kill Fee* is set.

Poppy's first encounter with the Russians is at the Russian embassy in October 1920. The embassy is staffed by an uneasy mix of Reds and Whites, as the outcome of the civil war has, as yet, been undecided. But as the war comes to a head in the Crimea – and in fact ends only a few weeks after the close of this story, on 7 November – the Reds are positioning themselves for a full takeover. The British government is also watching with interest to see which side will win.

If this were tennis, we'd be in the fourth set, with the Reds already having two sets marked on the scoreboard and leading 5:3. They are only a few serves away from match point…

CHAPTER 1

OCTOBER 1917, MOSCOW

Above the glow of gaslight a sprinkling of stars was beginning to appear. A man kicked at the golden leaves carpeting the pavement which would, by morning, have a dusting of frost. He pulled up the collar of his bearskin coat, wondering why, only that morning, he had felt overdressed. But he had been in Moscow long enough to know that things changed quickly in this city, very quickly, and a gentleman needed to be prepared for whatever the winds of change might blow his way. His fist tightened on his bone-handled cane and he allowed his thumb to rub against the secret clasp that would unsheathe the rapier closeted within.

His head swivelled towards a sudden blast coming from somewhere near the Kremlin, startling the swans that were accompanying him along the banks of the Moskva. He waited for the plume of smoke to rise on the skyline – he didn't wait long.

So Lenin's getting his way then, he thought bitterly, still smarting that the performance of *The Golden Cockerel* that he had been waiting months to see – and for which he had paid an emperor's ransom – had been cancelled so the little red gnome could address the joint Moscow Soviets in the grand Bolshoi auditorium.

Another bang and then another came from the direction of Red Square. The man clutched his cane and quickened his steps. If news from St Petersburg was anything to go by, he would not have long to pay a visit to the aristocratic family who lived in this neighbourhood before they too might be forced to flee with the other White Russian evacuees.

As he rounded the corner into the wealthy boulevard his heart sank. It was barricaded top and bottom, and manned by drunken soldiers in tattered uniforms, brandishing an assortment of weapons from rifles to pitchforks. Whether loyal to the Reds or the Whites he didn't wait to see, but ducked into a hedge before he was spotted. The sharp twigs clawed at his face and hands as he forced his way through the dense foliage; he emerged into a quiet garden, bathed in light spewing from a dozen windows. This was 67 Ulitsa Ostozhenka, home to a family with Romanov connections and, if the intelligence he'd received was correct, keeper of one of the prized Fabergé eggs.

The royal family had been under house arrest on the outskirts of St Petersburg since February, and their previous residence – the Winter Palace – was now guarded by forces loyal to the Duma, the new Russian parliament. Aides to the tsar and tsarina had managed to smuggle out the cream of the palace's treasures and had placed them with various "treasure-keepers". Rumours abounded that the family at 67 Ulitsa Ostozhenka was one of them. It was a dangerous task and the man in the bearskin coat feared for their safety.

Two years had passed since he had last been at the house and he wondered if the French window overlooking the herb patch still had the loose catch. It did. With a little jiggle he silently slipped into the conservatory.

Very little had changed. There were the same wicker chairs and pot plants; the teak card table with the découpage embellishment; the silver tea-trolley and white-tiled floor. As expected, at this time of night, the room was empty. The family, if at home, should be in the upstairs drawing room having their post-supper coffee; but he couldn't guarantee it, not with the children, and the servants of course could be anywhere. That is, if they had not already deserted the family. The Bolsheviks promised the world to the serving classes and he had heard tales of once faithful butlers and parlour maids turning on their employers. Loyalty could not be guaranteed and if the soldiers on the boulevard decided to break in and loot the place, they might not meet much resistance.

He ran his thumb over the secret catch on his cane and slipped from the conservatory into the hall. Down the hall, to his relief, he could see the front door was securely bolted shut – but there were other doors to the residence. He stopped to listen: murmurings from downstairs, but nothing above. He mounted the stairs.

His destination was the first-floor library where, he had been told, the family had secretly installed a new safe since his last visit two years before. Apparently not even the servants knew its whereabouts, but since his informant was the very person who had installed the safe, the man in the bearskin coat was confident he could find it.

He heard peals of laughter from downstairs: he paused, his hand on the doorknob. When he was certain the voices were not coming any closer, he slipped into the library and closed the door behind him. The room was dark, the bookcases hulking giants around him. Unwilling to turn up a gaslight he edged his way around the room until he reached the window. He pulled back the drapes enough to allow a shaft of moonlight into the library – until the bookcases softened to their normal form. He could now see enough to differentiate furniture from wall and through the silver glow located the Rembrandt he had been looking for. He paused again, listening, but all he could hear was his own breathing and the tick-tock of the library clock.

He unhooked the painting and propped it up on a nearby sofa, pausing a moment to ensure the masterpiece did not slip onto the floor. Then he turned his attention to the safe. It was a 1915 York Safe & Lock. He had broken into many security devices in his career and for a man of his considerable talent, the York was not the most complicated. It did not take him long to crack the code.

Inside were an assortment of jewels, bundles of cash and – the object of his search – an ornately jewelled egg, given to Queen Maria Federovna by her husband Alexander II. He pulled out an oilskin from his inside coat pocket and wrapped the egg in it, before inserting it back into his pocket. He perused the rest of the loot and selected a ruby and diamond ring and a pair of emerald teardrop earrings which, if he wasn't mistaken, had once belonged to the unfortunate Marie Antoinette. He put these in a velvet pouch which he tucked into his trouser pocket. He left the cash; it would be worthless in a few months if the revolutionaries had their way and the economy continued into free-fall. He closed the safe, spun the lock and then lifted the Rembrandt from its bed on the sofa. For a moment he considered slitting it out of its frame, but resisted. The missing painting would draw attention to the fact that the safe had been tampered with, and besides, his business was in jewels, not fine art.

A smash of glass and raucous laughter from somewhere downstairs made him stiffen: it was closer than before. The man shut the safe, replaced the Rembrandt and hurried to the library door to listen. The laughter grew louder; someone was in the hall below him. He checked his mind's eye to see if he had closed the French door properly – he had. Good. Confident he hadn't been noticed, he had no reason to doubt he could slip out as quietly as he had come in. Yet something stopped him.

Why was there no sound from the upper levels? No murmurs from the drawing room, no music, no crying of children and no sound of a bath being run above? Was it only the servants at home? Why then had they not turned out the upstairs lights? Since the February Revolution – and of course before that, during the war with Germany – fuel had been scarce. Even the wealthiest families were forced to economize. And he knew that this family – the Andreioviches – was no exception.

He remembered the dinner party he had attended here in 1915, where the lady of the house proudly announced to her guests that there would only be four courses rather than five as part of their "war effort" and apologized for the smaller portions of poultry and beef. Everyone had applauded her for her loyalty to Mother Russia and said they were praying for the safe return of her husband. The gentleman of the house – Sergei Andreiovich – was a special military emissary of the tsar, his whereabouts unknown.

Although the woman's husband was gone, she wasn't alone. Her unmarried brother lived with her, and her two boys would be in their mid-teens now. There was also her mother-in-law, a doughty cousin of the empress Maria Federovna, and of course little Anya. The man in the bearskin coat smiled as he remembered the girl's face when he had given her the present he had brought to the party: a dachshund puppy. The mother had frowned her disapproval, but relented when the little poppet begged her to let "Fritzie" stay.

But where were they all? The man knew he should leave, but his concern for the family prevented him. Another smash from below and a roar of laughter brought him to attention.

It sounded as if someone was in the cellar smashing bottles – accidentally or on purpose he had no idea. With his thumb on the secret catch, he worked his way down the landing, peering around doors, searching for the family. On the first floor was the library – from where he had just come – the music room and family drawing room; on the second the bedrooms, bathrooms and nursery. The ground floor held the more formal reception rooms and conservatory, and downstairs the servants' quarters, kitchen, scullery and cellar.

The library, he knew, was clear. He peered into the music room – that too was unoccupied. Only the drawing room remained to be checked. As he pushed open one of the double doors with his cane his stomach rose to his throat. Splayed across the Persian carpet, divans and coffee table were the bodies of half a dozen people. He rushed in and knelt beside a woman in a yellow silk gown – the Countess Andreiovich, her throat slit, eyes staring. He scanned the other bodies for signs of life: there were none. Two teenage boys – their chests blasted open by a shotgun – an older man, probably their uncle, with gunshot wounds to the stomach and head, and an old lady whose throat had been hacked rather than slit. The sixth body was of a man in his sixties wearing livery – a loyal servant, a butler perhaps – with defensive wounds on his arms and a bullet through his temple.

The man heard two people shouting: "Time to clear out; get what you can!" and then, "What should we do with them?" He could not fathom the reply. He flicked the catch on his cane and released the rapier, stepping over the bodies as he approached the door. He looked to left and right: the landing was still clear. Dare he try to go down the stairs? The voices sounded as though they were in the stairwell. Perhaps the window might be a better option. But as he walked back across the room his ears pricked at a sudden whimper and a stifled yap. It was coming from the sideboard. He checked over his shoulder, then approached the source of the noise. He listened again: silence. But he hadn't imagined it. And there was, after all, one body missing.

He carefully opened the door, whispering as soothingly as he could, "It's all right; don't be frightened," and to his immense relief was met by the large brown eyes of a little girl and the growl of a small dog.

"Shhh, Fritzie, shhh."

"Anya, don't be frightened. We need to get out of here. Come." He reached out his arms and the dog snapped at him. He pulled back.

"Where's Mama?"

"Mama can't come right now. But we need to get out."

"Are the bad men coming?"

"Yes, the bad men are coming. But I'll help you. Come."

He reached out again and grabbed the dog by the collar; it twisted around to bite him but couldn't reach. Then he held out his hand and took Anya's. Thankfully she came without any trouble. But as she stood up, her eyes widened in horror. She screamed. The man dropped the dog and slapped his hand over her mouth. Fritzie launched himself at him, baring his canines. He kicked him aside. Anya struggled against him. Then he heard someone running down the landing. Holding the child under one arm and clasping his rapier with the other, he turned to face the door.

But instead of a gang of Bolsheviks there was an old lady, her face battered and bleeding.

"Nana Ruthie!"

"Put down that child," said the woman in English.

Although he understood her, the man did not comply but pointed his rapier at the old woman's chest. She didn't flinch.

"Put her down," she repeated in Russian.

"The killers will be back. We have to go," he replied in the same language.

"And how do I know you are not one of them?"

"You don't. But you must trust me. I know the child's name is Anya and I know the dog was a gift from a dinner party guest."

"Everyone knows that."

"Oh, for heaven's sake!" He lowered the rapier and grabbed the old woman by the arm. "Take the girl and follow me."

The English nanny stood her ground for a moment, then complied. Anya ran to her and threw her face into the old woman's skirts. The dog jumped up, and the old woman caught him in one arm.

The man strode over to the doors, pulled them shut, then slotted a fire iron through the ornate double handles. It wouldn't hold for long, but it was the best he could do. Then he went to the window and slashed at the drapes with his sword. He opened the balcony doors and dragged the shredded curtain out onto the small patio, then called the old woman and the child to him. They came, Anya snivelling and sobbing as they manoeuvred their way around the dead bodies.

"I'll lower you down. Can you hold on to the child?"

The woman straightened her spine and stared at him with the condescension and forthrightness of her race: "I am an Englishwoman. I shall do whatever is necessary."

He didn't answer, but tied the curtain cord around her waist. She gave quick instructions to Anya to hold on to Fritzie and then picked them up. With a nod, she was ready.

The double doors rattled. A voice boomed: "Who's in there? Open up now!" Then a loud thump as someone threw his weight against the shaky barricade. More shouts and the sound of a crowd gathering.

The man hefted Nana Ruthie and the child onto the balustrade, braced his feet against the wall, and lowered them down. The doors to the room buckled, but he did not falter. Thankfully there was only one floor to descend and the cord slackened. As he looked down to see the old woman, child and dog safely on the lawn, the doors flew open. He gestured for the pair below to run, then turned, rapier in hand, and prayed that God would be merciful to his wretched, thieving soul.

CHAPTER 2

WEDNESDAY 17 OCTOBER 1920, LONDON

Poppy Denby shuffled along the row with apologies to the gentlemen who rose to allow her to pass. Why Ike couldn't have chosen a seat on the edge of the press pit, she didn't know. But as she sat on the reserved seat next to the West Indian political editor, she realized he had positioned them perfectly: three rows back and slap-bang in the middle. The man addressing the press briefing would not have to crane his neck up, down, left or right to see them. But why should she be surprised? Rollo would not have given Ike Garfield the most senior and influential position at *The Globe* – apart from his own job of managing editor – if he wasn't more than capable.

Poppy chastised herself for second-guessing the man and wondered if she still harboured a little jealousy that he had been given the job she had coveted. She who had only been a journalist five months! She smiled at her colleague – who was wearing a tartan bow-tie and tweed jacket – and whispered: "Sorry I'm late. Drama at the theatre."

Ike chuckled. "Don't worry. These diplomatic types never start on time. Now how diplomatic is that?" Poppy laughed with him as she took off her coat and hung it on her chair. As she settled into her seat she felt something poke the small of her back. She turned around to see what it was and came eyeball to eyeball with the arts and entertainment editor of *The Globe*'s rival newspaper, *The London Courier*.

The ferret like face of Lionel Saunders sneered at her and she noticed the toe of his highly polished shoe was poking into the back of her chair.

"Excuse me, Mr Saunders; if you don't mind…"

He curled back his lip to meet his moustache and said: "Why ever would I mind, Miss Denby?" and poked his toe further into the back of the chair.

Poppy was just about to put him in his place when Ike turned around and growled: "Back off, Saunders."

Saunders removed his foot. Poppy pursed her lips and bit back the "Thanks for the help but I had that in hand" retort, took a calming breath and retrieved her notebook and pencil from her satchel.

This was Poppy's first visit to the Russian embassy and as arts and entertainment editor she had been surprised when Rollo instructed her to accompany Ike. Politics wasn't her patch, but apparently the press call had included an invitation to "cultural journalists" too. So the plush room, decorated with the calibre of art usually found in the National Gallery, was filled with journalists from a dozen newspapers eager to hear what combination of political and cultural news the Bolshies were going to serve up today. On the bus over from the West End Poppy had done some background reading and learned that the embassy was officially being run by representatives of the Russian Provisional Government – a coalition of Whites and Reds – but in reality the Whites, loyal to the monarchy, were being forced out. And if news from the Crimea of the White army's imminent defeat was anything to go by, the embassy would soon be entirely Bolshevik.

The hubbub in the room subsided as a man with a black

goatee and slicked-back grey hair entered and took his place behind the lectern. He opened a file and placed some notes before him. Then, as if he were not keeping nigh on thirty journalists from his host country's media waiting, he picked up the notes, shuffled them and then repositioned them again, patting them this way and that until he was finally satisfied. A murmur rose in the room and one or two men coughed their dissatisfaction.

The man with the goatee did not respond but reached into his jacket pocket and removed a pair of wire-rimmed spectacles that he carefully placed on his nose. Then he perused his notes.

"Well I never. Outrageous manners!" Poppy recognized Lionel's voice.

"Get on with it!" someone else shouted.

Then one or two of the men started to get up to leave.

"I have summoned you here today…" The speaker's Russian accent was pronounced, but his English fluent. He did not look up and he did not issue a word of apology.

The men who were standing continued to stand with their arms folded, but did not leave.

"I have summoned you here today…"

"Summoned? *Summoned?*" It was Lionel again.

"To issue a statement from my government in Moscow – the Central Committee – that the planned exhibition of stolen Russian art at the Crystal Palace is an insult to the Russian people."

"What do you intend to do about it?" Lionel called out.

"The Central Committee has requested the British government declare the exhibition illegal."

"But the exhibition is being held at the behest of the royal family. The government will not interfere." Lionel again.

This time the man with the goatee looked up. "They can

and they must – if they want the new Russian government to sign the Anglo-Soviet trade agreement."

"And you have told Mr Lloyd George this?" Lionel's partner at *The Courier* enquired.

"I have. No doubt 10 Downing Street will be issuing a statement about this soon."

"And the palace?" Ike piped up.

"I have no interest in what the monarchists have to say. This is an issue between the people of Russia and the people of Great Britain, and their elected representatives."

"Correct me if I'm wrong, but the Soviet government has not been elected. You have taken over by force!" It was a voice from the back of the room. Poppy couldn't see who it was, but she thought it was the political editor from *The Times.*

"You are indeed wrong. The Central Committee has been elected by representatives of the people of Russia. And – as you say here in England – it's a jolly lot more democratic than the autocracy we had before."

A volley of questions was then fired from the floor and the man with the goatee answered them.

"Is that Vasili Safin?" Poppy whispered to Ike. "The People's Commissar for Foreign Trade?"

"It is," Ike whispered back, then rose to his feet. His basso profundo voice soon drowned out his fellow journos. "So, Mr Safin, to sum up: you have brought us here today to put pressure on our government to shut down the Crystal Palace exhibition. Is that correct?"

"I have brought you here today to –"

"But what if the exhibition goes ahead? What if the prime minister is unable – or unwilling – to convince the palace to withdraw their support? Will that put the Trade Agreement in jeopardy?"

Safin removed his spectacles and pointed them at Ike. "Those are your words, Mr Garfield, not mine, but if that's the line *The Globe* wants to take..." He gave a humourless smile. "Now, if there are no further questions I will –"

"I have a question," Poppy interjected, her voice loud, clear and high. If Safin was surprised, he didn't show it.

"Yes, the lady at the front."

"Poppy Denby, arts and entertainment editor at *The Daily Globe*." The snort from Lionel did not throw her, nor did the lone wolf-whistle from the back of the room. She continued: "If, in your view, the worst case scenario happens and the British government is unable or unwilling to shut down this exhibition, what contingency plans have you in place to reclaim your national treasures?"

"Well, I –"

"Because that is the point of all this, isn't it? These jewels and works of art are in the hands of private individuals – loyal to the late tsar and his family – and you believe they should be returned to Russia. Is that not correct, Mr Safin?"

Safin straightened up and nodded. "Indeed that is correct, Miss Denby. They are our treasures and we will reclaim them."

"And what lengths are you prepared to go to to get them?" All heckling stopped. Every man in the room looked at the young blonde woman in the red dress.

Safin smiled. Poppy didn't know if it was out of respect or condescension. She didn't really care as long as he answered her question.

"Let's just say we will not rest until they are finally returned to the people of Russia. We are indeed hopeful that the British government will co-operate with us on this. However, if they prove to be too weak to stand up to an old woman and her spineless son, we will demand the strictest security is implemented at the exhibition until such a time as we can negotiate their repatriation. And to that end may I introduce Comrade Andrei Nogovski, chief of security."

A tall, dark-haired man in his mid-thirties, dressed in a slate-grey suit, white shirt and black tie, emerged from the wings as if in a theatrical performance. He shook hands with Safin and they exchanged a few words in Russian. Then Nogovski turned to the assembled journalists and announced in perfect, Oxbridge English: "The Commissar has other business to attend to, so from now on – in relation to the exhibition – I will be your point of contact at the embassy." He raised both hands as if bestowing a spiritual blessing, and as he did, two secretarial assistants emerged, each carrying a pile of dossiers. They passed them out to the journalists.

"You are now being handed an overview of the security plan which will come into play if – as Miss Denby has pointed out – your government fails to stop this insult to the people of Russia from taking place." His coal-black eyes found Poppy's in the crowd and he continued speaking while holding her gaze, explaining the highlights of the plan. Poppy felt a red flush rising from her neck to her face but refused to look away. Andrei Nogovski was probably the most handsome man she had ever seen. He radiated a self-assurance that was both disarming and alluring. She found herself wondering if he were married and then stopped herself immediately. What was she thinking? She and *Globe* photographer Daniel Rokeby were just beginning to get their relationship off the ground after a number of false starts. Yes, life in the romance department was more than rosy, so if…

"Poppy, are you all right?" Ike interrupted her thoughts.

Poppy turned from Nogovski to her colleague and gave a wan smile. "Yes, of course. I was just wondering why the

Russians have gone to the trouble of having this security dossier printed for us if they are convinced they can influence Lloyd George to stop the exhibition."

"Exactly the question I will ask the prime minister when I see him later today."

"You have an interview with the prime minister?"

The West Indian man grinned broadly, showing a set of teeth to rival Stonehenge. "Indeed I do. Marjorie Reynolds set it up."

"What does she want in return?"

Ike laughed. "Ah, so I gather you've met the fearsome lady MP."

"She's a friend of my aunt."

"And why doesn't that surprise me?"

Poppy was just about to reply when a voice from the front announced: "I see Miss Denby and Mr Garfield are already bored with proceedings, so there's no need to drag things out. If you have any questions, contact my office; the number's in the dossier."

And with that Comrade Nogovski breezed out of the briefing room without a backward glance, leaving Poppy to nurse a curious sense of abandonment and disappointment. It must have shown on her face because Ike looked at her quizzically as he helped her into her coat. "Are you sure you're all right, Poppy?"

"Yes!" she said, in a voice far more blithe than she felt. "Can you give me a lift back to the office?"

"Of course. Not mobile yet?"

Poppy groaned. "My aunt's insurance company have declared I'm not yet competent to drive."

"Again?"

"Again."

Ike laughed and offered Poppy his arm. "So Miss Poppy Denby is not a natural at everything she turns her hand to."

"Of course not! Who says that?"

"Everyone," said Ike in a conspiratorial whisper and then cast a sideways glance at Lionel Saunders, who glowered back at his rivals. "Well, nearly everyone."

CHAPTER 3

Ike dropped Poppy off at the bottom of Fleet Street before heading to Downing Street. *The Daily Globe* was one of half a dozen newspapers that had offices on the street made famous by Samuel Pepys and Charles Dickens. It was also famous for its pubs, and as she passed, Poppy glanced into Ye Olde Cock Tavern – favourite watering hole of *The Globe* staff – to see if anyone was having a late lunch. In the five months since she had started work at the newspaper she had discovered that her boss – Rollo Rolandson – used the tavern as his second office. As the daughter of Methodist ministers Poppy had initially found this rather scandalous but soon learned that despite her boss's dubious intake of alcohol he still ran a tight ship and was one of the most astute editors on Fleet Street. It was Rollo she had to thank for giving her the job in the first place when most editors were still wary of women in the newsroom. But Rollo was a man used to social stigma and the last person to judge a book by its cover – however pretty.

True to form, there was Rollo. The red-haired man was perched on a bar stool, his dwarfish legs dangling two feet off the ground. Next to him sat a morose-looking Ivan Molanov, archivist at *The Globe*. Ivan was Rollo's physical opposite: a giant of a man with a great shaggy beard and a melancholic spirit. He was obviously in one of his moods today as Rollo was giving him a sympathetic pat on the shoulder. The editor looked up and saw Poppy in the doorway.

"Ah, Miz Denby. Sneaking in for a tipple?"

Poppy laughed at the long-standing joke between the two

of them. Poppy did drink, but only the odd glass of champagne or chardonnay on social occasions – and only in the evenings. However, when Rollo had heard that her previous employment had been at a Methodist mission, he had nearly not hired her. A native of New York, he had threatened to turn in his American passport when his mother country adopted Prohibition the previous year.

"Are you all right, Ivan?" she asked, noting that the Russian man was looking even more depressed than usual.

He sighed like a bear going into hibernation and shook his head. "I have just had some news, Poppy. From back home. It ees not good."

"Your family?"

"Yes. The rumours I heard were false. They have not been found."

"I'm sorry, Ivan. I will pray for you."

"Thank you, Poppy." He tried to smile but failed. Ivan's whole family had disappeared in 1917 while they were trying to make their way out of Russia to join him in England. The last Ivan heard they had left Moscow, but after that they were never seen again. Ever since news of the murder of the tsar and his family, no one was surprised to hear that yet another White Russian family had been killed. Yet as long as there were no bodies to prove it, Ivan still held on to a glimmer of hope.

Poor man, thought Poppy and made a mental note to light a candle for him at St Bride's Church on the way home.

"Did you want to speak to me, Poppy?" asked Rollo.

"Just to fill you in on the press conference at the –"

Rollo raised an eyebrow in warning.

"You know: the thing with Ike. He's off to see the PM and asked me to brief you."

"Righto. I'll be up in half an hour."

Poppy took that as a dismissal and left the two old friends to their pints.

She crossed the road and skipped up the granite steps – flanked by two marble globes – and into the black and white mosaic foyer. The foyer and reception area of *The Globe* was designed in the most up-to-date art deco style – with Egyptian motifs and statuettes – to set it apart from the more formal Edwardian and Victorian décor of the paper's rivals. "We're a modern paper with modern ideas," Rollo had explained on her first day on the job. "We blend the fun of jazz journalism with the social activism of the old pamphleteers. The Establishment may call us a tabloid, Miz Denby, but let me tell you something – this is the future. Are you with us?"

Poppy, who was only too grateful to be offered a job – any job – had said she was. She smiled as she remembered that day, but, as she always did, acknowledged that it was someone else's tragedy that had given her the break she needed. In fact, it was in this very foyer, on her first day on the job, that the death of one of the paper's most senior journalists had started her out on an investigation that shook the House of Lords and made the male journalists of Fleet Street take her seriously.

"Hello, Poppy!"

"Hello, Mavis!" Poppy waved at the motherly receptionist, Mavis Bradshaw, who was helping a man with three cigars sticking out of his breast pocket word a birth announcement.

"Are you sure it's spelt B-*i*-r-t-h-a?" asked Mavis.

Poppy smiled and left her to it.

She knew she probably should take the stairs up to the fourth floor, but guiltily headed towards the lift instead. It had been a long day already; she was tired…

"Hold the lift!"

Just as she was pulling the concertina gate closed a young

man in his late twenties with brown hair and twinkling grey eyes stuck out his hand and pushed it back. He had a camera box slung over one shoulder.

"Going up?" asked Poppy.

"I'm going wherever you're going," grinned *The Globe* photographer, Daniel Rokeby.

Poppy pushed the buttons for the correct floors: the art and photography department was on the second, editorial on the fourth. As the door closed on them, Daniel leaned in and planted a kiss on Poppy's lips.

"Mr Rokeby! We're at work."

Daniel gave her his wide-eyed puppy look. "Well, work is the only place I get to see you these days."

Poppy reached out her hand and took his. "I'm sorry. I know I've been busy – but after the White Russian Exhibition this weekend things should ease up."

"This weekend?" Daniel slapped the palm of his hand to his forehead. "Oh no! I forgot. I told Maggie you would be coming round."

Poppy inhaled sharply. "You *told* her?"

Daniel ran his hand through his hair, making him look like an overgrown schoolboy.

"Well, I didn't *tell* her. You can't tell Maggie anything. But… oh, you won't believe it – she actually asked when she could finally meet you, and I said this weekend."

"She – well – that's a turnaround."

"Isn't it just?"

"So what happened to the 'I'll never have that woman in my house' routine?"

"I don't know. I was too scared to ask. I'm just grateful she's finally coming around to accepting you."

"Well, it's only taken her four months…"

The lift shuddered to a halt on the second floor. Daniel didn't get out. After a while it shuddered to life again and continued its ascent. He put his arm around Poppy and drew her close. Even though she was breaking her own rules about no lovey-dovey stuff at work, she leaned her head against his chest. She could hear his heartbeat drumming steadily. She sighed and allowed the warmth of his body to seep into hers.

"So do you think she's finally accepting that it's time you moved on?" she mumbled.

Daniel caressed her shoulder with his thumb. "I don't think *I've* ever been the problem. It's the children. When Lydia died Maggie became more than their aunt. Her fiancé died during the war –"

"Oh, I never knew that," said Poppy, feeling ashamed that she had thought so poorly of Daniel's sister ever since the older woman had conspired to let her believe that he was married and simply dallying with her.

"Yes. It nearly broke her. Then when Lydia caught the flu…"

His thumb stopped its circular motion. Poppy waited for him to continue. He didn't.

"Look, Daniel, maybe Maggie's right. Maybe it is too soon. Maybe –"

He took both her shoulders in his hands, and looked intently into her eyes. "No, Poppy, it's not too soon. I'm ready to move on. With you. The children will love you, I know they will, and Maggie… well, Maggie will just have to get used to it." He grinned, the shadows of his past retreating again. Poppy's heart settled.

"Then I'd love to meet them. But can we take a rain check until next weekend? It's just going to be too hectic with the exhibition and everything."

"Of course. I'll tell Maggie I got the dates mixed up."

"Just tell her I'm working."

"Hmmm, that might not be the best thing…"

"And why's that?"

Before Daniel could answer, the lift stopped on the fourth floor. The door opened to reveal a young woman of around eighteen, with russet hair and green eyes.

"Miss Denby! Mr Rokeby! You coming out?"

"I am," said Poppy. "Mr Rokeby is going back down."

"Yes, I am. Need a hand there?"

Vicky Thompson, editorial assistant at *The Globe*, grinned widely. "Yes, sir, Mr Rokeby, that'd be grand."

Poppy held open the concertina gate while Vicky and Daniel manoeuvred a trolley-full of files into the lift.

"Got anything interesting there?" asked Poppy.

"You mean do I have any Jazz Files?" The girl winked. "Well, as a matter of fact I do. Mr Rolandson was just putting one together."

"Oh?" asked Poppy, intrigued to find out what latest gossip had been circulating Fleet Street. "Who is it?"

The girl looked mildly panicked as she tried to remember the name. "Oh, I know it, Miss Denby, I know I do. It's… oh, something Russian…"

Poppy laughed. "Why doesn't that surprise me?" She turned to Daniel. "Should we wager for it? A cup of coffee to the winner?"

Daniel grinned. "All right, you first."

Poppy took out her notebook and ran her finger down the page of notes she'd taken earlier at the Russian embassy. "I bet it's Andrei Nogovski," she said with a note of triumph, and stuck out her hand to take the file from Vicky.

Vicky quickly looked at the name on the file then shook her head. "Sorry, Miss Denby, that's wrong."

Poppy bit her lip. "Oh."

"Mr Rokeby?"

Daniel leaned against the lift door, stopping it from closing, straightened his tie and cleared his throat. "I bet it's Princess Selena Romanova Yusopova."

"It is!"

Vicky held up the file for both to see. "Well done, Mr Rokeby. Miss Denby, I think you owe him a cup of coffee."

"Hmmm, how did you know that?" she asked, raising an eyebrow at Daniel.

He patted his camera box. "I've just photographed her."

"At the Old Vic?"

"Actually, at your aunt's house, followed by the most splendid cream tea."

"So you won't be needing that coffee then."

Daniel grinned and looked as if he were just about to kiss her. Vicky giggled and Daniel pulled back. "Let's take a rain check, shall we?" He pulled the concertina gate closed, enclosing him and Vicky in the lift. Then, as he pulled the door, he asked: "Who's Andrei Nogovski?"

Poppy inexplicably felt herself blush. She tried to keep her voice nonchalant. "Just some bloke I met at the Russian embassy."

"White or Red?" asked Daniel. But before Poppy could answer, the door closed and the lift went down.

CHAPTER 4

Poppy let herself in to 137 King's Road, Chelsea. It was seven o'clock and she had stopped off on the way back from the office to have her hair trimmed. These fashionable bobs might look fabulous, but they needed regular upkeep. She also had a new frock in her bag, which had been on sale at Milady's. Thank heavens for her clothing allowance from *The Globe*! She would never have been able to keep up with her best friend Delilah Marconi without it. When Poppy first arrived in London, Delilah had resorted to clothing her from the wardrobe department at the Old Vic Theatre. Poppy never aspired to be the fashion aficionado that her actress friend was, but she did need to stay up to date to fit in with the jazz set with whom she now regularly rubbed shoulders in her job as arts and entertainment editor.

Number 137 King's Road, however, was far from "up to date". Her aunt, Dot Denby, had had her fashion hey-day in 1905 as a leading lady on the West End stage, and the stuffy Edwardian décor had not moved on since. Stuffy, though, was not a word that could be used of the lady of the house herself, whose most recent career had been as a suffragette and socialist activist. A bubbly giggle emanated from the townhouse dining room, buoyed by a hubbub of dinner party conversation. Poppy remembered that her aunt was entertaining this evening. Drat, she should have skipped the hairdresser and come home earlier. Her aunt had invited her, but as she had not been sure what time she would get home from work, she had been non-committal on her timeline; so non-committal that it had slipped her mind entirely.

"Join us when you can, then, darling!" had been her aunt's reply.

Poppy ran upstairs and got changed.

Ten minutes later she came down the stairs in her new emerald-green flapper dress and black boa. It might have been a bit risqué for a dinner party at home, but Poppy would be meeting Delilah later at Oscar's and she didn't want to get changed twice. Her aunt wouldn't mind, Poppy knew; her guests, though, might have other views...

Poppy pushed open the dining room door and heard a Mozart concerto playing on the gramophone. The table was set for eight people, and a further two – wearing a maid's and butler's uniform respectively – hovered around the periphery. Aunt Dot – who sat at the top of the table in a Chippendale chair, her wicker wheelchair pushed into the corner – was typical of the socialist-leaning upper middle classes of her era. She did not employ a full domestic staff but rather had a cleaning lady and cook during the day and hired in a butler and maid from an agency for special social occasions. And if it were not for the fact that she was paraplegic, that would have been all the help she needed or desired.

Unfortunately, Dot's long-term companion, Grace Wilson, was currently serving a prison term in Holloway, so her daily needs were now met by a Miss King, whose Christian name Poppy had yet to learn. Miss King, who sat primly to Aunt Dot's left, had once been governess to the prime minister's daughter, but now the child was grown, she was in need of new employment. Aunt Dot's old friend the MP Marjorie Reynolds – sitting this evening at the foot of the table – had recommended Miss King as a "stop-gap" until dear Grace came home. The fact that Grace was serving time for blackmail and perverting the course of justice was not enough for her faithful suffragette friends to turn their backs on her. And as Aunt Dot kept reminding Poppy, the former accountant would only serve half of her two-year sentence if she kept her nose clean.

"Poppy darling!"

Aunt Dot raised her glass and toasted Poppy as she came into the room. Two of the gentlemen at the table stood up to greet her; the third remained seated but acknowledged her presence with a nod.

Poppy went around the table and kissed her aunt on her highly rouged cheek. Aunt Dot laughed like a schoolgirl. "I didn't think you'd make it, darling. I thought you were chasing a deadline."

"Not this evening, Aunt Dot. Although I will be on Sunday night."

"My niece works at *The Globe*, you know. One of the new breed of women journalists."

"And doing a splendid job she is too," said Marjorie Reynolds, raising her glass to meet Dot's.

"Hello, Mrs Reynolds."

"Hello, Poppy. I believe you were at the Russian embassy this afternoon."

"Yes, I was. Did Ike tell you?"

"Indeed he did. In fact I –"

"Marjorie, darling, if you don't mind, you and Poppy can talk shop in a minute. But first I need to introduce her to everyone else."

"Of course, Dot. Forgive my rudeness."

"Not at all. The new minister to the Home Office can be forgiven anything. Did you hear of Marjorie's new appointment, Poppy?"

"I did. Congratulations, Mrs Reynolds."

"Thank you, Poppy. Perhaps we can arrange an interview sometime. But not tonight – your aunt's right, we shouldn't talk shop." Then she nodded towards Aunt Dot. "She's all yours, Dot."

Dot clapped her plump hands. "Splendid. Have you eaten, Poppy?"

Poppy shook her head.

Aunt Dot raised her finger towards the butler. "Is there anything left, Mr Brown?"

"There is, Miss Denby. If the other Miss Denby would like to take a seat…"

The butler pulled out the eighth chair for her and then served her. Poppy was seated between two gentlemen, both of whom nodded politely. She knew one, but not the other.

"Well, as you might have guessed, this is my niece Poppy. My brother's daughter. She's from Morpeth, Norman. Near your neck of the woods. Poppy, this is Norman Veitch from Newcastle. He runs a fabulous little theatre there called The People."

"It's the People's Theatre," said a kindly looking dark-haired gentleman in his forties. "Did you ever attend, Miss Denby? It's on Percy Street."

"Unfortunately not, Mr Veitch. My parents did not approve of the theatre."

Aunt Dot giggled again. "Oh, if they could see you now."

Poppy's heart sank. That was the last thing she would want. She had not seen her parents since she moved to London five months ago under the auspices of being her aunt's companion. Her letters to them had been scant on details and loose on truth. They knew about her job on the newspaper, but not all that it entailed. She wasn't quite sure how to put all that in a letter. So she was waiting until her next visit home to give them the full picture of her new life in London. She was not looking forward to it.

"Norman is a good friend of George's, isn't he, George?"

"Yes, he is. He and his brother Colin have been good enough to stage some of my plays," a gruff, bearded man in his sixties commented in a Dublin brogue.

"And this is George Bernard Shaw, the playwright. No doubt you'll be covering some of his work in years to come, Poppy."

"It would be my honour," said Poppy, trying to keep her voice casual. So this was the famous George Bernard Shaw. Poppy had read all about him in *The Globe*'s archives: socialist, supporter of women's rights, vegetarian, teetotaller, atheist... apart from his views on alcohol, Poppy's parents would have been appalled.

"George and I met at a Fabian Society meeting. Must have been nigh on twelve years ago now, George, wasn't it?" asked Dot.

"Thirteen."

"Yes, it was Gloria who introduced us. Were you there, Victor?"

"Unfortunately, I was not," said a suave, olive-skinned gentleman. "Lovely to see you, Poppy."

"You too, Mr Marconi. I'm going out with Delilah later. Did she tell you?"

Victor Marconi, the Maltese hotel magnate, laughed. "She might have, but I so easily lose track of my daughter's comings and goings."

"Have you met her new beau?" probed Aunt Dot.

Victor's eyebrows met in the middle. "I have."

"And do you approve?"

"The jury's still out – as you English say."

This brought a laugh from everyone at the table – including the gruff Bernard Shaw.

"Is he from a good family?" asked an exquisitely bejewelled fake-blonde, middle-aged woman sitting to the right of Victor Marconi, with the slightest hint of a Russian accent. She leaned in to him, her cleavage plump and white, offsetting a spectacular sapphire and diamond necklace.

"I have yet to meet his family, *principessa*."

Shaw laughed coldly. "If by good, Selena, you mean 'did his parents not send him off to boarding school or hire a nanny to make sure they hardly ever saw him?', then I think he might be so low down the social ladder that you would never approve of them. And what's it got to do with you anyway, unless you're planning on trapping poor Victor here?"

Princess Selena Romanova Yusopova – second cousin of Tsar Nicholas II, White Russian refugee and current guest star at the Old Vic Theatre – bit her lip and teared up.

Victor cleared his throat. "There's no need for that, Shaw."

"Yes, George, there's no need for that. Let's have a pleasant evening, shall we?"

"Come now, Dot, surely this was exactly what you were expecting. You know my views on class and yet you invite me to a dinner party with a distant cousin of a dead despot."

Selena's tears were becoming sobs. "Dear Nicky w-was not a despot. A-and there is no evidence that he – he's d-dead. It never seemed to bother you before that he was – how did you phrase it? – a *despot*, and you were all too happy to take his money for the Paris run of your show, and – and –" Selena choked up, unable to continue.

Victor patted her hand. "I think you should apologize, Shaw."

"Apologize? Whatever for?"

Aunt Dot's pretty pink nails tapped the damask tablecloth in mild annoyance. "For being rude, George. Selena is not responsible for her dear cousin's politics – and she is here as my guest. On the other hand, though, I too do not agree with the way the Russian aristocrats ruled –"

Selena gasped.

"I'm sorry, Selena, but it's true. You know my views on these things. And in George's defence, politics has always been on the agenda at this house. So forgive him too, my dear; he is just doing what he normally does when he is here."

"You mean not being a gentleman!"

"Well, yes –"

"Then you must excuse me." Selena stood up, nearly toppling her chair. Victor and Norman Veitch stood too. Shaw remained seated.

"Let me escort you, *principessa*." Victor looked at Dot. "Perhaps we can take sherry in the drawing room." Dot nodded her approval.

Selena simpered, raising a snort of derision from the Irish playwright.

Victor shot him a poisonous glare, then took the Russian princess by the arm and escorted her out of the room.

The butler, his face deadpan, opened then closed the door behind them.

"Oh dear, George, look what you've done!"

"Yes, George, that was very cruel, even for you," tutted Marjorie.

"Poor form, old man," contributed Norman.

Miss King and Poppy said nothing. What Miss King was thinking was difficult to tell – trained as she was to appear as wallpaper – but Poppy's mind raced. An interview with George Bernard Shaw on his views on Russian politics as a side-piece to her spread on Stanislavski's *Cherry Orchard*? She would run it by Rollo in the morning…

Shaw raised his hands in mock defeat. "All right, all right, I'm sorry. But really, Dot, what else did you expect?"

Dot sighed. "You're a rogue, George. An Irish rogue."

Shaw laughed. "Guilty as charged. Shall we have the pudding now?"

Everyone but Miss King laughed.

"Mr Brown. What delights has cook prepared for us?" Dot asked.

"Fruit salad, meringue and whipped cream, I believe, ma'am."

Aunt Dot rubbed her hands together in delight. "Oooooh, my favourite!" Then she frowned slightly. "We should keep some aside for Selena and Victor. Will you see to that, please, Mr Brown?"

"Of course, Miss Denby," said the butler and retreated from the room.

"Poor Selena," sighed Aunt Dot. "I didn't even have a chance to introduce her to you properly, Poppy. She's going to be staying here for a few weeks."

"She's *what*?" Shaw could not disguise his incredulity.

"Oh, do shut up, George," said Marjorie in her best House of Commons debating voice.

"Thank you, Marjorie," said Dot. "She has nowhere else to go, dear. Victor brought her over from Malta with barely more than the clothes on her back."

"Did she come on the *Marlborough* with the other Romanovs?" asked Poppy, who had been keeping abreast of developments in the Russian Revolution.

"She did. And Constantin – the dear man – has cast her to replace Bernice Boardman." She turned to Norman to explain. "The poor woman was suffering from a bout of vertigo and fell into the orchestra pit. Broke her collarbone!"

"Lucky for Stanislavski Selena was in town. She's from the Bolshoi, isn't she?" asked Norman.

"You've heard of her?" said Dot.

Norman grinned. "Newcastle does get the papers, Miss Denby. Things might have gone downhill since you left, but…"

"Oh, you flatter me, Mr Veitch. Do go on."

But Poppy wanted to know more about the Russian actress. "Excuse me, Mr Veitch, but is it normal for a Russian royal to be an actress?"

"A lesser royal, dear," said Marjorie. "But we mustn't judge. In her own way, Selena is quite a progressive woman. Emmeline met her when she was visiting Lenin. Although the two of them had a blazing row, apparently…"

"Did they really?" asked Dot, her eyes dancing at the thought of some gossip she had not yet heard.

"Oh yes, you should ask her about it when she returns from New York."

Norman looked puzzled.

"Emmeline Pankhurst," said Poppy, helpfully. "The president of the Women's Political and Suffrage Union."

"Of course," said Norman, folding his napkin into four then placing it in front of his dessert spoon. Shaw, on the other hand, was folding his napkin into a fan.

"Are we boring you, George, dear?"

"Not at all, Dot. I love hearing about the filthy rich and their filthy lives."

"Oh, I don't think she's that rich…"

"Didn't you see her necklace?"

"Of course, but perhaps that's all she managed to get out when she was fleeing for her life. A woman needs a little nest egg…"

"A Fabergé nest egg?" Poppy chirped.

Everyone looked at her. She blushed, but continued. "Apparently they had Rembrandts and Fabergés in their luggage, and jewels sewn into their underwear! There's going to be an exhibition this weekend. I think they're hoping to raise money to fund their exile…"

"Humph," said Marjorie.

"Humph, what?" asked Dot.

"That exhibition is causing a diplomatic furore. Isn't it, Poppy?"

"It is. The Russians – the Red Russians, that is – are furious. They are threatening to cancel trade agreements and everything."

"The PM was just saying today…"

But Marjorie's elucidation of the goings on at the House of Commons was interrupted by the arrival of the pudding.

Aunt Dot clapped her hands. "Tuck in, everyone!"

And they did.

CHAPTER 5

King's Road, Chelsea, was a hard place to get parked at night. At the top, opposite where Poppy and Aunt Dot lived, stood the Electric Cinema Theatre, which was currently showing *Pollyanna*, starring Mary Pickford; and at the bottom, two blocks from Delilah's flat, was the hottest club in town: Oscar's Jazz Club, which was showcasing the Original Dixieland Jazz Band on their London tour.

Poppy usually dropped by Delilah's flat on the way to the club, but this evening, due to the near-forgotten dinner party, she had rung her friend to tell her she would meet her inside – which was taking quite a while, as the queue for the club stretched halfway around the block. Delilah, a personal friend of the owner, Oscar Reynolds (son of Marjorie, whom Poppy had just dined with), always managed to jump the queue; but Poppy did not have the gumption to do so on her own. So it was nearly ten by the time Poppy got through the double brass doors.

She took a moment to soak in the warmth of the place and rub some life back into her freezing hands.

"Poppy! Let me take your coat. Surely you didn't stand in the queue, did you?"

It was Oscar, the host, in white tie and tails and wearing a gold monocle on one eye. Poppy passed him her black fur-trim overcoat, but kept her boa – partly to keep her warm, and partly to cover the alarmingly low plunging neckline that hadn't seemed quite as low when she tried it on in the shop.

"I did, Oscar; it was no trouble."

"But it's freezing outside!"

Poppy couldn't argue with that.

"Well, don't do it again. You know I consider you one of my best guests and I can't have you dying of hypothermia, now, can I? Your aunt would never forgive me. Or Mrs Wilson. How is she, by the way?"

"I haven't seen her for a few months, but Aunt Dot says she's well enough."

"As well as one could be in prison, I assume." Oscar shuddered. "Terrible business. Who would have thought she hid such secrets? Your aunt is a saint to forgive her."

"She and Grace are devoted to one another. And she did what she did out of misplaced loyalty." Poppy didn't want to talk about her aunt's incarcerated companion any more. Unlike Aunt Dot, she wasn't quite as forgiving of the former suffragette. Grace's actions had hurt a lot of people, not least Delilah. So she changed the subject. "Your mother's looking well. I just saw her at dinner."

"One of your aunt's soirees! Who else was there?"

Poppy went on to list the guests of the dinner party and, knowing Oscar delighted in vicarious gossip, told how George Bernard Shaw had just insulted the tsar of Russia's cousin. True to form, he was titillated, but pretended to be outraged. "Poor Selena! I was hoping she'd drop by tonight – she's quite a draw card – but apparently she won't be seen dead in the same room as…"

Oscar's words were drowned by a hubbub at the door. Two doormen stood shoulder to shoulder, trying to prevent the entrance of someone. Oscar immediately went over to help. Poppy decided to leave them to it and go into the club. As she did, she caught a glimpse of a dark-haired man in black suit and overcoat: Comrade Andrei Nogovski, the security consultant from the Russian embassy. Oscar and the two doormen blocked his entrance.

"He jumped the queue, governor!" explained one of the doormen.

Nogovski, struggling to contain his temper, reached into his coat pocket and retrieved some papers. He showed them to Oscar and whispered quietly to him. Oscar stood bolt upright and stepped back, ushering Nogovski in. The Russian shrugged off the restraining hand of one of the doormen and strode in, sweeping past Poppy and into the club. Oscar followed. Poppy caught his arm as he passed. "Is everything all right, Oscar?"

"Yes, yes, Poppy, don't worry." Then he cocked an ear and smiled, tuning in to the opening bars of a Dixieland ragtime number. "Ah, I see you're just in time. Get in; it'll be a showstopper!" He patted Poppy's hand, then hurried after Nogovski, who was heading downstairs to the basement, which housed Oscar's office and the club's wine cellar.

Poppy made a mental note to follow up Nogovski's visit with Oscar when he was less harassed. Whatever it was, it seemed official, and there might just be a story in it. She would mention it to Rollo and Ike Garfield in the morning.

For now, Poppy wanted nothing more than to relax and enjoy herself. She pushed open the swinging doors into the club proper to find two hundred people all turned towards the bandstand. As expected, the members of the Original Dixieland Jazz Band, all the way from New Orleans, lit up the stage; to Poppy's surprise they were joined by an olive-skinned elfin beauty, the up-and-coming West End actress Delilah Marconi. Delilah, in a Japanese-inspired outfit with wide, kimono-style sleeves and Asian eye make-up, stood in front of the microphone. She began to sing "Swanee" in a throaty alto that wooed every man – and nearly every woman – in the room.

As she brought the song to a close, Delilah threw herself off the stage into the arms of four men, who carried her around the room like a bird in flight. Had she prearranged it, Poppy wondered, or just jumped and hoped for the best?

After a full circuit of the room the men put Delilah down. The moment her feet touched the floor she began to dance – and the men followed suit. She started by doing the Black Bottom, a freestyle solo dance, then took a partner and broke into the foxtrot. Poppy clapped with delight. Delilah had taught her the basics of the foxtrot in her flat, but Poppy had never seen it performed at full speed.

Suddenly, a man was beside her: Adam Lane, Delilah's boyfriend. "Are you on your own, Poppy? No Daniel?"

"Unfortunately he's working. Trying to get some snaps of Mary Pickford, I think." And then, turning her attention to Delilah, "She's marvellous, isn't she?"

"She is indeed. I shall reclaim her in a moment. But until then, would you do me the honour?"

Poppy laughed. "You want to take a chance with my two left feet?"

"Oh, you're not that bad," he grinned, then swept her into his arms. "Just follow me!"

Poppy did her best not to stand on her partner's toes, and eventually, after two or three "sorries", she started to get the hang of it, and she and Adam were trotting around the room with the best of them. They intersected with Delilah and her partner; before she knew it, she and the young actress were swapped around and she found herself in the arms of another man, too exhilarated to notice who it was.

As the music came to an uproarious end she collapsed into the nearest chair.

Her partner stood over her and presented her boa, draped

over his forearms. She took it with thanks, covering her cleavage as quickly as she could. The man laughed, and she noticed he was wearing heavy eye make-up, like a woman.

"Here you all are!" Delilah skipped over to the table and plopped into the chair next to Poppy, closely followed by Adam. Then she called out across the dance floor to the bar: "Champers!" The barman waved to her.

Poppy looked up at the man and smiled. "Thank you for the dance, but I don't believe we've been formally introduced, have we?"

"Felix Yusopov," said the man with a bow and only the slightest hint of a Russian accent.

The name rang a bell, but Poppy could not quite place it. "Well, thank you for the dance, Mr Yusopov."

"That's *Prince* Yusopov," said a beautiful, dark-haired woman with a French accent. The woman placed her hand on the prince's forearm in such a way that Poppy could not help but notice an ostentatious wedding ring.

Suddenly realizing who the couple were, Poppy stood up and reached out her hand to the woman, hoping to defuse the situation. "I'm Poppy Denby. And I assume you are Princess Irina."

The woman nodded stiffly.

"Well, thank you for lending me your husband; although, as you could see, we were just swept along in the dance."

The man patted his wife's hand and smiled at Poppy. "Don't worry, Miss Denby; Irina knows she can trust me. However, with such a beautiful woman as yourself, I might be tempted..."

His wife glared at him.

Poppy cringed inwardly. Was he deliberately trying to cause bad feeling between her and the princess?

"Oh Felix, do stop it!" said Delilah. "Will you and Irina join us for champagne?"

Felix looked as if he were about to sit when his wife whispered something in his ear. He looked across the room and visibly paled. "Thank you, Delilah, but I think Irina and I should get back to Kensington Palace. The empress, I believe, wants to see me."

"Oh, the empress! Will she be at the exhibition on Saturday?"

"I believe she will," said the prince, still casting nervous looks across the room.

Poppy followed his gaze and saw, just behind the bar – near where she knew there was a private staff staircase to the basement – the dark figure of Andrei Nogovski. Their eyes met and she felt the same discomfort she had earlier in the day at the embassy. She forced herself to pull away as the Yusopovs bid a hasty retreat towards the club doors.

"What's put a bee in their bonnet?" asked Adam.

"Oh, who knows! More champagne for us." Delilah giggled as a waiter arrived with a bottle and five glasses. "Do you know who that is, Poppy?"

"I do indeed," she answered, nodding her thanks to Adam as he passed her a glass of bubbly.

"So what does it feel like to dance in the arms of an assassin?"

Adam nearly choked on his own champagne. "Whatever are you talking about, Delilah?"

"Don't you keep up with the news, darling? Felix Yusopov is one of the murderers of that dreadful Rasputin."

"Good heavens! Is that true, Poppy?"

"It is. Apparently he's never disputed it."

"Never," confirmed Delilah. "Rather proud of it, in fact. Which is one of the reasons why his cousin, Princess Selena, can't stand the sight of the man. Selena was very close to Tsarina Alexandra, and she was devastated when Rasputin died. At least that's what she's told my father…"

Poppy suddenly remembered what George Bernard Shaw had said earlier in the evening about Selena trying to catch Victor Marconi, and asked Delilah if it were true.

Delilah pouted. "Unfortunately, yes. She's been practically throwing herself at him since she and the other Romanov refugees landed in Malta. The top dogs all stayed at the governor's residence and the rest of them were put up in hotels. My father is still trying to figure out who to send the bill to."

"Surely the richest royal family in the world has enough to pay their hotel bill?" commented Adam.

"You would think so," Delilah agreed, "but they claim that everything was confiscated by the Bolsheviks."

"Everything apart from an entire exhibition hall of jewels and paintings," added Poppy.

"What are they hoping to achieve from the exhibition?" asked Adam.

"Well, there's a hefty entrance fee. I think they're trying to raise some cash."

"To pay their hotel bill?"

"To fund their exile. However long that will be..." Poppy looked across at the bar and noticed Andrei Nogovski in close conversation with Oscar. The Russian had an interrogative air; Oscar looked cowed. Then Poppy noticed another man approach the bar and stand beside Nogovski, causing poor Oscar to quake even more. If she were not mistaken, it was Vasili Safin, the trade commissar and interim ambassador. Whatever was going on? Poppy made a mental note to look into it as soon as she could. She turned to her companions and said: "Perhaps it's just to goad the Bolsheviks. They consider all the art the property of the Russian people."

"But isn't it privately owned by the Romanovs?"

"They're nationalizing everything. Don't you know?"

"Well, I had heard…"

"Oh, do stop talking politics, you two. It's deathly boring. Come, let's toast."

Adam and Poppy raised their glasses.

Delilah rolled her eyes melodramatically. "To dancing with assassins!"

Poppy and Adam laughed. "To dancing with assassins!"

CHAPTER 6

JULY 1918, YEKATERINBURG, RUSSIA

Ruth Broadwood had never been as cold in her sixty years on God's good earth as she had been during the winter of 1917/18. Even her first years back in England after the Boer War, when the change of climate from Africa to Northern Europe had frozen her to the core, were nothing compared to the seven months she had endured after fleeing from the house on Ulitsa Ostozhenka. But thank God it was now summer. Or at least what approximated to summer in the Russian Urals.

The pot of gruel on the campfire was coming to the boil. She used a stick to lift it off, and called out to her young charge: "Breakfast's ready!" Little Anya and the dog, Fritzie, were playing a game of tag between the abandoned railway carriages – one of which had been their home for the last week. But, thought Nana Ruthie, if the information she had overheard yesterday was correct, tonight they might finally sleep in a proper bed in a proper house. She shivered in pleasure at the thought.

She called again to Anya. The scamp pretended to ignore her, although the dog cocked its ears and looked up. Not a day had passed since she and the young aristocratic Russian girl had become refugees that she did not thank God for sparing the little dachshund. He kept the child occupied during the day and warm at night, and his chocolate-coloured fur soaked up her tears as she sobbed for her mama and brothers.

Nana Ruthie bent low and patted her thighs. "Fritzie! Come here, boy! Fritzie!"

The dog yapped and ran to her; then Anya, realizing her playmate had abandoned her, reluctantly followed.

"What's for breakfast, Nana?"

"Porridge."

The girl wrinkled her nose but didn't comment any further. In the seven months since she'd been wrenched out of her comfortable life in Moscow she had learned that complaining that she only liked porridge with cream and honey – and sometimes a sprinkle of almonds – did not advance her cause. In the first few weeks they had stayed with sympathetic middle-class friends of Nana Ruthie, and the food was close to what she was used to. But as word spread that a British nanny had murdered a White Russian family, stolen a royal Fabergé egg and kidnapped the heir to the fortune, it became increasingly dangerous to the friends – and the fugitives – for them to stay in Moscow.

So Nana decided it was best to head east, using the Trans-Siberian railway. Her intention was to get to the end of the line in Vladivostok on the Sea of Japan – which she heard was now held by the Allied navies – and then make her way to England. The western route through Europe was never an option, as the Great War still raged. From what Nana Ruthie had previously read in the papers, central Asia was largely untouched by the conflict and therefore the safer option. But it was months ago that she had read her last newspaper, and for all she knew the Mongols, Afghans and Chinese were now also blasting each other to pieces at the behest of their colonial lords.

She ladled a serving of watery oats into a tin cup and gave it to Anya, then poured some onto a tin plate and put it down for Fritzie. The little dog gave a yelp of delight, his stumpy tail wagging an accompaniment as he lapped at his food. Anya said a polite "thank you" – in French, as that was today's lesson – and sipped at the gruel.

Nana sipped at hers and contemplated the day ahead. Today, as soon as their breakfast and lessons were finished, they would go into town to see if they could find the house she had heard about yesterday. Nana had been lining up in the bread queue at the grain depot on the outskirts of Yekaterinburg – a mining city on the Trans-Siberian railway and as far east as she and Anya had managed to travel – when she overheard two women gossiping about the goings-on at a house at the bottom of their street.

"But I thought they were in Tobolsk."

"Apparently they were brought here in April. It's been top secret."

"Then how do you know?"

"My Yakov saw one of them when he was delivering coal. The youngest girl: Anastasia."

"Is he sure it was her?"

The older woman crossed one finger over another: "He swears by St Katerina."

The younger woman sketched a cross in the air. "Do you think they're all there?"

"Yakov said he heard the grand duchess call out to some others and then they came around the corner. All of them. He couldn't believe his eyes."

The women were distracted for a moment by the sound of heavy artillery in the distance, and drew their shawls closer in defence.

The Czechoslovaks are coming, thought Nana Ruthie. She and Anya had met some of them at their last stop along the railway when their train was halted and searched. The Bolshevik guards on board were outnumbered and removed, then replaced by Czechs, who accompanied the train to within fifteen miles of Yekaterinburg. There they joined another of their battalions and some White Russians moving in on the Red Russian stronghold. The Czechs barely noticed the old woman, child and dog, just two of the hundreds of thousands of displaced people in the middle of the civil war, and allowed them to alight unmolested. Nana and Anya waited a few days to see if another train would be allowed through – none were, so they decided to walk to Yekaterinburg along the track. It took them two days. Then, footsore and hungry, they slipped through the Bolshevik lines as easily as they had through the Czechs' and set up camp in the train yard to await the next locomotive east.

The bread line shuffled forward and Nana and Anya moved with it. The two women resumed their conversation:

"The Ipatiev House, you say?"

"Yes, the whole royal family, some servants and supporters – he thinks he saw Princess Selena too. You know, the famous actress?"

"Under guard?"

"Of course – just like the rest of them – but probably just for her protection. They'd never hurt them, would they?"

In the train yard Nana Ruthie slipped a hand under her shawl and into her bodice. She clutched a key hanging from a chain. If what those women had said was correct, and Princess Selena was with the royal family right here in Yekaterinburg, then she and Anya might have a way out of there. But she needed to see for herself.

"Hurry up and finish your porridge," she instructed her young charge. "Today we are going on an adventure."

CHAPTER 7

Poppy locked the front door of the Chelsea townhouse and hurried to the waiting taxi. Well, as much as one could hurry in four-inch heels and an ankle-length, figure-hugging white satin evening gown with fox-fur stole. If it weren't for the knee-high slit, she would have been hopping to the motor car like a white rabbit. Rollo, waiting to greet her, let out a long, slow whistle, took her hand and kissed it. "You look swell, Miz Denby, positively swell."

"Why, thank you, Mr Rolandson." Poppy flushed in pride and embarrassment as she stepped into the cab, ducking to ensure the ostrich feather in her headdress didn't get bent. The little editor jumped up beside her, closed the door, and instructed the driver: "To the Crystal Palace!"

Poppy greeted the other passengers, two of whom she knew, one she didn't: Ike Garfield and his wife Doreen, and a striking woman in her early forties with a black Eton crop and Middle Eastern features.

"May I introduce Miz Yasmin Reece-Lansdale? Yasmin, this is Poppy Denby, the new reporter I've been telling you about."

Yasmin reached out a long, elegant, gloved hand to Poppy. "The woman who finally put Melvyn Dorchester in his place. A pleasure to make your acquaintance."

"The pleasure's all mine," smiled Poppy as she shook the woman's hand. So this was the infamous Yasmin Reece-Lansdale. Poppy had heard that Rollo had been stepping out with her – or "dating", as the Americans called it – for the last three months. The daughter of a British major general and an Egyptian socialite, Miss Reece-Lansdale was not just an exquisite face. Behind those striking black eyes was a legal mind second to none. Trained as a solicitor, she was one of a handful of women hoping to be appointed to the Bar in the wake of the recent Sex Disqualification (Removal) Act. Having attended the various trials that emerged from her sensational journalistic debut, Poppy thought Yasmin would make an excellent barrister: intelligent, forceful and shrewd; but she would need every ounce of ability – and then some – to make her mark in the all-male Crown Court.

"Mind you, he should have got more than seven years for attempted murder."

"I couldn't agree more, Miss Reece-Lansdale."

"Please, call me Yasmin."

"Yasmin. And as for his son…"

"No surprise though, is it? Alfie Dorchester's got friends in high places."

"Most of them with holiday homes in Monaco," contributed the American editor.

"Is that where he's gone?" asked Ike.

"Last we heard. He should never have been given bail in the first place."

"Absolutely not," said Yasmin, with a look that said *she* would never have allowed the defence counsel to get away with it.

Poppy shivered at the thought of her nemesis roaming freely around Europe, and pulled the fox fur closer around her shoulders.

"His sister's in New York now, isn't she?" asked Yasmin.

"She is," agreed Poppy and wished they could change the subject. Her first story had been a raging success, but she did not want to be defined by it.

"Is Daniel not coming, Poppy?" It was Doreen Garfield, Ike's wife. Doreen was a short, plump West Indian woman with warm brown eyes and a smile to light up the West End.

Poppy smiled at her gratefully. "He's going to meet us there. He wants to be in position to photograph the guests as they arrive."

Doreen's eyebrows furrowed in sympathy. "That young man of yours works too hard. And so do you. How you two manage to find time to see each other, I'll never know. It's bad enough with Ike working, but if I did as well…"

Ike patted her hand.

"Oh, we manage," said Poppy.

"Well, don't you go giving up on your career for him, Poppy," said Yasmin with a sideways glance at Doreen. "I've seen it too many times: men being attracted to career women when they're single, but then expecting them to play second fiddle to them when they're married."

Rollo chuckled. "Is that a thinly disguised barb at me, Yazzie?"

"Of course not, sweetie," said Yasmin, stroking his cheek. "We'll never get married."

Rollo laughed even louder. Poppy wasn't sure if she was joking, but wouldn't have been surprised if she wasn't. Rollo – a notorious skirt-chaser – had met his match in Miss Reece-Lansdale.

Ike chuckled politely; Doreen glared at him and he stopped. Then she turned back to Poppy: "Have you met his children yet?"

"He's got children? Well, say no more! The word 'bargepole' comes to mind, Poppy. Stay well clear."

"I think you're the one who should stay well clear, Miss Lansdale," said Doreen. "Poppy needs to make her own mind up without your interference."

"Interference?" Yasmin spat.

"Yes, interference," said Doreen, sitting as straight as she could, but still only coming up to Yasmin's shoulder.

"Ladies, ladies!" drawled Rollo. "Let's not spoil the night before it's begun. It's going to be a corker, wouldn't you agree, Poppy?"

"It should be," said Poppy quietly, and looked out of the window as they pulled up to the Crystal Palace. They were met by a bank of camera flashes. And somewhere in that crowd was Daniel.

Poppy had never seen so many jewels in her life – both on and off the guests. The who's who of British high society wove their way through the exhibition hall, examining case after case of glittering artefacts, exquisite jewellery and objets d'art. On the walls were Rembrandts, Vermeers, Makovskys and Kramskois – and was that actually a Da Vinci? Poppy would need to check in her aunt's *Encyclopaedia of World Art* when she got home.

But it was the collection of Fabergé eggs on a raised dais in the middle of the hall that attracted the most attention: six of them – of various sizes – gilded and bejewelled with the finest craftsmanship the world of jewellery design had ever seen. According to the information card on the dais, they were all owned by members of the Romanov family.

"Aren't they just exquisite, darling?"

Poppy looked down to find her aunt beside her, wearing a violet gown of crushed velvet and taffeta.

"Almost as exquisite as you, Aunt Dot – you look gorgeous!"

Aunt Dot's cheeks flushed a delightful pink and her bluebell eyes nearly outshone the sapphires on her tiara. "It's a Jacques Doucet! It arrived from Paris just this morning. I almost thought I would have to air one of my old rags again."

"You would look spectacular in whatever you wore." Victor Marconi, with Princess Selena on his arm, joined Aunt Dot and Miss King, who was wearing a surprisingly elegant peach silk gown.

"Well, thank you, Victor. So which one is yours, Selena?" asked Dot.

The princess was wearing what looked like a Jean Paquin, but its simple lines were obscured by more jewels than were housed in the Tower of London. The question from Aunt Dot elicited a melodramatic hand to the side of the face and a stifled sob. "It is not mine, Dorothy. I am just a treasure-keeper. I am merely the custodian until dear Nicky and Alix and their children reclaim them."

Poppy, who believed reports that the tsar and his family had all been murdered, wondered if Selena really did think she was merely a custodian or was just "playing the pauper". She knew what Delilah would think.

"So which one is it?" asked Aunt Dot again.

"It's the large purple one in the middle, isn't it, *principessa*?" said Delilah's father.

Selena nodded her agreement, sniffing back tears. "Alix gave it to me herself, with her dear, sainted hands." Then she threw herself onto Victor's chest and sobbed. Victor patted her back gingerly. Poppy, who tried not to think the worst of people, was nevertheless finding it hard not to roll her eyes. Even Miss King, more practised in impassivity, raised an eyebrow at the pantomime.

Eventually Selena straightened up and dabbed a lace handkerchief at her eyes. "E-excuse me. I must go powder my nose." Then she flounced off, leaving Dot, Victor, Miss King and Poppy to admire the Fabergé eggs.

"You're a saint, Victor, a saint," said Dot and giggled.

"I hope she puts on a better performance in *The Cherry Orchard*," said Delilah as she joined the group, slipping an arm into her father's and kissing his cheek.

"Oh, she's marvellous on stage – just wait and see," said Dot.

"She's not showing much promise in rehearsals, is she, Adam?"

"Don't be unkind, Delilah; she's only been at it a few days," said Adam Lane as he too joined the group.

Delilah snuggled further into the crook of her father's arm. "It looks like she's been at it for years."

Despite herself, Poppy couldn't help chuckling at her friend's summation of Princess Selena Romanova Yusopova. One had to pity the woman – having to flee for her life from the Bolsheviks – but she wasn't doing much to endear herself to her prospective daughter-in-law.

Adam, the tallest of the group, suddenly stood up straight. "What ho, this looks like trouble… Didn't someone say Selena and that bounder Felix Yusopov – the fellow who offed Rasputin – couldn't stand the sight of each other?"

"*Loathe* wouldn't be too strong a word," commented Delilah, standing on her toes to try to see what Adam was looking at.

"Well, they're on a collision course."

Poppy, although taller than Delilah, couldn't see over the crowd either. "What's happening?"

"He's with the empress, and Selena is going to pay her respects… no, no… she's seen him and has changed direction… she's heading towards…"

"Adam dear, as delightful as you are at giving commentary, I think I'd rather talk about what I can see, not what I can't," said Dot and turned her chair to face the collection of Fabergé eggs. "What do you know about them, Poppy? You're bound to have researched them for your article."

Poppy gently nudged the chastised Adam. "She didn't mean it like that," she whispered, before raising her voice and answering her aunt. "I have actually. They were made by the jeweller Peter Carl Fabergé and commissioned by the late – the current – oh, you know what I mean – they were commissioned by Tsar Nicholas's father Alexander and then by Nicholas himself as presents for their wives and daughters. Every Easter since 1885 the Romanov women have received one of these splendidly jewelled eggs. There are around fifty of them in existence."

"Is it true some of them have secret compartments?" asked Dot, pushing her chair closer to the dais. One of the two guards flanking the Fabergé display stepped forward and politely asked Aunt Dot to move back. She did so, with a smile.

"So I've been told," said Poppy. "Apparently all of the imperial Easter eggs contained some kind of surprise. Did Selena mention anything about that to you, Mr Marconi?"

"She did not," said Victor. "But she only has one of them."

"What do you think it's worth, Papa?" asked Delilah.

"The big one could fetch around half a million pounds at auction. Perhaps more."

Adam whistled. "No wonder they're so tight with their security."

And no wonder the Bolsheviks want them back, thought Poppy. She assessed the guards in front of her: British, definitely British. In the days since the press conference at the Russian embassy there had been a tiff between the White and Red Russians about who exactly would provide security for the exhibition. The Whites claimed the Reds' offer to help protect the jewels – until such a time as their return to the people of Russia could be negotiated – was simply a ploy to steal them back. But the Reds insisted that the Whites could not be trusted with their nation's treasure either. So it was reluctantly agreed that the London Metropolitan Police and a security detail from the Queen Mother's Kensington Palace would be employed – although the latter was controversial, as the Queen Mother Alexandra was sister to the Russian empress Maria Federovna, mother of Tsar Nicholas II. However, as both of the royal sisters were attending the exhibition, the British government would not compromise on their safety – as Ike's article in this morning's *Globe* put it – and stood firm against the Bolsheviks' demands to have the Household Cavalry removed.

At that point Daniel arrived with his camera. "Daniel, darling! We've missed you," said Aunt Dot. "When are you coming around for supper again?"

"Whenever your niece asks me," said Daniel and gave Poppy a kiss on her cheek. "You look breathtaking," he whispered into her ear.

Poppy felt a shiver of delight run down her spine.

"Good to see you, old chap," said Adam. "I was just going to get us all some drinks. Do you want anything?"

"Not while I'm working, thanks," said Daniel as he changed the bulb on his flash. One of the guards stepped forward and questioned him. In reply Daniel produced his press card. The guard stepped back. Adam went to the bar.

"Do you need us to move?" asked Victor.

"Not at all, Mr Marconi. I've already taken pictures of the exhibits – before the doors opened. I want some shots of people viewing them now. I've managed to get a great one of the sister empresses in front of that Da Vinci. But," said Daniel with a wink at Poppy, "they are merely a warm-up act for the delectable Miss Dorothy Denby."

Aunt Dot threw up her hands in delight, then primped her hair and pouted her lips. "Ah, Mr Rokeby, I thought you'd never ask. Miss King, could you pass my compact, please? I do not intend to be outshone by an egg!"

Everyone laughed as Aunt Dot's companion dutifully passed her employer a mother-of-pearl make-up compact. But before Aunt Dot could start applying the powder the lights went out. A collective groan filled the room – just another in a series of repeated outages the guests had suffered throughout the autumn – followed by a litany of complaints about the London Power Company needing to get its act together. Then a momentary, deafening silence drowned by screams as a gunshot, and then another, echoed in the darkness.

CHAPTER 8

The sound reverberated in Poppy's ears, and she felt a dead weight on her chest. Beyond the ringing she could hear screaming and the crashing of bodies into furniture. A voice amid the chaos shouted: "Stay calm, stay calm!" *Easier said than done*, thought Poppy as she tried to shift the weight – it groaned. There was someone on top of her.

The lights came up and Poppy could make out a wheel about a foot from her. "Aunt Dot?"

"Poppy? Oh Poppy! Are you all right?"

The person on top of Poppy groaned again and rolled off. Or rather was lifted off. Daniel and one of the guards came into view.

"He's been shot!" said the guard. He settled his partner on the ground beside Poppy and began administering first aid.

Daniel leaned into her. "Are you all right?"

"I – I think so. I was just knocked off my feet."

"You're covered in blood!"

"Blood? Oh my! Has she been shot too? Poppy!"

Poppy looked down to see her white satin dress stained red. "I – I – it's not mine." She rolled onto her knees, then crawled over to the shot man. "Is he all right?"

"I think it's just through the shoulder, miss."

"Here, let me look." Daniel knelt down beside the man and examined the wound with the expert eye of a former soldier who had seen more than his fair share of bullet wounds. "He needs an ambulance."

"The shooter might still be out there," whispered the guard, and he and Daniel scanned the hall like two Tommies in a trench. Still on her knees, Poppy took in the scene around her.

The guests were milling around in varying degrees of confusion: some trying to catch the attention of the uniformed police swarming into the hall like stormtroopers; others helping friends who had fainted or fallen, and still others trying to take cover behind whatever makeshift barricades they could find. Poppy had heard two blasts, but she couldn't see anyone else who had been shot. Yet she couldn't be sure. What if one of her friends was injured? What if someone else needed help? Before Daniel could stop her, she got to her feet and was swamped by her friends: Delilah, Victor Marconi, Aunt Dot, and even Miss King, clutched her to them.

"Are you sure you're all right?" asked Delilah.

"I'm fine," said Poppy, relieved that they too were unharmed.

And Daniel, thank God Daniel was safe. He looked up briefly from helping the injured guard, and nodded towards the dais. Poppy followed his gaze: the cushion where Selena's Fabergé egg had nestled only minutes before was gone. So that's what this was all about: they were caught in the middle of an armed robbery.

Poppy looked around her, trying to judge whether they were in any further danger. The guard was right: the shooter could still be out there. She crouched down, pulling Delilah with her.

"What should we do?" asked the young actress, her brown eyes wide with fear.

"I don't know, I –"

Suddenly, armed Household Cavalry, with their characteristic horse-tail helmets, burst into the hall from every doorway, brandishing their rifles.

"On the floor!" shouted an officer, completely ignoring a plain-clothes policeman who walked up to him, showing him his badge. Some of the guests complied; others simply put their hands up.

A phalanx of cavalry officers swiftly located Queen Alexandra and Empress Maria Federovna, who had been herded into a corner by plain-clothes security guards. The two elderly ladies emerged from the scrum visibly shaken but unharmed, and were quickly ushered out of the hall.

The rest of the guests were not so lucky. It would be two o'clock in the morning before those who had not managed to flee before the Household Cavalry closed their cordon around the Crystal Palace would be allowed to leave.

Poppy and everyone else there knew that the body searches they were all subjected to were a waste of time. Whoever had shot the guard and stolen the egg was long gone, but the police still had to do their job.

Heading up the questioning was the Metropolitan Police's Detective Chief Inspector Jasper Martin from Scotland Yard, who happened to be at the exhibition with his wife and daughter. The ladies sat patiently in a corner, nibbling carrot sticks and sausage rolls, while DCI Martin took control.

The guests were ushered into an adjacent hall while the exhibition staff took an inventory of the jewels and art exhibits. It took them half an hour to determine what Poppy already suspected: only the Fabergé egg was gone. At this news Princess Selena fainted, falling into the arms of a gaggle of gentlemen, including Victor Marconi. Poppy wondered for a moment where the princess had been during the robbery, as she did not recall seeing her when the lights came back on. Also "missing" was Adam Lane, who had gone to get drinks moments before the blackout. But as she, Aunt Dot, Miss King, Delilah and

Victor shuffled into the adjacent hall Poppy saw him forcing his way through and sweeping Delilah up into his arms.

Already in the hall were Ike and Doreen Garfield, Marjorie Reynolds and her son Oscar, Yasmin Reece-Lansdale and Rollo Rolandson. The latter looked absolutely delighted to be caught up in the story of the season and lost no time gathering his news team around him. Daniel joined them as soon as he had handed the guard over to the ambulance crew. His war-scarred hands were covered in blood and shook slightly as he clutched his camera case. "Get that developed as soon as we're out of here," Rollo instructed in a whisper. Daniel nodded his assent.

Loud, foreign voices erupted in argument in the corner where Selena had fallen. Selena, no longer needing Victor's support, appeared to be venting her spleen in Russian at Prince Felix Yusopov, who was giving as good as he got. Then another voice, in French – which at least Poppy could partially follow – joined Prince Felix in his attack on Selena. It was Princess Irina: "I told you that strumpet would steal the egg for herself. Treasure-keeper, my eye!"

"Why would I steal it? How could I steal it?" demanded Selena in French, and flung her arms wide. "Search me, if you dare!"

She then switched back to Russian. Whatever she said merely inflamed Irina more and the assassin's wife threw herself at Selena. Rollo chuckled in delight and ordered Daniel to get some shots as Victor Marconi and Prince Felix vainly tried to keep the women apart.

"Utterly disgraceful," said Miss King; the first words she had spoken all night.

The catfight was finally broken up by uniformed officers on the instructions of DCI Martin, the ladies and their respective gentlemen dutifully corralled into separate corners. Victor Marconi tried to leave to return to his daughter, Adam and Aunt

Dot, but a burly sergeant stood in his way. The Maltese hotel magnate had the look of a hunted animal about him and visibly cringed as Selena clawed at his arm.

"Poor Papa," said Delilah.

Aunt Dot giggled. "There go Selena's wedding plans."

But then, as if there had not already been enough drama for one night, a set of double doors flew open and the dark figure of Comrade Andrei Nogovski burst in, flanked by two bodyguards who dwarfed every uniformed bobby in the room.

"Who is in charge here?" His voice was not loud, but it rose above the hubbub with an intensity and authority that demanded instant attention.

"Hmmm, who's that?" Delilah whispered to Poppy.

"Head of security from the Russian embassy," Poppy whispered back.

"Detective Chief Inspector Martin, Scotland Yard," said the rotund and moustachioed head of the Met without putting his hand out for Nogovski to shake. "And who are you?" DCI Martin was half a foot shorter than Nogovski and barely came up to the chests of the two bodyguards, but he held his ground with a calm authority. He too did not need to raise his voice.

"Comrade Andrei Nogovski, official representative of the People's Commissar of Foreign Trade for the Russian Soviet Federalist Socialist Republic."

"You mean the Russian Provincial Government," Martin corrected him like a schoolmaster.

"I mean what I said."

"White or Red?" asked Martin.

Nogovski's eyes narrowed. The bodyguards' backs tightened like drawn bows. "I am here to ensure the safe return of the missing egg to the people of Russia. I shall be joining your investigation."

Martin considered this for a moment, then said with a nod to left and right, "Red that corner, White that. Give your names to the constables and you'll be questioned in turn." He turned on his heel as if to walk away. Nogovski grabbed his shoulder. Instantly, half a dozen Met police officers launched themselves at the Russian, but were blocked by the giant bodyguards.

Poppy heard Rollo gasp in delight. Out of her right eye she saw Daniel ready his camera.

But all hopes of a rumble were dashed as Marjorie Reynolds, resplendent in a sapphire blue Jacques Worth creation, inserted herself between the two factions. "Marjorie Reynolds, minister to the Home Office. May I have a word with you, DCI Martin?"

Martin's moustache twitched; still, whatever he was thinking about being superseded by a woman he kept to himself. "Of course, Mrs Reynolds."

As the senior politician and policeman conferred, Nogovski and his men held their ground – and so did Martin's Bobbies. No one else dared speak until Aunt Dot whispered *sotto voce*: "Go get 'em, Marjorie." This elicited a few giggles from the crowd.

A few minutes later Marjorie and Martin returned.

"Mr Nogovski," said the DCI, "Mrs Reynolds has assured me of your credentials and has requested that you – and your superior, Mr Safin – be given special diplomatic status as observers in this investigation. However, I will need your assurance that that's all you will do: observe, not obstruct."

Nogovski thought about this for a moment and said: "I will do whatever is to the benefit of the people of Russia."

"That does not reassure me, Nogovski."

"Well, that is all –"

Marjorie Reynolds held up both hands. "Gentlemen, gentlemen, we can work out the parameters of Mr Nogovski's and

Mr Safin's involvement in the morning. For now, can we agree that this will be a two-way investigation by the Metropolitan Police and the Russian embassy?"

"A three-way investigation!" Marjorie, Martin and Nogovski spun around at the sound of a woman's voice. Yasmin Reece-Lansdale, flanked by Felix and Irina Yusopov, approached the central group.

Martin sighed. "And what's your role in all this, Mrs Lansdale?"

Yasmin, like a tawny desert lioness surveying its prey, narrowed her dark eyes. "It's Reece-Lansdale, Ms. And I am the legal representative of the Romanov royal family – to whom the missing egg belongs."

"Since when?" shouted Rollo.

"Since Prince Yusopov – at the request of Empress Maria Federovna – commissioned me."

"The Romanovs no longer have any legal standing in Russia. They do not represent the Russian people," Nogovski declared, his voice tight with anger.

"Ah, but they do have legal standing in the United Kingdom of Great Britain, where, Mr Nogovski, we still recognize the property rights of individuals. And," said Yasmin, in anticipation of DCI Martin's objection as he raised a finger in the air, "the British royal family will be paying for my services on behalf of their esteemed cousins. So if you have any further queries, Inspector, I suggest you take it up with them."

Martin looked at Marjorie. Marjorie shrugged.

DCI Martin ran his hand through his hair, exhaled through tight lips, and said: "Right, Whites to the left; Reds to the right and Pinkos in the middle. Let's get started."

The whole room let out another collective groan. It was going to be a long night.

CHAPTER 9

SUNDAY 21 OCTOBER 1920, LONDON

The newsroom was busy for a Sunday. Normally only Rollo stalked the halls of *The Globe* on the Lord's Day – and whichever hack had not managed to file their final copy on Saturday afternoon. *The Globe* did not have a regular Sunday release; the Monday early edition covered whatever happened on Saturdays, and the evening edition covered Sunday's news.

When the guests of the White Russian Art Exhibition were released from the Crystal Palace between two and three on Sunday morning, *The Globe* staff present at the sensational armed robbery had gone straight to Fleet Street to make sure their articles would get to press in time for the Monday edition.

But Rollo shocked them all by announcing they were going to print up a special short edition to be released Sunday lunchtime: a simple four-pager, produced on a skeleton staff. The bulk of the copy would be made up of pre-written personality profiles taken from the Jazz Files (the name given to archive material of celebrity gossip and background information) of three of the main players: Princess Selena and the Yusopovs. The rest would be made up of first-hand accounts of the robbery by Rollo and Ike. Poppy was to provide an overview of the art on display, including Selena's Fabergé egg, and there was to be a medical report on the guard who was shot.

Rollo planned to typeset the edition personally and print off ten thousand copies – only a tenth of the usual print run. "Better than nothing," he exuded as he jumped around like a leprechaun, directing the only print operator he could rouse in the wee hours of Sunday morning.

Poppy knew that Rollo was hoping to convince advertisers that *The Globe* could get the top stories ahead of its competitors – and hence attract more readers. *The Globe* was fair to middling in the readership stakes – on a par with *The Courier* but way behind *The Times* and *The Express*. Bringing out a Sunday morning edition would increase circulation, but it would be hard to lure readers away from the traditional broadsheets that normally caught their splodges of butter and marmalade over breakfast.

It was chicken and egg: *The Globe* needed additional staff to cover a weekend shift and extra money to pay the staff. Without more advertising it would be nigh on impossible to underwrite the payroll, but advertising would not increase until a Sunday edition became a feature and circulation grew. Poppy knew that Rollo had been looking at "alternative sources" of raising capital to tide the paper over, and she feared some of them involved gambling. Rollo had won the paper in a poker game; she hoped to high heaven he wouldn't lose it the same way.

As Poppy flopped into a chair in the newsroom, Ike Garfield handed her a welcome mug of coffee. She thanked him and sighed as the warm ceramic soothed her fingertips, which throbbed from hitting the typewriter keys for four hours straight. Typing was new to her and she had not yet mastered the touch typing technique that she envied in some of the older journalists, their fingers flying over the keys. Poppy was more of a search, point and thwack girl. But she was getting better, and she was relieved that the twelve-hundred word feature had not taken her longer.

"Are you done?" asked Ike, wedging his large frame into the chair next to Poppy.

"I think so. I've covered everything in the official exhibition catalogue, supplemented a bit with some background from my aunt's book on world art, and added a bit of hearsay at the bottom about the Romanov 'treasure-keepers'."

"Hearsay? Couldn't you corroborate it?"

"Not yet. I need access to the archives and some contacts in the Jazz Files, but Ivan isn't in."

Ike rubbed his temples as if trying to relax his overstretched brain. "He doesn't work Sundays. But I thought he would have been at the exhibition last night."

Poppy took a sip of her coffee, then shook her head. "No, I wasn't surprised he didn't come. Too many painful associations. I assume you've heard about his family…"

Ike nodded. "Of course. Completely understandable. Doesn't help with your article though, does it? But I suppose it can wait until tomorrow… I'm sure Rollo will ask you to do a follow-up."

"'Spect so. How's your piece coming on?"

"Nearly done. Just waiting for some comment from Scotland Yard." He looked over at the candlestick telephone on his desk. "I left a message with their press office asking them to ring back, but I doubt they will on a Sunday. I was also hoping to get a comment from Vasili Safin – what with all his grandstanding at the embassy about getting the Romanov art back for the Russian people. But no one answered when I called. I'll mosey over there myself after the ed meeting. Unless Rollo wants to go ahead without it."

The red-haired editor, wearing the same tuxedo he wore to

the exhibition, with the bow-tie hanging loose and the sleeves rolled up, bounded into the room. He quickly pinned four flat-plans to the board, then wiped his black-inked hands down the sides of his silk shirt.

"Right, it's –" he pulled a fob-watch from his trouser pocket "– eight o'clock. We need to get the press rolling by nine-thirty at the latest. I've set the personality profiles of Selena and the Yusopovs and the short piece on the guard. Danny Boy phoned something in to me from the hospital after he went to see the fella. Doing all right. Thank God. How's your piece coming on, Poppy?"

"Done," said Poppy with satisfaction, and slapped two pages of close typescript into Rollo's outstretched hands.

Rollo scanned it quickly and grunted his approval. "Well done, Miz Denby. Ike?"

"Still waiting on Scotland Yard and the Russian embassy."

"Forget it. Give me what you've got and we'll do a follow-up in the morning. I'll be seeing Martin anyway." He grimaced. "He's trying to subpoena Danny's film."

"Can he do that?" asked Poppy.

"He can with a court order. But he's struggling to get one on a Sunday. So –" he grinned, and Poppy noticed a bit of raisin from a Chelsea Bun he'd been eating stuck in his teeth "– we're just going ahead and printing what we've got. Which is another reason I wanted to do this Sunday special."

Not just about money then, thought Poppy with approval.

Rollo took his pointer and poked at the page flat-plans. "So as you can see, just Danny's front-page pic is missing. He's given me archive stuff of some of the high and mighties and a nice shot of the missing egg; now he's going through his film to see if we've got something *medias res* – in the action," he added, unnecessarily, for Poppy's benefit. "Actually, Poppy, can you pop down and get him to shake a leg? Ike, you can help me with the typesetting if you've finished your piece."

"Yes, boss," said Poppy and Ike in unison.

Daniel's darkroom was on the second floor at the back of the art and photography department. As expected, the door was shut. Poppy knocked. "You in there, Daniel? Rollo wants some snaps – snap-snap!" Poppy groaned at her own tired pun.

"Two ticks, I'll let you in."

Poppy heard the clattering of metal trays and some indeterminate shuffling, then the door opened a crack and one of Daniel's scarred hands – burned during a fire in the trenches when he'd hauled some men to safety – pulled her into a black-curtained atrium. The little tent – smaller than a changing room in a cheap department store – brought Poppy and Daniel chest to chest. He smelled of chemicals – acetates, nitrates, bromides. Poppy had heard him talk about them many times. They all seemed the same to her: acrid. But underneath it she could smell him: the familiar, warm, manly scent of Daniel. She sighed and laid her cheek on his chest. He held her close for a minute and then kissed her head. She longed to tilt her chin up to him so he could kiss her properly, but she knew Rollo was waiting for them.

"Do you have anything for the front page yet?"

"Yes, but in some cases I'm not sure what I'm looking at. Care to have a gander?"

"You bet!" said Poppy, wondering exactly what Daniel had managed to capture with his Kodak Brownie.

He pushed back the curtain and ushered her into the red-bathed light of the darkroom. On a bench there were three trays of chemical baths with emulsified paper floating in them. "They're still developing. But look at these."

He indicated a washing line with nine black and white photographs hanging from it. "I took two rolls with twelve exposures on each over the course of the evening. The first lot were of the exhibits – I took them before the guests arrived. I've given them to Rollo already. I think he's using the one of the missing egg."

Poppy said that he was. "But he wants a *medias res* shot now. Have you got anything?"

"You tell me."

Poppy examined the pictures from left to right. The first picture was a posed shot of Queen Alexandra and her sister Maria Federovna in front of the Da Vinci. "I think Rollo might want that one on the inside spread. They're the most important people there."

Daniel made a note and took the pic down.

The second, third, fourth and fifth photographs featured various socialites milling around the exhibits. Some were posed, some were frank "caught in the moment" shots. Shot number six caught Poppy's interest – it was of the Yusopovs, Felix and Irina, in close conversation with Vasili Safin, the Commissar for Foreign Trade from the Russian embassy.

"I didn't know he was there. Did you?"

"Who is he?" asked Daniel.

Poppy told him. "Thing is, I don't recall him being there when Martin interviewed us all, although Marjorie had mentioned that he and Nogovski would be part of the investigation. Did you see him anywhere?"

"No, I didn't."

"When was this taken?"

Daniel thought a moment and counted backwards and forwards along the line. "I have to change bulbs between each snap and have to wait around two to three minutes for the bulbs to cool before I can take them out. So on average, about five minutes between each pic. This was the reel I took in the run-up to the blackout. This one was halfway through, so I'd say half an hour before the robbery."

Poppy absorbed the information and did some calculations of her own. "Hmmm, so he must have left sometime before the robbery…"

"Or immediately after…"

"Or immediately after," agreed Poppy. Could Safin have stolen the egg back "for the Russian people"? He certainly had motive and quite clearly the opportunity, but did he have the means? Did he, somewhere under that dark suit, have a revolver closeted away? And what was he talking to the Yusopovs about? Their body language wasn't antagonistic, as you would expect from people on opposing sides of the political divide. But it was difficult to tell with just that one split second frozen in time. Oh, what she would have done to have photographs on either side of this.

Photograph number seven made them both laugh – Rollo being slapped in the face by an outraged Princess Selena Romanova Yusopova.

"Wonder what he said to her?" mused Poppy.

"Knowing Rollo, it would have been something wildly inappropriate. I'll ask him," Daniel chuckled.

They turned their attention to photograph eight. It appeared to be a dud shot – just the backs of some men, dressed in black tuxedos, standing at the bar. There was very little to distinguish them one from another. However, Poppy knew one of them – Adam Lane, his fair hair standing out from the rest – and he was talking to the barman. Nothing remarkable there. She was just about to move on to the next picture, when something caught her attention. She pointed to the barman. "I know him. The barman Adam's talking to."

"Adam?"

"Yes, that's Adam there. I'm sure it is. Look at the hair…"

"You're right; it's him. But how do you know the barman? Have you been frequenting drinking establishments without me, Miss Denby?"

Poppy laughed. "Hardly. Just Oscar's. But I think that's one of the barmen from there. I noticed him the other night when I was out with Adam and Delilah."

"Noticing barmen now, are we? Well, he is a good looking chap, I suppose…"

Poppy poked him in the ribs. "Jealous?"

"Should I be?" he asked, his voice suddenly serious.

Poppy turned to him and looked up into his grey eyes that seemed almost green in the red light. "Of course not. Where's this coming from, Daniel?"

He turned away and busied himself straightening some bottles of chemicals. "Nowhere. Forget it."

Poppy couldn't forget it. But neither did she have time to pursue it, so she shelved it away to be talked about when they both had some time off – together.

She cleared her throat. "Well actually, the reason I noticed him was that that night at Oscar's – last Wednesday – our Comrade Andrei Nogovski, the fella who tried to take over the investigation from Martin last night…"

Daniel nodded that he was following her.

"… made a big show of forcing his way into Oscar's."

"*Forcing* his way in?"

"Flashing credentials and all that. I'm not sure what he was after, but I saw him and Oscar talking and then Oscar took him downstairs."

"What's downstairs?"

"Oscar's office and the wine cellar."

"How do you know all this?"

Poppy chuckled and put on an American accent, mimicking Rollo. "I don't have the instincts of a first-class newshound for nothing, Danny Boy."

"Or the nose," said Daniel and bent down and kissed it lightly. Poppy relaxed. Whatever was bothering Daniel had been forgotten.

She giggled. "Or the nose."

"So what else did the nose sniff out?"

"Well, that's where the barman comes in. Nogovski – who's in charge of security at the Russian embassy, remember – came up the stairs from the cellar to the bar and was talking to this barman." She pointed to him on the photograph. "And then later the big cheese – that Safin chap – joined them. And now the same man – the barman – is at the Crystal Palace."

"Nothing surprising in that, though, is there? Oscar was probably asked to handle the catering for the exhibition."

Poppy nodded her agreement. "Probably. I'll ask him. But I also want to ask him why Nogovski – and Safin – were at the club. Oscar looked scared."

"Scared? That doesn't sound like our Oscar."

"Exactly. But that will have to wait for another day. We need a pic for Rollo – pronto!" Again she put on an American accent and drew an appreciative chuckle from Daniel.

"Well, the last one's not much to look at," he said, and Poppy agreed. It was just a wide shot of the crowd, taken from a slightly elevated level.

"Where were you when you took this?"

"On a chair in the corner. That's when I saw you and Aunt Dot."

"So the next one," said Poppy as she turned to the developing trays, "must be the one you took just after the lights went out. I remember a flash – just before the first gunshot."

"I took it just *as* the lights went out." Daniel's voice raised a decibel. "I was ready to take one of your aunt and her friends, but when everything went black, I pressed the shutter – by accident, I think – but I still managed to capture something."

He took some tongs and stirred the picture in the first tray, floating it around in the chemical bath. He nodded to the other two trays as he did so. "Those two were taken in the interview hall. One is of the Selena/Irina fight, and the other of DCI Martin. But now look at this…"

Daniel flipped over the picture and laid it out on a white towel alongside the tray. Poppy leaned in, but was desperately disappointed by what she saw. It was a blur. She couldn't figure out what was going on. "There's nothing there!"

"Ah, but there is. That blur is from the flash going off at the same time as the lights going out and the contrast being all wrong and losing focus. But look closer: there's a bit in the top right corner that you can just make out…"

Poppy looked, and gasped. Reaching into the frame was a bare forearm and, at the end of the forearm, a hand holding something that looked very much like a silver revolver. "Is that what I think it is?"

"It is," agreed Daniel, his voice tight with excitement. "And do you notice anything about the arm?"

"The arm…" Poppy gasped again. "Of course! It's a woman's. A *woman* shot the guard!"

CHAPTER 10

"**W**ell done, Danny Boy!" Rollo clutched the blurred photograph like a child with a present on Christmas Day. "Do you think *The Courier* or *The Times* got anything?"

Daniel was equally excited, but far more worn out than the hyperactive American. He yawned. "I don't think so. There was only one flash – mine."

"*And* I heard Lionel and his photographer having a tiff."

Daniel, Rollo and Ike turned to look at Poppy, still in her blood stained evening gown. She was just finishing her fourth cup of coffee of the morning.

"What about?" asked Rollo.

Poppy downed the rest of the coffee and winced at the bitter dregs. She put down her cup, stretched her neck to left and right, then answered her editor. "Lionel spent most of his time propping up the bar instead of interviewing guests. The camera chappie was having kittens. I heard him tell Lionel that if he wasn't going to bother doing his job properly, why should he? And then he stormed off. Left Lionel with a face like a slapped kipper."

The journalists chuckled. Lionel Saunders used to work at *The Globe* but had left in disgrace. Since getting hired by *The Globe*'s rival, he had gone out of his way to undermine every story Poppy worked on.

"Looks like you've scooped him on this one, Poppy," said Ike.

"Perhaps," said Poppy thoughtfully, "or perhaps not.

He's not a complete fool. He was talking to the barman from Oscar's... and like I said, I think there might be something going on there with him and the fellas from the Russian embassy. What if Lionel's thinking the same thing?"

"Talk to Oscar and see what you can get out of him, Poppy, and I'll talk to the barman," ordered Rollo, then he pinned the photograph to the flat-plan on the board. "Pity it's so blurred. Won't print well, but it's too big a scoop to leave out..."

"Why don't we crop it to a close-up on the arm – then use it as an inset on a bigger photograph?" suggested Daniel. "Such as –"

"Such as the catfight between the princesses! Brilliant, Danny Boy, brilliant! That way we imply that one of them might be the shooter."

Poppy frowned. "Is that fair, Rollo? It might not have been either of them. They could sue for libel..."

"Pwah! Let them sue. They won't win. Besides, Selena deserves it." Rollo took the photograph of the two women fighting and pinned it to the board next to the "smoking gun" picture, with the drawing-pin right in the middle of Selena's forehead.

"Now, now, Rollo; don't do anything out of spite. That wouldn't have anything to do with this, would it?" Daniel held up the photograph of Rollo being slapped by Selena.

Rollo went red in the face and cleared his throat.

"What's that about?" asked Ike, trying not to laugh.

Rollo busied himself rearranging the pages on the board. "She offered me a kill fee."

"For what?" asked Ike, Poppy and Daniel in unison.

"To not publish any interviews with the Yusopovs that claimed she intended to keep the Fabergé egg for herself."

Poppy was puzzled – and a little bit shaky. Too much coffee.

She struggled to concentrate. "But we haven't done an interview like that. Not yet, anyway... or have we?"

"She's convinced we have."

"Maybe it was Lionel."

"Maybe, but she's convinced we've got one ready to go to press."

"How much did she offer you?" asked Ike.

"Not enough," said Rollo, picking up his cup and examining it with disappointment. "Who's for more coffee?"

Poppy and Daniel declined. Ike poured a cup for himself and Rollo from a pot simmering on a little primus stove in a small kitchenette off the newsroom.

"Is that why she slapped you?" asked Daniel, stifling a yawn. "For turning her down?"

"No, she slapped me because I told her I expected more class from a Romanov dame, and –" Rollo grinned "– I asked her for more money."

"You *what?*" asked Poppy, more rudely than she'd intended. Nonetheless she was shocked that the editor had even considered burying a story. Did he really need money that badly? At the expense of the paper's reputation? At the expense of the reputation of every journalist who worked there?

Rollo seemed to read her mind. His bushy red eyebrows came together in disapproval. "Keep your judgments to yourself, Miz Denby. The day you take over the day-to-day running of this paper – dealing with advertisers and creditors and paying thankless reporters' salaries – is the day you can have opinions on such things."

Poppy lowered her eyes. She had spoken out of turn. She would not have done it if she hadn't been so tired. "I'm sorry," she said quietly, and doodled with her pencil on her notepad.

Daniel reached for her hand and squeezed it, then stared

daggers at Rollo. "Steady on, old man, the girl's entitled to her opinion."

Rollo sighed. "Yes, she is. I'm sorry. I think we all need to get some sleep." He caught Poppy's eye and smiled.

She smiled back, but was still a little hurt.

"However…" said Rollo, "no sleep until we figure out what to do next."

It was midday before Poppy left the office. While Rollo split his time between the print room and the newsroom, Ike, Poppy and Daniel discussed the story so far. The evidence seemed to suggest that a woman had shot the guard and stolen the egg. But which woman? There had been plenty at the exhibition. Irina Alexandrovna Yusopov was a front runner. She had publicly accused Selena of stealing the egg from the family and had every motivation for trying to get it back. On the other hand, what if Selena *had* stolen it – to keep it for herself? But why would Selena steal something that was already in her possession? And as she said herself, why wasn't it on her person? Or the gun for that matter? The same went for Irina who, when searched – with much protestation – was clean. Of course, the possibility existed that someone else was behind the theft – possibly the Red Russians – and that they had used a woman, someone as yet unknown to *The Globe* staff, to do their dirty work. There were dozens of suspects – practically anyone who had attended the exhibition and had been able to slip away before the Household Cavalry moved in.

Poppy agreed that after she had caught a few hours' sleep she would try to speak to Selena, who was a house guest of her aunt's. Then, after that, she would try to speak to Oscar.

Ike was going to cover the Russian embassy, as well as get some comment from Marjorie Reynolds on behalf of the Home

Office. Rollo would try to use his connection with Yasmin Reece-Lansdale to arrange a meeting with the Yusopovs. After that he would go for a drink at Oscar's and see if he could track down the barman. He also had a meeting set up first thing Monday morning with Scotland Yard.

It was agreed that Daniel had done more than his fair share and could go home to his children. Poppy kissed him on the cheek before he climbed on his motorbike.

"We'll have to rearrange meeting the family."

He looked at her, his eyes tired. "Not too long, though, Poppy; not too long."

Indeed, not too long, thought Poppy as she put on her fox-fur stole and stepped onto Fleet Street. She didn't have the energy to get the bus, so she decided to splash out on a cab. But as she was waiting for one to arrive, she saw a familiar figure on the opposite side of the road – the archivist Ivan Molanov, who looked as if he was going into Temple Church. Poor Ivan. For the same reason he had not attended the exhibition last night, he could not bear to be around people who reminded him of his family. The Russian Orthodox Church in Kensington was one such place. The well-meaning folk there would shower him with sympathy. Poppy knew that he sometimes slipped into Temple Church to worship – anonymously – and to light a candle for his loved ones.

Just before Ivan turned down the alley to the right of the Cock Tavern, leading to Temple Church, a man in a black trench coat and homburg hat intercepted him. Poppy caught a glimpse of a goatee beard. Could that be Vasili Safin? It was too far to see properly, but Ivan's body language was defensive. The large man's shoulders cowed as the goateed man spoke to him. They only conversed for a moment before Ivan turned down the alley and the man hailed a cab. As the black motor pulled up, the man glanced across the road and caught Poppy looking at him. Poppy stared back. Yes, it definitely looked like Vasili Safin. Perhaps she could get a comment from him for Ike's article… But before she could manoeuvre her way across the road he had climbed in the taxi and was driven away.

Poppy woke at seven o'clock that evening. She could hear the tinkle of cutlery being put out in the dining room below her. Was it supper time already? When she'd got home she had gone up the stairs without speaking to anyone and literally collapsed onto her bed and fallen asleep almost immediately. If it wasn't for her grumbling tummy – and the fact that she was beginning to smell like a navvy – she would have turned over and gone back to sleep. Oh, and the fact that she still had work to do. Poppy groaned and threw back the eiderdown. From the recesses of her mind she recalled Rollo asking her to interview Selena – and then Oscar, if she could. She really didn't have the energy for it, but she knew that Rollo meant tonight, not tomorrow, and that he would not be sleeping until he'd sent Monday morning's paper to press.

She showered as quickly as she could and put on a clean dress before going down to the dining room. Aunt Dot and Miss King were still at the table. Selena was absent and it didn't look as if a place had even been set for her.

"Poppy darling! What are you doing up? I was convinced you would sleep through to morning. Gertrude here –" she indicated Miss King – "brought a tray up to you around four o'clock, but she said you were sleeping like the dead."

Poppy sat down and reached for the tureen in the middle of the table. She lifted the lid – mmm, lamb casserole. She started ladling some of it onto a plate. "I would have," she explained, "but I still have work to do. Rollo wants me to interview Selena."

Miss King made a funny noise like a cat sneezing.

"Good luck to you!" said Aunt Dot, and produced the four-page Sunday edition of *The Globe* from under a napkin. "Fabulous article, by the way, darling, but Selena literally fainted – and I mean literally, don't I, Gertrude –" Miss King nodded "– when she saw the front page. I on the other hand have never laughed so much in my life."

Aunt Dot held up the picture of Selena and Irina clawing at each other like prize peacocks, with the headline: *Russian royals in hen fight over stolen egg.* "Classic Rollo! But Selena was not amused." Aunt Dot folded the paper and picked up her knife and fork. "How's the casserole, darling?"

Poppy, who was almost finished with her first plate and contemplating her second, had a mouthful of food but nodded enthusiastically. She swallowed carefully and then said: "So Selena won't talk to me, you think."

"Oh, I wouldn't take it personally, darling; it's just your association with *The Globe*. It's not you, per se, it's –"

"You think a woman did it." It was Miss King. Her voice was as thin and brittle as the autumn leaves scattered on the townhouse lawn. "The picture's not that clear…"

"It's clear enough," said Aunt Dot and put on her pince nez, which hung on a gold chain around her neck. She unfolded the paper again and scrutinized the inset photograph. "Yes indeed, it's clear enough. It's a woman holding a gun. No gloves, no jewellery that I can see –"

"No jewellery?" Poppy grabbed the paper from her aunt with a hasty apology and looked at the blurred photograph. Aunt Dot was right: there didn't appear to be any rings on the fingers or bracelets on the wrist. She looked again at the Selena and Irina picture and squinted to see their hands. But the angle it was taken from did not show what she needed to see. She would ask Daniel in the morning if he could go through his film again to see if there was a better shot of the women – or other women – that showed their hands.

"Well done, Aunt Dot. You might have given us a lead."

Aunt Dot flushed. "Really? How exciting!"

"You would have thought the police would have dusted us all for gunpowder residue." Miss King again. Aunt Dot and Poppy looked at her with a new-found respect. They waited for her to say more, but she didn't.

"They didn't do anything like that, did they?" said Aunt Dot. "Very suspicious…"

"Maybe they didn't see the need," said Poppy. "Maybe DCI Martin had come to the conclusion that the shooter must already have left. They did search us all for the gun and the egg, and no one found anything. So, ergo, the culprit had already escaped."

"Then it wasn't Selena or Irina." Dot sounded almost disappointed.

"I'm not saying that," said Poppy. "Only that that's what the police might have thought."

Miss King and Aunt Dot looked at each other and nodded. Then they all tucked into their casserole.

CHAPTER 11

JULY 1918, YEKATERINBURG, RUSSIA

Nana Ruthie, Anya and Fritzie walked down the high street of Yekaterinburg. It had so far been largely untouched by the war, despite its proximity to the strategic Trans-Siberian railway. Red flags flapped in the wind, declaring the town's allegiance to the Soviet committee that had taken control – without a shot being fired – back in October. And in case anyone was in doubt as to which side of the Red/White divide the citizens of Yekaterinburg were on, hammers and sickles, crudely painted on doors and shutters, marked the town as one wholly embracing the new Russia.

Before packing their meagre belongings into a carpet bag, Nana had tied a red ribbon into Anya's hair and wrapped a washed-out red scarf around her own, tying it under her chin. She ensured – for the third time that morning – that Anya had their cover story straight: they were domestic servants from Moscow. Their White aristocratic masters, of whom they wholly disapproved, had been arrested. Nana, calling herself Saskia Obledavich, claimed she had been the cook and Anya – renamed Mitza – was her granddaughter. The little dog had been the family pet, but Mitza was fond of it, so they had brought it with them. They were heading east to find some distant relatives whom they hoped would take them in. Who and where these relatives were changed the further east they went. But as they had only been asked their story once before, they had so far got away with it. The reality was, they didn't look important enough to stop, and no one east of Moscow knew who the Andreiovich family was – apart, perhaps, for the people at the Ipatiev House, and that's where Nana and Anya were headed.

On the two-mile walk from the train yard to the centre of the industrial town, Nana had made Anya recite nursery rhymes in Russian with a working-class accent. The girl was getting very good at it – perhaps she might have the makings of an actress, or, like Nana herself, a spy. Nana sighed as she remembered when she had first been approached to be the eyes and ears of His Majesty's government in the Russian court. If she had known then what she knew now, she would have turned down the offer and stayed in her comfortable semi-detached townhouse in Tower Hamlets.

In 1915, she had had a good job working as a translator of trade documents for the Chancellor of the Exchequer at number 11 Downing Street, while her friend, Gertrude King, worked there as governess to Lloyd George's daughter, Megan. It was well known that the Chancellor had his eye on moving in to Number 10, and he did in fact do so in December the following year. Asquith's approach to the war was attracting a lot of flak, and Lloyd George was not-so-secretly involving himself in foreign policy. So when Gertrude approached Ruth on behalf of the Chancellor, and asked her to meet with him about a "translation job abroad", Ruth suspected there was more to it than met the eye. And she was right.

Ruth Broadwood was the daughter of a famous linguist who had travelled the world with the British Foreign Service, writing "phrase books" for the diplomats, to help them get the basics of whatever lingo was spoken in Queen Victoria's vast colonies. Ruth, whose mother had died when she was young, had accompanied him until he retired after the Boer War. It was an exciting life but, as she approached middle age, she felt the need to set down some roots. She nursed her father until his death in 1910 and then, using his contacts in the Foreign Office, got herself a plum job with the Exchequer. There were a few male eyebrows raised that she was the "wrong" gender, but none of the other applicants could rival her vast knowledge of world languages. And it was this that had attracted David Lloyd George to her – that and the fact that she looked like a typical British spinster, straight out of a Brontë novel.

So after a bit of training in how to be a governess and the basics of espionage, she travelled to St Petersburg with forged references from some minor British royals. She was to be a back-up governess to the Romanov children in case the main governess fell ill. But as it turned out, the existing governess was in robust health and during the year she spent in the Winter Palace, she never got to see the children once. In 1916, the tsarina suggested her time would be better spent elsewhere, and sent her to the house of a distant cousin in Moscow.

Ruth was frustrated by the move but unable to say no to the Russian empress. The purpose of her deployment to the Romanov court had been because of Lloyd George's concerns that the tsarina's much-rumoured dalliance with the "mad monk" Rasputin would precipitate a Bolshevik-led revolt that would ultimately lead Russia out of the war, freeing Germany and the Austro-Hungarians to concentrate all their efforts on the Western Front. Lloyd George wanted eyes and ears in the court. Ruth reported what she could to her contact at the British embassy, but as she never quite got into the family's inner circle, she was limited as to what she could see and hear. Just before her redeployment to Moscow there was talk of "indisposing" the existing governess – much to Ruth's alarm. But it never came to that. And as it transpired, the Moscow placement turned out to be far more fruitful.

Count Sergei Andreiovich was a military advisor to the tsar. He had been sent to France as a liaison officer to the Western allies in 1914 and relayed information back and forth between the Russian government and the Allied military top brass. However, early in 1915 he disappeared – some said he was dead, some said he had gone undercover as a spy, but no one really knew. Until, that is, Nana Ruthie moved into 67 Ulitsa Ostozhenka to look after little Anya.

The house was much smaller than the royal palace and she had easy access to all parts of it. Using the training she had received from the Secret Service, she was quickly finding and copying letters and overhearing snippets of conversation that suggested Andreiovich had become disillusioned with the tsar and tsarina's increasingly autocratic style and had joined forces with some reformers, trying to influence Nicholas II to bring about democratic reforms before a revolution erupted. He had voiced his views to some fellow officers who, it seemed, turned on him. He was shot trying to get away. Allied troops found him, nursed him back to health and then he claimed asylum. He now feared for his family's future in Russia and wanted them to leave and come to Paris. However, his exact whereabouts were unknown.

Nana Ruthie relayed all of this information to her contact at the British embassy, who declared it to be "most useful" and instructed her to stay in place. Then, one afternoon in March 1917, she struck gold. The lady of the house received a visit from Princess Selena Romanova Yusopova. Nana had seen Selena on the London stage during a tour of the Bolshoi, and met her briefly at the Winter Palace in St Petersburg. She had also read a file on her, provided by the Secret Service, marking her as a "person of interest". Nana Ruthie could not imagine for a moment why the silly, affected prima donna might be a person of interest to British Intelligence, but after reading the file she changed her mind.

Princess Selena had once been completely and inexplicably in love with Vladimir Lenin, despite him being happily married with children. It seemed as if Lenin had seen Selena on tour in Paris and presented her with a bouquet of flowers in appreciation of her performance in Shaw's *Arms and the Man*. Selena read a coded romantic overture into the gesture and started following Lenin's career. She attended a few Bolshevik meetings, hoping to catch a glimpse of him, and in London tried to get Emmeline Pankhurst and Dorothy Denby to introduce her to him. She eventually did get to meet him and he, thinking she might genuinely be interested in Bolshevism, politely entertained her.

Back home in Russia, she kept up a casual association with local Bolshevik intelligentsia who frequented theatrical circles. Her family were surprisingly unalarmed by Selena's flirtation with left-wing politics, seeing it as just another expression of her "eccentricity", and turned a blind eye to her pale-pink leanings. The file did not suggest that she was a serious Bolshevik, just that she had friends in Bolshevik circles who might try to use her connections with the royal family to further their aims. It never occurred to whoever compiled the file that Selena might genuinely be complicit in an anti-royal plot.

A few weeks after the February Revolution, which had forced through reforms and the abdication of the tsar, but not yet brought in full Bolshevik rule, Princess Selena visited Countess Sofia Andreiovich. As soon as Nana Ruthie heard the two women were going to take tea in the conservatory she slipped in ahead of them and positioned herself behind an elephant fern. She was far enough away for them not to hear her breathing, but close enough, with the acoustics of the tiled floor and glass walls, to hear whatever confidences they might share. And after a little bit of chit-chat, they got down to business...

"It really shouldn't have come to this; if only Nicky and Alix had listened to people like Sergei," commented Sofia.

"Yes, Sergei would never have wanted them to abdicate. They just needed to be a bit more sensible about everything. Now look where we are," observed Selena.

"In the middle of a revolution."

"Surely not the middle, Sofia. Last month's goings on will be the last of it, I'm sure."

"Are you? I can't say I'm convinced of that – not at all. The people are angry. It won't be long until the Red Gnome –"

"If you mean Vladimir –"

"Lenin. Of course. Don't look at me like that; you know what he's capable of."

Selena sniffed and took on an offended tone. "He is capable of great things."

"Don't be a fool! This is not one of your silly plays. You cannot take off your costume and go home after the curtain falls. This is the new Russia. There is no going back. And by the looks of things, there's going to be bloodshed... oh, for heaven's sake, Selena. Sit down."

"I will not have Vladimir spoken of like that!"

Sofia's voice softened as if speaking to a child or a startled pony. "All right, I'm sorry. I hope you're right about him. But that's not why you came, is it? To discuss the – to discuss Lenin."

From her vantage point Nana Ruthie could only see the two women's feet. Selena reached down and opened her bag.

She took out something about the size of a grapefruit wrapped in cloth. She sat up, taking the object out of Nana's eyeline. Whatever it was made Sofia gasp.

"How did you get that?"

"Alix gave it to me. She asked me to make sure it was kept safe. She's scared that the Bolsheviks will loot the palace. I told her, of course, that they would do no such thing... What? Oh, do stop it, Sofia, or I shall leave. I came here needing your help, and this is the way you treat me –"

Sofia sighed. "I'm sorry. That was uncalled for. You were saying... about the egg..."

Selena humphed and Nana Ruthie could imagine her folding her arms over her spectacular chest.

"I'm *sorry*, Selena..."

"All right. Apology accepted. So Alix has got it into her head that all the Romanov treasure is going to be looted and scattered to the masses. So she's asked me – and a few others – to ensure some key pieces are kept safe. Will you be a treasure-keeper, Sofia?"

"You want me to keep a royal Fabergé Easter egg?"

"Just until things settle down. Will you?"

"I suppose so. At least until Sergei and – at least until I have decided whether or not the family is going to leave."

"I'm so sorry. I forgot about poor Sergei. Is there any news?"

"No."

"Do you fear the worst?"

"I do not, Selena, and I would appreciate it if you did not voice such morbid thoughts."

"Of course. That was quite insensitive of me. So... the egg... will you?"

Sofia sighed again. "Yes, I'll do it. Give it here."

"Before I do, there is something you should know. In case –

well – in case Alix is right and things get – well, things get out of hand. I'm sure they won't. Vladimir won't let it, but…"

"What is it?"

"Let me show you."

Nana Ruthie repositioned herself, desperate to see. She risked the women seeing her, but…

"It's a key! A tiny key!"

Nana still couldn't see. If she shifted a little this way…

"A very important key. So important in fact that the old tsar – Uncle Alex – asked Monsieur Fabergé to hide it in one of these eggs."

"What is it a key to?"

Nana Ruthie could finally see. Just a little bit, but enough. Sofia held a ruby and diamond encrusted golden egg on her lap. A tiny compartment was open and she held an equally tiny key in the palm of her hand. Nana wished she had seen how the compartment had been opened, but she would have to figure that out later. If she ever managed to see the egg again. For now she needed to concentrate on what Selena was saying…

"It's a key to another egg. And in that one there's a map."

"Do you have that egg too?"

"No. Someone else does. Alix and Nicky thought it wise that each treasure-keeper does not know who has the companion egg to their own. The contents of the map are – how should I put it? – incendiary."

"Oh?"

"Oh yes. They show the location of a secret vault." Selena's voice took on a theatrical timbre. "If the contents fall into the wrong hands…"

Nana saw Selena take the egg and key from Sofia and close the secret compartment. She opened and closed it again for good measure. *Ah, so that's how it's done; that ruby there…*

Sofia had an incredulous look on her face. "No offence intended, Selena dear, but why would Alix and Nicky entrust this to you? They fear the Bolsheviks, and they know you have – well – Bolshevik friends…"

Selena sat bolt upright. "My loyalty to the family has never been brought into question! And never will. Alexandra trusts me, she always has, even though she and I differed over Rasputin – as did you and she…"

"Indeed. I for one was glad he died. Shocked by the way it happened – whatever was Felix thinking? – but not unhappy that he had finally gone. Which is my point exactly. We saw things differently. Why then is she trusting you – and me – with my husband a known reformer?"

"For exactly that reason. No one would suspect us. It's genius!"

Sofia did not look convinced, but curiosity got the better of her. "So… what's in this vault?"

"I can't tell you."

"You don't know."

"I most certainly do. I told you: Alix trusts me. And just to prove how much, let me tell you." Her voice became *sotto voce*; Nana Ruthie could imagine her on stage at the Bolshoi or the Royal Albert Hall. "There are secret documents pertaining to all the royal houses of Europe. You know that between them Nicky and Alix are related to them all. Well, so was the late tsar – and Empress Maria Federovna."

Sofia's voice was disdainful. "Of course, everyone knows that!"

"But what they don't know is that Tsar Alexander had been collecting incriminating evidence that could bring down every monarchy on the continent. He kept it for insurance. Just in case he needed their help or they decided one day to turn on him."

Sofia opened her mouth to speak and then closed it again. She was an intelligent woman – far more so than Selena – and Nana realized that she was weighing up the probability of whether or not Selena was telling the truth. And if she was, what it might mean to her circumstances.

"So, if I help you…"

"Not me – Nicky and Alix…"

"So if I help Nicky and Alix, will they help me?"

"I'm sure they will. If they can."

"Indeed. If they can. And that's a big 'if'. However, I have nothing to lose. Sergei is still missing and I will need all the help I can get to find him. I believe the tsar knows where he is. So yes, go and tell them I will help them. I will keep the egg – for now – but in return I want everything Nicky knows about Sergei's whereabouts."

"And if he does not know…"

"Oh, he knows. And if he wants his little secret kept secret, he will have to help me. Do we have a deal?"

Selena looked at her cousin and handed over the egg. "We have a deal."

Nana Ruthie, Anya and Fritzie walked past the wrought iron gates of the Ipatiev House, flanked by two Bolshevik guards. Nana instructed Anya not to look in. They would not be entering the residence the conventional way. This was just a reconnaissance.

Nana felt the little key on the silver chain, cool against her chest, and gripped Anya's hand more tightly.

CHAPTER 12

SUNDAY 21 OCTOBER 1920, LONDON

The man with the bearskin coat whistled to himself and swung his cane as he headed to his next meeting. His previous meeting on the Chelsea Embankment had gone exactly the way he had hoped. Green had been recommended to him by an associate as an efficient courier who – as long as you could meet his eye-watering fee – would take whatever items you desired from A to B. In this case A had been the White Russian Art Exhibition at the Crystal Palace and B a park bench on the Embankment.

The previous night, Green had paid someone to flip the switch – someone who would pocket his fee and seal his lips – and waited for the egg to be passed to him. There was to be a signal when the man in the tuxedo – not his bearskin coat – got close enough to the dais to make his move, then the lights would go out. When they did, the man grabbed the egg and passed it to Green, who had been dressed as a waiter. Green then exited the exhibition hall before the cavalry had time to cordon it off. All of that had gone to plan. But what hadn't been expected was the gunshot. Neither Green nor the man in the tuxedo had a gun with them, nor – so they swore to each other – did they know who had.

"Must've been someone else after the egg, guvnor," said Green as he passed the treasure, innocuously wrapped in an oilcloth, to the man in the bearskin coat. "But we's the ones what got it."

"Indeed, 'we's the ones'," agreed the man as he handed over an envelope full of cash and thanked Green again for his service. Green ran his thumbnail over the bills, doffed his bowler hat, and walked away. The man did not wonder why Green hadn't counted the money; he knew that men like Green knew people who knew people and his life would not be worth living if he had short-changed him. Besides, he had a reputation to protect. He was a "gentleman thief", not a common scoundrel, and honour must always be upheld.

That was why he had risked his life to save the old lady and the child in Moscow three years earlier. He wondered, though, why these eggs attracted such violence. First the massacre of the Russian family, now the wounding of the guard – and he was lucky he was only wounded. Who else was after these eggs? He'd thought in Moscow that it had been sheer coincidence that the Bolshevik thugs had broken into the house at the same time he had. But now, with the events of the previous night still fresh in his mind, he began to wonder if they too – or whoever had sent them – had actually been after the egg as well.

The man looked to left and right and, apart from a lonely dog walker on the towpath, he was alone. He sat on the bench under the gaslight and opened the oilskin to reveal the purple enamel egg with the silver filigree hatching. A large pearl, like a bobble on a hat, topped the egg, and hatching radiated from it. At the cross of each hatch was a diamond – thirty-six in all – each worth more than the man earned in a year in his day job.

The egg rested on a silver tripod. He turned it this way and that, trying to see if he could find any evidence of a secret compartment – but he couldn't. Not all Fabergé eggs had the compartments, but he knew some did. He had found one in the egg in Moscow – but it was empty. Either there had never been anything in it or someone had taken whatever was in it before he broke into the safe that night. Regardless, his client had not been well pleased. At least, that's what his "fence" had told him to justify why he was not getting the full fee they'd agreed.

The man in the bearskin coat was not well pleased himself at that, particularly because he had nearly been killed on the job. After the old lady and the girl had fled across the lawn he had held off the thugs with his rapier until he had a chance to jump over the balcony, holding on to the drape with one hand and his weapon with the other. He had lowered himself down to the lawn while the Bolshevik thugs argued about which one of them was to follow him. And then he made his escape. But before he did he looked up to see a man in a dark suit looking down at him. He had seen the same man last night at the Crystal Palace – had he been the one to fire the gun? Had the man spotted him and realized what was about to happen? Had the bullet been meant for him? The man in the bearskin coat shuddered at the thought, but then dismissed the idea. No, that was highly unlikely. Since he had shaven his full beard and washed out the dye and cut his hair short, he was not easily recognizable as the man who was in Moscow. But he didn't want to take any chances. The first thing that needed to go was the bearskin coat. He took it off and threw it into the river below the Embankment. He shivered, and pulled his light dinner jacket closer around him.

As soon as this job was over and he had handed over the second egg to his fence, it would be time to move on. Venice was nice at this time of year… the opera would be worth the trip alone. Or perhaps he could get another foreign placement with his day job – as he had in Russia. But first things first.

He turned the corner from Oakley Street into King's Road and was soon standing in front of the double brass doors of

Oscar's Jazz Club. He resisted the urge to pat the wrapped egg in his inside pocket, in case he was being watched. Instead he flashed a smile at the doorman.

"Shocking what happened at the Crystal Palace last night, wasn't it, guvnor? I read about it in *The Globe* this morning. You was there, wasn't you?"

"I was, yes. Shocking. Absolutely shocking."

Poppy knocked on Princess Selena's bedroom door. Despite being told that the Russian woman would not want to see her, Poppy was determined to get some kind of statement from her to file with Rollo before deadline.

"Who is it?" came the answer, thick with tears.

"It's Poppy. Can I come in?"

"No, you cannot! How could you do this to me?"

"I did nothing. It wasn't my decision to print the picture. It was my editor's."

"But you wrote the article. The one about the treasure-keepers."

"Yes, but there was nothing in there that –"

"I have nothing to say to you, Miss Denby. Now leave me alone!"

Poppy sighed, reluctant to give in, but she didn't have much choice. She would try again in the morning. Selena would have to come out of her room sometime.

The man who had once owned a bearskin coat walked into the jazz-soaked atmosphere of Oscar's and headed straight for the bar. But as he did he noticed that someone had got there before him and was talking to his fence. It was Rollo Rolandson, the editor of *The Daily Globe*, nursing a tumbler of whisky. He doubted that Rollo knew the barman was a fence – only a handful of people did – and it was probably just a coincidence that the American was there. Still, better not risk it. He'd have to deliver the egg another day. He went into the men's cloakroom and wrote a quick note, using the code he had been given by the fence, and asked to rearrange their handover day. He placed the note in the crack behind the hatstand just outside the men's cloakroom, as per instruction.

And then he heard a woman singing – ah, Delilah Marconi. Such a pity he couldn't stay.

Poppy smiled at the doorman at Oscar's as he pushed open the doors for her. "Evening, Miss Denby, ma'am. Miss Marconi is already here."

"So I hear," she said as the alto broke into the final chorus of "Avalon" by Al Jolson.

Poppy walked across the dance floor as Delilah brought the song to a close. The club was only a quarter full, but there was still a good round of enthusiastic applause. Many of Oscar's regulars had been at the Crystal Palace the night before, so Poppy wasn't surprised to see most of them had decided to have a night in. She stifled a yawn, shunning thoughts of her nice warm bed and eiderdown comforter, and joined Rollo at the bar.

"Evening, Poppy. Glad you could make it," said the red-haired editor, signalling for the barman to bring Poppy a drink. "Chardonnay, is it?"

"Just soda water tonight, Rollo; I have a headache."

Rollo chuckled and put in the order. He waited for the barman to serve a customer at the other end of the bar before continuing his conversation with his reporter.

"Did you get anything?"

Poppy sipped her water and shook her head. "Sorry, no. She wouldn't talk to me. Wouldn't even let me in her room." Then she went on to tell Rollo what Aunt Dot and Miss King had told her about Selena fainting when she saw the picture of her and Princess Irina fighting.

Rollo threw back his head and roared. He had a loud, sonorous laugh that still surprised Poppy. Other customers looked over and smiled. Rollo raised his glass in their direction. "I didn't do much better," he said. "The barman couldn't shed much light. Like we suspected, he'd just been hired in to cater the exhibition. Oscar had provided all of the staff – waiters, waitresses and bar staff."

"Is Oscar here?"

"No. He's taken the night off. We'll have to try and catch up with him tomorrow. Can you handle that? I've got a meeting lined up with the Yusopovs and Yazzie. Ike is talking to Marjorie Reynolds at the Home Office and Vasili Safin at the embassy."

Poppy agreed that she could. "I'll try Selena again too. I might go and see her at the theatre. Maybe I can slip into her dressing room before she can lock me out. I'll speak to Delilah and see what she suggests."

"You using my name in vain?" Delilah swanned over to the bar and sat down on a stool, crossing her silk-clad legs.

Rollo looked at them appreciatively. "Beautiful song, Miz Marconi."

"Well, thank you, Mr Rolandson. Written by one of your countrymen."

"He was originally Russian, you know, or Lithuanian. Same thing."

"I didn't know that. How fascinating! Did you know that, Poppy?"

"I didn't."

"But they're everywhere, these days, aren't they?"

"They certainly are," said Poppy, looking over her friend's shoulder at the man talking to the barman at the other end of the bar. It was Andrei Nogovski, head of security at the Russian embassy and assistant to the interim ambassador, Vasili Safin. She couldn't hear what he was saying, but his body language was interrogative. And though the barman was trying to look nonchalant, the set of his shoulders told Poppy he was tense. Then, without touching his drink, Nogovski slipped off his stool and left the dance hall.

"Excuse me, you two. I'll be back in a minute."

"Where are you going?"

"To follow a lead."

CHAPTER 13

JULY 1918, YEKATERINBURG, RUSSIA

Nana Ruthie pushed her carpet bag into the bush and told Anya to share the bread between herself and Fritzie. "Now, what did I say?"

"That I mustn't leave here until you come back."

"That's right. I might take a little while, but don't come looking for me. Promise?"

"I promise, Nana."

"Good girl. You can play patience if you get bored."

"And Fritzie?"

Nana patted the little dachshund on his head and he snuffled her with his wet nose. "Fritzie can have a snooze. Don't let him leave the hedge though – promise me."

"We promise, don't we, Fritzie?" Fritzie pawed the air.

Nana chuckled and spruced up the tall grass in front of the blueberry hedge to disguise the child's whereabouts, before picking her way back through the wood to the perimeter wall of the Ipatiev House. The house backed onto woodland. Guards stood only at the front gate, so after she checked that the coast was clear, she chose a spot covered in ivy and pushed her way through. The six-foot wall had plenty of footholds for her, but it was still a tricky climb for a sixty-year-old woman; for the hundredth time that week she wished she were back in Tower Hamlets. Oh, how she wished she were there now.

Safely over the wall, she straightened her back, groaning with the effort. Woodland surrounded her and she headed in the direction of where she thought the house should be. She had not fully worked out what she was going to do when she got there; she would reassess when she had a clearer view of the house and gardens.

The women in the bread queue had said that the royal family and their attendants – including Princess Selena – were free to roam the grounds. If her suspicions were correct, Selena was not really a prisoner, and was still being used by the Bolsheviks to get close to the royals. After overhearing the conversation with Countess Sofia Andreiovich, Nana Ruthie had gone to the embassy to meet her contact. He had told her that a mole inside the Bolshevik inner circle had informed him that Selena had been press-ganged into working as a double agent. She had been promised that no harm would come to anyone in her family as long as she fed them information about what the Romanovs were planning and thinking. Nana Ruthie realized that this line would only work with a stupid person – and fortunately for the Bolsheviks, Selena was just that. So when Selena was imprisoned along with the tsar, tsarina, children and attendants, Nana strongly suspected she was still acting as a mole.

Nana's plan was to attract Selena's attention and to tell her she knew the whereabouts of the key – which she had taken off and hidden under a stone on the other side of the wall. She would tell Selena that the key was in London – taken there in a diplomatic pouch – and if the Russian princess were to arrange safe passage for Nana and Anya, she would hand it over once they reached England. She calculated that Selena would not tell the Bolsheviks that she had the key, as the actress would want it in her hand before she did and would relish the influence it would give her with Lenin. And if she didn't think like that already, Nana would convince her that that's what she needed to do. It was imperative though that Nana catch Selena on her own. She could assess, face to face, whether her theory about the woman was right. If it wasn't, she would be able to outrun the overweight actress, but not any accompanying guards.

Nana neared the edge of the tree line and the house came into view. Out of nowhere two people ran towards her. She froze, then slipped behind a shrub hoping she hadn't been spotted. Peering through the foliage she saw it was a man and a woman, their clothes and hands splattered with blood. They stopped a few feet from her. She knew one, but not the other.

The woman held out her hands like Lady Macbeth. "You promised, Nogovski! You promised! You promised they wouldn't be hurt."

"It wasn't my doing, Selena, I swear. It was out of my control."

"But they're dead! They're all dead! Even little Alexei. Oh God, oh dear God!"

The man, Nogovski, tried to placate her, looking over his shoulder as if checking they weren't being followed. "It was out of my control," he said again, his voice hollow.

Selena's voice grew shriller and shriller: "They're dead! You killed them!" She flung herself at Nogovski and clawed at his face. He grabbed her hands and wrestled her to her knees.

"I did not kill them, woman. If anyone did it was you."

Selena threw her head back and glared at him. He was holding her wrists above her head. "*Me*? What did I do?"

"If you had told them where the key was they might have spared them. It might have distracted them."

"But I didn't know. I told them it was at the Andreiovich house –"

"It wasn't there."

"But it was. That was the last place I saw it, I swear. But that's not the reason they killed them. It's because they're royal. They'll kill me next, they'll –"

Selena's words were knocked out of her mouth as Nogovski struck her hard across the face. She looked at him, still kneeling, like a victim before her executioner.

"Are you going to kill me too?" she whispered.

"No," he said, as he took a handkerchief and held it over her mouth and nose until her body went limp. "No. I'm going to save you."

Nana Ruthie smelled the sickly scent of chloroform. She held her hand to her mouth as she watched Nogovski struggle to pick up the body of Princess Selena Romanova Yusopova and carry her back to the house. When they were gone she stumbled back to the wall, leaving behind all hope of salvation at the Ipatiev House.

SUNDAY 21 OCTOBER 1920, LONDON

Poppy slipped off her bar stool and as nonchalantly as possible followed Andrei Nogovski as he crossed the dance hall and went into the foyer. To her disappointment he went into the men's cloakroom. The clerk at the coat-check asked if she would like her coat. Not knowing what else to do, she said "yes". As she waited for the man to return with her red mackintosh, Nogovski came out of the men's room. *That was quick*, she thought. He looked to left and right, and slipped his arm behind the hat stand. When he pulled it out again he looked up and caught Poppy's eye. Drat, she needed to work on her surveillance technique. *Not quite Secret Service material*, she thought wryly as she slapped a false smile on her face.

"Have you lost something, Mr Nogovski?"

He peered at her, as if trying to place her face, then answered: "No." He put the piece of paper in his pocket and then waited in line for his coat. The clerk soon appeared with Poppy's mac and then took Nogovski's chit for his.

"So, Mr Nogovski, I was wondering if –"

"I have an appointment with Ike Garfield in the morning." His coat arrived and he shrugged into it, then plucked his hat from the hatstand.

"Yes, but –"

"Good evening, Miss Denby." And with that he walked out of the club, leaving her smarting.

CHAPTER 14

Poppy arrived at *The Globe* office at 9 a.m. the following morning. After a solid eight hours' sleep she felt almost human again. She greeted Mavis and took the stairs. On the second floor she cast a glance into the art and photography department and noted that Daniel's hat was on the stand. Good, she would try to meet up with him later for lunch. On the third floor she bumped into Ivan Molanov as he was coming out of the lift and opening the archive.

"Good morning, Ivan. How are you today?"

The Russian man had large bags under his eyes. "I could do with another weekend, Poppy," he said and put the key into the lock.

"I know how you feel. I assume you've heard all about the drama at the exhibition?"

Ivan grunted.

"Actually, I'm glad I caught you. Can you pull out a couple of Jazz Files for me?"

"Which ones?" asked Ivan as he pushed open the double doors. Poppy followed him in and waited as he took off his black mackintosh and homburg hat.

"Princess Selena Romanova Yusopova and Felix and Irina Yusopov. They're all related," she explained, unnecessarily. Ivan,

117

being Russian, was bound to know that already, she reminded herself.

He nodded thoughtfully. "Yes, I will get them out for you. I will send Vicky up with them later."

Poppy expressed her thanks and headed for the door. But then she remembered something. "Oh, and while you're at it, do you have a file on Andrei Nogovski? He's the security consultant for the Russian embassy. Not a society type, so it's a long shot, but I thought you might –"

Ivan's brows met in the middle as he growled his response. "Stay away from him, Poppy. That man is dangerous."

"Oh," said Poppy, suddenly interested. "How do you know that?"

Ivan put down his briefcase on his meticulously organized desk, then turned back to the young reporter.

"I know him from my life in Russia. You know I was a reformer."

Poppy nodded. Rollo had told her as much.

"Well, the tsar and his police – the *Okrana* – did not like reformers. Nogovski was *Okrana*. He is dangerous man. Him and his new boss, Vasili Safin. They are both snakes. Be very careful, Poppy."

"But it can't be the same Nogovski. This man is a Bolshevik."

"It is the same," said Ivan and sat down, pulling his desk diary towards him. "Now you excuse me, I have work to do."

Poppy knew that Ivan would not volunteer more information when he was in this mood. She would have to wait for the Jazz Files to come up and then ask Rollo to use his influence to get more out of the archivist on Nogovski. *How interesting*, she thought, *a gamekeeper turned poacher. Or perhaps he was still a gamekeeper…* Poppy would definitely be speaking to Comrade Nogovski again.

Four hours later and Poppy had put in a solid stretch at her desk in the newsroom. There was not much to add to the collection of articles to follow up the robbery at the exhibition, so Poppy typed up her research to date for the proposed interviews with George Bernard Shaw and the theatre director, Constantin Stanislavski. She had just about exhausted that when Vicky brought up the Jazz Files she had requested. She thanked the young woman, got herself another cup of coffee, and opened the files to read.

She started with Princess Selena. She noted that Selena had starred in *Arms and the Man* in Paris – and, according to the Jazz File on her, she had met Vladimir Lenin. There was a note in the file, pinned to the back of a grainy photograph of Selena holding a bouquet of flowers that Lenin had sent to her. *How odd*, thought Poppy, *that a Russian aristocrat would be associating with an anti-royal revolutionary*. However, the date on the photograph was 1912, and from what Poppy had read, the true extent of the Bolshevik ambitions was not widely understood at the time.

Another photograph showed Selena with the Chelsea Six (the suffragist cell that Aunt Dot and her friends had belonged to) and Emmeline Pankhurst. The attached note said that when Selena was in London, starring in a West End show, she had become friends with leading suffragist leaders and had even considered setting up her own cell in St Petersburg. What was it that Marjorie Reynolds had said the other night? That Selena might appear silly but it had taken courage to follow a career as an actress and that she was a feminist in her own way? The Jazz File seemed to back this up. But Selena was a contradiction: on the one hand she was part of the richest royal family in the world – and, from her comments about "poor Nicky and Alix" the other night at dinner, fiercely loyal to them – but on the other, she associated with Marxists, socialists, feminists and reformers. Poppy concluded, however, that the two were not mutually exclusive. Aunt Dot was a feminist, socialist and reformer, but she was also comfortably upper-middle class and saw absolutely no contradiction in it.

In the file Poppy also found a note from a "source in the Home Office" that Selena was considered a "person of interest" and had been under observation by the British embassy in St Petersburg. She wondered if Marjorie Reynolds might be able to shed some more light on this. She would mention it to her.

She was just about to close the file when a hand-drawn sketch, coloured with pencils, caught her eye. It was of an elaborate pendant necklace of rubies and emeralds. The note on the back informed her that the garish trinket had been stolen from Princess Selena in Paris in 1912 during the *Arms and the Man* run at the Paris Opera House. It had been on loan to her from the Russian empress Maria Federovna. Selena was reportedly "devastated". There was no record in the file to suggest that the jewel, or the jewel thief, had ever been found. *How interesting*, thought Poppy as she leaned back in her chair and nursed her coffee cup. Surely this couldn't be a coincidence: two separate incidents where two separate jewels, both of them on "loan" to Selena from the Romanov royal family, had been stolen. *Hmmm*, thought Poppy, *we might finally have a lead.*

Just before the editorial planning meeting, Poppy outlined her findings to Rollo. They both agreed that before she could share the information at the staff meeting, she should try to find out more. She said she would go to the theatre after lunch to see if she could speak to Selena. The planning meeting was wrapped up in half an hour, and as the journalists sloped out, she sidled up to Daniel. "Want to go out for lunch?"

Daniel looked down at her and smiled. "You mean I get you all to myself for a couple of hours?"

"One hour," corrected Poppy. "I've got a job, you know."

He gave a wry grin. "Well, it's better than nothing. Picnic outside Temple? We can pick something up from the sandwich shop on the corner."

Poppy looked out of the window and saw that the sun had come out. Autumn would soon turn to winter, so best they enjoy what was left of it. "It's a date."

An hour later, Poppy reluctantly said goodbye to Daniel with a kiss on the cheek and jumped on the next bus to Waterloo. They had agreed to Sunday lunch at Daniel's house the following weekend, when she would finally get to meet the formidable Maggie and Daniel's two children. Poppy had suggested they first meet on neutral territory – perhaps a picnic in Battersea Park – but Maggie would have none of it. No doubt she wanted to have the home advantage. Poppy wished Daniel had sided with her instead of his sister and agreed to the day out.

She remembered what Yasmin Reece-Lansdale had said the other night in the cab – that a man with children would mark the end of her career. Golly, what a thought. She was struggling to come to terms with the notion that she even had a career, never mind that it might end. Five months ago she had arrived in London with the simple ambition of being a companion to her aunt. But then… oh my, what a whirlwind! She'd never dreamed that her life could be anywhere near as exciting as it was now. Surely it wasn't going to come to an end. Was it really impossible for her to get married and have a job at the same time?

She'd had a friend back in Morpeth, a girl called Mary, who had studied at teacher training college. She had told Poppy that the reason there were so many spinsters in the teaching profession was not that these women did not want to get married, but that there was a marriage bar in place – a practice backed up by law – and they would be forced to resign if they did. It was believed that they would soon be taking time off to have children, and that simply would not do. Would it be the same for her as a journalist? She couldn't imagine Rollo holding to such outdated notions; but Daniel? She wasn't so sure about him.

Daniel loved his children above all else. And that was as it should be. But the bottom line was they weren't *her* children. Would she really be expected to take over the role of mother if she and Daniel ever got married? And what if they had children together? Is that what Daniel would expect? Perhaps. Perhaps not. It was probably something she should find out. Daniel respected women and their right to a career if they chose to have one, but he was no feminist. She knew he would never contemplate the notion that perhaps *he* should stay home to look after his own children – or perhaps work part-time and share the childcare duties so she could also follow her career. However, if she were entirely truthful, the notion was alien to her too. She remembered when she first came to London and listened incredulously to her aunt's suffragette friends speculating that one day that's how the world would be. But it wasn't the world Poppy lived in, and she had to face the reality of what would be expected of her now, not in some utopian feminist future. Would she really be prepared to leave her children – her stepchildren or her own – in the care of another woman (paid or otherwise) while she went out to work? She wasn't sure, but she was certain of one thing: she didn't want to lose Daniel.

The bus pulled up outside Waterloo station and she got off, then waited for a gap in the traffic to cross the road and head down to the Old Vic Theatre. After a lovely blue Aston Martin passed, she was on her way. *One day*, Poppy thought, *I might drive something like that. Or is that also a dream…*

Since her appointment as the arts and entertainment editor at *The Daily Globe*, she had become a familiar face at the Old Vic Theatre, and thanks to her positive reviews and thoughtful, balanced journalism, she had free access to backstage. She entered the foyer and waved to the clerk in the box office, who was selling advance tickets to *The Cherry Orchard*, which was opening in three weeks.

Chekhov's famous play about the demise of a Russian aristocratic family first played in 1904 in Moscow, on the eve of the 1905 Russian uprising. It sounded a warning to the tsarist regime that if it did not reform it would die. Now, sixteen years later, Chekhov's prophecy had come to pass and the London performance was being met with great anticipation. How would the old text read in light of recent events? Would Stanislavski make any overt references to the Bolshevik takeover through staging, costume or set? Would Peter Trofimov – played by Delilah's boyfriend, Adam – move from being a mere left-leaning reformer to a full-on Bolshevik? Poppy doubted the famous Russian director would go as far as amending the text – which would be tantamount to theatrical heresy – but there were other ways of building sub-text into the production. Poppy was eager to see what these would be and she could hardly wait for the press preview in a fortnight.

In the meantime, she reminded herself, she was working on another story, which coincidentally starred the same leading lady: Princess Selena Romanova Yusopova. Poppy headed for the actress's dressing room. En route she passed the Green Room, where some members of cast and crew were smoking and drinking tea. Adam spotted Poppy and waved. She waved back, but didn't go in. Unperturbed, Adam returned to his conversation with a man Poppy recognized as the prop manager. Past the Green Room Poppy could hear the sultry tones of Delilah Marconi, then a deep Russian voice admonishing: "Too sexy. Far too sexy. Be an innocent, Delilah. Try to remember what that was like!"

Gosh, Delilah's not going to like that, thought Poppy. As she passed the rehearsal room and spotted Delilah's red-flushed face as she turned away from Stanislavski, she knew she was right. Poor Delilah. She would talk to her about it later. The man had practically called her a floozy! And although the Maltese girl was a fun-loving bright young thing, she was certainly not a floozy.

Eventually Poppy came to the dressing room. Selena was obviously in, as a sign hung from the door: *Do not disturb*. Well, disturb her she must. This cat-and-mouse game had gone on far too long. Poppy had a job to do and she wasn't going to allow a prima donna like Selena to stand in her way.

She decided against barging in unannounced and instead knocked lightly. Perhaps too lightly, as only silence answered. She tentatively turned the knob – it was unlocked, good – and pushed open the door. "Selen–" she began, then gagged on her own scream.

There, sprawled across a pink chaise longue, was Selena, her white satin dressing gown splayed to reveal a pair of fleshy thighs and an ample bosom drenched red with blood.

CHAPTER 15

The amber liquid burned Poppy's throat. It was the first time she'd tasted cognac, and she hoped it would be the last. Stanislavski had thrust the drink upon her after he had responded to her screams. A man used to drama on and off the stage, he seemed to take the death of his leading lady in his stride. To him the dressing room was a theatre that needed to be managed; the unfolding events after Poppy's discovery of the body, a play to be devised.

The central character lay in repose like the Swan Queen with an arrow in her heart. But there was no arrow; only a red stain over her chest. "Stabbed through the heart" was Stanislavski's diagnosis, as if he had seen a myriad other victims with similar fatal injuries. The rest of the cast and crew that came in and out of the dressing room before the police arrived confirmed the great director's assessment.

"Certainly looks that way," said Adam, offering Poppy a refill of the cognac. She declined.

Delilah came in and announced that the theatre manager, Lilian Baylis, and the police had been called and they were on their way. No one should touch anything – she had been instructed – and the dressing room, but not the theatre, was to be evacuated.

"Evacuated? I shall not be evacuating anything," declared Stanislavski, and he plopped himself down on the dressing table stool and folded his arms. "The rest of you, though, should go."

"But the policeman said –"

"I do not give two hoots what the policeman said, Miss Marconi. My Lyubov has been murdered. *My* Lyubov. And we open in two weeks! I knew it was a mistake to rehearse at the same time as the auditions for the Scottish Play." He shuddered.

Poppy recalled the name of the Shakespeare directed by Robert Atkins that was to follow *The Cherry Orchard*.

"First Bernice falls into the orchestra pit, and now this!" Stanislavski gestured to Princess Selena with a sweep of his arm, then rested his forehead on the heel of his hand, as despondent as Macbeth on the edge of Birnam Wood.

Adam gingerly patted him on the shoulder and then picked up a box of chocolates from Selena's dressing table and offered them to him. "Come on, old chap – er, Monsieur Stanislavski – I'm sure we can find another Lyubov. Here, have a chocolate. She won't be needing them any more."

"Er, Adam, maybe you shouldn't do that," suggested Poppy. "It might be evidence."

"Evidence of what?"

"I don't know. Maybe the killer brought them in with him – or her. They haven't been eaten yet, and –"

But it was too late. Monsieur Stanislavski plucked a foil-wrapped chocolate from the box and started unwrapping it.

Adam gave Poppy an apologetic shrug and looked as though he was about to continue offering them around the room.

Annoyed, Poppy snatched the box from Adam and put the lid firmly back on, placing it, as best she could, in its original spot.

"Sorry, Poppy," he muttered.

"Hmmm," said Poppy. "Well, let's not move anything else, shall we? The police need to find everything as close to –" she cast a glance at the unfortunate Selena and bit her lip – "as close to the time of death as possible."

Everyone looked at her expectantly, as if she were now an authority on crime scene investigation. Golly, what did she really know, apart from what she'd read in detective novels? A woman had died! Should they really all be standing around discussing it as if it was simply a rehearsal for a murder mystery play? But what else could they do? Poppy felt that perhaps she should not be taking such a leading role in this. Surely Monsieur Stanislavski should be in charge. She tried to catch his eye, to defer to him, but the director was too busy trying to pick a fiddly piece of foil wrapping off his chocolate to notice. Should she tell him *not* to eat the chocolate? Did she have a right to?

But before she could finish her musings on the chain of command, the director flicked the piece of foil away and popped the chocolate into his mouth.

Oh well, thought Poppy, *that's that then.*

But that wasn't that. Stanislavski gagged and clutched his throat.

"You all right, Monsieur?" asked Adam and patted him on the back. The gagging continued and the director started turning an alarming shade of puce. Poppy suddenly recalled a scene from *The Mysterious Affair at Styles* involving poisoned coffee. Good heavens, could it be…? Poppy leapt up and threw her arms around Stanislavski's waist, clutching both hands into a fist, and pushing upwards into his solar plexis again and again until a glob of half-eaten chocolate truffle cannoned out of his mouth and splattered against the dressing-room mirror. Poppy then thrust the tumbler of cognac at him and instructed him to gargle and spit it out. He did.

"Bravo, Poppy! Bravo!" said Delilah to the accompaniment of applause from the cast and crew.

As the director gulped down the cognac, Adam helped him sit down, enquiring as to his health. *His health? If it weren't so serious it would be comical*, thought Poppy. But then she started shaking. Golly, had she just done that? Her heart was beating ten to the dozen and she steadied herself against the dressing table.

Stanislavski slumped beside her, his face as white as cold cream, his shapely lips an unnatural blue. Adam patted his hand, muttering worried platitudes.

"Where did you learn to do that?" asked the props master, edging in to see the action.

"First aid training when I helped out at the convalescent home during the war," Poppy mumbled, then took a swig of cognac herself. She braced herself as the burning liquid lined her throat. Then she remembered something else from *The Mysterious Affair at Styles*. She opened the chocolate box lid and sniffed. *Golly, could that really be…?* "I think you'd better call an ambulance, Delilah. We should get Monsieur Stanislavski checked out. I can smell almonds in the chocolate box. Can you?"

Delilah had a sniff. "Yes. So what? There are usually almonds in chocolate boxes."

Of course, Delilah was right. But Poppy was not going to take any chances. Stanislavski did not look well and there was, after all, a murderer on the loose…

"Yes, but just in case."

"You mean…" whispered Stanislavski.

"I'm afraid I do, sir. There's a chance these chocolates might have been poisoned."

Adam snorted. "I know this is a theatre, Poppy, but don't you think you're being a tad melodramatic? Monsieur Stanislavski simply swallowed without chewing properly. He's fine now, aren't you, sir?"

"I'm not sure, Mr Lane," said Stanislavski. "I feel quite ill."

"But surely that's just –"

"Oh, for heaven's sake, Adam, what if Poppy's right? Selena's already dead; we don't want two corpses on our hands." Delilah nodded an apology to Stanislavski, then lowered her voice. "Better safe than sorry, anyway. I'll call the ambulance."

Relieved that at last someone was taking her seriously, Poppy picked up the box of chocolates again and examined it. She used a silk handkerchief to hold it, aware that whatever fingerprints were left after Adam and Stanislavski had man-handled it – and she to rescue it – needed to be preserved. It was an expensive-looking package with a small card tucked into the corner of the ribbon wrapped around the lid. She doubted anyone had touched the card during the recent debacle, so she extracted it carefully using the corner of the handkerchief. It might be the best chance of getting some clear fingerprints. In small, earnest handwriting was inscribed: *"To Princess Selena Romanova Yusopova, the Old Vic Theatre. From a repentant fool."*

How very strange, thought Poppy. She read the card again; not to make sense of the message but to try to dispel the nagging feeling that she had seen the handwriting before. Surely it couldn't be… Poppy looked around. The rest of the theatre folk were attending to Stanislavski, the body of the leading lady no longer centre stage. The police would be here soon. She should hand the card over for evidence. But instead of slipping it back into the ribbon she wrapped it in the handkerchief and deftly slid it into her coat pocket, hoping no one had seen her. She felt a wave of guilt, but then justified herself immediately with the thought that she just needed to check something before the police put two and two together and came up with five. And as she did, the dressing room door opened and Lilian Baylis and Detective Chief Inspector Jasper Martin entered, followed by half a dozen Bobbies.

Martin took in the scene immediately. "Get that man to hospital!"

"Someone's gone to call an ambulance," offered Adam.

Martin knelt down and examined Stanislavski, sniffing the air around him like a bloodhound. "No time for that," said Martin, gesturing his men to pick Stanislavski up. "Take him in the Black Mariah. Go with him, Miss Baylis." Then he swept the room with an interrogative glare. "As far as I can tell, you are the only one here who isn't a suspect."

As Stanislavski was carried from the room, followed by a visibly shaken Lilian Baylis, Martin turned his full gaze on Poppy. He sneered. "I see the press are here already. Escort her out of here, sergeant, but don't let her out of the theatre just yet."

Poppy took a step back. "But Inspector Martin –"

"But nothing. I don't want details of this in the papers before I've even had a chance to examine the crime scene. Sergeant…"

"But Poppy was the one who found the body," offered Adam, stepping between Poppy and the advancing sergeant. "Surely she should stay."

Martin grunted, sticking his thumbs in his waistcoat pockets and thrusting out his chest. "Just my luck," he muttered before barking orders to his team to clear everyone from the room. He held up his hand. "Not you, Miss Denby. I want to talk to you."

Two hours later, Inspector Martin declared that he was finished with the witnesses for now, and let them all go. Poppy declined Delilah and Adam's offer to accompany them to Oscar's to steady their nerves.

"No, I need to get back to the office. Rollo will never forgive me if we get scooped by *The Courier*." Poppy spotted Lionel Saunders standing on tip-toe, trying to look over the police cordon that now surrounded the theatre – and behind him was Daniel. She motioned for the photographer to meet her across the road from the theatre. As she waited to cross, a maroon Chrysler pulled up, and out stepped the interim Russian ambassador Vasili Safin and his security chief Andrei Nogovski. Although there was a break in the traffic, Poppy lingered to see if there would be any drama between the Russians and the constabulary. She was disappointed that there was not.

Safin demanded to see DCI Martin. A Russian national had been killed and he wanted answers. The Bobby didn't argue, and ushered him in. Nogovski followed, his face grim.

Poppy looked up to see Daniel already across the road, waving to her. She waved back, quickly crossing to join him, then filled him in on everything that had happened.

"Good golly, Poppy! You mean you were there from the very beginning? You discovered the body? Rollo will be on cloud nine!" Then he looked at her, his face concerned. "Are you all right? It must have been a bit of a shock."

Poppy smiled, grateful for his concern. "I'm fine, thanks." She almost added: *Don't worry, I've had some cognac*, but wisely held her tongue. Instead she said: "I'd better get to Rollo. When you're finished here can you go to the hospital to check on Constantin Stanislavski, then telephone the office to tell us how he is? I hope I managed to get most of the poison out of him, but he might still have ingested some, and he wasn't looking very well."

Daniel looked into her eyes, clearly still worried, but then nodded. "Of course. I've got all the shots I can now anyway, since they've removed the body. And the police aren't letting us in any closer."

"Righto. I'll see you back at the office later." She said her goodbyes and waved down a cab. There was no time to waste on waiting for buses, and a story like this would be worth the expense.

CHAPTER 16

Daniel was right: Rollo was on cloud nine. "This on top of the Crystal Palace robbery? What are the odds, Poppy? What are the odds?" The little editor was pacing to and fro across the small area of clear space that surrounded his desk, among the sea of files and paraphernalia that filled the rest of his office. Vicky Thompson, who had been hired to replace Poppy as his assistant after she had been promoted to arts and entertainment editor, had made little headway in bringing order to the American's domain.

He rubbed his large hands together in glee.

Poppy frowned. "Let's not forget that someone actually died today, Rollo. I know it's a good story, but…"

Rollo's shaggy red eyebrows came together in contrition. "Of course, you're right, Poppy, and I realize she was a friend of your aunt's —"

Her aunt? Oh crikey! She'd better ring Aunt Dot, or she'd have her guts for garters. The older woman would never forgive her if someone else in her social circle heard the news first.

"Can I make a telephone call, Rollo? Before we continue?"

"Of course," said the editor, his momentary chagrin forgotten as he began to make frantic notes about how *The Globe* was going to announce to the world that a White Russian princess had been murdered. He crossed out a word and wrote another. No, how a White Russian princess had been *assassinated*. He quivered in delight.

***

"Oh Poppy! How absolutely ghastly!" declared Aunt Dot from the other end of the telephone line. "Poor, poor Selena. Someone will have to tell her family. Should I do that, darling?"

"The police might have done so already, Aunt Dot, but there's no harm in you contacting them too."

"Then I shall. Felix, Irina and Selena might have had their differences, but in the end, blood is thicker than water."

Poppy wondered if it was, but kept her suspicions to herself.

"I'm sure they will break it to the empress gently. The poor woman has had enough tragedy to deal with lately. This on top of poor Nicky and Alix and the children…"

Poppy heard her aunt sigh, and although fraught with theatricality, she didn't doubt its sincerity.

"And then there's poor Victor Marconi… he and Selena were close for a while… And George, Norman and Marjorie… To think we only had dinner together less than a week ago!" Aunt Dot started to cry.

"Are you all right, Aunt Dot?"

The ageing actress sniffed. "I am, my dear. Don't worry about me. I'll get on letting everyone know and then I'll go and visit Constantin. Are you sure he's all right?"

"I hope so," said Poppy quietly, the enormity of what had happened suddenly dawning on her. She'd discovered a murder victim and then potentially saved the life of another within the space of fifteen minutes. She closed her eyes and took a deep breath, then tuned in to the familiar, comforting voice of her aunt.

"I hope so too. Do let me know if you hear anything more. Lilian must be beside herself. And what are they going to do about Lyubov?"

"Lyubov?"

"They'll be needing a new lead. First Bernice, then Selena; there are not many actresses with sufficient experience to fill in at the last minute."

"I should imagine not," agreed Poppy.

"But I think I might know of someone who could do it."

"That's good," said Poppy, but her mind was not on who, if anyone, would replace a dead actress in a theatre play, but rather on the person – or persons – who had killed her.

Poppy went back to Rollo's office carrying two mugs of coffee. Rollo grunted his thanks as she placed a mug on the concentric stains on his desk, and then sat down with her own.

"Danny Boy's been on the blower. You were right. Cyanide. They pumped the director's stomach and they think he'll be all right. They say your quick action probably saved his life."

Poppy flushed, proud and grateful that Stanislavski was going to be fine.

Rollo smiled at her, then made some notes. "So, moving on… The cops think that the dressing room had been searched."

"That's right," said Poppy, then took a sip of the sweet, dark brew in her mug. "They said there were signs that Selena's effects had been disturbed – even before half the theatre staff waltzed in to watch the show."

"Was this before or after she was stabbed through the heart with a rapier?"

"They're not sure."

"But they're sure it was a rapier?"

"They strongly suspect. It will be confirmed later, once the chief medical officer has had a look."

"And you definitely heard Martin instructing his lads to seal off the props room? Particularly the armoury?"

"I did. Obviously they suspect that the killer might have

used one of the theatre's swords. But I'm not sure yet if they realize that the swords they use on stage have been blunted."

"I don't imagine the boys in blue attend much theatre, Miz Denby."

Poppy imagined that if anyone did, it would be Detective Chief Inspector Jasper Martin with his society wife, but she didn't offer her opinion.

"So Selena was stabbed through the heart with a rapier and Stanislavski was poisoned with chocolates – which no doubt had also been meant for her. The same killer? Why would he –"

"– or she…"

"Or she, have two means of assault. In case one didn't work?"

"Maybe the chocolates were delivered first, but Selena didn't eat them. I did hear her say she was trying to lose weight to fit into her costume," offered Poppy.

"Maybe, maybe not. How did the killer – he or she –" he grinned at Poppy – "know that Selena *hadn't* eaten the chocolates?"

"Perhaps he – or she – came to check and saw them uneaten."

"Which suggests Selena knew the killer. Why else would she let them into the dressing room?"

"And put up a *Do not disturb* sign on the door."

"It could have been put up after the killer left."

Poppy conceded that was true. "I suppose they could have done it to buy themselves time to get out of the theatre before the body was discovered."

"Who says they left the theatre?"

Poppy put down her mug with a shaky hand. "Surely you're not saying…?"

"Anyone in the theatre could have done it. And then stayed

in the building. It could have been an inside job." Rollo leaned back on his seat and cradled the back of his head in his hands. Poppy wished he didn't look as if he were enjoying this as much. But if she were honest, she was too. She shook off the self-revelation and turned her attention back to her editor.

"But what would have been the motive?"

Rollo moved his head from side to side, stretching his neck. "She was a prima donna. No one liked her. She could have insulted, offended or humiliated any one of her co-workers until they snapped. You know what these theatre luvvies are like – highly strung."

Poppy shook her head. "There needs to be more to it. Remember, the police said the killer appeared to have been looking for something... and let's not forget this is only two days after the theft of the Fabergé egg from the exhibition."

Rollo grinned and Poppy could not help thinking he looked like the Cheshire Cat from *Alice in Wonderland*. "Now you're thinking like a journalist, Poppy. I agree. The two events are inextricably linked. Who at the theatre was also at the exhibition?"

Poppy thought for a moment. "Well, obviously there was me, Delilah and Adam, and I think Stanislavski was there too..."

"He was. And Baylis. They came in together – fashionably late."

"You don't think they're suspects, do you? Firstly, Lilian Baylis wasn't there when Selena was killed."

"Wasn't she?" asked Rollo.

"No."

"How do you know that? All you know is that she wasn't there when the body was found. But she could have been there earlier and then left... we'll only know for sure who's in the picture when the senior medical officer gives us a time of death."

Poppy shook her head. She wasn't buying it. "But even then, I very much doubt she or Stanislavski did it. They have too much to lose. They're already beside themselves wondering who is going to play the lead now."

Rollo chuckled. "A nice little side-bar there, Poppy."

Poppy grinned too. She couldn't help herself. "I know."

"What about the Russians?" asked Rollo. "Safin and Nogovski. They were both at the exhibition. And didn't you say you think Safin left before the cavalry got there?" He paused, drumming his fingers on the desk. "Hmm, although at least a dozen other people left too. And we still haven't been able to pin them all down…" He stopped drumming and templed his fingers, raising them to his chin. "Didn't Safin and Nogovski declare they would not stop until the art and jewels were restored to the Russian people? I wonder how far they would go?"

Poppy admitted that was the very line of thought she'd been following on the taxi ride over from the theatre. But there was one inconvenient truth: Safin and Nogovski had arrived at the theatre *after* Selena had died. She shared her musings with Rollo.

"True," agreed the editor, "but wasn't it two hours *after* the police arrived? They could have left the theatre secretly and then returned."

Poppy thought about this for a moment, then shook her head. "No. I would have remembered that maroon Chrysler – it's very distinctive. It definitely wasn't parked outside the theatre when I arrived. And I had to walk down Waterloo Road, so I would have spotted it if it was driving away."

Rollo cocked his head. "You're very confident in your powers of observation, Miz Denby. How sure are you really?"

Poppy blushed, realizing how boastful she sounded, but she really was sure that she hadn't seen the expensive car anywhere in the neighbourhood. She'd noted it outside the Crystal Palace on Saturday night, so she was sure she would have recognized it again. She pursed her lips and looked Rollo directly in the eye. "Quite sure."

Rollo grinned. "All rightee, so they didn't arrive in the motor to kill Selena. They could have come on public transport."

"They could have," agreed Poppy, "but it's a very thin line of enquiry with scant evidence."

Rollo nodded in agreement. "It is. I think for now we have bigger fish to fry. So let's look at who we *know* was at the theatre and who was also at the exhibition."

Poppy went through a mental checklist and finally replied: "Miss Baylis, Monsieur Stanislavski, Delilah, Adam and me." She shrugged. "Can't imagine any of us did it. Can you?"

Rollo chuckled. "You never know, Poppy. You never know. But even if we can't imagine it, the police just might. Watch your back, and tell Adam and Delilah to do the same."

Poppy nodded soberly. "I will."

Rollo got up and began to pace. "So if it wasn't anyone at the theatre – although I'm not one hundred per cent convinced the embassy crew are off the hook yet – who are our other suspects?"

Poppy thought of the card in her coat pocket and knew exactly who would be first on the list if the police ever saw it. She thought of telling Rollo about it, but decided against it. She wanted to do some checking first. Lots of people had similar handwriting. Surely she was mistaken. She needed to think it through before she brought the card into evidence.

"Poppy? Are you with us?" Rollo was looking at her intently.

"Sorry, yes. I think I'm still reeling from the shock. It's not every day you find a dead body, is it?"

"No, it's not. But back to the suspects at the exhibition…"

"Well, there's the Yusopovs – Felix and Irina," offered

Poppy. "They publicly accused Selena of trying to steal the egg for herself. It's highly feasible that they tried to steal it back, to keep her from pilfering it." Poppy then told Rollo what she had read in the Jazz File about a Romanov pendant being stolen from Selena in Paris. "It seems like she has a track record in this. Add to that Felix's history as an assassin…"

"Surely he's too clever for that," observed Rollo. "He'd know he would be the first suspect because of his connections with Rasputin."

"He poisoned and stabbed the monk, didn't he?" probed Poppy.

"Felix and his accomplices, yes. One of them was a Brit. They also shot him. And drowned him. He was a tough critter."

Poppy shuddered. "So, a modus operandi of multiple means of murder…"

Rollo laughed. "Ooooh, that would make a stonker of a headline! But… unfortunately, I don't think we can use it in connection with Felix. Apart from the fact that he'd get Yasmin to sue the pants off us, I always got the impression he was trying to put all that behind him. He's not a killer at heart. He just did what he thought was necessary for Russia at the time."

"Is that what Miss Reece-Lansdale has told you?"

Rollo raised one eyebrow at Poppy's uncharacteristic jibe. "I'll let you off with that one, Miz Denby, seeing you've had a shock today and all, but you should know I'm a man who forms his own opinions and won't let any skirt influence them. Any skirt," he said pointedly.

Chagrined, Poppy smoothed down her own skirt and apologized to the editor.

Rollo cleared his throat. "So, who else is in the picture?"

Again, Poppy thought of the card, but immediately pushed her suspicions aside. "Well, we'll only really know when we've determined who was where when Selena died. Whose alibis hold up and whose don't. Any fingerprints that might emerge from the police search, and so on. But there's one person who was definitely there when Selena died."

Rollo looked at her intently. "And who's that?"

"Selena herself."

Rollo thought about this, his intelligent eyes blinking rapidly as he computed the hypothesis. "Go on," he said, eventually.

"Well, I won't know for certain until I've had another look at the photographs from the exhibition, but my aunt and her companion, Miss King, said something the other evening that made me suspect that Selena might have been the one to pull the trigger –"

"Good God in heaven!"

Poppy frowned at his blasphemy, but let it pass. Instead, she went on to tell him about the shooter not wearing any jewellery or gloves and the theory about the gunshot residue still being on the hands.

"Selena wasn't wearing gloves." Rollo rubbed his cheek. "I remember, because she slapped me."

Poppy grinned. "I remember too. But the thing is, I think she might have been wearing gloves *after* the robbery. I need to have another look at the photograph of her and Irina having the fight to confirm it…"

Rollo reached across his desk and opened a file. Inside were the photographs for the Sunday edition. He flicked through them and selected three: Selena slapping him, Selena and Irina fighting, and the phantom arm holding the gun. Poppy leaned in, tingling with excitement.

"I was right! No gloves before the robbery. Gloves afterwards. But…" she frowned. "Selena was wearing jewellery.

Rings and a bracelet. And the shooter had none." Poppy let out a disappointed sigh.

Rollo cocked his head in sympathy, then he straightened up as a thought struck him. "But she could have taken off the jewellery to fire the gun."

"Why would she do that?"

"I don't know. Maybe she felt they would get in the way. Maybe they made a noise against the metal."

Poppy nodded. "That's certainly plausible. I don't like wearing jewellery when I'm working with my hands either. It gets in the way when I'm typing. I've never tried shooting, but..."

Rollo laughed. "And let's hope you never do, Miz Denby. Like with everything else, I bet you'd be a crack shot."

Poppy flushed, grateful that she appeared to have been forgiven for her previous rudeness.

Rollo gave her a paternalistic smile, then got back to business. "There's one thing that bothers me with this theory, Poppy. Why would Selena put gloves on *after* the shooting?"

Poppy had already thought about this and offered: "To hide the gunshot residue."

"But surely it would have made more sense to do it the other way round. To wear the gloves, then take them off and dispose of the residue at the same time as she disposed of the gun... however she did that... and of course the egg."

"It would have made more sense, yes, but while not wishing to speak ill of the dead, Selena was never the sharpest knife in the drawer, was she?"

Rollo cocked his head again. "Well, if this theory is correct, she was sharp enough to get rid of all the evidence linking her to the crime."

Poppy thought about this for a moment, then said: "Perhaps, or perhaps not. I wonder how long gunshot residue lasts on the skin – or under the fingernails. It will be interesting to see what the medical officer comes up with. Do you think you might be able to give DCI Martin a call and prompt him to look for residue?"

Rollo stuck out his bottom lip and rubbed it back and forth for a while. "I could... I'll chew on it for a bit, though. This is a big news point – strong enough for a story on its own. We need to pace the release of these articles throughout next week. And I need to time them correctly to make sure I can get something from Martin in return – and of course to ensure we scoop *The Courier*."

"Don't leave it for too long, though; they'll be doing the post-mortem as quickly as possible," advised Poppy.

"Yes, but they won't be disposing of the body immediately."

"True," agreed Poppy.

"There's one more thing that's bothering me, though."

And me, thought Poppy, as the card again took centre stage in her mind.

Rollo spread the photographs out on his desk. "If Selena was the shooter, then she could not have been acting alone. She had to have had an accomplice to get rid of the gun and the egg. Agreed?"

"Agreed."

"And look here. In this picture – pre-robbery – she has an evening bag, big enough to hide a small revolver and a pair of gloves."

Poppy looked at the photograph and nodded her agreement.

"But in the post-robbery pic there is no bag. Could that have been where the gun and egg were hidden?"

"It could have been," agreed Poppy. "The revolver, definitely, but not the egg. I don't think the bag is big enough for both."

"But if she didn't have the bag, the revolver or the egg on her person after the robbery, she must have passed them on to someone. Or hidden them somewhere."

Poppy shook her head. "No. Martin's men searched the place – and everyone in it – thoroughly after they arrived."

Rollo again looked like the Cheshire Cat. "Exactly. *After* they arrived. Could Selena have passed them on to him – or her – in the chaos between the robbery and the arrival of the police, while the Household Cavalry were struggling to take control?"

"That's highly plausible. It's always been my theory that the robber got away during that time. But if the robber was Selena, then it had to have been an accomplice."

"And if that's the case, then isn't it also highly plausible that the accomplice might have been her killer?" asked Rollo.

"A fall-out among thieves?"

"Something like that. Perhaps the thief wanted to keep the egg for him – or her – self. It's worth a fortune, after all."

Poppy nodded. What was it that Victor Marconi had said? Nearly half a million pounds? "Yes. Perhaps Selena had simply hired someone to help her. And that person got greedy. They came to the theatre and asked her for more money."

"Or simply to get the egg back. Remember her effects had been searched."

Poppy sat bolt upright. "Do you think Selena could have had the egg in her dressing room?"

"If this theory is correct, I suspect she might have. Better than at your aunt's house with a snooping reporter in residence." Rollo winked at her; Poppy grinned, but then became serious as she thought about the card.

She took a deep breath. "The thing is, Rollo, none of this explains the chocolates."

Rollo frowned. "I thought we'd covered that. They were probably from the killer."

Poppy exhaled slowly, and thought to herself: *Oh, I do hope not.*

CHAPTER 17

The man who once owned a bearskin coat stepped out of the Art Deco lift and onto the landing outside his Kensington penthouse flat. He scratched around in his new sheepskin coat pocket and found the key to the rented accommodation. He opened the door and immediately checked to see if the cigarette paper he had left in the lintel was still there. It was. Good, no unwelcome visitors. Unless of course they had come in through the balcony door... He flicked the secret catch on his cane and released the rapier, holding it like a French fencer as he approached the sliding glass doors. Seeing that neither the blinds nor the windows had been disturbed, he lowered the razor-sharp blade, sheathed his rapier and placed it with his hat and coat on the stand near the door. Then he poured himself a large whisky.

Whisky in hand, he went into his bedroom, kicked off his Italian leather shoes and slipped on a pair of slippers, then plucked a red satin smoking jacket from a hanger behind the door. The man was looking forward to a night in. He had been working non-stop in the run-up to the exhibition, the exhibition itself and then in the aftermath, trying to get the egg to his fence.

He had tried again tonight, but once more Oscar's was filled with people who might recognize him. Perhaps he would go in the morning, before his day job; he wasn't due in until around eleven, so that should give him plenty of time. The man was starting to get very anxious. It did not usually take this long to pass on merchandise. The longer he had it on his person, the greater his chance of getting caught. And now this business with

Princess Selena. Good grief. Why couldn't that woman keep her nose out of other people's business? Even in death she was causing trouble. Or at least Poppy Denby was. Just his luck that the reporter was the one to find the body. That girl would never stop digging until the truth was out. Hopefully he'd be gone before it got to that. Hopefully...

He ignited a gas wall-heater, took a cigarette from an ivory and onyx cigarette box, bent down and lit it from the blue flame. Sucking the nicotine into his lungs, he started to relax. The clock on the mantelpiece struck nine. Yes, a night in would do him the world of good. He ran a finger down a pile of gramophone records, stopping at a Tchaikovsky – no, he'd had his fill of Russians. How about some Brahms? Or – ah – yes, some Gershwin. Something New World. He opened the leather folder, took out the disc and placed it on the turntable. Then he wound up the lever, lowered the arm and smiled as the crackle and hiss turned into a melody.

He topped up his whisky, then lay out full stretch on his leather sofa, sucking on his cigarette until his heart rate steadied and the stresses of the last few days ebbed away. But then a knock at the door jarred him back to his former state.

"Who is it?" he called. No answer. Another knock.

Sighing, he sat up, swung down his legs, perched his cigarette on a black marble ashtray, and shuffled towards the door. He made sure his left hand was in easy reach of his cane, put the security chain on the latch and then opened the door.

A beautiful, dark-haired elf stood outside, her eyes wide with fear.

"Delilah? What is it?" He immediately unhooked the chain and opened the door.

She threw herself at him, sobbing.

July 1918, Yekaterinburg, Russia

Nana Ruthie scaled the wall around the Ipatiev compound and forced her way through the brambles and ivy, not caring that thorns tore her flesh and ripped at her clothes. She was greeted by a yapping dachshund and a sleepy child. She wasted no time gathering their meagre belongings and hurrying them in the direction of the railway yard, not forgetting to retrieve the key from under the rock where she had hidden it. But as she stood up, brushing the Ural dust from her knees, Fritzie started barking and pulling on his lead. Little Anya struggled to hold him, and he broke free, running along the wall, following a scent or sound only he could detect. Anya ran after him. Nana Ruthie called out for her to stop, but the child did not obey.

Cursing in English and Russian, Nana Ruthie ran after her. They scampered around the corner of the wall and then through a hole in the masonry that Nana had not seen before. Oh dear God, they were going into the Ipatiev grounds where – if Nana was not mistaken – the Russian royal family had just been murdered.

"Anya!" Nana screamed.

"I'm getting Fritzie," Anya yelled back. "I won't be long."

Nana clawed at the stone and mortar, trying to make the hole big enough so she too could crawl through. "Come back now!"

But the only answer was a scream from Anya and furious barking from Fritzie – which was silenced with a thud and a yelp. "Fritzie!" screamed Anya.

Nana sat on her backside, lifted both legs, and kicked at the loose brickwork with her hobnail boots. Pain shot through both her ankles and knees, but she kept on kicking.

"Don't worry, Miss Broadwood. I've got them."

Nana stopped kicking and looked up to where she heard a male voice speaking in English. It was the man Selena had called Nogovski. He was perched on the wall, looking down.

"Tell her you're safe, Anya." The man spoke to the child in Russian.

"I – I'm safe, Nana, but Fritzie –"

"Fritzie will be fine, my little poppet, as long as you do what you're told."

Nana could not see Anya through the hole, but she didn't sound as if she were far.

"It's all right, Anya, I'm here. Don't be scared. Everything will be all right." Nana tried to keep her voice calm.

"Indeed it will," said Nogovski, his voice light and playful. "As long as your Nana gives me her key. Now, Miss Broadwood, don't waste our time by telling me you don't have it. What good fortune that little Anya should stumble across my path! I knew her father well. She has his eyes, you know. And I can't believe she still has that little dog! Now, Miss Broadwood," he continued in English, "I think it would be best if you came through the front gate – it's much more decorous for a lady of your age. Anya and I will meet you there. Come, poppet! And yes, you too, Fritzie!"

MONDAY 22 OCTOBER 1920, LONDON

Poppy was glad to be heading home. After her meeting with Rollo she had typed up the lead for the following morning, filed it with the editor and left him to choose a front page pic from Daniel's photos. Daniel was at a parents' evening at his eldest child's school.

It was 9.30 p.m. when Poppy got off the bus at the top of

King's Road and walked to her aunt's house at 137, opposite the Electric Cinema. A crowd was gathered outside the cinema, including some police cars. Poppy wondered which moving picture star was making an appearance tonight. But as she got closer, she realized the crowd was not outside the cinema but her house. And on the pavement, wrapped in a blanket, was Aunt Dot with her companion Miss King, who was pouring tea from a flask and offering it to her employer.

"Aunt Dot! What are you doing out here?" Poppy ran the last few feet and knelt down beside her paraplegic aunt.

"Oh Poppy! You wouldn't believe it. But these – these – *monsters* arrived an hour ago and tossed us out!"

A line of Bobbies blocked the entrance to the townhouse and Poppy could see shadows moving behind the curtains of the three-storey building.

"We didn't toss her out, miss," said one of the Bobbies. "We asked her to vacate the premises so the forensic lads could do their job."

"The forensic lads?" queried Poppy.

"They're searching Selena's bedroom. And the rest of the house. What they expect to find, I have no idea!"

"Fingerprints, gunshot residue, Fabergé eggs..." offered Miss King.

"Surely if there had been a Fabergé egg in my house I would have seen it. Besides, it has already been stolen from Selena. Don't the police read the papers?" She glared at the Bobby who had spoken, daring him to contradict her. His unfashionable handlebar moustache twitched, but he didn't speak.

Poppy sighed. "Excuse me, constable. My name is Poppy Denby. This is my aunt, and I also live in this house. I have had a long day at work and I would like to go inside and have my supper."

"I know who you are, miss. You're the press, and you're not allowed in."

"But it's my house!"

"Actually, darling, it's my house, but they don't care about that either."

Poppy took her aunt's hand and squeezed it – it was freezing. Poppy saw red. "Now listen here. I demand to speak to DCI Martin immediately. My aunt – sorry, Aunt Dot – is not a well woman and it will not look good for the police if tomorrow's morning paper reports that an invalid was left to freeze to death on the street while the police stood by and did nothing."

"She has a blanket. She has tea. She –"

The door behind the three Bobbies opened and Detective Chief Inspector Jasper Martin and a team of men carrying briefcases and bags – the forensic lads, Poppy assumed – filed out of number 137.

"DCI Martin!"

Martin held up his hand. "Not now, Miss Denby. Anything I have to say to the press will be to your editor, not to you. And that will be at an official briefing, at my convenience, not his."

Then he stopped in front of Aunt Dot and Miss King. "I apologize, Miss Denby, Miss King, for the inconvenience. You may go back in now."

"Did you find anything?" asked Miss King.

"That has still to be determined," said Martin, and he led his team to the nearest Black Mariah and climbed in. After the police had pulled away, the crowd began to disperse, until only Poppy, Aunt Dot and Miss King remained.

"Well, we'd better get in then," said Poppy.

"Actually, darling, could you do me a huge favour?"

"Of course, Aunt Dot."

"Can you go and check on Delilah?"

"I can telephone her. Why?"

Miss King cleared her throat and busied herself screwing the lid back on the flask.

Aunt Dot twirled a curl of hair around her finger. "Er, no you can't. You see, I'm in a bit of a fix with that. Since Grace left I've had some trouble keeping up with paying all the bills – who knew there were so many? – and our telephone's been – it's been –"

"It's been cut off," said Miss King, packing the flask into a basket hanging from the back of Aunt Dot's wheelchair.

"Ah, I see. Why didn't you say something before? I could have done that for you," said Poppy.

"I didn't know! But look, can we sort that tomorrow? I'm worried about Delilah."

Poppy felt a cold chill seep through her red mackintosh. "Why? What's happened to her?"

Aunt Dot squeezed Poppy's hand. "Oh nothing! Nothing like that. But these – these dreadful policemen – scared her, I think. She popped around here after coming from Oscar's and saw us being tossed out. She objected, just like you did, but then that awful constable with the moustache – you know, you could hang twins from that thing – told her that they were there because a killer was on the loose and she should be thanking them, because she could be next."

Poppy stifled a giggle.

"It's not funny, darling. You might have taken it with a pinch of salt, but Delilah is like me, she's got a fertile imagination – it's what makes her such a good actress – and she, well –"

"She got spooked," finished Miss King.

"Spooked?"

"Yes, that's a good word for it, Gertrude, a very good word. She got spooked. She ran off. Can you pop down the road and see if she's all right? It shouldn't take more than half an hour…"

Poppy considered that in half an hour she could have had a light supper, a shower and be preparing for bed; but her aunt's large blue eyes, filling with tears, won her over. As they always did. Poppy let out a sigh that sounded more like a groan. "All right, Aunt Dot. I'll go. But can you rustle something up for me when I get back?"

"I will," said Miss King and then pushed her employer up the ramp and back into her ransacked home.

CHAPTER 18

Poppy arrived outside Delilah's apartment building ten minutes later. It had originally been a Georgian townhouse, like Aunt Dot's, but a property developer had converted the three-storey building into six tasteful flats catering to Chelsea's well-to-do single set. The rent was far more than your average young actress could afford, but Delilah also had an allowance from her father, who owned a string of hotels in Malta. Poppy knew that when the time came for her to leave Aunt Dot's and get a place of her own, it would never be anywhere as grand as this. Delilah had asked her recently if she might consider moving in. But she couldn't think of leaving Aunt Dot while Grace was still in prison. After she was released, it might be a different story…

With these thoughts in mind, Poppy rang the bell for Delilah's second-floor apartment. No answer. She rang again. Still no reply. She looked up to see if Delilah's lights were on: darkness. Poppy was not worried. Delilah had a colourful social life and could be out at any number of clubs or friends' houses. Certain that Selena's death was linked to the Fabergé egg, Poppy didn't consider for a moment that the young actress may have fallen foul of the "killer on the loose". Her father, of course, had been stepping out with Selena, but Delilah had told Poppy at the theatre that he had sailed back to Malta the day after the exhibition.

Poppy scratched in her satchel and pulled out a notepad and pencil. She wrote a quick note asking Delilah to let Aunt Dot know that she was all right at her earliest convenience, and could she do it in person, as the telephone at number 137 was out of action? Poppy folded it and pushed it through the bronze flap of Flat 3's post box, then turned to walk away – straight into a man's chest.

"Oh, pardon me, I didn't see you there –"

"Miss Denby?"

Poppy took a step back as she realized who it was she had bumped into: Comrade Andrei Nogovski. Her heart skipped a couple of beats.

"Mr Nogovski!"

Her omission of "comrade" was deliberate. She waited for him to correct her; he didn't. Instead he raised his hat in greeting.

"Good evening, Miss Denby. Have you also come to visit Miss Marconi?"

Poppy busied herself buckling up her satchel. "Also?"

"Yes. I'm here to see her too."

"At this time of night?"

"As you know, Miss Denby, Miss Marconi doesn't always keep sociable hours."

Poppy couldn't argue with that, but she resented the implication that her friend's character might be considered questionable.

"Well, I doubt Delilah would let you in at this time of night – if she were in, which she isn't."

"Ah, that's a pity. I needed to speak to her about her father."

"Her father?"

"Yes. And his association with Selena Romanova Yusopova."

"And what has that to do with you?" she blurted. Poppy was tired and easily irritated. If Andrei Nogovski took offence at her tone, he did not show it. Instead he smiled and offered her his hand.

"Miss Denby, I believe we have got off on the wrong foot. I apologize for being so rude to you at Oscar's last evening. Like you, I was tired. It had been a long day. I should not have taken it out on you."

Poppy was uncertain if he was truly sorry, but her curiosity got the better of her. This, after all, was the man who had attracted her attention by playing both sides in the Russian power game. She wanted to talk to him with regard to the exhibition story – and of course the subsequent murder of the former keeper of the infamous Fabergé egg. She would be a fool to snub his olive branch, whatever his motive for giving it. She reached out her hand and shook his. "Apology accepted, Mr Nogovski."

He smiled and crooked his arm. "Then, Miss Denby, may I escort you home? We can talk on the way."

"Thank you, Mr Nogovski. That's very kind." She refrained from adding that King's Road was as safe as a schoolyard at this time of the evening, with so many theatre, cinema, club and restaurant goers walking by. Instead, she slipped her arm into his and allowed him to match her stride as she turned towards her aunt's house.

Their shoes crunched through the autumn leaves that spilled through the wrought-iron railings encircling the oak trees lining King's Road. The wind was picking up and Poppy thought they'd just get back before it started to rain. Nogovski appeared only to have a cane with him, not an umbrella. Perhaps she would lend him one.

"It looks like rain," he observed.

"It does," agreed Poppy.

Weather out of the way, silence resumed. She wondered if she should fill it or wait for him. She had a lot of questions, but she instinctively knew a man like Nogovski would feel more comfortable if he directed the conversation. It would make him feel in control. It suited Poppy's purposes to allow him to feel that, so she held her tongue.

"So, Miss Denby..."

Poppy smiled to herself.

"How well do you know Victor Marconi?"

"Not too well. He's a friend of my aunt's and, of course, Delilah's father. I've met him a few times socially."

"Ah yes, your aunt. If I am not mistaken, was she not a famous suffragette?"

"She was."

"And what was Victor Marconi's association with the women's suffrage movement?"

Poppy expected Nogovski already knew this. But she played along. "Nothing, apart from that his wife was a member of the WSPU and belonged to the Chelsea Six, the cell that met at my aunt's house before the war."

"The wife that died."

"That's right. Gloria. Delilah's mother."

"Yes," observed Nogovski, with a tinge of humour in his voice, "I read all about it in *The Daily Globe*."

"I didn't know *The Daily Globe* reached Russia," countered Poppy, matching his tone.

"Not the newsstands, no, but my department receives special deliveries."

"So you knew all about me before you arrived in London."

"Not *all* about you, Miss Denby. Only what you wrote in *The Globe*."

Poppy doubted that very much.

"It was quite a scoop, wasn't it, the Dorchester exposé?"

"It was a tragic story that needed to be exposed."

"Well, Miss Denby, I think you did an admirable job."

"Thank you, Mr Nogovski."

Poppy and Nogovski stepped aside to allow a group of giggling Bright Young Things in fancy dress pass by. One of them – dressed like an Egyptian pharaoh – greeted Poppy. She couldn't place where she'd met him – some exhibition or book launch, probably, or possibly out on the tiles with Delilah. She wished him and his friends a good evening.

Nogovski did not appear impressed.

"Bourgeois excess?" Poppy teased.

"Indeed. Back home, people their age are fighting to have a just society."

"We've had enough of fighting here," observed Poppy, a note of irritation creeping into her voice. It was time to take control. "What is your interest in Victor Marconi?"

Nogovski's arm tensed. No, he did not like it when someone else took the lead. She did not give a fig. It was after ten o'clock and she had been at work since nine that morning. And she still needed to catch up on her lost sleep from Saturday night.

"I've told you. It's in connection with Selena."

"And what is your interest in Selena?"

"You mean other than she might have been involved in the theft of treasures from the Russian people?"

Ah, so she had been on the right track with that. "Yes, other than that."

Nogovski stopped walking. His arm tightened on Poppy's. She would not be able to break free if she chose to. She told herself to stay calm.

"Selena Romanova Yusopova was a Russian national. Her death is naturally of interest to the Russian embassy. I am simply doing my duty in trying to find out what happened to her."

"So you're helping the police with their enquiries?"

Nogovski chuckled. His arm relaxed. "As much as I can. DCI Martin has lots of questions."

"Somehow, Mr Nogovski, I don't think you will give him many answers."

"And why do you think that, Miss Denby?"

"Because you have another agenda."

"As do you."

She could not deny that. They were approaching 137 King's Road and she still did not have much information from him. "So, Victor Marconi…"

"Ah yes. Do you not find it strange that Marconi left the country the day after the theft at the exhibition?"

"I do not. He would have had his berth booked for weeks. Hang on, are you implying…"

"That Victor Marconi might have been in cahoots with Selena to steal the Fabergé egg?"

Poppy wrenched her arm from Nogovski's and perched her hands on her hips. "I've never heard such codswallop in my life!"

Nogovski threw back his head and laughed. "Codswallop? Oh Miss Denby, you are a breath of fresh air."

Poppy sucked in her breath, preparing to give Nogovski a piece of her mind.

He held up his hand. "Hold on, hear me out. Let me get one thing straight. I do not think your friend's father had anything to do with this, but I know for a fact that that is a line of enquiry the Metropolitan Police are following."

Poppy started to release her breath, slowly.

"So I have a proposal for you."

"A proposal?"

"You are a formidable investigative journalist, Miss Denby, for one so young. I was highly impressed with what you did on the Dorchester story. I reckon you will no doubt get to the bottom of this one in due course too. So I would like to work with you."

Poppy squared up to him and crossed her arms in front of her chest. "And what's in it for me?"

"Access to information. I'll tell you whatever I can. Selena was a Russian national. We have files."

Poppy considered this for a moment. No doubt those files would be highly redacted, but they could prove useful. As could a source in the Russian embassy – whatever his true motives for courting her. She doubted that Lionel Saunders from *The Courier* had been made the same offer. But if she didn't take it, perhaps he might be next on Nogovski's list. Rollo would never forgive her if she let this one slip. She chewed her lip. "And you? What do you hope to get out of it?"

"I've told you. You have a knack of getting to the bottom of stories. We need to wrap this up as quickly as possible. We need to retrieve the Fabergé egg and return it to the Russian people."

She doubted that was his only reason, but she let it pass. Her newshound nose was twitching: he'd laid a scent and she couldn't wait to follow it.

"All right, Mr Nogovski. Let's see if you can put your money where your mouth is. Bring your files to *The Globe* office tomorrow and my editor and I will see if there's anything in there worth following."

Nogovski laughed as a cream Jaguar pulled up to the kerb. "I don't think that would be the best way of approaching it."

Marjorie Reynolds stepped out of the motor as Nogovski continued: "I'll tell you what: meet me at Oscar's tomorrow night for a drink and we can talk about the parameters of our – er – relationship then. Good evening, Mrs Reynolds." He doffed his hat at the Home Office minister.

"Comrade Nogovski. Poppy. Is everything all right here?" asked Marjorie, approaching the two young people.

Poppy fixed a smile on her face and turned to the older woman. "Of course. Mr Nogovski is just answering a few questions I had for him for a story we're running. As a – er –

representative of the Russian embassy. About Princess Selena."

"Poor Selena," said Marjorie. "I'm sure your aunt is devastated. Is she in? I heard about the police search."

Poppy looked at her watch. It was half past ten. "She is, Mrs Reynolds, but it's rather late…"

Marjorie hooked her arm through Poppy's and turned her towards the door. "I know, Poppy, and I won't stay long, but I simply must see if Dot's all right. Goodnight, Mr Nogovski."

Nogovski doffed his hat. "Goodnight, Mrs Reynolds. Miss Denby. Shall we say eight o'clock tomorrow?"

Poppy was tired and hungry and beyond annoyed with the presumption of it all. From Marjorie and Nogovski. "I'll ring the embassy tomorrow and let you know," she said tersely, pulled her arm from Marjorie's and strode towards her front door. As she put her key in the lock it started to rain.

CHAPTER 19

TUESDAY 23 OCTOBER 1920, LONDON

"Poppy, ma'am?" Poppy looked down, surprised to hear her name coming from a Fleet Street pavement. She was met by an outstretched hand holding a paper poppy.

"Good morning, Sarge. What have you got there?"

Sergeant "Sarge" Hawkins was one of Fleet Street's regular beggars. He had lost both legs in the war and, like many returning servicemen, injured or otherwise, had not been able to find work back on Civvy Street. He lived in a home for veterans run by the Salvation Army and made his way to this patch of pavement between the entrance to St Bride's Church and the Empire Tea Rooms every day. He carved small crosses out of wood and sold them for a handful of pennies. Poppy had at least a dozen of them, being unable to say no to the crippled soldier who reminded her of her brother, who had died during the war.

"Did you make that just for me?" asked Poppy, touched.

Sarge grinned, revealing a new gap in his sparsely toothed mouth. "I would like to say yes, Miss Denby, but that wouldn't be the truth. And I know how you like the truth. No, it's a new thing us old Tommies are doing. For the coming Armistice anniversary. Some blokes thought it would be a good idea to make these poppies as a reminder of, well, you know…"

As Poppy's brother was buried under a field of poppies in

Belgium, the young journalist knew exactly what he was talking about.

"How much?" asked Poppy, taking the paper flower and pinning it to her turquoise lapel.

"As much as you'd like to give, miss," answered Sarge.

Poppy opened her purse and took out some coins, making sure she kept enough back for her breakfast meeting in the Empire. She thanked Sarge, then pushed open the door to find Marjorie Reynolds seated and waiting for her with a pot of tea and a plate of buttered toast. Despite it only being eight o'clock in the morning, Marjorie's salt and pepper hair was immaculately set with finger waves.

"Snap!" said Marjorie, pointing to the paper poppy on her tweed jacket lapel.

Poppy smiled as she pulled out the vacant seat opposite the Home Office minister and took off her cloche hat, hanging it, with her satchel, on the back of her chair. A waitress arrived and removed the hat to its proper place on the hatstand. Poppy smoothed down her blonde curls, expressed her thanks, then turned to her breakfast companion. "Morning, Mrs Reynolds. It's a nice idea, this, isn't it?" she said, fingering the flower on her lapel. "Although the paper won't last that long."

"I don't think it has to. It's just for the few weeks up to Armistice Day. I hope it will catch on."

"So do I. But people like Sarge need a lot more than the few pennies they can get from a paper poppy or a wooden cross. Can't the government do something to help them? If it wasn't for charities like the Salvation Army and the Royal British Legion they'd be starving to death on the street."

"A tad melodramatic for this time of the morning, Poppy."

"Do you think so? I'd say it's spot on."

Marjorie looked down her nose at Poppy as she poured the

younger woman a cup of tea. "I didn't know you'd switched beats to politics, Miss Denby. The last time I checked, Ike Garfield still had that job. And don't forget you're preaching to the converted here." She pushed the sugar bowl across the table. "In the last two years I have backed every social reform bill brought to parliament by the Liberals – and even more that were blocked by the Conservatives." She sniffed and picked up her cup.

Poppy, who hadn't slept well the night before, realized her rudeness. Marjorie Reynolds was one of the good guys – as Rollo liked to say – and an invaluable source who needed to be kept sweet. And that, after all, was why she was here. Last night, before Marjorie left, she had asked to meet Poppy for breakfast. She said she had some information on Andrei Nogovski. Naturally, Poppy was curious and readily agreed. However, Poppy reminded herself, besides her usefulness as a source, Marjorie was also one of her aunt's oldest friends, and a veteran of the women's suffrage movement. Social justice was in her veins. "I'm sorry, Mrs Reynolds; I've been living on stale air and coffee since the robbery at the exhibition."

Marjorie put down her cup and reached across the table and patted the young reporter's hand.

"I'll have a word with Rollo. He's working you too hard."

Poppy laughed and plopped two sugar cubes into her tea. "But not as hard as he's working himself."

Marjorie acknowledged that with a wry "I can believe it", and then called over the waitress.

"What will you have, Poppy? I'm just having toast. They feed us well at –" she paused – "the office."

"A bacon sandwich, please." Poppy smiled to herself. She was beginning to suspect that "minister to the Home Office" was a euphemism for what Marjorie Reynolds actually did, and that pause just added fuel to her suspicions. She'd heard rumours about a Secret Service that had been set up during the war to root out German spies. And as far as she knew, it was still going – but now the focus was on scuppering Bolshevik influence. Just two months earlier, her aunt's old acquaintance, Sylvia Pankhurst, had helped establish the Communist Party of Great Britain. Aunt Dot had been invited to join; she had declined, and so, apparently, had Marjorie Reynolds. "Sylvia's gone a little too far this time," declared her aunt, who, although left-leaning, enjoyed her middle-class comforts too much to be a serious supporter of Bolshevism. Was it a coincidence that Marjorie wanted to speak to her about Comrade Andrei Nogovski? Poppy didn't think so.

"So," she said, stirring the sugar into her tea, "Andrei Nogovski…"

Marjorie sipped on her tea, then put down her cup. "Indeed. Andrei Nogovski. You met with him last night."

"I didn't *meet* with him. I bumped into him outside –" she stopped, realizing that Marjorie was getting information from her before they had set out the parameters of their engagement. It was one of the cardinal rules of journalism, according to Rollo, and he had drilled it into her. "Information is our currency, Miz Denby. You can buy it or sell it, but don't give it away."

"Buy it?" asked Poppy. "Do you pay people to tell you things?"

Rollo had raised a shaggy red eyebrow. "Not under normal circumstances, no. It taints what we've been given and limits what we can print. No, we buy the information in other ways. Everyone has a price, everyone has an agenda. It's your job to figure out what it is. Some people are just lonely and want the attention. Others want revenge on someone and use us to out them. Then there are the crusader types who want us to further their cause, or publicity hounds who need to keep themselves in the public eye – for vanity or profit, it doesn't really matter."

"But how do we know what they are telling us is true, Rollo?"

"We don't, initially, but we can sift it later. At this stage of the interview you need to suss out whether they've got something worthwhile to tell you and whether it's worth the price they're asking."

"Will they tell you what they want in return?" asked Poppy.

"Sometimes," answered Rollo.

Sometimes. Poppy looked at Marjorie and wondered what it was she wanted. Poppy had known her long enough to understand that she valued forthrightness, so she decided to take the direct route.

"Forgive me, Mrs Reynolds, but I thought you were going to give *me* some information about Comrade Nogovski; not the other way round."

Marjorie raised her teacup in mock salute. "Ah, I see Rollo's been training you."

Poppy raised her cup in return. "You've got something to tell us about him, but I doubt the information will come without strings. What is it you want from us, Mrs Reynolds?"

Poppy and Marjorie both leaned back as the waitress arrived with the bacon sandwich and enquired if Mrs Reynolds would like more toast. The older woman declined. Alone again, Poppy busied herself with cutting the sandwich in half, the rashers crunching satisfyingly as she pressed the bread down.

"So, you want to know my motivation in all this?" asked Marjorie.

"I do."

Marjorie finished her toast and dabbed at her lips with her napkin. "And it isn't enough that I'm worried about an old friend's niece?"

Poppy thought about this for a moment as she chewed her

first bite of bacon. The juices melted into her mouth. She wished she had more time to savour it. She swallowed. "I appreciate that, Mrs Reynolds, but if this was just personal you would not have arranged to meet me at *The Globe*."

"I didn't. I arranged to meet you here."

"Not at first. Your first thought was that it was a business meeting. Something to do with the newspaper. Then you changed your mind."

"Can't it be both?"

"I'm sure it can, but we won't know until you tell me."

Marjorie's sharply pencilled eyebrows met in the middle. "I do appreciate forthrightness, Miss Denby, but you are bordering on rude." She folded her napkin and reached for her briefcase. "I think I'd better speak to Rollo about this directly. You're right, it is business; but you're also wrong. I do have a personal concern for you. And I'd appreciate some gratitude."

Again, Poppy pulled herself up for her brusqueness. She was new at this game and struggling to balance her natural, trusting personality with the suspicious stance her profession now demanded of her. No doubt she would err on both sides of the divide many more times before she found a style that was true to herself and not just a facsimile of Rollo. She put down her sandwich. "I'm truly sorry, Mrs Reynolds. Marjorie. Please forgive me. You've been friends with my aunt for a long time and I know you would never do anything to hurt her or anyone close to her. It's just that with my new job…"

Marjorie put her briefcase down and waved back the waitress who was preparing to swoop in. "I know, pet," she said. "It's a learning curve. I've been on it – as an MP and now in my new job. But we mustn't lose ourselves. We mustn't try to do things the same way our male colleagues have always done them. We need to find our own way."

Poppy gave a tight smile. "Rollo said you'd want something."

Marjorie matched the smile. "He's right. I do. Well, not me personally, but the people I represent. That's how it works. We want certain information in the press and we want other information kept out of it. But that doesn't mean I don't have something very valuable for you – professionally and personally. And there is a personal dimension, Poppy. I *am* worried for you."

The bell on the tea-room door rang and a group of men walked in. Poppy recognized them as journalists from *The Courier*. "Let's finish up here and go for a walk around St Bride's, shall we?"

Marjorie assessed the group of journalists and nodded. "Good idea."

A cleaning lady was polishing the brass candlesticks on the altar when Marjorie and Poppy slipped into the chancel. They took a seat at the back, near the stone stairs spiralling down to the underfloor crypt. Marjorie opened her briefcase and extracted a manila envelope. She placed it on the pew between her and the young journalist.

"What I've got here, Poppy, is some information on Andrei Nogovski."

Poppy reached her gloved hand out to take the envelope.

Marjorie edged it away from her. "First, though, I need to tell you what I would like in return."

"Well, Rollo's really the one to –"

"No. It's you I need a favour from. It has nothing to do with the newspaper."

"Then why –"

Marjorie raised her hand. "Well, some of it does, but I'll get to that later. First I need to get the personal stuff out of the way. It's about my son, Oscar."

"Oscar? What about him?"

"I think he might be in trouble." Marjorie lowered her voice to a whisper as the cleaning lady walked past them carrying her bucket and rags. Poppy nodded to the woman and smiled. She received a warm smile in response.

Marjorie drummed her fingers on the back of the pew in front of her. Poppy had never seen the Member of Parliament and minister to the Home Office so agitated. Aunt Dot always said she had the backbone of Genghis Khan, having withstood personal and public attacks in her rise to power that would have cowed a lesser human being.

"Why do you think he's in trouble, Mrs Reynolds? Have you spoken to him about it?"

Marjorie flexed her fingers and then folded them softly in her lap. She steadied her breathing and visibly forced herself to appear composed. "I've tried, but you know what children can be like with their parents. He thinks just because he's thirty-five I don't have a say in his life any more. And he's right, of course. But I'm his mother. And since his father died, he's all I have. You understand that, don't you?"

Poppy did, but perhaps not in the way Marjorie would have hoped. At twenty-two she was trying desperately to break free of her parents' influence, knowing that they didn't fully approve of her new career. But she knew that wasn't what Marjorie wanted to hear. She smiled. "Of course I do, Mrs Reynolds. It's only natural for a parent to worry about their children – however old they are. But what is it that's worrying you?"

Marjorie picked up the envelope and slipped out a photograph. Poppy recognized the setting immediately; it was the bar at Oscar's Jazz Club and three men were in deep discussion: Oscar, the barman and Andrei Nogovski. Poppy had a sense of déjà vu. She had seen this picture before. Or had she?

Oh, hang on, it wasn't the photograph she'd seen; it was the real-life tableau. This was taken the night she had danced with Prince Felix Yusopov. The night Andrei Nogovski had muscled his way into the club and had gone downstairs with Oscar. She had noticed then that Oscar looked uncomfortable. She had intended asking him about it. And now here was his mother, apparently worried about the same thing.

"Who took this picture, Mrs Reynolds?"

Marjorie shrugged. "It doesn't matter. But it came to my attention at the Home Office. Some of my colleagues were concerned that Oscar might be involved with Nogovski and Safin in some way. Apparently the interim ambassador arrived soon after this picture was taken. And this, apparently, is not the first meeting they've had."

"But surely it's just a matter of a host speaking to one of his patrons," said Poppy.

"Yes, that's what I told my colleagues. But they're not entirely convinced. And neither am I."

Poppy paused again as a man in a clerical robe nodded to them as he passed. "But why do you assume it's something underhanded or illegal? Nogovski and Safin are legitimate representatives of the Russian embassy. Oscar does catering. Perhaps they were arranging a reception or something."

Marjorie straightened her tweed skirt with brisk strokes. "You don't believe that, and neither do I."

Poppy sighed and told Marjorie what had happened the other night.

Marjorie listened, her mouth in a tight line. "He was scared, you say?"

"That's how I interpreted it, yes. It appeared as if Nogovski was intimidating him in some way."

"That's what I'm afraid of. Nogovski is not a man to be

trifled with." Her hand quivered slightly as she withdrew another photograph from the envelope. She offered it to Poppy. It was a family portrait. A well-to-do aristocratic family: a powerfully built middle-aged man in Imperial Russian military uniform, a woman in her mid-thirties, two boys of around ten and twelve, and a small girl of about two with a halo of black curls and puppy-dark eyes.

"The family of Count Sergei Andreiovich, previously of Moscow, Russia. This was taken in 1912." Marjorie pointed at each of the family members in turn. "The count, his wife Sofia, their two sons Boris and Jakov, and the baby, Anya."

"They look like a lovely family," said Poppy, not knowing what else to say.

"They were. But now at least three of them are dead. The mother and two boys – along with their grandmother, uncle and family butler – were massacred in their home in October 1917."

"By Bolsheviks?" asked Poppy.

"That's what we think, yes, but the Russians have put out a rumour that one of our lot did it."

"Our lot?"

"A Brit. A woman by the name of Ruth Broadwood." Marjorie slipped another photograph from the file. Poppy looked into the plain, sensible face of a woman of around sixty. She reminded Poppy of her aunt Daphne in Morpeth. Poppy could not imagine for one moment that this Aunt Daphne lookalike was capable of murdering an entire family. But appearances could be deceiving…

"She doesn't look the type, does she?" said Marjorie, reading her mind.

Poppy shrugged. "Not really. But stranger things have happened."

"They have," agreed Marjorie, "but when you consider that

two grown men and two strapping teenage boys were among the victims, some of whom had been hacked to death before they were shot, I think it is highly unlikely that a woman of Ruth Broadwood's age and physical stature could have done it."

Poppy felt the bacon sandwich in her stomach churn. She imagined the horror of the scene and was grateful that she had not been presented with a photograph of it. "Indeed," was all she managed. She picked up the photograph of Ruth Broadwood again and looked intently into her eyes, trying to read something of her story. "Who is she?"

"Well, the Bolsheviks are right – she is one of ours. In fact, she's a friend of your aunt's new companion, Miss King."

"*Really?*" asked Poppy, incredulous.

"Really. They both worked for David Lloyd George when he was Chancellor of the Exchequer at 11 Downing Street. Ruth was a translator, Miss King a nanny." Marjorie then went on to recount how Ruth had been recruited by Lloyd George for the secret mission to the tsar's household in St Petersburg and how she had later transferred to the house of the reformer Count Sergei Andreiovich in Moscow.

Poppy looked at the photograph of Ruth Broadwood with renewed respect. A spy? At her age? Good for her! "So do you think the Bolsheviks knew she was a spy?"

Marjorie leaned back her head and stretched her neck from left to right. "Probably. They raided the office of our Moscow attaché around the same time the Andreioviches were murdered. That was the office Ruth used to send us her reports in the diplomatic pouches. Our attaché managed to get out, as did the ambassador in St Petersburg, but a lot of sensitive information was lost in the process."

"Why would the Bolsheviks raid our offices?" asked Poppy. Marjorie raised one eyebrow at Poppy. "It's because of how our royal families are connected. As you know, the Queen Mothers, our Queen Alexandra and Empress Maria Federovna, are sisters; their brother is the king of Denmark. Their sons, our King George and Tsar Nicholas, are – were – cousins."

Poppy noted the change in tense. So Marjorie and the Home Office also believed the stories that the Russian royal family had been murdered, even if the old Queen Mother – and poor, deluded Princess Selena – did not.

It was now approaching nine o'clock and members of the clergy were beginning to set up for the morning service. On another day, Poppy might have stayed, but today she was far too interested in the story of the dead Russian family, the British spy and how – if at all – it was connected with Andrei Nogovski.

"Perhaps we should go outside," she suggested.

CHAPTER 20

Marjorie and Poppy sat together on a bench in the graveyard of St Bride's, a dour yew tree hunched above them. The photographs were laid out between them.

"So," said Poppy, "let me see if I've got this straight. A Russian family – known for its reformist sympathies – was murdered during the Russian Revolution. You believe the Bolsheviks did it, but they say it was one of our spies, a woman posing as a nanny. They did this, you believe, because they were paranoid about British interference with the Russian royal family. Which turned out to be unfounded, because in the end our King George failed to send anyone to rescue them and in fact denied them asylum when they first asked."

Marjorie took a sharp intake of breath. "Well, I don't want to criticize the royal family…"

"Of course not," said Poppy, wishing that more people would. She took a deep breath and pushed the critical thoughts about the failings of the royals out of her mind. "So, where is this Ruth Broadwood?"

Marjorie picked an autumn leaf off the bench and pressed it between her gloved palms. "Well, no one knows for sure. But we suspect she is with the youngest member of the Andreiovich family – the girl Anya, who will now be about nine. She was the only member of the family not found at the house. We think she and Miss Broadwood managed to escape and – if they're still alive – are on the run."

Poppy touched the face of the little cherub in the

photograph, imagining what she would look like five years on when her family were murdered, and then now, three years after that, if she were still alive. Then she touched the barrel-chest of the father – Count Andreiovich – and examined his clean-shaven face bracketed by impressive mutton-chop sideburns. He had the same dark eyes as his daughter and a mouth that although firmly set for the photograph had a slight upturn at the corners, suggesting a man who easily laughed. The fairer boys appeared to take after their mother, a beautiful woman in the prime of her life. But they were all gone. Or were they?

"What about him? The count. You didn't list him among the dead."

Marjorie let the leaf fall to the ground and land in a small puddle on the churchyard path. It floated on the trapped water.

"No. Count Andreiovich was not killed with the family. He was on the Western Front, as far as we know, when it happened. At least we think he was. We lost track of him in 1916."

A chill wind had picked up and was playing with the churchyard leaves. Poppy pulled up the collar of her turquoise mackintosh to meet the rim of her cloche hat. "You lost track of him? Why were you keeping track of him in the first place?"

Marjorie cleared her throat and straightened her posture on the bench. "Well, it was before my time at the Home Office, but I believe it was because we hoped he might work for us."

"Another spy?" Poppy tried to keep the delight out of her voice. Oh, this was turning out to be more exciting than a detective novel.

"Not exactly, no. He had reformist sympathies and we thought we might be able to use him to influence the tsar. The writing was on the wall for the regime if it didn't change; we were hoping to avoid what happened in 1917. But as it turned out, the tsar and tsarina dug in their heels in the face of criticism. If they'd listened to the likes of Andreiovich instead of Rasputin, things might have turned out very differently in Russia."

Poppy absorbed this. She wondered if things would have been different, or whether the Bolshevik Revolution was inevitable. Which reminded her again of Andrei Nogovski. "So what has any of this to do with Andrei Nogovski?"

Marjorie looked to the left and right, as if checking for eavesdroppers. There was only an elderly woman tossing chunks of bread to a flock of gathering pigeons. "I'll get to him in a minute. But first I need to tell you how we think all this fits in with the murder of Princess Selena." Two of the birds started squabbling over a crust. The old woman flicked her scarf at them. They flew off and dropped the bread, which was picked up by an opportunistic youngster that flapped its wings in victory.

Poppy was assailed by a memory of the actress dead on her dressing-room couch. Yes, she mustn't forget in all this titillating intrigue that there was a dead woman at the centre of it. "I assume Selena was connected with the Andreioviches in some way."

"You assume correctly," confirmed Marjorie. "Selena was sort of a double agent."

"Sort of?" asked Poppy, trying to reconcile the silliness of the dead princess with the image of an international spy.

"Yes, sort of. She had Bolshevik friends from her days in Paris."

Poppy remembered the photograph of Selena with Vladimir Lenin in Paris. It was also taken around 1912, if she remembered correctly.

"Yes, I know," said Poppy.

Marjorie raised a curious eyebrow, suggesting she was surprised that Poppy knew anything about it at all. Poppy was slightly miffed, but let it pass.

"But Selena, being Selena," continued Marjorie, "did not really know what it was all about. Her family realized this and did not take her pseudo-socialist views too seriously. Both sides, it seems, tried to play her. The royals tried to get information out of her about developments in Bolshevik circles; the Bolshies used her to get intel on the royals. Fortunately for us, because she was such a renowned gossip, neither side could trust her and just used her to spread misinformation."

"How do you know all this?" asked Poppy.

Marjorie stamped her foot to chase away a pigeon that was edging towards her. "We – the Home Office – had informers. One of them was Ruth Broadwood. She sent us information while she was inside the Winter Palace in St Petersburg. Then again when she was with the Andreioviches in Moscow. As I said, we lost track of the count in 1916. We never knew, though, whether he had died or had decided that blood was thicker than water and gone on some secret mission for his cousin the tsar. We were hoping Ruth would be able to find out."

"Did she?" asked Poppy.

Marjorie checked her watch. "No. She didn't. It seemed that the countess was just as much in the dark as we were. In fact, she agreed to do something, very foolishly, in order to get some information out of the tsar. She believed Nicholas knew where her husband was. Whether he did or didn't, we don't know. But she agreed to become a treasure-keeper in return for information on her husband's whereabouts."

Poppy's ears pricked at the familiar term: a treasure-keeper. That's what Selena had claimed to be. The rest of the royals, it seemed, thought she was just a simple thief. Was she? Poppy remembered the information in the Jazz File about the missing necklace in Paris. Was that just a coincidence? She decided not to mention it to Marjorie.

"Look, Poppy, time's getting on. So let me wrap this up. Very quickly: Selena took a Fabergé egg to Sofia Andreiovich for safe keeping on behalf of the tsarina. Ruth Broadwood sent a despatch to us to say that she believed the egg contained a key and that the key opened another egg that held very sensitive information that might expose our royal family to scandal." She picked up the photograph of the dead family. "We believe the Andreiovich egg was stolen the night the family was murdered. And we believe the egg stolen at the exhibition last Saturday might have been the egg containing the information. Or at least the thief thought it might be."

Poppy was stunned. So that was how it was all connected. "All right…" Poppy took a deep breath, then exhaled. "So, whoever it was who stole the egg has access to the information. What will they do with it?"

Marjorie raised her hand. "We don't know if they do have the information yet. Firstly, there are nearly fifty Fabergé eggs in circulation. Any one of them could contain the secret. We think that perhaps the thief just assumed Selena's egg would be the correct one. But we would be very surprised if the tsarina had entrusted something so sensitive to her silly cousin. We have been told that other eggs have been stolen too: in Paris, Venice and New York. We also don't know if the Moscow thief even has the key. You see, we think Ruth Broadwood managed to get it from the egg first. And that's why the Bolsheviks put out word that she had killed the family. So she could be hunted down."

Poppy picked up the picture of the elderly spy. "But she hasn't been found yet?"

"No. Not that we know of."

"And are you certain it's the Bolsheviks who are after her – and the eggs?"

Marjorie shrugged. "My colleagues seem to be. But let's just say it serves their purpose to believe that – and to let others believe it too."

Poppy looked at the older woman, surprised at her candour. She had all but admitted that the British government had a policy of smearing the communists. She let it pass. "But in reality it could have been someone else. Someone with another agenda."

Marjorie nodded. "It's possible, yes."

The clock of St Bride's struck half past nine. It was time she got to the newsroom. And time she got to the point. "So, Mrs Reynolds, let's get to it. What has all this to do with Andrei Nogovski and Oscar?"

Marjorie started packing up the photographs. "Oscar, I'm not sure, and that's what I'd like you to try and find out. He won't tell me anything, but he likes you. And you seem to have a way of getting information out of people. Can I ask you, if you find anything out, to tell me about it first, before it gets into the papers?"

Poppy sucked in her breath. Was Marjorie trying to dictate to her how she did her job? She looked at the older woman and the worry lines around her eyes. No, that wasn't what she was doing – at least not in relation to Oscar. She was just a mother, trying to protect her son. "I could, yes," agreed Poppy. "But I will need something else in return."

Marjorie's mouth twisted into a half-smile. "Of course you will. You're Rollo's girl."

Poppy shrugged, choosing to take the jibe as a compliment, not an insult. She opened her satchel and took out the greetings card that had been attached to the chocolate box in Selena's dressing room. She held it between thumb and forefinger. "Tell me, Mrs Reynolds, does the Secret Service hold fingerprint files on leading figures and other 'persons of interest'?"

Marjorie's mouth relaxed into a full smile accompanied by a twinkle in her eyes. "The Secret Service, Miss Denby? Why, I have no idea what you mean. However, the Home Office may have access to certain files, yes. Why do you ask?"

Poppy passed her the card. "I need to know who, if anyone's, fingerprints are on this card."

Marjorie reached into her inner jacket pocket and took out a pair of spectacles, and perched them on her nose.

"*To Princess Selena Romanova Yusopova, the Old Vic Theatre. From a repentant fool.*"

She read the card and then looked at Poppy with unbridled surprise. "Have you been withholding evidence from the police, Poppy?"

Poppy flushed. Yes she had, was the truthful answer. And she would hand it over if her suspicions about who had written the card attached to the poisoned chocolates proved to be false. But if they weren't... A shiver ran down her spine. Well, she would decide what to do then. For now though, she needed some information from Marjorie. And Marjorie needed her help to protect her son. It was an arrangement they both knew they would agree to. And they did.

Marjorie wrapped the card in a handkerchief and put it back with her spectacles into her pocket. Then she picked up her briefcase and readied to leave.

Poppy reached out her hand and took the older woman's arm. "But Mrs Reynolds, you haven't told me what all of this has to do with Andrei Nogovski."

Marjorie again looked to right and left, then motioned for Poppy to walk with her. They headed out of the graveyard and through the gate of the church. Marjorie stopped and again looked around her. Poppy was beginning to get annoyed. Why couldn't she just spit it out?

"Well, Mrs Reynolds?"

"You need to be careful, Poppy; you really do. He seems to be taking an interest in you, and I'm not entirely sure it's all professional."

"I –" interrupted Poppy.

Marjorie raised her hand. "Andrei Nogovski is a dangerous man. We believe he might have been responsible for the murder of the Andreiovich family. And the Romanovs – although their deaths have not been confirmed."

Poppy felt the hairs rise at the back of her neck. "And Selena," she whispered.

"Yes," said Marjorie, reaching out and taking Poppy's hand. "We think he might have done that too."

CHAPTER 21

Adam Lane stretched out his long limbs on the king-sized bed in his Kensington penthouse apartment, then curled them back around the soft body of the delectable Delilah Marconi. Delilah stirred and snuffled like a warm, sleepy puppy, then wriggled herself deeper into his arms – but she did not awake. Adam pressed his face against her tousled black hair and inhaled her scent. She smelled of orange blossom – hmmm, he loved that shampoo.

He looked across at the clock on his dressing table and saw that it was half past nine. He should be getting up soon if he still wanted to shower and breakfast before leaving for the theatre – and perhaps drop by Oscar's on the way. He should probably wake Delilah up too, but if he did he would have to face the questions he had managed to quench the night before with his kisses. Questions such as: why was he holding a sword to answer his door? And wasn't that the same kind of sword that had killed Princess Selena? She had also noticed his new sheepskin coat on the hatstand and had playfully asked if he was now a bear in sheep's clothing. And then she had tried to put on the coat, and he had snatched it from her, knowing he had not yet removed the Fabergé egg from the inside pocket. His brusqueness was completely out of character from what Delilah knew of him, and the girl was concerned by his change of demeanour. He had put it all down to having had a fright at the theatre and the fact that he was still recovering from seeing a dead body.

Delilah had tutted in sympathy and said she completely

understood and now that she thought about it, she was glad he had a sword with a murderer still on the loose. Which was why she was here in the first place. She absolutely could not stay alone until the killer was caught! Could she stay with him? He thought of the complications this might cause until he'd managed to pass on the egg, but could think of no plausible reason to turn her down. And now, after the night they'd had, he was glad he hadn't. But it would still be tricky. He'd have to play this very carefully indeed…

Adam Lane was used to playing things carefully. Lane was not his real surname. He didn't know his real surname, having been abandoned as a baby in a provincial theatre. His mother, a vaudeville dancer, had left him behind when she moved to her next job, and the wardrobe mistress, a spinster who couldn't resist his googly charms, had taken him in. She took him to work with her every day for four years, but then she died of consumption. The theatre manager had declared he should be taken to the Sisters of Mercy, but neither the manager nor any of the staff had got around to it. Little Adam was a scamp, and knew every nook and cranny of the theatre. Whenever there was talk of "getting rid of the lad" he would hide until the person tasked with looking for him gave up. Eventually they gave up completely, and Adam took on the same role as the theatre cat. He knew how to find food and make himself useful folding programmes or helping to sweep up after a show. He knew how to make himself scarce too.

The props master took a particular liking to him and in his spare time would let Adam play with the stage weapons. He even taught him how to sword fight. And to steal. The props master moonlighted as a jewel thief, hiding the stolen merchandise among the paste and tat of the theatre collection until the heat had died down. Many a time a leading lady would be wearing a real diamond pendant without even realizing it – sometimes with the owner sitting in the audience. Adam was the Oliver to his Fagan, with some key differences: Adam liked the life and the props master was never cruel.

Adam learned to act by watching the cast rehearse. As he got older he began to audition for minor roles; by the time he was eighteen he was getting leads. He could turn his voice to any accent and mimic the style and demeanour of any class. When the props master retired and the replacement was not as kindly disposed to him, Adam decided to continue his education elsewhere. He joined a travelling theatre company and moved from city to city, then country to country. Wherever he went he plied his dual trade of acting and thieving, first using his mentor's network, then developing one of his own. Now at thirty-two his act was so refined that no one suspected he was anything else than the only son of a minor aristocrat. Alas, his parents had died on the *Titanic*, and no, he didn't have any other family. Adam easily won people over, and whatever he lacked in bloodline he made up for in charm and talent.

He had met Delilah in the summer, when he was playing Demetrius, and she a fairy, in *A Midsummer Night's Dream*. They had both then auditioned for Stanislavski's version of Chekhov's *Cherry Orchard* and were cast as the young lovers. Soon life began to imitate art.

Adam felt Delilah stir against him. He pulled her closer. He had not meant to fall in love with this girl. She had been a summer dalliance. But now that summer had turned to autumn his feelings for her had grown. It was too dangerous for them to continue, however. For him and for her. Delilah had no idea about his alternative life. As far as she was concerned he was a young travelling actor. And he knew Delilah was no innocent wallflower; she had had lovers before and that was one of the reasons he had chosen her. She was not quite as likely to have a broken heart when he left. But what about him? He felt his own heart pounding against her back, her body absorbing and amplifying the sound. And with his hands pressed against her chest, he could feel hers beating too: they were in rhythm.

Adam hoped that all of this bother with the eggs would not force him to leave before he had fulfilled his contract to Stanislavski. Assuming, of course, the director did not succumb to the poison that had not been meant for him – or at least Adam hoped it hadn't been. No, how could it be? Surely it had been meant for Selena. A back-up plan in case the killer failed. Or had the chocolates been Plan A? Adam didn't know. He also didn't know why Selena had been killed. But he could guess. She had been the one to fire the gun at the exhibition – he was sure of that now. Why she had done it, he didn't know, but he wouldn't put it past the woman to be trying to steal the egg for herself. What a coincidence that it was on the same night he had been paid to do the same. Or was it a coincidence? Perhaps his employer – whom he had never met and with whom he mainly communicated through his fence at Oscar's – had hired her too. In case he failed. Or perhaps to ensure that he didn't... Was he working for a murderer? It was time he had a talk with his fence. This was getting far too dangerous. The guard, Selena and now Stanislavski...

The last he'd heard, the world famous director was stable and the doctors were confident of a full recovery. But what if they were wrong? Adam's stomach tightened. What if he died? Adam admired Stanislavski immensely, and not since the wardrobe mistress in the theatre where he was first abandoned had anyone seen value in him – Adam Lane, or whatever his real surname was. Stanislavski – the leading acting teacher of his generation – had seen that Adam had talent. Stanislavski had not given him the part because he was the best of a bad bunch, or because he was the best looking boy in the ensemble. No, dozens of hopefuls had auditioned, and Adam was the chosen one. Stanislavski had faith in Adam that he could make it as an actor on the world stage. That he was worthy. Stanislavski believed in him. Delilah believed in him. And for the first time in his life, Adam was truly beginning to believe in himself.

But it was becoming too dangerous to stay. Too many people were looking for the egg and the person who had stolen it. Would it be possible to simply pass it on to his fence like he normally did and then resume his life as if nothing had happened? He doubted it. Adam felt a lump in his throat. He did not want to leave. Not when this potential new life had just begun. Perhaps he should confide in Stanislavski. He was a man of the world; he knew how things worked and was not likely to turn him in to the police. Like most Russians of his generation, Stanislavski had an intrinsic mistrust of the police, no matter which country they were from. No, Adam did not think he would turn him in. Poppy Denby, on the other hand, was not as easy to predict. What would she do if she found out? And the longer Adam spent with Delilah, her best friend, the greater the chance he would come on to Poppy's radar during her investigation.

Adam eased himself away from Delilah and lay on his back, his forearm draped across his forehead. No, it would not be as simple as confiding in Stanislavski. And besides, it was no longer just about some stolen jewels: people were dying… or nearly dying. The guard, Stanislavski, Selena, the family in Moscow…

Adam wondered for the umpteenth time since that horrific night whether or not the little girl and the old woman had got away. He hoped they had, but there was no way of finding out. He had briefly met the child when he had been to a dinner party at the family home back in 1915 on his first Moscow tour – which was when he had first met Stanislavski too. Adam had been invited to the Andreiovich home by Stanislavski, who was a friend of the family. On a whim he had bought a puppy at a pet shop on the way to the party and given it to the little girl. Were they still alive? The child and the dog? He prayed that they were.

Adam and his creator had a complicated relationship. Adam believed in God and, despite being a thief, tried to live as good a life as possible. He graded sins according to the harm they caused to others and in his mind relieving a wealthy woman of jewellery did not rank at all. It was – how did the Marxists term it? – merely a redistribution of wealth. He had a suspicion that God did not quite agree with him. Ah well, they'd just have to agree to disagree on that one.

And on this... he thought as he contemplated waking Delilah and making them both late for rehearsal. It was tempting, very tempting. "Oh Delilah, darling..."

An hour later, Adam and Delilah were both showered and heading towards Adam's motor car, parked down a side alley near his apartment building. They were due for rehearsal at eleven and it was now a quarter to. They knew they'd be late, but calculated that as Stanislavski was still in hospital, and the theatre was a crime scene, no one would be too fussed.

Delilah suddenly pulled up. "Oh drat!"

"What?" he asked.

"I think I've left my ciggies in your flat. Can I have the key, please?"

"I'll get them."

"No," said Delilah, her hand outstretched. "We don't have time. You get the motor cranked while I get the ciggies. We need to multi-task, darling!" She flashed her beautiful smile and cocked her head to the side.

He chuckled. "All right, but make sure you lock the door properly on the way out."

"Of course!" she declared, took the keys, and scampered off.

He continued towards the motor car. As he did, someone stepped out of the shadows, blocking the path to the vehicle. It was a man dressed in a black overcoat and homburg hat, carrying a cane. The hat was pulled low over his face.

"Good morning, Mr Lane," he said in Russian. "I believe you have something that belongs to me." The man's fist tightened over the cane handle.

Adam's tightened over his own. "I have no idea what you are talking about, sir," said Adam in English.

"No?" said the man, and raised his head, allowing Adam to see his face.

Adam gasped inwardly, but did not allow it to show. It was the man he had noticed at the exhibition. The man he had first seen on the balcony of the Andreiovich house as he was escaping over the lawn.

But Adam was not going to let on that he recognized him. He drew on his years of acting experience and asked nonchalantly, "Have we met?"

"Not formally," said the man in English. "But we have a number of acquaintances in common."

"Oh? Such as?"

"The Andreiovich family, Princess Selena Romanova Yusopova... oh, and Poppy Denby." The man smiled coldly. "And I am also on first-name terms with your fence."

Adam took a step back; the man took a step forward. Adam's thumb rested on the catch to his rapier.

"Give me the egg, Lane, and no one else will get hurt. Your lovely little Delilah, for instance…"

Adam saw red. He flicked the catch and unleashed his weapon. The Russian man did the same: a rapier of the same design as Adam's. For a split second, Adam thought of Selena and the rapier wound to her heart, then he thought of Delilah. He'd be damned if the same was going to happen to her! He thrust forward, the Russian parried, he stepped to the left, then thrust again. The Russian matched him move for move. The two men circled around the alleyway in an intricate, deadly dance.

"Got them," Delilah's voice trilled down the alley. "Adam! What's going on?"

Adam, distracted for a moment, let his guard down. The Russian took the gap. Adam felt the rapier slice into his forearm. But he held on to his weapon and blocked the next thrust.

"Get out of here!" he yelled over his shoulder.

"Help! Help!" screamed Delilah, running out onto the street. "Officer! Over here!"

"We'll finish this later," the Russian man said. Then he ran back down the alley, away from where Delilah and a uniformed Bobby were coming to Adam's aid.

Adam quickly sheathed his rapier and dropped it to the ground. No one but an expert would know that it was anything but a cane. He clutched his forearm as blood seeped through his fingers.

Delilah ran up to him and took hold of his arm. She pulled up his sheepskin sleeve, took a silk scarf from her neck and wrapped it around the wound, encouraging Adam to sit down.

The Bobby, breathless, returned from giving chase to the Russian. "He's gone, sir. What happened? Are you all right?"

Adam steadied his breathing and got into character. He was a mugging victim. Some scoundrel had jumped him, no doubt hoping to steal his motor car. The man had a long knife. No, not a sword. It must have just looked like that from a distance. Adam defended himself with a cane. Yes, that's the one. Of course he was sure there were no swords. His lady-friend must have been mistaken.

His "lady-friend's" eyes narrowed as she listened to his statement, but she didn't contradict him.

"I'll take you to the hospital then, sir."

"It's just a flesh wound; my coat took the worst of it. The lady here can drive. I'm sure you've got more than enough to do, officer."

"Well, I was on the way to checking out reports of a break-in at the greengrocer's... the two might be related."

"Well, there you go," said Adam. "I'll pop in to the station later and make a full statement, shall I?"

Assured that an official route would eventually be followed, the policeman agreed. He stayed long enough to help Adam get the motor cranked and then waved the young couple off as they headed to hospital.

After Adam had been stitched up, he and Delilah sat together in the hospital canteen having a cup of tea. Delilah looked at him, her cat-eyes shrewd and knowing.

"What's going on, Adam? Who was that man? And why did you tell the policeman you didn't have swords? I'm not blind. Don't pretend I am."

Adam sighed. He should never have let things go this far. "I know you're not, darling. And I promise I will explain everything, truly. But for now you need to trust me. The less you know, the safer you will be."

"Safer? Are you in... am I... and Selena? Has this got something to do with Selena? Did that man..." Delilah's voice was rising in panic.

Adam took her hand and squeezed it tightly. "Shhh. I'll tell you everything, I promise. But I need to do something first. You go ahead to the theatre; I'll meet you there later."

"But what if that man –"

"Take a cab. Go directly there. There'll still be police all over the place. You'll be safe."

"And what about you?" Delilah was near to tears.

"I can look after myself, sweetheart."

"But –"

He put his finger on her lips. "Shhhh. Please. Just do as I say."

189

"Oh Poppy, you've got to help me. I don't know what to do." Delilah threw herself, sobbing, into Poppy's arms.

"Whatever's the matter, Delilah?"

"It's Adam. I don't know where he is… or what's happened to him. You see, there was this man with a sword —"

"*A sword?*" Poppy – and every journalist in the newsroom – dropped what they were doing and waited for Delilah to tell them more.

To the disappointment of the news hacks, Poppy took her friend's arm and led her to a private interview room and shut the door. If there was a story to be had it was going to be hers. Besides, she didn't like the way they were all ogling the young actress.

She sat Delilah down, pulled out her notepad and said: "Right, let's start at the beginning…"

Twenty minutes later and Poppy had as full a picture as she could possibly get from Delilah, but it still wasn't clear. Why was Adam sword fencing with a man in an alley? Who was the man? Why had Adam lied when the police arrived? And why had he not turned up at the theatre as he had said he would?

"What could have happened to him, Poppy? Do you think I should go to the police?"

Poppy circled her notes about Adam not giving the Bobby the full story and said: "Adam didn't want the police involved. Perhaps we should respect that for now. At least until we've heard his reasons."

"But what if he's hurt? Or worse! The police will know what to do. They'll help find him."

Poppy smiled sympathetically. "They will only consider filing a missing person's report if he's been missing for longer than forty-eight hours. And it's only been an hour or two, hasn't it?"

Delilah nodded through her tears. "Yes. But he said he'd be straight there. As soon as he'd dealt with something."

"Well, there you go. He's obviously still busy. Did he say what it was?"

Delilah shook her head, then dropped it onto her forearms and sobbed.

Poppy put down her pencil, walked around the desk and wrapped her arms around her friend. When the sobbing slowed, she stroked her sleek black hair and said: "I'll tell you what. Let's go to his apartment. He might be there. Did you check?"

"N-n-no."

"Then that's the best place to start. I'll just have to tell Rollo where I'm going. Here…" She passed a handkerchief to Delilah, who took it with a grateful smile and blew her nose.

"Thanks, Poppy. It's probably nothing, but you can't blame me for being worried, can you? I mean there *is* a murderer on the loose. Selena was killed with a sword and this man had one. *And* Adam had one. I saw it last night and I saw it this morning. No matter what Adam says, I saw it. I know I did."

Poppy patted her on the shoulder. "I believe you. It does look as if Adam's got himself involved in something."

Delilah's brown eyes widened. "Oh, I'm sure he's got nothing to do with it. He's a victim. Or he might be. They're trying to kill off the cast of *The Cherry Orchard*. But why? They haven't even seen us perform it yet."

Poppy stifled a smile. "I don't think anyone's killing off the cast of *The Cherry Orchard*, Delilah."

"But Selena, Monsieur Stanislavski – all right, he's not dead, but he might have been – and now Adam." Her hand went to her throat. "Oh my, do you think I might be on the list too?"

This was getting out of hand. Poppy pulled back her shoulders and in her most no-nonsense voice said: "Now let's not get ahead of ourselves. There's something going on here, but I don't think it's the mass murder of actors. Look, Delilah, I know you're worried – and you have a right to be – but I really don't think this is as bad as it seems."

"No?" asked Delilah, her eyes still fearful but her voice a touch calmer.

"No," said Poppy, relieved that Delilah appeared to be coming back from the brink. "Now, let me just go and tell Rollo –"

But before she could finish, the door flew open and Rollo burst in, followed by Daniel. "There you are, Poppy! Let's get going. There's a story breaking."

"Sorry, Rollo, I can't; I promised I'd help –"

Rollo put up his hands. "Whatever it is it can wait. It's not every day there's a murder at Oscar's Jazz Club."

Whatever Rollo said or was about to say after that was drowned by an ear-splitting scream. And then Delilah fainted.

On the drive over to Chelsea, Poppy filled Rollo and Daniel in on what Delilah had told her. Daniel was driving the company motor and she and Rollo were in the back. They had left Delilah in the care of Vicky Thompson and Mavis Bradshaw, who were to tell her, when she woke up, that Poppy promised to telephone as soon as they got to the club and found out the identity of the victim.

"Great Scot!" declared Rollo. "They were actually sword fighting?" He was so excited that bubbles of spittle sprayed the seat in front of him. Poppy leaned back as far as she could into the corner of the Model T Ford.

"That's what Delilah says. And she'll have seen enough of it play-acted in the theatre to know what she was seeing."

"Maybe that's all it was," offered Daniel from the front seat. "Adam might have been staging some theatrical stunt. You know what these actor-types are like: melodramatic to the extreme."

Poppy thought of her Aunt Dot and Delilah, and knew exactly what he meant. But she didn't think this was the case here. "He was injured, Daniel; he needed stitches. And last night Delilah said he looked scared when she arrived. Why would he answer the door with a sword – or a rapier?"

"Why would he be carrying one around in the first place?" asked Rollo, wiping his mouth with the back of his hand. "Sorry, Poppy."

Yes, this was puzzling Poppy too. Delilah had mentioned something about a cane that sheathed the rapier. She remembered the cane. Adam carried it everywhere with him. She had thought it was just a dandy fashion statement, but now she was beginning to wonder if Adam was not quite all he seemed. What did she know about him, after all? What did Delilah? They'd only known him a few months. Perhaps Lilian Baylis or Constantin Stanislavski could shed some light on his background. She made a mental note to visit the hospital as soon as she'd finished at the club. She'd been meaning to go and see the director anyway.

Daniel turned right outside Charing Cross station onto the Victoria Embankment. It was a Tuesday lunchtime and office workers were eating their sandwiches overlooking the Thames. A pleasure boat bobbed at its moorings: not too many tourists were around this late in October.

"A rapier, eh?" repeated Rollo. "The same weapon that killed Selena."

"The same *type* of weapon," corrected Poppy. "No one is suggesting Adam killed her."

"Aren't they?" asked Rollo with an apologetic shrug. "That's exactly what I'm suggesting. I know this Lane fella is a friend of yours, but from an objective viewpoint, he's now the prime suspect."

Poppy opened her mouth to object.

"Let me finish, Miz Denby."

She closed it.

Rollo cocked his head and grinned. "You might not like it, Poppy, but a journalist has to lay aside personal feelings and follow the scent no matter where it takes them."

This irked Poppy. Had he forgotten that she had done exactly that only four months earlier, when her investigation into the Dorchester story struck right at the heart of her own family? But Rollo was in mentor mode and would not be detracted from pressing home his point.

"You said he was at the theatre?" he continued. "That he was first on the scene when you called for help?"

Poppy acknowledged that this was true.

"Well, there you have it: motive, means and opportunity."

"I don't see a motive, Rollo," Daniel said. They had just passed New Scotland Yard, Big Ben and the Houses of Parliament, and were turning right onto Victoria Street.

Rollo grinned. "Maybe Miz Denby can work that one out. Where else was Adam Lane, Poppy?"

Poppy knew exactly what he was getting at, but she was peeved at him and was trying to control her feelings before she answered.

Before she could speak, Rollo chipped in: "We discussed it yesterday afternoon, Miz Denby. Remember? Who do we *definitely* know was at the theatre on Monday when Selena was killed and also at the exhibition on Saturday night?"

His patronizing tone was annoying, but Poppy knew he

was right. These were exactly the types of questions a journalist should be asking. She sighed and bit the bullet. "Me, Selena, Delilah and Adam."

Rollo didn't bother trying to hide his smug expression. "Exactly."

"Well, Selena definitely didn't do it," said Daniel. "And I don't think Delilah or Poppy did either… Or did you, Poppy?" His tone was playful, but Poppy resented him appearing to take sides with Rollo in giving her an object lesson in investigative reporting. She looked out of the window and noticed some Bobbies on the beat. She pulled herself up. *Don't be so childish, Poppy; go with the flow. People's lives are at stake here. And you know the police are also going to think Adam did it if they find out about this. We – you, Rollo and Daniel – need to get to the truth before they do. It's the only way to protect Adam, if he's innocent, or Delilah if he's not.*

She turned to look at Rollo and said: "If Adam's guilty, we'll find out. I agree, it looks like he's the prime suspect, but we still need proof that he did it."

"Or that he didn't," offered Rollo in a gentler tone.

"Indeed, if he didn't." Poppy smiled at him. And then at Daniel as he gave her a wink over his shoulder.

"So," she continued more chirpily, "the exhibition. They're inextricably linked: the theft of the egg and the murder of Selena. And Adam was at both."

"Do you remember where he was when the lights went out, Poppy?" asked Daniel.

Poppy thought about this and then remembered Daniel's photograph of the men at the bar. She had noticed Adam there talking to the bartender from Oscar's – speaking of which, who had been murdered? Rollo's source hadn't said. Could it be Oscar? Poppy shuddered. They'd find out soon enough. But for now, they had a puzzle to work out.

"He went to get drinks for us all."

"Aha!" said Rollo. "Once again, opportunity."

"Yes, but it was a woman who pulled the trigger. We've proven that," corrected Poppy.

"Almost proven it," said Rollo. "I'm still waiting on my source in Scotland Yard to tell me if the forensic boys found any gun residue on Selena or inside her gloves – if they found them in the search last night."

"But who says the shooter and the thief were the same person?" offered Daniel. "There could have been two of them."

"True," said Poppy. "It's highly likely Selena was trying to steal the egg for herself. But it would have been difficult to shoot the gun and then steal the egg and then dispose of both the gun and the egg in the aftermath. She probably had help."

"Adam?" asked Daniel. "It's hard to believe. He's such a nice bloke."

"I know. I feel the same. And Delilah will be devastated if it's true, but he does seem to be caught up in something. That man in the alley…"

"Who also had a rapier," observed Rollo, "so could also have been Selena's killer. What's going on here, Poppy?"

Poppy thought about it for a moment. "What if there were three of them? The shooter, the thief and then the person who took the gun and the egg away. For argument's sake – and I'm not convinced it's true yet, but let's go with it – if Adam was the thief it would follow that a third person *had* to be involved."

"Why's that?" asked Rollo.

"Because both Adam and Selena remained behind and were searched by DCI Martin."

"Bingo!" said Rollo.

"So what we're suggesting then," summed up Daniel as he turned left onto King's Road, "is that Adam, Selena and this mystery man were in cahoots, and that Selena's death was a result of a fall-out between thieves. One of them wants the egg for himself. He's already killed Selena and he's attempted to kill Adam –"

"Or Adam's attempted to kill him," Rollo interjected.

Poppy frowned, but reminded herself that they needed to follow this train of thought to its logical conclusion before they could prove or disprove Adam's guilt. "Whichever way, we need to find out who this mystery man is."

"Did Delilah recognize him?" asked Daniel. They were driving past Aunt Dot's house and approaching Delilah's apartment block.

"No," said Poppy. "She said he was dressed all in black with an overcoat and homburg hat. She couldn't see his face. But she said he was a similar height and build to Adam."

They passed Delilah's building and Poppy remembered Andrei Nogovski waiting for her there last night. Hadn't he been in a black ensemble? And hadn't he too been carrying a cane? He was about the same height and build as Adam... Poppy felt an icy chill run down her spine. Yes, it would fit with what Marjorie had told her about him at breakfast. She still hadn't had a chance to fill Rollo in on her meeting with the Home Office minister – she had been busy writing up her notes as Delilah arrived – and now they were pulling up to Oscar's Jazz Club.

And there was Marjorie Reynolds standing talking to DCI Martin. She looked as pale as a ghost.

CHAPTER 23

A police cordon surrounded the jazz club. King's Road neighbours and passers-by were hemming in, trying to see what was going on inside, particularly because a mortuary van had just pulled up. Poppy, Daniel and Rollo tried to slip through, but were prevented by a line of Bobbies. Poppy recognized the one with the handlebar moustache from last night. If she were not mistaken, he actually smirked at her.

She called out to Marjorie who was in animated conversation with DCI Martin. "Mrs Reynolds! Marjorie! What's going on?"

Marjorie turned away from Martin, her face a combination of worry and fury as the Detective Chief Inspector went back into the club. "Poppy, Rollo, thank heavens you're here."

"Do you know what happened?" Rollo asked Marjorie.

"Apparently there was an altercation. Oscar had a row with one of the staff."

"Oh no, it isn't –" asked Poppy, thinking of their conversation that morning.

Marjorie looked close to tears. "No, it isn't. It's the barman. But – but – they think Oscar did it."

Poppy gasped. "But why?"

"Because a delivery man heard them arguing and then saw Oscar running out of the cellar with blood all over his shirt and hands. When the delivery man went in he saw Watts – the barman – dead."

"How?" asked Rollo as he nodded to Daniel to start taking photographs of the scene outside the club.

"Stabbed, I think. But Martin didn't say what with." Marjorie bit her lip. "Oscar's still being questioned."

"Inside?" asked Rollo.

Marjorie nodded in confirmation. "All rightee," said Rollo with an exaggerated drawl. "Let's go and find out what the neighbours saw, Poppy. Danny Boy, you stay here and get a pic of the body when they bring it out. Miz Reynolds, we'll see you later." He raised his hat and took hold of Poppy's arm and led her up the street, away from the club.

"Shouldn't we be staying to see what happens?" asked Poppy. "The neighbours are all there anyway."

"Very observant of you, Miz Denby," said Rollo, under his breath. "But it's not the neighbours we're going to see. It's Oscar."

"And how do you propose to do that?" whispered Poppy. "The coppers have got the place locked down tighter than the Tower of London."

Rollo smiled up at her with his best Cheshire Cat grin. "Watch and learn, Miz Denby; watch and learn."

When they were about a block away from the club, Rollo pulled Poppy into a side street behind a newsagent. A *Daily Globe* delivery van was just pulling out. Poppy recognized the driver. He smiled and waved to Rollo and Poppy as he drove off. When the van had turned onto King's Road, Rollo flicked his head left and right to see if the coast was clear, then took Poppy's hand and pulled her behind a line of dustbins and skips. He squatted over a manhole cover, inserted his stubby fingers into the holes and began to pull.

"What on earth are you doing? You'll never lift it; you need one of those crowbar thingies," observed Poppy.

But Rollo just grinned and pulled the cover up with ease. Instead of coming out in its entirety, the metal disc hinged back like a trapdoor. Underneath Poppy could see that it was made of wood with a thin layer of metal on top to make it look like a manhole cover.

"What on earth…"

"I'll explain on the way," said Rollo, motioning for her to get in. "Quick, down the ladder. I'll close the door after us."

As the afternoon sun was blocked by the closing hatch, Rollo called for Poppy to wait for him at the bottom of the ladder. With no clue as to where she was going, she had no intention of heading off without him anyway. She stood in what she had briefly glimpsed as a tunnel, girded with wooden supports and a compacted earthen floor. Poppy was five feet five inches tall and the ceiling only cleared her head by an inch – if that. She instinctively stooped, and wondered how someone like Daniel would have fared. Rollo, being a good foot shorter than Poppy, had no such problems. He struck a match and squeezed passed the young reporter, gesturing for her to follow him.

The match cast giant shadows on the walls, and the periodic crunch of discarded matches underfoot – no doubt dropped by previous tunnellers – amplified Poppy's fear. She did not like enclosed spaces. The Tube lines of London's Underground were already too much to bear – this was nearly intolerable. Add to that the squeak and scuttle of the tunnel's regular occupants, and it was approaching nightmare proportions.

Rollo, oblivious to Poppy's phobia, led the way, chattering over his shoulder as he went.

"*The Globe* owns half a dozen paper shops around London. I started buying them to improve our distribution outlets. I acquired the one up there just over a year ago. When I was given a copy of the blueprints I noticed something strange. There appeared to be a cellar on the prints, but there was no cellar under the actual shop. I thought it was just an error in the plans, but when I queried the previous owner about it he tapped his nose and said I should speak to Oscar Reynolds. So I did."

The match sputtered out. Poppy squeezed her fingernails into the palms of her hands. Rollo struck another match and they continued.

"Oscar told me that he hadn't known the shop had been sold and that he hoped it wouldn't cause any problems. 'Why would it?' I asked. We were a block away from the club and as far as I could tell there was no connection between the two. Well that, Miz Denby, is where I was wrong. Oscar swore me to secrecy – promising me tip-offs when leading socialites visited the club – and then took me down to the club cellar. Behind a wine rack there is a door that opens up into this tunnel. It leads, for a quarter of a mile, under King's Road, and comes out just behind the newsagent."

"But what's it for?" asked Poppy, her fear beaten into submission by her curiosity.

Another match expired. Another was lit.

"Prohibition," said Rollo. "Or at least the fear of it. During the war there was talk of introducing a ban on alcohol on the home front – or if that failed, raising the price of a liquor licence so high no one would be able to afford it. Tommies on leave were drinking themselves motherless and it was considered unpatriotic for civilians to be partying while the boys abroad were dying in droves. Then across the pond, the great U S of A announced plans to start banning the commercial sale of alcohol, and many thought it would come here too. If you recall, Miz Denby, that was one of my concerns at your job interview when I heard you were a Methodist."

Poppy did indeed recall it. She had wondered at the time why Rollo appeared more concerned by her religious convictions than her journalistic knowledge.

"But why the tunnel, Rollo?" she asked as they rounded a bend and felt the floor cant upwards.

"Insurance," said Rollo as his match went out. Poppy froze, trying to control her breathing. Rollo lit another. With a rasp and a hiss, the tunnel was illuminated again. Rollo peered up at her. "Are you all right, Poppy?"

"Uh-huh," said Poppy, not very convincingly.

Rollo smiled sympathetically. "Don't worry, we're almost there."

Something scuttled over Poppy's foot. She yelped. Rollo took her hand and hurried her along, going into lecture mode to distract her. "So, as I was saying, when Oscar bought the club three years ago, he, like many others in the hospitality trade, feared they would go out of business if prohibition came in. He arranged for this tunnel to be dug to ensure he could still get deliveries. He did a deal with the former owner of the paper shop and has kept the tunnel a secret ever since."

Just before the next match went out, they rounded another bend and came face to face with a wooden door. Poppy reached out over Rollo's head and touched it, willing it to open. Rollo squeezed her hand and then felt around for the latch. Seconds later the door edged forward, flooding the tunnel with light. Poppy let out the breath she hadn't realized she'd been holding.

Rollo raised a finger to his lips. "Quietly. We don't know who's on the other side. Let me look first." He did, easing the door open an inch at a time. "Looks like the coast's clear. But –" he looked up at Poppy – "don't get a fright, Miz Denby; they haven't moved the body yet."

Poppy nodded. She had seen dead bodies before. She would cope. She followed Rollo through the gap in the door into Oscar's wine cellar. Rollo pushed the door closed behind them and Poppy noted that it was disguised as a wine-rack. At first glance no one would suspect the rack actually swung open. If someone entered or exited the cellar by the tunnel they would need prior knowledge of the secret doorway; it was not likely to be found by accident.

The door from the club to the cellar was closed and there was no living person in the room. However, on a bed of broken glass and spilled wine was the corpse of the barman illuminated by the paltry glare from the overhead light. His eyes had been closed, posthumously. He lay on his back, his limbs splayed and his white shirt soaked red. It was difficult to tell how much of it was blood and how much wine. But his face had a long slit down the cheek, suggesting a blade had been used.

"Do you think it was the rapier again?" whispered Poppy.

"Possibly," said Rollo, tiptoeing across the carnage towards another wine rack. He pulled up a whisky barrel and clambered on top of it, then peered through the rack.

"Over here, Miz Denby."

Poppy followed, careful not to get her shoes wet in the blood and wine.

"Look here," whispered Rollo. He pulled back his shaggy head to reveal a peephole through the wine rack and into the room beyond. Again, without prior knowledge no one would have known it was there. She peered through into what she assumed was the club manager's office. Seated at a desk, flanked by two uniformed Bobbies, was Oscar Reynolds. His usually immaculate attire was in disarray, his bow-tie undone and his gold-rimmed monocle, usually perched cockily in his eye socket, hanging limp against his blood-soaked shirt.

Across the desk was DCI Jasper Martin, his hands folded across his rotund belly, with his thumb hooked into his pocket-watch chain.

"How did you know?" asked Poppy.

"Oscar showed me. He had it put in to keep an eye on the cellar."

"Because of the tunnel?" asked Poppy.

"Because of theft," said Rollo. "It happens in all pubs and clubs. Oscar wanted to keep an eye on his staff."

Poppy looked over her shoulder at the body on the floor. What had Marjorie said the man's name was? Watts? As Poppy had suspected, it was the same barman who had been at the exhibition – a man in his early forties, of medium height and build. Beyond that, Poppy knew nothing about him.

"Do you think Oscar found him stealing alcohol and they had an altercation?" asked Poppy.

"No, I don't," said Rollo, close to her ear. "I've known Oscar for years. He's incapable of hurting a fly."

"But what if the fly was attacking him?" asked Poppy, peering at the defeated-looking man through the peephole. But even as she said it, she knew it wasn't the case. Oscar did not appear to have any injuries. If he had been attacked, surely there would be some kind of visible wound. There was blood on his shirt, yes, but that was most likely the barman's. "So what's the alternative? A third man?"

"That's what I think, yes. And whoever it was must have known about the tunnel. How else could he have got away without the delivery man seeing him? And another thing: I smelled cordite before I lit my first match back there. Someone had been through the tunnel not too long before us."

Poppy shuddered, thinking she had been walking in the footsteps of a murderer. "Then why haven't the police searched the tunnel?" asked Poppy.

Rollo shrugged. "Oscar probably hasn't told them. He won't want the police to know about it. I doubt he'd reveal it unless he really had to."

"Well, I should think clearing your name of murder would qualify as a good 'had to'," observed Poppy.

Rollo shrugged again, then his hand gripped Poppy's shoulder. "Coppers at the door," he whispered.

Poppy cocked her head to listen. She heard a "Give us a hand with the stretcher, Bill."

"They're coming to get the body," said Poppy.

"We don't have much time," agreed Rollo.

Rollo jumped off the barrel, toppling it in the process. His ripe expletive was drowned in the crash. Poppy helped him up and they ran to the secret door. On tiptoes Rollo reached up and released the catch, then pushed Poppy into the tunnel as the door to the club opened, revealing a pair of Bobbies holding a stretcher.

"What the –"

"Run!" hissed Rollo. "I'll hold them off."

"But –"

"Run! That's an order. And tell Ike he's in charge."

Rollo pulled the door shut behind them. Poppy heard bottles smashing and the door to the tunnel rattling.

Poppy ran. She didn't have any matches, so she had to feel her way along the wall. The floor sloped downwards, the tunnel turned. She heard smashing and swearing behind her and someone shouting, "It's the Yankee dwarf!" And then more shouting, some of it in an American accent. The tunnel angled upwards and turned again. It must be close, it must be – "Ow!" Poppy collided with the metal ladder. Her cheek bone throbbed, but she didn't stop. Up the ladder she went, then she pushed on the hatch and it swung open. She pulled herself up into the fresh Chelsea air, then slammed the fake manhole cover shut, silencing the commotion in the tunnel. She heaved an overfull bin on top of the cover, realizing as she did it that she would be trapping Rollo inside too. But she knew the dwarf had no chance of outrunning the policemen. He would be arrested. Again.

Poppy caught a glimpse of her reflection in the glass panel of the paper shop back door. She looked a mess. But no time to worry about that now. At full pelt she ran down the alley and into King's Road, and back towards the front of the jazz club. As she approached, she slowed to a walk, trying to be as nonchalant as possible. She spotted Daniel, corralled with a group of reporters and photographers, Lionel Saunders from *The Courier* among them.

Daniel's eyes widened as he saw her. "Poppy! What the –"

"They're coming out!" shouted Lionel.

"Get the pic," said Poppy to Daniel. "I'll explain later."

Daniel frowned but readied his camera and muscled his way to the front of the pack, using his height to get the best vantage point. Poppy stayed behind, listening to the flash of bulbs and the barrage of questions hurled at the police and their prisoner.

"Where's the body?"

"Why did you kill your barman, Oscar?"

"Can we have a statement, Inspector?"

Suddenly, a collective gasp went up from the journalists, and Poppy heard an incredulous: "It's Rollo Rolandson in handcuffs!" And then all hell broke loose.

CHAPTER 24

Once Rollo and Oscar were bundled into the Black Mariah – Oscar looking morose, Rollo grinning from ear to ear and winking at Poppy and Daniel – the photographer pulled Poppy out of earshot of the other journalists and demanded to know what was going on.

Her cheek throbbed, and the dust and cobwebs on her hat and coat from her subterranean adventure burned her eyes, making her sneeze. She dusted herself off as best she could, spanked her hat and examined the welt on her face in her compact mirror. *Ouch.* That was going to leave an impressive bruise.

"So?" demanded Daniel. "What happened?"

"I'll tell you on the way back to the office." Poppy took his arm and led him back to the motor, ignoring the curious stares from rival journalists.

"Where's Marjorie?" she asked as he opened the passenger door of the Model T.

"She's off to Scotland Yard to demand Oscar's release. But don't change the subject; I want to know what happened to you and Rollo. Why do you look like you've been run over by a bus, and how on earth did Rollo get inside the club – not to mention get himself arrested?"

He shut her door, put his camera in the boot, cranked up the engine and then climbed into the driver's seat. Poppy used the time to consider her options. Was she able to tell Daniel about the tunnel? Rollo said he'd been sworn to secrecy. But he'd told *her* about it – on a need-to-know basis. Could she tell Daniel? Would she be betraying a confidence? Surely the tunnel was no longer a secret. The police now knew about it, so Oscar's contingency plan for getting booze into the club was obsolete. Yes, she decided, she'd tell him. It had caused no end of problems the last time she had to keep something from him when she was working on a story. She didn't want a repeat of that. There was more than their professional relationship at stake.

"Rollo took me through a secret underground tunnel."

"He *what*?" asked Daniel, incredulously.

Poppy explained what had happened in the tunnel and the cellar. "And then I ran into a ladder," she said, gingerly touching her cheek.

"Is that a euphemism for Rollo putting you in unnecessary danger?" asked Daniel, barely controlling his fury.

"No, it's exactly what happened. I ran into a ladder. And it hurt. A lot." She pouted, giving him the little-girl-lost look that he normally found so amusing.

But it didn't work. His knuckles were white on the steering wheel, his lips tight. "I will kill that stupid little Yankee when I get my hands on him! He'd better pray the coppers keep him in jail, because he'll be looking at the inside of a coffin if they ever let him out!"

"It's not his fault, Daniel. He was just following the story. We both were."

"By putting you in danger."

"I wasn't in danger. And neither was Rollo."

"He got arrested!" shouted Daniel.

"And look how happy he was about it." Poppy's voice rose to meet his. "I wouldn't put it past him if that was his plan all along. At least now he's on the inside of the investigation and will have a chance to speak to Oscar about what really happened."

Daniel slowed down and turned right onto Victoria Street. When they got back into the flow of traffic he turned to Poppy, his face still flush with anger.

"But he had no right to drag you along with him."

"He didn't *drag* me. I chose to go with him. I could have said no at any point. I didn't. And besides, he made sure the police didn't catch me. He protected me. Not that I needed protecting…"

"But you do need protecting. You're just a –" He stopped speaking and bit his lip.

Poppy felt a rush of anger. "I'm just a what? A woman?"

Daniel drummed his fingers on the steering wheel. "That's not what I was going to say. I was going to say you're just new on the job. You've got a lot to learn."

"And I am learning. On the job. And I'm grateful that Rollo doesn't molly-coddle me the way you do."

Daniel turned to her and momentarily took his eyes off the road. A taxi blared its horn as the Model T veered too close. Daniel swore and got the vehicle under control as they passed the Palace of Westminster and approached the intersection to the Victoria Embankment.

"I molly-coddle you, Poppy, because I love you. I *will* worry about you. I *will* be angry with anyone who puts you in danger. And that includes you. But if that's not what you want…"

He left the ambiguous threat of break-up hanging in the air while he slowed down to allow a family to cross the road at a pelican crossing. The children were squabbling and the mother tried to intervene while carrying a big bag of shopping.

Is that my future? thought Poppy. *If I marry Daniel, will I be expected to give up work to be a mother to his children? Would he consider it inappropriate for his wife to be gallivanting around London following news stories?*

"That's not fair, Daniel. Don't make this about us. It's not about us."

"Isn't it?" he asked.

She crossed her arms over her chest and looked out of the window.

Poppy and Daniel arrived back at Fleet Street in silence. As they parked in the alley behind *The Globe* offices Daniel looked across at her with furrowed brows, but looked away again when she tried to meet his eye. He was cross with her. And she was cross with him for being cross with her.

But she didn't have time to deal with it now. As Delilah had pointed out there was a killer on the loose, and Poppy had an article to write before deadline.

She got out of the motor and without a backward glance walked through the basement where the printing presses were churning out the evening edition, and pressed the lift button for the fourth floor.

"Poppy!" Daniel called. But she ignored him, pulling the gate shut and leaving him to field the knowing looks and comments from the printer staff.

Poppy examined her swollen cheek in the lift mirror. It was beginning to turn purple. She thought of covering it with a bit of make-up, but decided against it. First, it was too tender to touch; secondly, she was rather proud of it. It was her war wound from the journalistic trenches and she would wear it like a badge of honour.

The lift stopped at the third floor and Poppy braced herself to meet whoever came in. It was young Vicky Thompson, carrying some files.

Vicky gasped. "Miss Denby! What happened?"

"I had a run-in with a ladder."

"Golly! Are you all right? Do you need to see a doctor?"

"No, I think I'm fine, Vicky. It's just bruised."

"Cor blimey, you're gonna have a right shiner!"

Poppy chuckled at Vicky's slip back into Cockney. The seventeen-year-old was the daughter of a window cleaner and a washer woman from the East End of London. Poppy had met her on the Dorchester story in the summer and had given the girl a chance to have a career. Vicky had jumped at it and for the last few months had been trying to sound as posh as she thought she ought to for a job on Fleet Street. Poppy – who had a Northumbrian accent herself – had tried to tell her that she needn't be ashamed of who she was or how she spoke, but to no avail.

"Actually, Vicky, I'm glad I've caught you. I need a couple of Jazz Files."

Vicky grinned. "Way ahead of you, Miss Denby." She passed the files to her. They were for Adam Lane, Oscar Reynolds, Andrei Nogovski, Vasili Safin and Arthur Watts.

"How did you know?"

The lift stopped at the fourth floor and the two women got out. On the landing Vicky cocked her head towards the newsroom and said: "Mr Molanov sent me up with the Rusky ones. Then the darkie asked for the rest."

Poppy frowned. Vicky had not quite got over the fact that she was working with a West Indian gentleman who was her senior. Where Vicky came from in the East End, boarding houses had signs outside declaring "No Jews, Irish or Negroes". Come to think of it, some of the posher establishments in the West End had the same.

"You mean Mr Garfield," she chastised.

"Sorry, yes, Mr Garfield." Vicky looked at her feet and muttered: "And I'm sorry about Miss Marconi too."

"What about her?" Poppy slapped her hand to her mouth. Oh no! She'd forgotten about Delilah. She'd forgotten to telephone as she'd promised to tell Delilah the name of the murder victim at Oscar's – to assure her it wasn't Adam.

"Mrs Bradshaw and me couldn't stop her. When she woke up she wanted to know where you were. We told her what you'd said about telephoning from the club. She said she couldn't wait for that and would go and see for herself. We couldn't stop her, miss, I swear. If you don't believe me, ask Mrs Bradshaw. She'll tell you. We tried our best. We –"

Poppy patted Vicky's shoulder. "It's all right. It's not your fault. The whole British Army couldn't keep Delilah from doing what she wants to do. Did she say where exactly she was going?"

"She didn't, miss. I'm sorry."

Poppy sighed. That's all she needed. A hysterical Delilah trying to find Adam – a man who may or may not have just killed someone in a cellar in Chelsea. Poppy held the files to her chest. She needed to get to work. There was no point trying to track down Delilah. She'd no doubt go to Oscar's and find out that Adam was not the victim. Hopefully that would calm her down and she would go home. Her flat was just a couple of blocks up the road. She would telephone Aunt Dot and ask Miss King to pop down and see if she could find her. Yes, that's what she would do.

Vicky was still looking at her anxiously.

Poppy smiled. "Don't worry, Vicky, you did your best. And thank you for these files. You've been a grand help."

Vicky flushed at the compliment and the forgiveness it implied. "Thank you, Miss Denby. Is there anything else I can do for you?"

Poppy smiled. "A cup of coffee would be lovely. Can you bring it to Mr Garfield's desk?" she asked.

"Of course, miss. And I'll bring one for him as well, shall I? Do you know how he likes it?"

Pleased that her lesson in tolerance had been taken on board, Poppy gave Vicky the coffee order and then opened the door to the newsroom. Through the nicotine haze she spotted Ike Garfield on the telephone. After fielding a few concerned queries from some of the other journalists, she sat in the spare chair at his desk to wait for him.

He finished his call at the same time as Vicky arrived with the coffee. He looked surprised. "Thank you, Miss Thompson; that's very kind of you."

Vicky flushed. "You're welcome, Mr Garfield, sir." Then she hastened a retreat.

He gave a knowing look at Poppy, then pulled up when he saw her cheek.

"Heavens, Poppy! What happened?"

Poppy sighed, leaned back in her chair and sipped her coffee. She waited a moment for the sweet, warm brew to work its magic and then she launched into her explanation.

As she wrapped up she finished with: "Rollo said to tell you you're in charge."

He grinned, his large square teeth like piano keys. "I know. That was Yasmin Reece-Lansdale on the blower. Rollo used his one telephone call to bring her in as his solicitor. She's working on getting him out now."

"On instruction to not work too quickly, I bet," said Poppy, winking at Ike.

Ike laughed. "You know Rollo too well, Miss Denby."

Poppy gave a lopsided grin, trying not to engage her cheek muscles on the bruised side of her face. "So what did she say?"

"Rollo's fine. He managed to talk to Oscar in the Black Mariah before they were told to shut up by the old bill. It didn't make sense when I first heard it, but now you've told me about the tunnel it does. Oscar says he heard a commotion in the cellar, looked through his peephole and saw Arthur Watts, the barman, having an argument with someone. He couldn't see who the person was. By the time he got from his office to the cellar, Watts had been attacked and the assailant had disappeared. Oscar had tried to save Watts, but it was too late. He ran out of the cellar to get help, and was seen, covered in blood, by the delivery bloke. Seems like this chappie has it in for Oscar, as he was planning on changing suppliers. Oscar claims he fudged his statement to the police, saying he'd heard Oscar and Watts fighting before Oscar ran out covered in blood. But that couldn't have happened, because Watts was already fatally wounded by the time Oscar got in. Allegedly."

"Allegedly?" asked Poppy, raising her eyebrow over the coffee mug.

"Well, we've only got Oscar's word for it," clarified Ike.

"But Rollo believes him."

Ike nodded thoughtfully. "Yes, he does. But there is no evidence to support it."

"Isn't there?" asked Poppy. "Then where's the weapon? If Oscar stabbed Watts with a... do they know what it was yet?"

Ike nodded. "Probably a rapier again. The medical officer will still need to confirm it."

Poppy nodded in agreement. "Well, if Oscar stabbed Watts with a rapier, where is it? There was no sword when Rollo and I were there. The police could already have taken it, of course..."

"They didn't. Apparently the murder weapon has not yet been found."

"So that backs up Oscar's story of the third man," concluded Poppy. "And of course there was the tunnel."

Ike put down his empty coffee cup and leaned back in his chair, his hands clasped behind his head.

"Well done, Miss Denby. I think we have enough for a story." He chuckled. "The other papers will be going with Rollo Rolandson and Oscar Reynolds being arrested for murder and conspiracy to pervert the course of justice. We'll go with 'Jazz club murderer escapes through secret tunnel'."

Poppy frowned. "I don't know if Oscar will want that to be made public."

Ike pursed his lips. "I'm sorry, Poppy; I can't ignore it. It's too strong a story."

Poppy sighed. She knew he was right. "Fine. But don't reveal the location of the tunnel entrance if you don't have to."

Ike smiled. "We don't have to." He straightened his notebook and put a sheet of paper in his Remington typewriter. "Right, you work through those files, Poppy, and see what you can come up with. I'll get the lead done for the morning's edition."

He didn't wait for her to leave before his fingers started pounding the keyboard.

CHAPTER 25

Back at her own desk, and after unsuccessfully trying to telephone Delilah's flat, Poppy telephoned home and spoke to Miss King – thankfully the bill had now been paid and the phone was reconnected. But Aunt Dot wasn't there. She was at the hospital, visiting Monsieur Stanislavski. Miss Baylis, the theatre manager, had said she would drop Dot home later. Poppy filled Miss King in on the goings on at Oscar's and asked her to pop down the road to see if she could find Delilah. The operator had told her the telephone had been disconnected that morning. Poppy thought this odd, but then reminded herself that Delilah was much like her aunt and probably hadn't gotten around to paying her bill either. After being assured that the sensible and surprisingly daring Miss King would do her best to find Delilah, Poppy put down the telephone and readied herself for work.

As had become her daily habit Poppy first watered her potted begonia and marvelled at its ability to survive in the smoke-filled newsroom. Neither Poppy's parents nor Aunt Dot smoked. Grace had enjoyed an occasional cigarette in the garden. Delilah, of course, loved her "ciggies" and used a foot-long tortoiseshell and onyx cigarette holder. It had probably cost the girl – or whoever had bought it for her – more than Poppy would earn in six months at *The Daily Globe*.

Delilah earned her own income as an actress, but far exceeding that was her stipend from her rich father and what she inherited after her mother's death. However, despite being a very wealthy woman, Delilah rarely spent any of her own cash. She didn't have to, as she was never short of suitors who showered her with gifts. Which was why Poppy and everyone else who knew the young actress were so surprised at how hard she had fallen for Adam Lane. Delilah had been monogamous since she met the handsome young actor in the summer. Poppy had even caught her flicking through the wedding pages in the latest *Vogue*, drooling over the photographs of the hitching of actress Beatrice Lillie and Sir Robert Peel.

Everyone who was anyone, apparently, had been invited to attend, but Delilah had turned it down in favour of a weekend away in Monte Carlo with Adam. That was most unlike Delilah. She would have heart palpitations if she thought she were missing out on the latest gossip and goings-on of high society. Poppy had not been invited, although she had joined the press scrum outside the gates of the churchyard with Daniel. Only the *Vogue* photographers had been allowed access into the church grounds. And a moving picture photographer too.

Poppy had later watched the newsreel with Delilah and Aunt Dot at the Electric Cinema in Chelsea. They all declared that Beatrice had looked "scrumptious" and Sir Robert "very spiffing indeed". Aunt Dot, accompanied by Marjorie Reynolds, had not attended the church service either; there was no wheelchair access and she declared that she would not be carried in front of the *Vogue* photographers; but she had made it to the reception in the evening.

Poppy pulled herself up. This was no time to be thinking about society weddings. She straightened the edges of the five Jazz Files on her desk, then checked her watch and noted that it was half past three. It had been a jam-packed day. First the morning meeting with Marjorie Reynolds at the Empire Tea Rooms, followed by the intriguing discussion in St Bride's Church, where Poppy heard about the murdered Russian family, the missing British spy Ruth Broadwood, and the possibility that Andrei Nogovski had murdered Selena. And then Delilah's sudden visit with the news that Adam had "disappeared" after a sword fight with a mysterious man: all of this before her near arrest at Oscar's Jazz Club! Poppy sighed; it had been an exhausting day and it wasn't nearly over. She would just have to keep going on caffeine and adrenaline.

She shuffled through the five files and extracted Vasili Safin's. Only a single sheet of notes and a photograph – taken on the steps of the Russian embassy when Safin had arrived to assume the post of interim ambassador and trade commissar three weeks earlier. He looked impatient to get inside, his mouth set above his goatee. The notes told her very little. He was a widower, a close associate of the leading Bolshevik Josef Stalin and a card-carrying member of the Russian Communist Party. He had, apparently, spent a number of years in a Siberian work camp due to his involvement as an agitator in the aborted 1905 revolution. His wife had sadly died in his absence. He had no children. As far as his London connections went, none were recorded. *Not much there then, other than a good reason to hate the Russian royals. Let's see if there's anything on his partner in crime,* thought Poppy, and turned to Andrei Nogovski.

She reminded herself that this was a Jazz File containing celebrity gossip and not a Secret Service dossier. She did not expect to find evidence in here linking the Russian to the deaths of the royals, but she did hope to find something linking him – or perhaps Safin – to Selena and the Fabergé eggs.

Inside was a single typed sheet of paper and two photographs. The sheet confirmed what she already knew about Nogovski: he had arrived in London in early September to take up an appointment as a security consultant for the Russian embassy. Poppy noted that the timing was unusual, as the old ambassador – a White Russian – had still been in residence at the time. It was only with recent events in the Crimea, where it seemed near certain that the Whites would lose the civil war, that the ambassador had resigned and been temporarily replaced by Comrade Safin. So why had a Bolshevik been given the appointment of security consultant? Perhaps it was a compromise on behalf of the interim government in Moscow. Or perhaps it was because of the next note – that Nogovski had formerly been a member of the tsar's not-so-secret police – that he had been appointed. He knew the royals and he knew the revolutionaries. He was uniquely placed to deal with both sides. There was nothing to indicate why Nogovski had changed from White to Red; only that he had.

Then there was a paragraph about his personal life. Or lack of it. He was thirty-four years old and single, or at least with no known family. The author of the report – Rollo? Ike? Ah, it was both of them; the initials RR and IG appeared at the bottom of the page – had noted with some disappointment that there were no known "dalliances". He had not been seen at any celebrity parties apart from events hosted by the Russian embassy.

He had, however, been part of the welcoming party to greet the Romanov refugees off the ship from Malta. And there was a photograph to accompany it. Nogovski was standing next to a man Poppy assumed was the former ambassador. They were being introduced to Empress Maria Federovna and her entourage, including Prince Felix Yusopov and Princess Irina. Poppy could tell little from the static image, and wished there was a moving image with subtitles. Was Felix looking directly at Nogovski? Was Nogovski looking back? It appeared that way, but it was hard to know for sure. And what if they were? Were they summing one another up? Did they know each other from back in Russia? They must have if Nogovski formerly worked for the royals. She wondered when Nogovski had "turned" – the file didn't say – and she had no way of knowing which side he was on when Rasputin was murdered. Had he been involved in the cover-up? Had he been part of the police detail that had cleared Yusopov and his fellow assassins of murder and declared there was no charge to answer? She made a note to try to get some more information from Ivan Molanov. The Russian archivist would hopefully be able to fill in some of these gaps – if he was willing to talk about it. It would probably be wise for her to wait for Rollo to get out of the slammer and ask him to talk to his old friend.

Poppy picked up the second photograph and was surprised to see that it was another photograph of Princess Selena in Paris back in 1912, starring in the George Bernard Shaw play. It was the photograph of her standing with a bouquet of flowers next to Vladimir Lenin – it must have been misfiled. It belonged in the Selena file, which Poppy still had in her drawer from yesterday's research. She pulled out the dead woman's file and took a paper clip to attach the photograph to the duplicate.

But then she noticed that the photographs were not exactly the same. The second picture had been taken from a different angle and included some people in the background behind Selena. She turned the photograph over and read the caption: "Princess Selena Romanova Yusopova and her security guards with Vladimir Lenin, Paris, June 1912. *Arms and the Man* run, Paris Opera House." Security guards? She hadn't seen them in the other photograph. There were two of them: one a slim, middle-aged man with a thin face, the other... the other...

Poppy scrabbled around in her drawer to find a magnifying glass. She peered through the glass at the younger, bearded man and tried to look beyond the facial hair. Could that be Andrei Nogovski? She looked intently into his eyes and for a moment it felt as though he were looking back. A shiver ran down her spine. She had looked into those eyes before – and they into hers – at the press conference at the embassy last week. It was indeed a younger Andrei Nogovski in his mid-twenties. Of course it was. This was his file. But why had it been put there? He was not named in the caption. Rollo and Ike were not likely to have picked it up. It must have been Ivan. Again, Poppy made a note to speak to the man.

So, Andrei Nogovski had been Selena's bodyguard back in the day. How interesting. He hadn't mentioned it. But why would he? Their conversation last night had surrounded Delilah and her father, and the possibility that the police would be pursuing that line of enquiry. She wondered for a moment who had set the police looking in that direction. Could it have been Andrei Nogovski himself? She wouldn't put it past the man.

Poppy slipped a page into her Remington typewriter and typed up the new information she had received on Nogovski that morning from Marjorie Reynolds, initialled it PD and added it to the file. Then she closed it.

Her stomach rumbled. It had been a long time since breakfast and she had missed lunch with all of the drama at Oscar's. She didn't really have time to take a break. Then she spotted Vicky walking across the newsroom, carrying a bouquet of flowers.

"Oooh, Vicky, they're lovely. A secret admirer?"

Vicky blushed. "No, Miss Denby. I found them in Mr Molanov's bin and thought I'd rescue them. They've still got life in them."

Poppy frowned. "Why were they in Mr Molanov's bin?"

Vicky shrugged. "I don't know. I couldn't ask him. He's gone out." She paused, then asked: "You don't think he'll mind me taking them, do you?"

Poppy smiled. "Why should he? He'd already thrown them away, hadn't he? I wonder who they were from. Was there any note?"

"Nothing," said Vicky and went into the little kitchenette just off the newsroom, where the journalists made their coffee and tea. When she emerged with the flowers she placed them on top of a filing cabinet. "There. That brightens the place up, doesn't it?"

Poppy agreed that it did, then asked Vicky to pop out and get her a sandwich. Vicky, always eager to please "Miss Denby", said she'd get right to it.

Poppy's stomach grumbled again. She set aside the Nogovski file and then picked up Arthur Watts's. There were only two items in it: a half-page of text with the initials IG, and Daniel's photograph of the exhibition with Watts serving a line of gentlemen, including, Poppy could now see, Adam Lane. The caption on the back confirmed that it was Watts.

Poppy picked up the file and strolled over to Ike's desk. The political editor was still pounding the keys.

"Ike, did you write up this Jazz File on Watts?"

Ike nodded, his mind still on the story he was writing.

"Where did you get the information?"

"My contact in the police. All they told me was that he'd been a person of interest for a while and that they suspected him of being a fence. But they had no hard evidence. Sorry there isn't more."

"No, that's fine. There's enough for me to follow up. Very interesting about his uncle being the props manager at the Old Vic, isn't it?"

Ike stopped typing. He reached out his hand and took the file from Poppy. "You know, I hadn't noticed that before. I typed this up a couple of days ago, obviously before he died. I was just trying to get some profiles on those present at the exhibition. Didn't really take much notice. But now that he's dead, this fence thing sounds very interesting. That may be why he was killed."

Poppy nodded in agreement. "I think I'll have a wander over to the Old Vic and see if I can speak to his uncle."

Ike frowned. "Don't go on your own, Poppy. There's still a killer on the loose. Why don't you take Daniel with you?"

Poppy pursed her lips and fought the urge to tell Ike that she didn't need Daniel or anyone else's protection. She took a calming breath, telling herself that Ike meant well.

"I'll tell you what: I need to drop by the hospital shortly anyway. If Lilian Baylis is there, I'll go back to the theatre with her. If not, I'll wait until tomorrow."

Appeased, Ike nodded. "I think that's wise." He turned back to his typewriter, his mind already moving on.

Poppy thanked him and went back to her desk. A fence, eh? That would explain a lot. That and the fact that she remembered Andrei Nogovski talking to Watts the previous week at Oscar's, the night he had barged in, flashing his credentials. She'd thought then he had had a very interrogative air about him. No wonder Oscar had been so nervous. Had he known about Watts? Had he turned a blind eye to what was going on at the club? Or was he more involved than that? She struggled to reconcile the image she had of the urbane club owner with his gold-rimmed monocle and some kind of criminal mastermind.

She pulled Oscar's file towards her. It was as fat as Watts's was thin. Oscar knew everybody and there were photographs of him with royalty, show business celebrities and politicians. There was so much to wade through, Poppy didn't know where to begin. Fortunately, Vicky and the sandwich arrived at that moment and Poppy took her time mulling it all over as she munched her cheese and tomato roll.

Five minutes later, Poppy had decided that trying to find evidence in Oscar's file would be like looking for a needle in a haystack. She already had enough to go on with: Watts and his uncle at the theatre, as well as interesting avenues of enquiry with Nogovski. She needed to speak to Yasmin Reece-Lansdale in that regard, to see if she could get an interview with Prince Felix. Poppy wondered how Yasmin was doing getting her other client – Rollo Rolandson – out of the slammer. Poppy chuckled, remembering Rollo's cheeky face as he was manhandled into the Black Mariah.

The final file she turned to was Adam Lane's. It consisted of a few pages of text, mainly dealing with his theatre career and the various famous women he had stepped out with, including Delilah. Poppy learned that he was the son of Sir Walter Lane of Guisborough. She had never heard of him and made a note to look him up in Burke's Peerage. She also read that Sir Walter and his wife Ethel had been killed on the *Titanic*. Poor Adam. What a terrible way to lose both parents. In Poppy's previous big story – the Dorchester case – one of the main players there had also lost a parent in the shipping tragedy. In fact, if she wasn't mistaken, she had seen a list of the deceased at the time... she made another note to check the Elizabeth Dorchester file for the list. It wasn't urgent, she had plenty to do, but it might give her a nice little filler. She hoped for Delilah's sake that was all Adam's involvement in this was: just a little filler.

She continued paging through his file. Adam, as she already knew, was a travelling actor. In the last three years he had been in plays in London, New York, Venice and... hello, hello, Moscow. It seemed Adam had been in a show that had to close because of the October Revolution. Hmmm, there was the Russian connection again. She really needed to speak to Monsieur Stanislavski. She checked her watch; it was half past four. She'd just finish reviewing Adam's file and then she'd head over to the hospital. Right, where was she? Ah yes, Adam had been in London, New York, Venice and… hang on… New York, Venice… Where had she heard that before? Aha! Marjorie Reynolds this morning. Marjorie had said Fabergé eggs had been stolen in New York and Venice, as well as London and Moscow. Someone was trying to find the egg with the key and match it with the egg with the information that could damage the royal family. Could that someone be Adam?

Poppy sat back and touched her cheek. Oh, it was too horrible to contemplate. If Adam was the thief, could he also be the murderer? Of that family in Moscow? Of Selena? Of Arthur Watts? He did have a rapier. And he was in the theatre when Selena was killed. He had been talking to the props manager when Poppy saw him. The props manager! The uncle of Arthur Watts. Yes, it was all beginning to fit together into some grotesque puzzle. And he had been in Moscow when the family were killed…

Oh dear God! Delilah! She needed to find her friend soon. Should she go to the police and tell them what she knew? She looked across at Ike's desk, wondering if she should pass it with him first, but he wasn't there. He was probably down in the typesetting hall getting his lead story mocked up. She didn't have time to look for him. If Delilah's life was in danger she needed to get help now. She shoved four of the Jazz Files into her drawer, and put the fifth – Adam's – into her satchel. As an afterthought, she retrieved Nogovski's file from the drawer and slipped that into her bag too. She was not ready to let Comrade Nogovksi off the hook just yet.

CHAPTER 26

It was nearly half past five when Poppy reached New Scotland Yard. She walked up the steps, into the charge office and approached the front desk. To her dismay it was manned by the handlebar moustachioed sergeant from the previous night. Oh dear. She took a deep breath, pulled back her shoulders and approached.

"May I speak to Detective Chief Inspector Martin, please?"

The sergeant peered at her from under his bushy brows, then pulled his upper lip to meet his nose as if she were a smudge of dog poo on his shoe.

"No press allowed."

"I'm not here as the press; I'm here as a private citizen and I –"

"No press allowed," he said again.

Poppy sucked in her breath and released it slowly. "I'm sorry, sergeant, but I must speak to DCI Martin."

The sergeant said nothing, but pushed a sheet of paper across the desk.

Poppy looked at him, waiting for further instructions. He then pushed an inkwell and pen towards her.

"You want me to write it down?" she asked.

He grunted.

"And then what?"

"I'll pass it on to DCI Martin." The sergeant folded his arms over his barrel chest.

Will he indeed? Poppy wondered. *And if he does, will it be too late for Delilah?*

Just then, the door behind the desk opened and a constable stepped aside to allow the tall, elegant figure of Yasmin Reece-Lansdale and the squat figure of her client, Rollo Rolandson, to pass through.

"You'll just need to sign this," said the constable to Rollo.

Rollo took the form, signed it with a flourish, then looked up with a huge grin. "Miz Denby! How kind of you to visit! Too late though; they're letting me go."

The constable and sergeant looked at each other with expressions that suggested that if it had been up to them they would have tossed the diminutive editor in the deepest holding cell and thrown away the key.

"Well, gentlemen," said Rollo with a grin, "it's been a pleasure."

The sergeant grunted and lifted the flap over the desk to let Yasmin and Rollo through. Then he turned back to Poppy. "Well, have you written it yet?"

"Written what?" asked Rollo, standing on tiptoes to get a better view of what was on the desk.

Poppy wasn't sure what to do. She really needed to speak to DCI Martin to tell him of her suspicions about Adam and her fears for Delilah, but she didn't want it to slip into file thirteen. She looked at the high-powered pair of lawyer and editor and decided she had a better chance of getting the police to listen to her if she had them on her side. And there was Marjorie Reynolds too. Yes, that's what she'd do. She needed to beef up her arsenal. She put the pen down and pushed it and the sheet of paper back across the desk to the sergeant.

She smiled tightly. "Don't worry. I'll arrange to speak to him personally later."

The sergeant shrugged, sat down and crossed his ankles, his hobnails pointing the way to the door.

Poppy turned on her heel and walked out, followed by a curious Yasmin and Rollo.

Outside the station Rollo took Poppy's elbow and pulled her aside.

"What was that about?" he whispered, keeping an eye out for potential eavesdroppers going in or out of the station.

"Is there somewhere we can talk privately nearby?" Poppy whispered. "I need to speak to you and Miss Reece-Lansdale urgently."

Yasmin leaned in. "Yes, my chambers are just down the road in Whitehall. Let's go."

12 NOON, TUESDAY 23 OCTOBER 1920, LONDON

Adam Lane left the hospital, and after making sure Delilah got the cab to Waterloo, he drove to Oscar's Jazz Club. He needed to get rid of the merchandise once and for all. This whole affair was becoming far too dangerous. Time to ditch the egg and run. It would be sad to leave Delilah, but after the attack earlier, it would probably be safest for her anyway. The last thing he wanted was for her to be hurt in this madness.

Adam had clarified Arthur Watts's shifts with Arthur's uncle at the Old Vic. In fact, it was through Uncle Jimmy – a friend of Adam's own surrogate father – that Adam had heard Arthur was the best contact for moving stolen merchandise in London. He had passed this information on to his employer – the person who had hired him to steal the eggs in Moscow, Venice and New York – when he arrived in London.

Adam had never spoken to his employer in person. He was first approached at the Bolshoi Theatre in Moscow in 1917 by a man who told him his employer had been impressed by his work in Paris in 1912 – his first commissioned theft on mainland Europe, on his very first foreign theatre tour. The man briefed him about the Andreiovich egg and arranged for the handover before Adam left Russia, just as the nation exploded into revolution. Adam thought he would never hear from the man or his employer again. But he was wrong.

He was approached again in Venice in the spring of 1919. Not in person, but by telegram. The employer, apparently, knew his touring schedule and wanted him to do some work for him while he was there. It was another Fabergé egg – held in the collection of a Prussian prince; a distant relative of the Romanovs. He was told to telegraph when the job was done and money would be wired to him. The same thing happened in the autumn of the same year when he was doing a short run on Broadway, New York. Again, another egg, from the home of a White Russian émigré in downtown Manhattan. Like in Moscow and Venice, Adam decided to take other jewels too – first to hide the fact that it was a targeted hit and secondly to make sure he got a bit extra out of the job. He couldn't rely on the patronage of this mysterious man forever.

The employer now appeared to be in Malta. Whether permanently or temporarily he had no idea. It was pure coincidence, Adam thought, that Delilah was also Maltese by birth. At least he hoped it was a coincidence... Wasn't her father on the police radar? Wasn't he a suspect in the exhibition robbery? Hadn't he hightailed it back to Malta the very day after the heist? Hadn't he been ogling the egg ever since he met Princess Selena back in his hotel in Valetta? No, he was just being paranoid. Delilah was not a plant. They just happened to fall for each other. Call it fate, if you must.

The man – if in fact it was a man – went by the nom de plume of Senor Swart, a strange mix of Spanish and German.

Adam never thought for a moment it was his real name. He just sent the telegrams to the Valetta post office and waited for the reply. When he had telegraphed that he would be in London for the summer and autumn of 1920 and would be available for jobs, he was told to wait for instructions of how to continue. He waited four months before he was told – in code – that the White Russian Art Exhibition at the Crystal Palace was to be his next target. He had also been instructed to use the time to find a suitable fence. Hence his trip to see Arthur Watts.

Adam parked about a block away from the club, not wanting to draw attention to the fact that he was there in case the man he had met in the alley earlier was watching. Hadn't he said he knew Adam's fence? Of course he did. Adam had seen him talking to Watts at the exhibition on Saturday night. Was Watts double-dealing? Was that why he had been so elusive?

How many times had it been now that he had tried to get to Watts? He tapped his gloved fingers on the steering wheel… was this the third? It shouldn't be this hard. Not with a professional like Watts. But perhaps Watts had been turned. Was he working for the man in the alley as well as his and Adam's mutual employer? Adam wondered for a moment whether he should try to track down Mr Green, his assistant for the robbery who had taken the egg out and given it back to him on Sunday at their meeting on the Chelsea Embankment. What Green didn't know about the London underworld was not worth knowing. Green had been another old contact of his surrogate father.

Adam considered his options for a minute. In the time it would take for him to send word to Green and set up a meeting, this whole thing could have spiralled out of control. It was only a matter of time before the Bobby who had stumbled to his aid earlier went back to the station and discovered that the young man from the alleged sword fight had not come in to report it.

And just a matter of time before Delilah realized he wasn't going to meet her at the theatre. And just a matter of time before the man in the alley tracked him – or her – down. Adam had no doubt the man would follow up on his threat to "finish this later". Adam swallowed, his throat tense. He would have to do a long warm-up before he was able to go on stage for rehearsal later...

What was he thinking? There would be no rehearsal later. This was the end of the road for him and his acting career. He had come so close. He had been chosen by Stanislavski himself. Adam felt tears well in his eyes.

But he couldn't allow himself to be overcome. He shook himself, patted the parcel in his inside pocket and got out of the motor. He turned towards Oscar's.

The club normally opened at 1 p.m. for lunch and then stayed open until the wee small hours of the morning. It was too early for the front door to be unlocked, but Adam knew there would be people inside getting the place ready. Arthur had told him he could always get in through the service entrance. As Adam rounded the back of the club he had to step back for a man heaving a barrel on his shoulder and carrying it inside. Adam held the swinging door open for him. The man grunted his thanks. Adam expected to be challenged by a member of staff – and had an excuse ready about telling Arthur Watts his uncle at the theatre had taken ill – but he didn't need it.

He followed the barrel man down a corridor, past the kitchen, and towards what Adam assumed was the cellar. The man put down the barrel outside the door and turned around to go and get the next one. "Scuse me, mate."

Adam stepped aside to let him pass. He heard voices coming from the cellar. One of them sounded like Arthur's. He carefully pushed the door open a crack and saw Arthur talking to a man in a black coat and homburg. Wasn't that the man he'd sparred with in the alley? He felt his hands go clammy at the thought and leaned against the wall, out of sight. What the hell was he going to do? Was Arthur in cahoots with the Russian? Would it be safe to pass on the merchandise? If he did, would Arthur give it to the Russian, or would he forward it to his employer as arranged? Needless to say, he wouldn't get paid if the egg didn't make it to his employer. But Adam was beginning not to care. He just wanted rid of it. As the barrel man was coming down the corridor with his second load, Adam went up the stairs to wait for Arthur in the bar. He greeted a cleaner running a mop over the dance floor, and muttered something about waiting for the barman. The cleaner didn't seem to care. Adam took a seat on a stool.

Ten minutes passed and still no Arthur. Adam was contemplating going back downstairs when he heard a commotion: a clatter of barrels, shouting and then stomping up the stairs. A breathless barrel man ran into the bar pointing back down to the cellar. "He's killed him! Call the police! Oscar's killed Arthur!" The cleaner just stood there, mop in hand, with apparently no intention of calling anyone. The barrel man ran up to Adam. "He's killed him I tell ya! Look for yourself." Then he ran out of the bar towards the foyer and the rest rooms calling out his terrible news to whomever would listen.

Unable to resist seeing if it was true, Adam picked his way down the stairs, his heart in his mouth and his thumb on the secret catch on his cane. He walked straight into a hysterical Oscar, his white shirt front drenched with blood, his monocle hanging limply from his pocket. Oscar grabbed Adam by the lapels and looked wildly into his eyes. "Arthur's dead. I couldn't save him. I tried. I swear I tried. There was too much blood."

Adam looked over Oscar's shoulder and into the cellar. And there, splayed on the floor, was Arthur, with a wound to his chest that was still seeping blood. Adam took Oscar's hands firmly in his and tried to still the shaking. "Who did it, Oscar? The barrel man said it was you. Was it?"

Oscar tried to pull away from him, but Adam held him firm. "No! I tried to save him. I swear. It was someone else. I heard voices. I came to see what was going on."

"Did you see who it was? Was it a man in a homburg hat?"

"I didn't see. I didn't see," repeated Oscar.

"Where did he go?"

"I – I –" Oscar faltered, his eyes flicking from right to left. "I –"

"For heaven's sake, man! I'm trying to help you."

Oscar's eyes came into focus and he looked at Adam. "You're Delilah's friend, aren't you? Mr Lane."

"I am," said Adam.

"And Poppy's. You know Poppy Denby, don't you?"

Adam nodded, wondering where this was going.

"Then can I trust you not to tell the police what I'm going to tell you now?"

Adam wondered if Oscar was about to confess to him that his club was used to fence stolen goods. Did Oscar know all along? Arthur had always thought the dandified owner didn't have a clue. But to Adam's surprise, Oscar showed him a tunnel, dug in case of Prohibition.

As the secret door swung open, Adam heard the barrel man come back down the stairs with someone in tow. "He's in there. That's where it happened."

Adam was just about to pull Oscar into the tunnel with him, when the club owner whispered: "Find the man in the homburg. He's my only alibi," and then shut the secret door and turned to face his accusers.

CHAPTER 27

Adam made sure he was out of earshot of the cellar before he struck a match. Yes, it was indeed a tunnel. He had been in New York when Prohibition came in there and had no doubt that half the establishments in the city wished they had made similar contingency plans. He applauded Oscar on his forward thinking. However, it seemed as if the tunnel had recently been used for more nefarious purposes than slipping in a bit of illicit booze. How had the man in the homburg known about it? Had he come in that way and met with Arthur? Had Arthur known about it and used it for his fencing activities? Had he arranged to meet the Russian in the cellar? Adam had no way of knowing. Nor did he know what he would do if he came face to face with the Russian in the tunnel.

There had been no light before he struck his match. Or had there? He allowed his match to go out, then waited. Listened. Just the scuttling of rats. Adam calculated that by the time it took the barrel man to go upstairs and for him to go down and hear Oscar's explanation, it must have been about five minutes. Before that, according to Oscar, he had been trying to revive Arthur. Another five minutes perhaps? That would have given the Russian at least ten minutes, possibly more, to make his escape. And unless he intended to come back into the club in the immediate aftermath of Arthur's murder, there would be no reason for him to stick around.

Adam lit another match and continued along the tunnel, trying to figure out what was going on as he went. Why had he killed the fence? Why had he killed Selena? Was it because they didn't have the egg? That clearly wasn't the reason he'd killed – or orchestrated the killing – of the family in Moscow. The egg had still been in the safe when Adam arrived at the residence, and the family were already dead. If all the man had wanted was the egg surely the lady of the house would have given it to him. Or perhaps she had and he had found what Adam's employer had found: that there was something missing. And then had he put the egg back into the safe? It didn't make sense. Unless he was trying to cover his tracks. No, the Russian did not want the eggs – he wanted what was inside them. And for that he was prepared to kill.

This man was not going to stop until he had found whatever he was looking for. With a shudder, Adam thought about all the people in London close to him – Stanislavski and Delilah chief among them – and one of them had already had an attempt on his life, however inadvertent. Adam still could not figure out why the chocolates in Selena's dressing room had been poisoned, but they had been, and the man he admired most in the world had nearly died. Intentionally or not, people close to him were being picked off by this mad Russian and it was time to stop him. But first he needed to check that Delilah was safe.

The tunnel began to slope upwards and Adam sensed it was coming to an end. The match went out just as he reached a metal ladder. He stopped to listen again. Was that the sound of sirens? Adam felt his way up the ladder and pushed on the hatch above. As light flooded into the tunnel, Adam unsheathed his rapier and climbed out, fully alert and ready for any possible attack. But none came. He found himself behind a line of skips and bins near the back entrance of a paper shop, the hatch cleverly disguised as a manhole cover. Did the proprietor of the paper shop know about the secret tunnel? He must. And he must have been paid to turn a blind eye. Good. That's just what Adam needed.

Checking again to make sure the coast was clear, his ears ringing with the wail of sirens from police vehicles pulling up at the jazz club, he slipped down the alley and followed the back streets to Delilah's apartment building. She lived on the second floor. He didn't risk going around the front in case the police or any nosy neighbours spotted him. Instead, he climbed the fire escape and used the key she had given him to slip in through the back door.

He didn't expect her to be there; he just needed to use her telephone to call the theatre to check that she was all right. But as he stepped into her kitchen he knew something was wrong. Delilah's flat was usually immaculate. Mrs Jones the cleaning lady kept the place spotless, and Delilah, despite her laissez faire attitude to the rest of her life, was exceptionally organized in her domestic sphere; so open kitchen cupboards were not to be expected. Adam unsheathed his rapier as he pushed the door open to the rest of the flat. It was chaos.

Bookshelves and stacks of gramophone records had been overturned, cushions and sofas sliced open and their guts spilled. Adam searched frantically through the carnage, but to his relief Delilah was nowhere to be found. His breathing slowed… a little.

The telephone lay under a scattering of *Vogue* magazines, its cord cut. Why? Had the Russian – and Adam had no doubt that it was the Russian in the homburg who was responsible – been hoping that Delilah was home and had cut off all chance of her calling for help? His stomach tightened. Had she been home? No, it was impossible. He had seen her get into the cab to Waterloo and there wouldn't have been time for her to go there and get back, surely. Or had there? He checked his watch.

Quarter past one. Yes, it was possible. His stomach clenched even further. He needed to get to the Old Vic to find out. He checked the bedroom and bathroom one more time – just in case he had missed something – and then headed back down the fire escape and towards his motor car.

He thanked God for his foresight in parking away from Oscar's. A glance down King's Road told him the police had moved into the jazz club with force. Poor Oscar. His only hope was to prove there was another man in the cellar. And Adam would help him do that, if he could, but first he needed to find Delilah. His arm, slashed by the Russian's rapier, ached, and the Fabergé egg in his inside pocket burned. The thing was a curse, he was sure of it. And as soon as he found Delilah he was going to get rid of it – even if it meant tossing it in the Thames.

He cranked the motor of his Model T Ford and jumped in as the engine burst into life, then headed in the direction of Chelsea Bridge.

It was nearly two o'clock by the time he had negotiated the London lunchtime traffic and pulled up outside the Old Vic. As he passed the Waterloo railway station he realized it would have been quicker to catch the train or a bus. Too late now.

He parked the car outside the stage door on Webster Street, and slipped into the theatre. It was quiet backstage, far quieter than it usually was in the middle of rehearsals. The rehearsal room itself was empty, as were the dressing rooms, including Delilah's. A handwritten notice had been posted on Selena's door – "Stay out. Crime scene. Entry only with permission from DCI Martin, Metropolitan Police" – signed by the theatre manager, Lilian Baylis. Adam tried the handle. It was locked.

Then Adam heard voices coming from the Green Room. Of course. That's where they'd all be, having a late lunch. Adam pushed open the door to find half a dozen or so crew and cast members lounging around. A couple were playing cards, another was going over his lines between bites of a sandwich. But no Delilah. There was, however, the props manager, Jimmy Watts, reading a copy of *The Daily Globe*. *Oh dear*, thought Adam, *no one has told him yet*. He would have to be the man to do it, but first he enquired whether or not anyone had seen Delilah. The consensus was that she had been there earlier but was very "out of sorts". She had paced around for a good hour then left.

"She was waiting for you, Lane," said the man with the sandwich, running his tongue along his lip to mop up any stray crumbs. "Where the deuce have you been?"

"Who was running rehearsal?" asked Adam.

The card players chuckled. Then one of them said: "Miss Baylis asked Roy to do it, but he refused, saying as assistant director he might be next on the killer's list. We told him Selena was a one-off. It was probably a crime of passion and the chocolates had been meant for her too."

The card players didn't seem too worried about a homicidal maniac on the loose and turned from their amateur sleuthing back to their game of pontoon.

Ah, but they don't know about Arthur Watts yet. It's not a one-off. But neither are they likely to be the next targets. They know nothing about the egg. But Uncle Jimmy might... and the killer might have come to the same conclusion...

"So," he continued, "any idea where Delilah might be?"

The occupants of the Green Room shrugged and grunted. No one knew where the girl had gone. The knot in Adam's stomach tightened even further as his mind flicked through various scenarios. But the thought that was still uppermost in his mind was Arthur Watts lying dead on the cellar floor.

"Er, Jimmy, might I have a word with you please? In private?"

Jimmy lowered his newspaper, the front page ablaze with the news of Princess Selena's death under Poppy Denby's byline. "What's afoot?" he asked.

Adam left the theatre at the same time as Jimmy Watts. He had offered the props manager a lift to Chelsea, but the man had declined, saying it would be quicker to catch the train. After first absorbing the shock of the news of his nephew's death, Jimmy had asked why Adam had been allowed to leave the scene of the crime so quickly. Surely he would have been held there with everyone else to be questioned by the police?

I never thought of that. I'll have gone and made myself a suspect now. He tried to recall the people, apart from Oscar, who had seen him there: the barrel man, the cleaner and possibly some of the kitchen staff. *Great Scott! The police will be after me in no time.*

He had to get out of London – and soon. But he couldn't go without first finding Delilah and ensuring she was safe. He gave a wishy-washy explanation to Jimmy – that the props man seemed to take at face value – then parted ways with the grieving uncle.

As Adam cranked the motor, he swore with every turn. "Where the hell is Delilah?" Then Jimmy Watts's newspaper came to mind. *Poppy Denby!* he thought, and plotted his route to Fleet Street.

CHAPTER 28

Yasmin Reece-Lansdale's chambers were as swish and exotic as Poppy had expected. They were greeted by a doorman wearing top hat and tails, who welcomed them into the foyer of one of the best addresses in Whitehall. The polished white marble floor and walls acted like a prism, bouncing the reflected light emanating from recessed alcoves. Poppy felt as if she were in an ice palace. But as they exited the lift into the suite of offices occupied by Yasmin and her legal partners, the globe spun from the arctic north to the sultry Middle East. The walls were hung with silk tapestries made – Yasmin told her – during the classical period of the Ottoman Empire, and Poppy's scuffed shoes sank into the plush pile of a Turkish carpet. Poppy thought she should be walking in stockinged feet, but as Yasmin didn't, neither did she. Inside Yasmin's chambers, the globe shifted ever so slightly again, to Egypt. Poppy knew that the renewed interest in the archaeological excavation of the pyramids was causing a fashion flurry in London – exemplified by Delilah's apartment and wardrobe – but this was the real thing. Yasmin was half-Egyptian and the décor and objets d'art were all original, not a reimagining of an art deco designer.

Rollo flopped onto a divan uninvited, kicking off his shoes and tucking his short legs under him, but Poppy waited. Yasmin smiled at the younger woman, acknowledging the courtesy. She indicated a suitable seat and Poppy took it. Then she picked up her thoroughly British telephone and requested tea and sandwiches be sent in. It was nearly six o'clock, but clearly Yasmin's assistants worked as late as she did.

While they were waiting for the tea to arrive Yasmin opened a cocktail cabinet – greeted by grunts of approval from Rollo – but shut it firmly after removing an ice bucket and a linen napkin. "Put that on your cheek, Poppy. You won't be able to see out of that eye soon unless you get the swelling down."

Poppy took it gratefully. She filled Rollo and Yasmin in on what had happened in the tunnel and outside the club as she pressed the cool, damp cloth to her face, then, as the tea arrived and was poured, listened to Rollo's retelling of his stint in the slammer. As she had already gathered from Ike Garfield, Rollo had heard Oscar's version of events that there was a third man in the cellar, but that he hadn't seen who it was.

"If Oscar is to be let off, we need to find that man," said Yasmin, adding a slice of lemon to her tea. Poppy, like a good northern lass, reached for the milk jug. "As he is now my client," Yasmin added.

"Hold your horses," Rollo interjected. "Oscar's your client as well? Is there anyone in London who isn't your client, Yazzie?"

Yasmin smiled at him indulgently. "No one who matters, sweetie, no."

Behind her napkin, Poppy smiled at the repartee between the couple. They really were a good match for each other.

She put down the ice pack, her cheek sufficiently numbed, and sipped her tea. The cups were rimmed with gold leaf. She had no doubt that it was genuine.

"So," continued Yasmin, "what were you trying to tell the police?"

Poppy put down her cup and reached for her satchel. She took out Adam Lane's Jazz File and outlined her suspicions about the young actor – highlighting the fact that he had been in the same cities at the same time as the Fabergé eggs had been stolen.

She then went on to discuss Arthur Watts and the possibility that he was a fence. Rollo grunted at this, saying his sources had told him much the same thing. They all agreed that it was highly probable that Watts had been killed by someone hoping to get his – or her – hands on the stolen Fabergé egg.

Then she told Rollo and Yasmin the highlights of her conversation with Marjorie Reynolds that morning and the hypothesis that one of the eggs contained sensitive information that could negatively expose the royal family, and another egg, the key to open the first. Rollo's ears pricked at "sensitive information" and Poppy could see him ruminating over the juicy gossip that it might contain.

Could Rollo be trusted not to splash the information all over the morning newspaper if it came into his hands? Probably not. And why should he not? She knew that his view – which she partially shared – was that the royals should not have any kind of special privilege when it came to reporting the truth. If they'd got something to hide, and *The Daily Globe* found it, why shouldn't they expose it? But what if that information was as sensitive as Marjorie Reynolds had suggested and royal families could actually fall? The ripple effect might cause such social and political unrest that Europe could be thrust back into war. Poppy shuddered at the thought.

"Well, go on," said Rollo, sitting up on his divan and leaning forward, eager to hear what else Poppy had discovered.

"How certain is Marjorie that that's what's in the eggs?" asked Yasmin.

Poppy shrugged. "I'm not sure. I doubt she shared with me everything the Home Office has on this, but I think her words were "we believe they contain". So I think the probability is high that that's what's in them."

"Or that's what people think is in them and they are prepared to kill because of it," offered Rollo. "In the end it doesn't really matter. Wars have been started on less."

Yasmin and Poppy nodded in agreement. Rollo's ominous words echoed Poppy's own thoughts on the matter. The eggs were dynamite.

"You're representing the Russian royals on this, aren't you?" asked Poppy.

Yasmin pursed her lips. "I'm giving them legal advice during the investigation into the exhibition theft, yes. But I'm afraid, Miss Denby, that I can't divulge any information about what they've told me regarding the eggs, if that's what you're after."

"Of course that's what she's after. That's what we're all after, Yazzie. Come on, toss us a bone. Do the Romanovs and the Yusopovs know what was in the eggs? Do they suspect that was the reason they were stolen? What do their spies say?"

"Mr Rolandson," said Yasmin with mock chastisement. "This is a refugee family who fled a war zone with only the clothes on their backs!"

"Oh really?" said Rollo, turning to face his girlfriend. "So the rumours about rolled-up Rembrandts and jewels sewn into bodices are all false?"

"Scurrilous lies!"

"So you'll be doing all this pro bono then?"

Yasmin scowled at him.

"Just as well Oscar and Marjorie Reynolds can afford a few bob. Your fee for keeping Oscar from the gallows might just keep you from the poor house too."

Poppy chuckled, imagining the elegant solicitor in one of the city's poor houses.

"Oh, that reminds me," said Yasmin, opening her briefcase and taking out a sealed envelope. She passed it over the table to

Poppy. "Marjorie asked me to give this to you earlier. She said it was the thing you'd asked her to do."

Rollo craned his neck to have a look. "What's that then, Miz Denby? Top secret files from the Secret Service?"

Poppy laughed. Her cheek didn't hurt quite as much as it had earlier. "No. Just something I asked Marjorie to look into. It's –" Poppy paused, stopping herself from blurting out exactly what it was. Perhaps it was best that she look at it privately first, before Rollo and Yasmin got the wrong end of the stick. Or the right one... and that was more worrying. "I asked her to look into something on my aunt's behalf," she lied lightly, hoping her bruised face would mask her deception. She slipped the envelope, unopened, into her satchel. Yasmin and Rollo didn't look worried. Poppy breathed a sigh of relief. "So, how is Marjorie?" she asked, trying to steer the conversation away from the contents of the envelope once and for all.

Rollo grinned. "Spitting nails. She read the riot act to Martin about arresting Oscar."

"Yes, she did," agreed Yasmin, then frowned, her beautifully shaped eyebrows touching over the bridge of her Egyptian nose. "But she admitted to me that she realized Martin didn't have a choice. Oscar was in the wrong place at the wrong time. And seeing that it's his place, well..." she motioned with her manicured hands.

Poppy tucked her own short-nailed fingers, cracked and split due to hours of pounding her typewriter, into the palms of her hands. "Have they found the murder weapon yet?" she asked.

"No," answered the solicitor.

"Then surely that's the hole in their case."

Yasmin smiled at the young reporter. "Have you ever thought of going into law, Miss Denby? Your mind works in very clever ways."

"Back off, Yazzie; she's mine," growled Rollo. And they all laughed.

"Poppy's right though. That's exactly what I'm going to be using to get Oscar out. And as soon as we're finished here I'll be drawing up my deposition to a judge to accelerate Oscar's bail hearing." She sat up straight in her chair. "So, if you'll forgive my directness, Poppy, can we hurry this up please? What else have you got for us?"

Poppy took out Nogovski's file and opened it on the desk, the picture of him in Paris with Selena uppermost. "Comrade Andrei Nogovski. Seems like he used to be Selena's bodyguard. She pointed to the younger bearded man behind the princess."

"By Jove it is!" declared Rollo, picking up the photograph and examining it closely. "Amazing how a beard can change the look of a man."

"And the feel," purred Yasmin. Rollo chuckled. Poppy blushed.

"So you didn't put this picture in the file?" observed Poppy. "It must have been Ike… or Ivan." Poppy chewed her lip, sorting through the problem. "But why would he have…"

"Hello, Miz Denby!"

"Sorry. There's something I've been meaning to ask you but haven't had a chance with all the recent drama. Ivan warned me to stay away from Nogovski. He told me he was a very dangerous man and that he'd known him back in Russia when he was a member of the tsar's secret police. Ivan was a reformer," she added for Yasmin's benefit. "But Ivan being Ivan is not too forthcoming with information. I was wondering if you could have a chat with him, Rollo, to see what he knows. It might not be any more than is already in here, but there's a chance…"

Rollo nodded. "Will do. He's been more glum than usual – because of what he's heard about his family – but I'll take him out for a drink and see what I can get out of him. Do you mind if I give him a ring, Yazzie?"

Yasmin passed him the phone. He picked up the earpiece and spoke to the operator, asking for a number. The Russian answered. Poppy could hear his gruff voice across the room as he grumbled and groaned that he was too tired to go out. Rollo quipped that this was the first time he'd ever known a Russian to turn down a free drink. Ivan's tone lightened as he asked whether Rollo was offering to buy them. Rollo said he was, but only if Ivan was man enough to take off his slippers and meet him at the Cock. This seemed to do the trick and they agreed to meet at Ye Olde Cock Tavern in an hour. Rollo put the phone back in its cradle and meshed his fingers behind his head. "Spiffing. Righto. Let's wrap up here and I'll give you a lift back to the office, Miz Denby."

"Well, yes, I suppose I can tell you the rest in the motor…"

"Splendid!" said Rollo and slapped his thighs. He got up, went around the desk and kissed Yasmin on the cheek. "Later, toots!"

Yasmin gave a mocking scowl at the provocative, sexist slur and raised her eyebrows towards the door. Then she pulled out a legal pad and started making notes.

"Sorry, Miss Denby; time is of the essence if I'm going to get a hearing for Oscar tomorrow morning."

"Of course," said Poppy congenially, and started to gather her things. However, she hadn't had a chance to discuss her suspicions about the connection between Andrei Nogovski and Adam Lane, and which of them might be the killer. Nor why she was trying to give this information to the police. Delilah! She needed to telephone Miss King to find out if she'd located the young actress, but Yasmin had already picked up the receiver and was asking for a number at the Old Bailey. Poppy closed her files and put them in her satchel. As she did, a sheet of paper slipped out and fluttered onto Yasmin's desk. The solicitor's eyes widened when she saw what was on it – the sketch of the sapphire and ruby necklace stolen from Selena in Paris in 1912.

Yasmin asked the operator to wait a moment and turned to Poppy: "Where did you get this?"

"It was in the Jazz Files," said Poppy.

Yasmin took the paper. "Do you mind if I hang on to this?"

Rollo snatched it from her hand, folded it up and put it in his breast pocket. "I'm sure you've got enough to deal with this evening, toots."

She glared at him, but then was distracted by a voice from the telephone. "Ah, yes, good evening. May I speak to Judge Denvers please... Yes, yes, I know it's gone six o'clock, but..."

Rollo took Poppy's elbow and steered her towards the door as Yasmin continued her conversation.

"What was all that about?" asked Poppy in the black cab on the way back to Fleet Street. Rollo checked to see that the glass division between the driver and the passenger compartment was firmly shut.

"Yazzie was very interested in that necklace. She's obviously seen it before."

"But how could she? It was stolen eight years ago."

"Exactly, Miz Denby, exactly. But I've known Yasmin Reece-Lansdale long enough to read her expression."

"Why didn't you just ask her about it?"

"She was on the telephone. And besides, even if she wasn't, she wouldn't have told me. Not if it had something to do with one of her clients. Which I suspect it has."

"With Oscar? Oh, you don't think he is involved with this after all?"

"No, I don't. I feel it in my water, Miz Denby. Call it a newspaperman's sixth sense."

"Then who? The Yusopovs?"

Rollo nodded. "Very possibly. I need to do some more digging. I'll start with Ivan and see if he can suggest someone else to speak to."

"You don't think that Felix Yusopov could be the killer after all, do you? Have you changed your mind on that?"

Rollo shrugged. "I'm keeping my options open. What do you think?"

Poppy touched her cheek. "Well, I'm not sure now. The Felix Yusopov connection has put a spoke in the wheel…"

"It has. But before you heard his name, who else did you think was involved in this?"

Poppy leaned back in the cab and pressed her head into the leather upholstery, stretching her neck. "Well, that's why I was at the police station, you see. It's possible that Adam could be the killer, and that puts Delilah in danger."

Rollo snorted. "Adam Lane? A killer? Come on, Poppy. Do you really think that? What's in your water? What do you really feel?"

Speaking of water, Poppy had not had a chance to visit the restroom at Yasmin's chambers and really needed to go. She crossed her legs as subtly as possible. Then she thought of Adam, the man she had come to know since the summer. Handsome, charming and good-natured, he clearly thought the world of Delilah. But from the evidence she had seen so far, he seemed to be a man with a secret. Was the secret that he was a killer? She didn't really think so, but whether this was a newspaperman's sixth sense or a woman's intuition she didn't know. Perhaps it was neither. Perhaps it was just wishful thinking – wanting to think the best of Adam for the sake of her friend. The cab dipped into a pothole. Poppy's bladder lurched. She crossed her legs the other way.

"I think Adam's involved with the theft," Poppy said eventually, "but I don't think he's the killer. However, the chances are that he knows the killer. Or perhaps is even in partnership with him. And I think Selena was involved too. I think there were three of them in on the exhibition theft: Adam, Selena and someone else."

"And might this someone else be Andrei Nogovski?"

Up until a few minutes ago, Nogovski had been her prime suspect. But the mention of Felix Yusopov added another possibility. Both men had a motive to get the eggs – or more likely, what they contained. Yusopov's motivation would probably be to protect the royal families – the British and Russian; Nogovski's, as a Red, would be to expose the corruption (or whatever dirty secrets the egg contained) to discredit the royals once and for all to sway public opinion towards the revolutionary cause. Could they be working together? No, it wasn't possible. One was White, the other Red. On the other hand, Nogovski *had* been working for the Whites until a few years ago... Was his conversion fake? Possibly, but then Poppy remembered the evening she had danced with Felix Yusopov, and he and his wife Irina had seen Nogovski talking to Watts at the bar. They had looked terrified and left immediately. Why? Were they scared Watts was going to expose them as jewel thieves? Were they jewel thieves? Had they commissioned Adam to steal the egg? It couldn't have been them personally; they were both still at the Crystal Palace after the police arrived. And what was their connection with Selena? Was all of that arguing and catfighting just a smoke screen? *Very possibly*, thought Poppy.

For the rest of the journey Poppy expounded her thoughts on the matter. Rollo nodded in agreement with her line of thinking. "We need more information, Poppy, but I think we're on the right track. I'll see what I can get out of Ivan. And you?"

Poppy wasn't sure what to do now. She needed to find Delilah. She also needed to see Monsieur Stanislavski in the hospital. Which reminded her: the envelope... her first priority was to see what information Marjorie had dug up on the fingerprints on the chocolate box card. "I'm not sure. I'll go back to my desk, write up some notes and take it from there."

"Righto," said Rollo as the cab pulled up outside *The Daily Globe*.

CHAPTER 29

Poppy and Rollo went up to the fourth floor together and entered the newsroom. Ike was still at his desk and Rollo went over to catch up with him. Poppy listened to Ike's good-natured ribbing of Rollo the Jailbird as she slipped into the restroom. When she emerged she saw Rollo examining Vicky's flowers on the filing cabinet, a scowl on his face. "How did these get here?" he growled.

Poppy was surprised at his tone. She hadn't thought Rollo would be so offended by flowers. Perhaps it was a feminine touch too far in the previously all-male newsroom. Which reminded her: she really needed to speak to him about getting a separate restroom for ladies installed on the fourth floor. The only ladies' lavatories were on the ground floor, just off the foyer. So she and Vicky had to go all the way down and up to spend a penny if they didn't want to use the communal facilities in the editorial department. But perhaps now was not the best time.

"Vicky found them in Ivan's bin. She thought they had some life in them still, so she brought them up here. I think they're lovely."

"In Ivan's trash can? What were they doing there?"

"Exactly the question I asked. She didn't know. Perhaps you can ask him about them when you see him tonight."

"Perhaps I shall," said Rollo through pursed lips. "Well, Miz Denby, I'll be off to warm a stool at the Cock. Drop in before you go home, will you, and let me know which line of enquiry you'll be following next." He looked around the near empty newsroom. "Oh, and Poppy, don't stay after Ike's left. We don't want a repeat of the Saunders incident."

Poppy shuddered at the memory of what had happened during her last big story, when she had been working alone – or so she thought – in *The Globe* offices after hours, and was attacked. Why on earth would Rollo be thinking of that now?

Poppy frowned and then lowered her voice to a whisper. "What are you suggesting, Rollo? Do you think we have another mole?"

Rollo shook his shaggy red head. "No, not that. But people are dying, Poppy. I –" he cleared his throat. "I just don't want you to be hurt, that's all." He reached up and touched her cheek. "And I don't want to be responsible for it."

Poppy was taken aback. First, by the emotion in his voice and secondly that he had touched her so... so personally. It wasn't like Rollo. What was going on?

"Are you all right, Rollo?" she asked.

He was gathering his things and preparing to leave. "Right as rain, Miz Denby, right as rain." Then he left the newsroom.

Still puzzled, Poppy waited until she heard the lift open, close and then start its descent to the ground floor. She thought of mentioning Rollo's odd behaviour to Ike, but he was engrossed in typing and she didn't want to bother him. He was already behind deadline on tomorrow's lead and he wouldn't thank her for the distraction.

She walked quietly to her desk and sat down. Poppy had already submitted her copy for the morning's edition, so she was free to have the night off. But she couldn't possibly go home, not yet. There was too much up in the air. Delilah, Adam, Oscar, Daniel... she shook her head. No, she was not going to think about Daniel now. She needed to patch things up with him, yes, but she was still too angry – and too busy – to do so. It would have to wait until the morning. Perhaps they could thrash it out over lunch.

She refocused on her desk, reaching for the small pile of memo notes from the receptionist, Mavis Bradshaw. It was nothing unusual; there were often messages waiting for her when she'd been out following a story – people who had called to see her, sources passing on leads and occasionally a visitor who had dropped by on the off-chance she was there, like Delilah had done earlier that day.

The first message was from Miss King, who asked Poppy to give her a ring. Poppy did, anxious to hear how the older woman had got on in her search for Delilah. Poppy checked her watch – it was a quarter to eight, and Aunt Dot and Miss King would be having dinner. The telephone was in the hall outside the dining room, so it didn't take long for someone to answer.

"The Denby residence. May I help you?"

"Miss King? It's Poppy."

"Poppy," Miss King answered, lowering her voice. This was not a good sign; clearly Miss King did not want Aunt Dot to hear what she was going to say. Poppy's stomach tightened.

"What is it? Did you find Delilah?"

There was a pause, then: "No. I didn't. Firstly, I rang the theatre to see if she was there, but she hadn't returned after visiting you. So then I popped down the road. She wasn't at Oscar's – the place was still crawling with police – and she wasn't at the flat. I knocked and there was no answer. However…"

"What?"

"I thought I heard a clatter, like someone was going down the fire escape."

Poppy could just imagine the situation. She had once fled Delilah's flat the very same way when an undesirable had come calling. Although Delilah's apartment was swish, it was not large, and it was quite feasible that Miss King had heard someone on the fire escape from the front door.

"Did you see who it was?"

"No. By the time I got around to the back of the building he – whoever it was – was gone."

"Why do you say *he*, Miss King? It could have been Delilah." Then she told the older woman what had happened during the Dorchester story and how she had left Delilah's flat via the fire escape. "Delilah told me she occasionally let suitors out that way when she didn't want the neighbours to see who had been calling."

Poppy could hear the disapproval in Miss King's voice. "Well, that's as may be, but I had the distinct impression that it was a man – and that he was up to no good."

"What gave you that impression, Miss King?"

"I have not always been an invalid's companion," she said primly. "I have – how should I say? – a certain *background* in such things."

A certain background? Poppy's head spun with possibilities. But they would have to wait until she had more time. Miss King's shady past was the least of her worries now.

"I'm sure you're right," said Poppy in a conciliatory tone. "Did you alert the police?"

Miss King sucked in her breath. "I did not. In my experience the police are not always the best port of call in such circumstances. There is no evidence that a crime has been committed and – well – after the way they behaved here at your aunt's house last night, I think they would be more likely to think of "our lot" as suspects, not victims."

Our lot. Poppy stifled a giggle. The phrase encompassed so much: suffragettes, socialists, theatre folk, journalists…

"Well, thank you, Miss King. And obviously, if you see or hear anything, let me know. I – I'm still concerned about Delilah. And it may require a telephone call to her father in Malta. His boat should be docking tomorrow, I think. Let's see what the morning brings and we'll decide then, shall we?"

"I think that would be wise, Poppy. And I wouldn't mention anything to your aunt yet either. Considering Miss Marconi's track record, there could be a perfectly reasonable explanation for her whereabouts."

Poppy agreed that there could be, thanked Miss King again, then hung up the telephone. *There could be, but what if there isn't?* thought Poppy, recalling how distressed and out of character Delilah had been earlier in the day. And there was also the odd coincidence of Delilah's telephone having been disconnected. Poppy needed to see for herself. She had a key to her friend's flat – she occasionally house-sat when Delilah was out of town – so she might just pop by and check things out for herself. Yes, that's exactly what she would do. She just needed to go through the rest of the messages from Mavis and then she'd be on her way.

The next note was to say that Andrei Nogovski had called to remind her that they had agreed to have drinks this evening. *Agreed? I don't remember agreeing to anything. I said he could call the office and we could make an arrangement, but I didn't agree...* There was a telephone number for her to call. She was peeved at his presumption, yes, but intrigued to hear what he had to say. He had suggested he might have information for her. And of course, she had quite a few questions for him as well...

She took hold of the candlestick telephone and lifted the ear piece. Then she replaced it. No, she didn't have time. She needed to see to Delilah first. If Mavis had still been there she would have asked her to return Comrade Nogovski's call and tell him she would speak to him during office hours tomorrow.

But Mavis wasn't there. And neither was Vicky. And Ike was too busy… She lifted the receiver and dialled. A woman answered, announcing that she had got through to the Russian embassy. That was a relief. She didn't have to speak to him directly. She left a message.

The next note was in a different handwriting – Daniel's. It read: *Adam came to see you. He's worried about Delilah. We weren't sure what time you'd be back so we've gone to look for her.*

Poppy caught her breath. Daniel was with Adam, the man who may or may not be a killer. Although her gut had told her no – he was more than likely a thief – her gut could be wrong; Daniel could be in danger. What was she to do? So much lay out of her control. What else *could* she do but pray? *Oh God, I'm in a bit of a fix. I need your help. Will you protect Daniel, please; and Delilah, wherever she is? Help Daniel and Adam to find her. And Adam… I don't know what to pray about him… Give me wisdom to know what to do next and who to trust. Amen.*

She sat for a few moments allowing the prayer to settle in her soul. Gradually, her breathing calmed and her thoughts slowed down. "Thank you, Father," she whispered.

Right, it was time to go. No ideas other than the one she already had – to go to Delilah's flat – had come to mind, so she packed her things into her satchel… *Hang on, I've forgotten about the envelope from Marjorie.* She pulled it out, laid it on the desk and reached for a letter-opener.

Inside was the gift card from the chocolate box in Selena's dressing room that she had asked Marjorie to have fingerprinted. She read the message again – the message in the familiar handwriting: *To Princess Selena Romanova Yusopova, the Old Vic Theatre. From a repentant fool.*

Surely it was just a coincidence. Lots of people had similar-looking handwriting. But fingerprints were unique. Modern science had proven that. She unfolded the single sheet of paper in the envelope, stamped with the Home Office moniker. On it were glued four square pieces of card, each with a copy of an inked fingerprint. They were labelled A, B, C and D. Under them was a typed paragraph:

> *Three full prints (A, B & C) were retrieved from the exhibit, and one partial (D). A does not match any prints on record. B is a match for Count Sergei Andreiovich (P674) and C & D for the same person, Roland Bartholomew Rolandson (T437).*

A rush of bile gushed into Poppy's mouth. She swallowed it, then reached for a glass of water, her hands shaking. She took a gulp, then put the glass down with a clatter. *Roland Bartholomew Rolandson. Rollo.* The handwriting had belonged to Rollo; she wasn't wrong. But why? Why had he sent poisoned chocolates to Selena? Assuming, for argument's sake, that the poison was added later (*and, please God, let him not have known about the poison*) why had he sent the chocolates in the first place? *A repentant fool...* To say he was sorry? She had slapped him at the exhibition on Sunday night when he had asked her for a higher kill fee to quash any stories suggesting she was thinking of stealing the Fabergé egg for herself. That was before the actual theft. The chocolates must have been sent yesterday – Monday – as gift delivery services were not open on Sundays. Why was he saying sorry? For being so ungentlemanly? Possibly. But Rollo didn't usually apologize for deliberately provocative behaviour unless he was hoping to get something in return. What did he want in return? Money? A cut of proceeds from the theft? Rollo was always looking for new ways to make money. He was a gambler. And he always seemed to be in need of more income to keep the paper going.

Poppy took another sip of water, her hands steadier now. She simply couldn't imagine Rollo as a killer. But how well did she really know him? She'd only worked with him for five months...

Focus, Poppy, focus. There are two other fingerprints on this card. Either of them could be the killer... Yes, but Rollo is still involved somehow... Focus!

Someone whose prints were not on record... that could be anyone. The delivery person perhaps? Not very helpful. But Count Sergei Andreiovich was. She'd heard that name only this morning. He was the father of the Moscow family that had been murdered. What had Marjorie said about him? He had been spying for the British? No, that wasn't it. They'd been hoping he'd spy for the British. He was a reformist sympathizer who held sway with the tsar. They hoped he would use it to influence the despot into making reforms. But they'd lost track of him. He was last seen during the war, somewhere on the Western Front... Well, it seemed that Sergei Andreiovich was alive and well and right here in London. Another connection. Another Russian. Another potential murderer...

Poppy felt a chill run down her spine. She looked around her. She was alone in the office apart from Ike, his bowed black head and the click-clack of typewriter keys comforting. Should she tell him? Tell him what? That their boss might be a murderer? No, she needed more evidence. She really needed to speak to Marjorie. She pulled out her contact book and found Marjorie's number. She rang it. No one answered. Poppy let out a long, deep sigh. What was she to do? She closed her eyes and prayed again. *Oh God, I'm completely stumped. What must I do? I ask for your guidance. I ask for your help. Please.* She opened her eyes and closed them again. *It's Poppy, by the way. I've been meaning to go to church, I really have; it's just that... I'm sorry, God. Can we talk about this later? I promise I will. Can you just help me with this for now? Please. Amen.* Then she waited for an answer. Nothing came other than the word "Delilah" – which is what she'd been thinking before she opened the envelope anyway. Should she still go to her flat?

After a few more moments of waiting for divine revelation, nothing else came. She packed her satchel, said goodbye to Ike, and went out into the October night.

CHAPTER 30

On the way to the bus stop, Poppy passed Ye Olde Cock Tavern. Through the window she could see the little and large duo of Rollo and Ivan on their usual bar stools, Ivan laughing at something Rollo had said. It was good to see the sombre archivist so relaxed. He normally wore the tragedy of his past like an old mackintosh, but Rollo somehow had the knack of helping him shrug out of it – just for a while.

It was a strange and unlikely friendship, forged in a field hospital in Belgium during the war. Poppy wondered what Ivan would say if she told him Rollo might be implicated in some way in the death of Selena. She shook her head at the thought. It was ridiculous, surely. And yet… No. She wasn't going to go down that path just yet. She needed to speak to Marjorie first to discuss the involvement – and possible whereabouts – of Count Sergei Andreiovich. And then of course there was the unidentified fingerprint on the card, which could belong to a delivery person or to someone else. Too many variables meant she was not yet prepared to condemn her editor and mentor. There was every possibility that the chocolates were intercepted by Andreiovich – or the mystery person – and the poison added after Rollo had sent them. That was the hypothesis Poppy was going to work with – the only one that made sense.

Poppy hadn't been sure if she would go into the pub as Rollo had requested, uncertain whether she could face him with a cloud of suspicion hanging over him. But now that she had a feasible explanation worked out in her mind – one that felt increasingly comfortable – she decided to go ahead. Should she ask him why he had sent chocolates to Selena? To do so she would have to confess that she had kept a piece of evidence secret and gone behind his back to have it fingerprinted. He would not be pleased. She took a deep breath and pushed open the door.

The olde worlde pub was about half full. Over the summer months it would have been standing room only, as tourists from across the globe wanted to have a drink in the establishment formerly frequented by Samuel Pepys and Charles Dickens. But on this late October night it was comfortably bubbling with the after-work conversation of lawyers and clerks from Temple Bar and journalists and publishers from Fleet Street. Poppy approached her two colleagues. Ivan immediately got off his stool, removed his homburg from the seat next to him, and reached out his hand to help her onto it. Poppy smiled. Despite his fearsome facial hair and bear-like build, Ivan truly was a gentleman from a bygone age.

"Can I get you drink, Poppy?" asked Ivan.

"No thanks. I'm not staying. Just checking in with Rollo before I head off."

Ivan nodded. "Yes, get early night. It's been busy days. Rollo told me goings on at Oscar's. All fuss over jewelled eggs. Poor Mr Reynolds. I hope police catch real killer soon."

Poppy looked at the archivist, remembering his warning about Andrei Nogovski and what a dangerous man he was. She decided to take advantage of his generous mood, and the back-up of Rollo, and probe him a bit further.

"Ivan, yesterday you told me to be careful about Andrei Nogovski. Do you think he might be the killer? Both Selena and Arthur Watts were killed with a rapier and I have –" she thought of what Delilah had told her about Adam's rapier concealed in a cane, a similar cane to the one Nogovski carried "– possible evidence that he might be in possession of a rapier. Do you think he could have done it?"

Ivan's jolly mood dissipated in a flash. A cloud came over his face, and his eyes seemed to sink even deeper into their sockets.

"Is possible," he said, then sipped his beer, turning his shoulder away from the young reporter. Poppy sighed; she had known the archivist long enough to know that that was the end of the conversation. Oh well, she'd tried.

She turned to Rollo, who had almost finished his pint. Poppy hoped it was still his first. She needed to tell him that she was going to look for Delilah. But to do so, she knew both men would start to worry. And Poppy did not want to have to deal with their well-meaning paternalism on top of her nagging concern for her friend. If it turned out Delilah was sleeping over at a friend's place, or dancing in a nightclub, or catching a reel in the cinema – all very possible scenarios for a girl who dealt with stress by having as much fun as possible – then she would have worried them unnecessarily. No, she'd keep that to herself.

Instead she said: "So I've been over my notes and I think the next port of call will be the hospital. Visiting hours are until nine o'clock. I still haven't had a chance to speak to Monsieur Stanislavski."

"He the one who get sick from poison chocolates, no?" asked Ivan.

"Yes. But we think they were meant for Selena. Actually, that reminds me: there's something I need to tell you –"

"Rolandson, you old dog! How are you?" They were interrupted by a jovial chap in a pin-stripe blazer, wide-legged Eton trousers and a boater. "We haven't seen you at the club for a while. Licking your wounds, are you?"

"Evening, Bertram," said Rollo. "May I introduce Miz Poppy Denby and Mr Ivan Molanov, colleagues of mine from *The Globe*. Bertram is a poker pal. A real card sharp if you ever met one!"

Bertram grinned at what he considered to be a compliment and shook hands with Ivan and then Poppy. He held on to Poppy's hand a bit too long and then started caressing it with his thumb. "Ah, the delectable Miss Denby. I have heard so much about you..."

Poppy pulled her hand away. "Well, pleasure to meet you, Mr Bertram, but I was just leaving." She slipped off her stool. "Have a good evening, gentlemen."

"Oh, but Miss Denby, I was hoping we could –"

Rollo jumped off his stool too. "I'll walk you to the door."

Ivan wished her a good evening and then distracted Bertram from following her by offering to buy him a drink. Bertram took off his boater and placed it on the stool Poppy had just vacated and asked for a double whisky.

At the door Poppy buttoned her turquoise mackintosh, tucked a stray blonde curl behind her ear and straightened her cloche hat. "Have you had a chance to question Ivan yet about the Yusopovs?"

"Not yet," said Rollo. "But I will as soon as I've got rid of old Bertie. I have, however, asked him about the flowers."

"The flowers?" Poppy was again surprised that Rollo was so concerned about a passing fancy.

"Yes. I never mentioned it before, but I've been waiting for the police to come calling about them."

Poppy stepped back to allow a young couple past her. The man unclipped his umbrella. It was starting to rain.

"The police? Why on earth would they be interested in Ivan's flowers?"

"Because," said Rollo, keeping his voice low, "they're my flowers, not Ivan's. I sent them to Selena on Monday morning by way of apology for my behaviour on Saturday night. I was hoping to get her back on side. She is – was – a useful source on the exhibition heist story and it wasn't doing us any good having her peeved with me. So I sent the flowers. Or at least I thought I did. And I've been waiting for the police to come and question me about it. But they didn't mention it during my... interrogation today," he grinned, still relishing the drama of it all, "and of course I didn't mention it to them. I assumed they would have found the flowers and the card, and questioned the delivery company. The card didn't have my name on it, but surely a few calls around some local florists would have given them the information they needed. I thought they simply weren't doing their job properly. But then I saw the very flowers I'd picked out in the office and you told me they'd been found in Ivan's trash can. So obviously they hadn't got there. I'd asked Ivan to arrange for them to be sent over yesterday morning because I was going to be in a meeting. He'd said he would."

Poppy looked over at Ivan, who was beginning to lose interest in "old Bertie" and was staring into his pint. Bertram didn't seem to care and chattered away. He noticed Poppy looking at him and raised his whisky glass with a caddish smile.

Poppy shuddered. He reminded her of Alfie Dorchester, whom she had had the misfortune of meeting on her previous big story. She turned back to Rollo.

"So why didn't he send the flowers then?"

Rollo shrugged. "He said he'd read in Selena's Jazz File that she had a pollen allergy. He said he thought it would be counter-productive if I sent them and would only turn her further away from us if she had a hay fever or asthma attack and couldn't go on stage."

Poppy absorbed this. It didn't quite fit, but she wasn't sure why. There was something at the back of her mind – about Selena – but she couldn't quite recall what it was. For now though she was faced with another door opening; it was not one she wanted to go through. Someone else whose fingerprints weren't on file… She looked over again at Ivan, but then averted her eyes as soon as Bertie tried to catch hers. "So he replaced the flowers with chocolates…"

"Oh no, he didn't bother doing that. He just didn't send them. Typical Ivan. Making executive decisions without consulting me. He's never taken very well to being a mere employee. Did I ever tell you about the time – hang on, did you say chocolates? He replaced them with chocolates? Oh Poppy, you're not saying…"

Poppy looked down glumly at her editor. "Can you walk me to the bus stop, Rollo? There's something I need to show you. And tell you. And I'd rather not do it here."

He nodded. "Righto, I'll just get my hat and coat –" he looked out of the window "– and brollie. Back in two ticks."

Poppy held the large black umbrella over both of them as they walked down Fleet Street to the bus stop. Rollo had told Ivan and Bertie he would be back in a few minutes, after he'd seen the lady onto the bus. Poppy wondered if that had made Ivan suspicious. Rollo was not much of a gentleman and wouldn't usually bother seeing her off like that. And normally Poppy wouldn't mind; in fact it was because her editor did not hold traditional views about women that he had thought her worthy to accompany him through the tunnel earlier that day.

At the bus stop, Rollo held the umbrella as she scratched around in her satchel and took out the gift card and letter from the Home Office. She took the umbrella back from him so he could read the report for himself. When he had finished, he glared up at her, his face like thunder.

"What the hell did you think you were doing, Miz Denby? You should have told me!"

Poppy swallowed, her throat tight. "I – I – I was trying to protect you. I recognized the handwriting – or thought I did – and my first thought was that the police didn't get hold of it and get the wrong end of the stick."

Rollo's shoulders rose and fell as he struggled to keep his temper under control. "Well, at least you realized it was the wrong end of the stick!"

Poppy nodded meekly, thankful she didn't have to confess that for a while she thought Rollo had actually done it.

"So then you thought you'd get it fingerprinted. Well, I must say, Miz Denby, I'd take my hat off to you if it wasn't raining. That showed some gumption."

Poppy's heart lurched. Was that forgiveness?

Rollo's shoulders had settled on his squat frame. "So, there are three potential suspects for the poisoning – correction, *attempted* poisoning – of Princess Selena. Count Sergei Andreiovich, an unknown person and… well, and me." He chuckled.

Poppy breathed a sigh of relief.

"And the police haven't seen this?" he asked.

"No," answered Poppy. "And I don't think Marjorie would have let on to the Home Office forensic department where she had got the card."

"You don't think, or you know?"

The rain was easing. Poppy pulled down the umbrella. "I don't think," she answered. "I tried ringing her from the office, but there was no answer."

Rollo nodded. "She might still be at the police station. And if not there, out and about trying to use her influence to get

Oscar free. You should try her again later. Doesn't she live near your aunt somewhere?"

Poppy said she did – just a few streets away – and she'd try to drop in to see her at home later. And if not this evening, tomorrow morning. "She's got to sleep sometime," she observed. Rollo grunted his agreement.

"I also want to ask her about this Count Andreiovich." She reminded Rollo of what Marjorie had told her this morning, the highlights of which she had already outlined in Yasmin's chambers. She told him about the murdered family in Moscow, the missing count, and the connection with the Fabergé eggs. "And now it seems we have evidence that this Andreiovich is right here in London. Although we have no idea where."

Rollo sighed deeply and looked up at his young protégée. "Actually, Miz Denby, we do. Count Sergei Andreiovich is currently in Ye Olde Cock Tavern, having a beer."

CHAPTER 31

Two buses to Chelsea passed while Rollo told Poppy all about Count Sergei Andreiovich and how he became Ivan Molanov, archivist at *The Globe*. As Poppy already knew, Rollo had met Ivan in a field hospital in Belgium, and after the war Rollo had given him – and Daniel, whom he had also met there – jobs at *The Globe*. Ivan had been a White Russian reformist and, in 1917, had heard that his family had been killed back in Russia, so there was nothing left for him to return to. He had come to London as a refugee. Over the last three years there had been intermittent rumours that his family might not have died but were caught up with the masses of displaced people trying to get out of the war zone to safety. But there was no evidence of that, and the previous week Ivan had heard that yet another rumour had come to naught.

All this Poppy knew, but what she didn't know was that soon after Ivan started working for Rollo he had confessed that his true identity was that of Count Sergei Andreiovich of Moscow, distant cousin and military adviser to Tsar Nicholas II. His story then began to dovetail with what she had heard that morning from Marjorie. He had gone to the Western Front as a military adviser but disappeared in 1916. No one knew whether he had defected to the German side or been killed and his body never found.

But Rollo apparently knew. "He was shot by some other White Russian generals who had got it into their heads that he was spying for the British. Although Britain was technically

Russia's ally in the war, there was still a lot of mistrust, and many Russians thought Britain was using the war to extend its empire at Russia's expense. And of course, there might be some truth in that," Rollo told her, leaning against the bus-stop post. Poppy remembered what Marjorie had told her that morning about the British Home Office trying to recruit Ivan to influence the tsar. But she didn't want to interrupt Rollo's flow.

The editor straightened up, dusting droplets of water from his shoulder. "But Ivan – I'll continue to call him Ivan, because that's who he is now – thought the real reason was because he had recently been suggesting that Russia pull out of the war; that he had adjudged the real battle was taking place in Russia itself and that talks needed to start between the Imperial government, the reformers and – and this was the clincher – the Bolshevik leaders. He had sent a report back to the tsar to advise him to consider this course of action. The generals had intercepted the despatch and confronted him with it. When he confessed that this was indeed his opinion, they shot him, leaving him for dead in a ditch."

Rollo then went on to tell Poppy that Ivan had been found by British soldiers and brought to the field hospital where his photographer for *The New York Times* was being treated. "That's where I met him – and Danny Boy, of course – and the rest –" he splayed his overlarge hands – "is history."

Poppy chewed on her lower lip, absorbing the new information. It made sense. Most of it. But she couldn't quite see how a few loose ends worked into the picture.

"So why is he pretending to be someone else? Why not just live openly as Count Sergei Andreiovich here in London?"

Rollo shoved his hands into his overcoat pocket. It was getting cold at the bus stop and Poppy wished they'd taken a table in another public house instead.

"Because," answered Rollo, "he felt his life was still in danger from the Russian generals and he didn't want the British to use him as some kind of diplomatic pawn."

That made sense to Poppy: in her mind's eye she wove one of the threads into the tapestry, then took hold of another. "But why settle in Britain then? It's like walking straight into the lion's den. He could have left Belgium and settled anywhere. Why come here and risk being unearthed by the Secret Service?"

Rollo shrugged, his hands still in his pockets. "I don't rightly know, Miz Denby. You know what Ivan's like – keeps his cards close to his chest – so the most I could get out of him was that he felt the best chance he had of keeping his ear to the ground regarding events back in Moscow was here in London. Due to the connections between the two royal families, Britain would have been the likely destination for any Romanov refugees. Paris too, of course, has attracted a lot of them, but the Brits were the best option for getting Nicholas and his family out."

"And look how well that went," observed Poppy wryly.

"Indeedy," agreed Rollo. "But in 1917 when Ivan first came here, it was thought that the tsar and his family would be arriving any day. Perhaps Ivan was hopeful that he would be able to get some information about his family. It seems that his wife and the tsarina were quite close as children."

Poppy tried to imagine the bear-like Ivan Molanov as a pre-war Russian aristocrat. She attempted to picture the photograph Marjorie had shown her that morning. There had been no beard, and the shaggy hair had been cut short. He was eight years younger too. She struggled to see the resemblance. But then she remembered the eyes – the same eyes that had stared at her from the face of his young daughter – and yes, she could see Ivan in them. She would ask Marjorie to show her the picture again when – or if! – she ever managed to get hold of the woman.

How much of this should she tell her? She didn't want to blow Ivan's cover.

As if reading her mind, Rollo said: "Best you don't tell Marjorie any of this for now. We don't want to get Ivan into trouble."

Poppy's cheek was beginning to hurt again. She touched it gingerly. "I think Ivan's already in trouble, Rollo. Whether we like it or not, he's somehow caught up in this whole Selena/Watts/Fabergé egg thing."

Rollo cocked his head and looked up at her. "How d'ya reckon that, Miz Denby?"

"The chocolates, of course. Somebody poisoned the chocolates – intending them for Selena, and then poor Stanislavski got them instead."

"You reckon he did it, then?" asked Rollo, folding his arms over his chest.

Poppy sighed, and it was her turn to lean wearily on the bus-stop post. "Well, his fingerprints are on the card..."

"So are mine..."

Poppy scowled at Rollo. "Are you trying to implicate yourself?"

Rollo laughed, but there was no humour in it. His demeanour was subdued, worn down. *I wonder if he's beginning to consider that Ivan could really have done it?* Poppy thought.

"Let's not forget there's a third set of prints. Someone unknown..."

Rollo brightened a fraction. "Indeed there is, Miz Denby. And we need to find out who they belong to."

"And," she added, matching his tone, "we need to find out the real reason Ivan replaced the flowers with the chocolates. There's something about the hay fever story that doesn't fit. Selena stayed at our house and – I've just remembered – there were fresh flowers in her room every day. She asked for them herself. And I didn't hear so much as a sniff. If Selena had –" she stopped suddenly, realizing the one thing she had not thought to do "– I haven't searched her room. The police have, but I haven't got around to it yet. There might be some evidence in there."

Rollo perked up a little more.

"If the police have left anything…" observed Poppy. "But what if the evidence implicates Ivan?"

Rollo reached out and patted her shoulder. "Follow your nose, Miz Denby, follow your nose. Just like you did on the Dorchester story, even if it implicates people you know and love."

You mean people you *know and love,* thought Poppy. Poor Rollo. He wanted desperately for his friend to be innocent. She knew exactly how that felt. In all of this she'd forgotten Adam and Delilah. She needed to find them. Her stomach clenched into the familiar knot. The lights of another bus turned the corner into Fleet Street. She reached into her pocket for her purse.

"I think I'd better get this one, Rollo. I've got a few things to do – and people to see – in Chelsea."

The editor agreed. "I'll go back to the pub and see what I can wheedle out of Ivan, and then I'll try to get Yasmin to set up a meeting with the Yusopovs. Even if they're not directly involved, they must know something about this."

Poppy agreed. Rollo asked her to ring him later at the office so they could compare notes. She said she would, then got on the bus. As she settled down, she wiped condensation from the window and watched as Rollo's already small figure hunched even lower in the dim streetlight.

CHAPTER 32

Poppy didn't get off the bus at King's Road but stayed on it – past Aunt Dot's house, past Delilah's flat (the windows were dark – still no one home?) and past Oscar's Jazz Club – and turned right into Edith Road. She rang the bell and got off at the corner of Edith and Fulham with the lights of Fulham Road Hospital a beacon to her right. It was now well after nine o'clock and visiting hours would be over. However, this would not be the first time she had "broken in" to a hospital after hours, avoiding interrogation by staff, and soon she was slipping unnoticed, wearing a white gown and Sister Dora headscarf she had dug out of a laundry hamper, into the room of Constantin Stanislavski.

The theatre director was sleeping. She pulled up a chair and settled down, taking his hand in hers. It was clammy. She whispered his name until he stirred. He mumbled something first in Russian, then in French. Poppy knew enough of the latter to know he thought she was a nurse. "No, I is not nurse; I Poppy Denby," she answered in her schoolgirl French.

Pale and weak though he was, he managed a smile and said in near-perfect English: "You have an appalling French accent, Miss Denby. Has anyone ever told you that?"

She grinned. They had.

His eyes now fully open, he looked at his visitor. He did not ask why she was dressed as a nurse; he simply went along with the theatricality.

"I'm sorry I haven't visited earlier, Monsieur Stanislavski, but I've been busy trying to find out who did this to you."

"Have you made any progress?" he asked.

273

"A little," admitted Poppy. She wasn't sure yet how much she was going to tell him, but she needed to tell him something in order to get something in return. "But first, how are you feeling? What do the doctors say?"

Stanislavski coughed hoarsely. Poppy poured him a glass of water and held it as he sipped. He sank back onto his pillow, closed his eyes for a moment and then opened them again. Poppy feared he was going to go to sleep, but his eyes were fully awake and holding her gaze.

"Despite appearances, Miss Denby, they think I will make a full recovery. Thanks mainly to you. They all agree that undoubtedly it was your quick thinking to get the chocolate out of me that prevented the toxin from taking hold."

Despite herself, Poppy flushed with pride. "It's what anyone would have done under the circumstances."

"But anyone didn't – it was you. And for that I am grateful. So if there's anything I can ever do for you…"

Poppy was going to brush this aside with the usual "Oh, there's no need for that" when she remembered there *was* something he could do for her. Or at least for someone she knew. But it could wait. She had urgent business to attend to first.

"So have they identified the poison? Was it cyanide?"

Stanislavski nodded. "It was. Injected, as you suspected, into the chocolates. No doubt meant for poor Selena."

No doubt. But who had meant it for her? Poppy decided not to tell Stanislavski about Rollo's and Ivan's fingerprints. But she would tell him a little. And she hoped he could tell her a little too.

"The question that's on my mind," he continued, "is why the two different murder attempts? If there was one killer, why would he – or she – send poisoned chocolates and then stab her with a rapier?"

Poppy screwed up her nose. "I think that's what we're all wondering, Monsieur Stanislavski. The police too, no doubt. The best I can come up with is that the killer sent the chocolates – perhaps even watched as they were delivered – and then went in to check that the job had been done. But Selena was on a diet. I'd heard her mention it to my aunt. She was struggling to fit into her costume and was too embarrassed to ask the wardrobe mistress to let it out. So she had resisted the chocolates. So when the killer went in –"

"He saw that Plan A hadn't worked and resorted to Plan B," finished Stanislavski.

"Yes, I think so," agreed Poppy.

A little more colour was coming into Stanislavski's cheeks. Sorting through this muddle was invigorating him rather than tiring him out. "However," he added, "stabbing her so brutally and publicly doesn't seem to fit with the character's modus operandi. The poisoning was murder by stealth. It must have taken a lot of planning. But stabbing is immediate, passionate even, risking discovery if Selena screamed for help."

Poppy smiled at Stanislavski's use of the word "character". He was slipping into director mode, analysing the script to get to the heart of the writer's intentions.

"But Selena didn't scream for help. Or if she did, no one heard her. You were not far away in the rehearsal room and you didn't hear her," Poppy observed.

"Ah, but that's because the rehearsal room is soundproofed."

Poppy absorbed this for a moment. When she had arrived to speak to Selena she had seen Stanislavski and Delilah in the rehearsal room and Adam and the props manager – Arthur Watts's uncle – in the Green Room. If there were other people backstage she hadn't seen them. After she screamed it was those four who came first, joined afterwards by other theatre folk from elsewhere in the building. Yes, the dressing room had definitely filled up. So there were other people around. But who were they? The police no doubt would have got a full list of them. She never thought at the time to do so. When she and Rollo were trying to identify suspects they focused on the people who would have been at the exhibition *and* the theatre. And the only person, apart from herself, Delilah, Stanislavski and Selena, was Adam. Adam had been in the Green Room – the closest room to Selena's dressing room. She doubted the Green Room would have been soundproofed, as actors need to hear when they are being called. And Adam, she believed, had a rapier. However, Arthur Watts's uncle was there too. A relative of a now-known criminal. A props man with access to weaponry. Stage weaponry, but a blunted rapier could easily be sharpened…

"Penny for your thoughts, Miss Denby."

"I'm sorry. I was just thinking about who was there at the time. When I first arrived at the theatre."

"Do you think the killer was still there?"

"It's possible, yes."

"But it's also possible that he – or she – slipped out before you arrived. The police told me Selena had been dead for under an hour before we found her. They can't say how much 'under an hour' – it might have been as little as fifteen minutes, apparently. Their science cannot be that accurate. But a quarter of an hour is still ample time for someone to leave the theatre undetected."

Poppy chastised herself: another thing she'd forgotten to check. She didn't have sources in the police, but Rollo did. Did Rollo have this information?

As if reading her thoughts, Stanislavski picked up a newspaper on the bedside table and placed it on the bedspread. "Your editor's article says the same."

Poppy flushed. She hadn't actually read Rollo's article this morning. She had been so busy with Marjorie and then the drama at Oscar's and the meeting at Yasmin Reece-Lansdale's chambers…

Stanislavski patted her hand. "Don't worry, Miss Denby; I can see it's been a long day. I hope you are going home to get some sleep soon."

Sleep. And supper. Wouldn't that be nice?

"I will, Monsieur Stanislavski, but I was wondering if you could help me with something first. There is obviously a Russian connection with this and I was hoping you could give me insight." She smiled wryly. "And you are the only Russian in London who is clearly not the killer."

Stanislavski smiled too. "Have you ever thought of writing a murder mystery, Miss Denby? I think you'd give your Miss Christie a run for her money."

Poppy chuckled and at that moment decided Constantin Stanislavski was a man she could trust. She went on to tell him as much as she knew about Selena and the Fabergé eggs, the connection with the royals and the possible involvement of Vasili Safin, Andrei Nogovski and the Yusopovs. The only Russian she didn't mention was Ivan Molanov. She needed to give Rollo time with him first. But she did mention Count Sergei Andreiovich.

"Sergei Andreiovich," said Stanislavski. "He and his wife were great fans of the Bolshoi before the war. We all thought he was dead. But now you're saying he might be here in London?"

"He might," said Poppy. "But what his motivation might be for stealing the eggs I have no idea. He seems to have been trying to avoid being used by either the Russian or British government. So why he would be interested in the eggs I can't fathom."

Stanislavski readjusted his shoulders on the pillow and said, "If I were directing this play I would say that Andreiovich is part of a sub-plot, not the main."

"What do you mean?" asked Poppy, intrigued.

"You are assuming that the same person who stole the eggs is the killer."

Poppy nodded her agreement.

"But what if they are two different crimes with two different motives?"

Poppy straightened up. The thought had crossed her mind, but she had not been able to figure it out. "Go on," she said.

"What if Andreiovich had a vendetta against Selena?"

"Such as?"

"Such as it seems like it was she who got Andreiovich's wife involved with the eggs in the first place. And ultimately, if what you say is correct – God rest their souls – that is what led to their murder. Andreiovich might have blamed Selena for it and killed her simply out of grief. This man is acting in his own tragedy. He is a Hamlet."

Poppy thought of Ivan and the sadness he carried. Yes, he was a Hamlet – not a Macbeth. If he killed, he killed out of pain, not to further a cause or ambition. She felt a cold chill run down her spine. But he had killed nonetheless… perhaps.

"It's strange you should mention the Andreioviches," Stanislavski continued. "Do you know that I introduced Adam Lane to them back in 1915? Or to the countess, at least. The count was on the Western Front at the time."

Poppy had not mentioned Adam's name yet. Her ears pricked up. "Oh?"

"Yes," continued Stanislavski. "I'd met Adam at the Bolshoi and was very impressed with him – both as an actor and a man. It was his first time in the city, so I invited him with me to the Andreioviches for dinner. He was charming. He took the little girl a puppy. And now it seems the child might still be alive. I wonder if Andreiovich knows?"

Poppy wondered the same. Did Ivan know his little Anya was still alive? Or that she might be? Was the information he'd received last week about his family possibly having got out of Moscow really just information about his daughter? But then, Rollo had said, it turned out to be false. Could this rising of hope and then the dashing of it have pushed Ivan to lash out at the woman he blamed for his family's death?

"I have no idea," she answered truthfully. "But," she took a deep breath, "now that we're on the subject of Adam, I have something else to tell you." She went on to recount what she knew – or suspected – of Adam's activities as a jewel thief, and surmised that he was involved in the theft of the Fabergé eggs.

Stanislavski closed his eyes and listened. When she had finished he opened them again and said, "If you expect me to be surprised, I'm not."

Sensing that Stanislavski had a story to tell, Poppy leaned in closer.

"I once met a manager at a provincial theatre, here in England, who told me his former props man had raised an orphan lad to be a thief. The manager thought this was highly amusing and told me to keep a look out for the lad, because he was now grown up and on the acting circuit. I don't know what he expected me to do with the information – the fellow was drunk at the time – but I thought it an interesting tale. He told me the boy's name was Adam, and that he was blond, but couldn't remember the surname."

Poppy gasped. "Adam! Adam Lane!"

Stanislavski nodded sagely. "That's what I've come to believe, yes. I first met him in Paris in 1912 –"

"Selena's necklace!"

"Indeed. There have been rumours in theatrical circles that jewel thieves often target wealthy theatregoers and hide their loot among the props until it is safe to move it. And although Selena was an actress not an audience member, I wouldn't be surprised if that's what happened there. And perhaps what happened here."

"You mean the egg could be in the props room at the theatre?" asked Poppy incredulously.

"It could be, but it seems in this case the props man – Watts – has taken his fencing activity off-site. His poor nephew at Oscar's…"

Yes, it was all beginning to make sense. The killer, assuming it was a different person to the thief, had come to the theatre looking for the egg, assuming, like most people did at the beginning, that Selena herself had staged the theft at the exhibition. She wondered if the police were pursuing this line of enquiry too or – what was it Andrei Nogovski said? – were they still considering that Selena passed the egg on to Delilah's father, Victor Marconi, who in turn took it to Malta? If so, no doubt the authorities would be waiting for Mr Marconi in Valetta when he docked tomorrow. Poor Mr Marconi. She sincerely doubted that he was involved, but who knows what a man might do for a woman he had been infatuated with?

"However, it does seem that whoever killed Arthur Watts believed that he had the egg, or knew where it was," continued Stanislavski. "Which suggests that the egg was not found at the theatre."

"But that brings us back to the theft and the murder being connected after all," observed Poppy.

"Oh, I'm sure they are connected," clarified Stanislavski, "but I just have the feeling they may have different causes."

Poppy agreed that they might. But there was something else bothering her. "Monsieur Stanislavski, you said that Adam had impressed you as an actor and as a man. Do you still feel the same now that you've heard he might be involved in all this?"

Stanislavski thought about this for a moment and then answered, "Yes, I do still feel the same. If what I've heard about him is true – that he was raised by a thief in the theatre – then the boy didn't really have a choice. He was bred to be a thief. But murder is a very different thing. And the man I know would not choose to willingly kill someone. Would you agree?"

She'd been over this before. And still she had no definitive answer. "I don't know," she answered truthfully. "I would like to speak to him personally and then I'll judge."

Stanislavski nodded. "Yes, I think that would be wise. But assuming that he is the thief, I think it's pertinent that he hasn't yet left town. The question is why?"

"Well, as far as I know, he's currently out looking for Delilah."

"Exactly. He's a man with a heart. Could a man like that possibly be a cold-blooded killer?"

Poppy hoped not. She thought of how happy Adam and Delilah were together… and then a shadow passed Stanislavski's door. It was a nurse, looking in. Poppy turned her head, hoping not to be challenged. She wasn't, but it was just a matter of time. She needed to wrap this up.

"There's just one more thing, Monsieur Stanislavski. What do you know about Andrei Nogovski?"

Stanislavski's eyes flicked to the door and back, then he lowered his voice to a whisper. "A very dangerous man."

"So I've been told," whispered Poppy in return. "But is there anything else you can tell me about him? Anything that might be useful to this investigation?"

Stanislavski fell silent for a moment, accessing his memories of Nogovski. Then he looked up at Poppy. "He was Selena's bodyguard. When she was in Paris. It was there that he met Lenin and was turned – so Lenin told me in later years. Nogovski became a communist soon afterwards but kept it a secret. After Paris he was recruited into the *Okrana*, the secret police. He'd kept his political leanings to himself and we can only assume he worked for the Reds as a double agent. But it must have become too much for him, because sometime in 1915 he resigned from the *Okrana* and became a card-carrying member of the Communist Party. And as you know, he's now high up in their intelligence service. He is a trained killer, Miss Denby. But – and this is strange – he always remained devoted to Selena. No one could figure out why. We all thought, initially, that it was because he'd been assigned to be her handler. From what you've told me you already know that the royals indulged her dalliance with Bolshevism, and both sides used her to spread misinformation –"

Poppy nodded. Yes, Marjorie had told her the same thing.

"But in my opinion, it was more than that. I saw Nogovski and Selena together. There was something there I could never quite put my finger on. Some kind of sub-text…"

The hairs on the back of Poppy's neck were beginning to stand up. Was Stanislavski suggesting Nogovski and Selena had – or were having – an affair?

"When he visited her at the theatre last week –"

The door opened and a nurse came in, pushing a medicine trolley. "Time for your nightcap, Mr Stanislavski," she said. And then, on seeing Poppy: "And who are you?"

Poppy muttered something about being on the way to see another patient and pretended she was straightening the sheets.

"Goodnight, Monsieur Stanislavski. I'll see you tomorrow. Sleep well."

"Goodnight… nurse," Stanislavski winked at her.

"I haven't seen you before. Are you new?" The real nurse

stepped from behind her trolley and looked at Poppy full on. "And what is that get-up you're wearing?"

"I... well..." But before Poppy was compelled to answer, the theatre director started coughing and spluttering, and the real nurse rushed to his aid.

Poppy slipped out.

CHAPTER 33

Poppy walked home up Fulham Road. She felt light-headed from hunger and needed to get some supper. Yasmin Reece-Lansdale's sandwiches seemed a long time ago. However, Marjorie Reynolds lived on Fulham Road and Poppy decided to see if she was home. She could always beg a biscuit. Marjorie lived in a well-to-do four-storey townhouse complete with butler, live-in maid and cook. The butler answered the door and informed her that Mrs Reynolds was not yet home. The elderly man looked tired and more than a bit worried, failing to hide it behind his mask of servitude.

"Don't worry, Mr Samuels. I'm sure everything will work out fine."

The servant allowed himself the hint of a smile. "I do hope so, Miss Denby. Mr Oscar has got himself into quite a fix. He's too old to be worrying his mother like this." Poppy remembered her aunt telling her that Samuels had been with the Reynolds family since before Oscar was born.

"I'll be praying," said Poppy.

The old man thanked her. "Is there anything I can help you with, Miss Denby? You look tired."

A ham sandwich, a cup of tea and some divine inspiration to sort out this muddle, thought Poppy. But instead she answered: "If you could just ask Mrs Reynolds to give me a ring when she gets in, I'd appreciate it. On second thoughts," she looked at her watch, "I'll only be home for about the next half an hour…"

Samuels raised an eyebrow at the suggestion that a young lady like Poppy would still be out so late at night.

"So better she call Rollo Rolandson at *The Globe*. He'll be doing an all-nighter. We very much need to speak with her."

"I will do, Miss Denby. Would you like me to walk you home?"

Poppy smiled at his kindness. "No, thank you, Mr Samuels. It's just around the corner and there are plenty of people out. Living just opposite a cinema has its advantages."

Mr Samuels didn't look fully convinced, but he let her go, and shut the door.

Five minutes later, Poppy was putting her key into her aunt's front door. It was just after ten o'clock and across the road the evening picture show had just finished. Men and women – dressed to the nines in fur coats and top hats – spilled onto the pavement, comparing notes about the performances of John Barrymore and Martha Mansfield in the apparently terrifying *Dr Jekyll and Mr Hyde*. She and Daniel were planning on going to see it next week. She had received review tickets, but they had clashed with a gallery opening in Piccadilly, so Ike Garfield had taken the tickets and written the review on her behalf. Good old dependable Ike; he was a real asset to the paper. Him and Daniel... Her heart lurched as she thought of the press photographer. She had cooled down since their fall-out and all she wanted to do now was fall into his arms and say she was sorry. But was she sorry? Hadn't she had a right to object to his controlling attitude? She felt irritation stir again, but she quenched it. There would be time to think about that later. For now, she only had one thing on her mind, and that was food.

She let herself into the hall and called up the stairs that she was home. Aunt Dot's wheelchair was at the bottom, so Poppy assumed Miss King had helped her aunt into the stair lift to get her ready for bed.

"Poppy, is that you, darling?" called her aunt.

"It is, Aunt Dot. But I'm not staying. I'm still working on a story. Just need to get some supper first though."

"Oh bother!" called her aunt. "I was hoping for a good chinwag before bedtime. There's so much going on."

"I know, Aunt Dot. I'll tell you as much as I can at breakfast. I'll pop in and say goodnight before I go though."

"All right then, darling. See you in a jiff."

Poppy smiled at her aunt's remarkably tolerant attitude to her comings and goings. Her parents would have a cadenza if they knew. But Aunt Dot had encouraged Poppy to get a job as a journalist and was supportive of everything she did. Which was just as well, because on the arts and entertainment beat it wasn't unusual for Poppy to shuffle in after midnight. If Aunt Dot weren't so laissez-faire Poppy would have had to consider getting a place of her own. Or taking a room with Delilah. That reminded her – she needed to pop up to her room to get Delilah's spare key. Poppy kept it in her dresser drawer. But first, supper…

Fifteen minutes later, Poppy had polished off a slice of Melton Mowbray pie, a jacket potato and a pile of limp green leaves, cucumber and chopped tomato that the cook charmingly referred to as salad. The cook was a temporary stand-in. Aunt Dot's faithful companion Grace Wilson – who was now serving time in Holloway – had been nursemaid, cook and friend. Miss King, on the other hand, drew her boundaries far more clearly. She would aid Aunt Dot with her personal ablutions, cater to her medicinal needs and provide social companionship, but cooking, cleaning and, well, anything else was not in her remit. So Aunt Dot had had to hire a cook and a cleaner, despite her semi-socialist views. Poppy was not fussy. Limp salad and cold pork pie filled the gap, washed down by a hot cup of tea.

Feeling satisfied, Poppy popped up to her third-floor

bedroom to change, bypassing Aunt Dot's second-floor room where she could hear the older woman chattering away to Miss King. She'd drop in on the way back down. Poppy looked at herself in the full-length mirror and saw that her turquoise outfit was looking rather worse for wear. Not surprising after all she'd been through today. So she opened her wardrobe to look for a change of clothes. She reached for her poppy red dress, but then changed her mind. It was twenty past ten and she was not going out on the tiles. Instead she took a grey skirt and dark blue jersey top off the hanger and slipped into some sensible shoes. She scratched around in her drawer and found Delilah's key, which she dropped into her skirt pocket. She just needed to go to the bathroom and she was ready.

A few minutes later she stepped onto the landing. She noticed that the door to the guest bedroom – recently occupied by Selena – was slightly ajar. She pushed it open and went in. She did not have much time, as she really needed to get to Delilah's flat, but she'd have a quick look. She flicked the light switch and was not surprised to see that the room was topsy-turvy. The police had done a good job of pulling everything out and leaving it where it shouldn't be. Selena had a surprising number of belongings for a woman who had allegedly fled a war zone with only the clothes on her back. Poppy had read reports of the warship HMS *Marlborough* that had been sent to Yalta to evacuate the empress and her entourage. Apparently it had taken the captain two days to load the refugees – with all the luggage they had managed to bring from their Black Sea holiday villas, where many of them had been in exile. One or two of them arrived with just a suitcase each, but most of them had trunks and hampers filled with household goods. And of course the famed Rembrandts, Fabergé eggs and other works of art that had been made public at the weekend's exhibition. Some of the crew of the *Marlborough* had allegedly been given gifts of priceless Russian artefacts to keep them sweet. The captain eventually had to call time on all the luggage, as the Red Russian army was literally at the gates of the city and starting to shell the harbour.

Poppy began to pick through all that was left of Selena's worldly goods: a nightdress here, a camisole there and a box of cosmetics. At the bottom of the make-up box Poppy spotted the corner of what looked like a photograph. She extracted it with thumb and forefinger and realized it was two photographs that had been glued together. On one side was a picture of a baby in Victorian-era clothing. The child – Poppy could not tell if it was a boy or a girl – was propped up against a pile of cushions and looked as if it was just about to drop off to sleep.

The second photograph nearly took Poppy's breath away. It was a more recent snap (if the quality of the image and card was anything to go by) and on it was a picture of an elderly woman dressed in Russian peasant garb and a young girl of about seven or eight. The girl too was dressed as a peasant; but Poppy recognized them both from pictures she had seen earlier today: Ruth Broadwood and Anya Andreiovich. In the right-hand corner of the photograph was scrawled "Yekat'brg 1918". Poppy had no idea where or what Yekat'brg was, but it appeared that she finally had proof positive that Anya Andreiovich had survived the Moscow massacre and was still alive up to, at least, two years ago. She needed to speak to Marjorie and Rollo and –

"What do you have there?" Miss King was standing in the doorway. Poppy's instinct was to hide the photographs, but she realized it would look silly to do so. Miss King had already seen that she had something in her hands.

"Some photographs of Selena's."

"Oh," said Miss King. "I was going to tidy this lot up

tomorrow. Your aunt has invited the Yusopovs to dinner and we're going to ask them to collect Selena's things. They're her nearest relatives – at least the nearest that are in London – and your aunt thinks they should have them. May I see?"

Miss King reached out her hand and Poppy had no good reason not to give them to her. The older woman looked first at the baby and commented "circa 1885 by the bromide", once again surprising Poppy with her forensic knowledge. Then she turned over the picture and gasped, her free hand going to her throat. It was the most emotion Poppy had ever seen her aunt's companion emit. "Ruthie!" declared Miss King and turned towards the door.

"Wait! I need the pictures!"

"I'm sorry, Poppy, but these are now the property of His Majesty's government."

"They're what?"

"I have to hand these in. You probably don't know, but the woman in this picture has been missing for three years. She works for the government, and –"

"Ruth Broadwood. I know. She was spying for us at the Russian court."

Complete shock registered on Miss King's face. "However do you know that? It's top secret."

Poppy reached out her hand and took hold of the photograph. Miss King continued to hold her side.

"If it's top secret, Miss King, how do *you* know? I know you were friends with Ruth when you both worked at Downing Street, but how do you know about this?"

"And how do you know about Downing Street?"

"Marjorie Reynolds told me."

"Marjorie... oh." Miss King sank onto the bed. Poppy, now with the photograph in hand, could easily have left, but she was intrigued by Miss King's past and wanted to know more. She sat on the bed beside the older woman.

"You weren't just a nanny for the Chancellor, were you? Were you trained as a spy too."

Miss King had begun to recover herself. She straightened her shoulders and adopted her familiar deadpan look. "I'm afraid I can't tell you that, Poppy. But let's just say that my appointment here wasn't an accident. Your aunt is very well connected in all sorts of circles."

Poppy was incredulous. "You're here to spy on Aunt Dot and her friends?"

"Not spy, no. But Marjorie Reynolds thought it might be prudent to have someone in the house to keep an eye on things. For your aunt's protection."

"Marjorie what?" Poppy's voice rose in outrage.

"Gertrude! Poppy! Are you coming down?"

Poppy walked to the door, still holding the photograph. "I'm not going to tell Aunt Dot about this now – I've got too much else to do this evening – but I think when things quieten down, you, Aunt Dot and I need to have a little talk."

Miss King nodded. "Fair enough. But please, promise me one thing: get that photograph to Marjorie Reynolds. If there's a chance Ruth could still be alive…"

Poppy agreed that she would, then scampered down the stairs to see her aunt. She made the visit as quick as she could, careful not to be drawn into Aunt Dot's efforts to have a "little chat", then headed downstairs to the hall. She put on a slate grey mackintosh and hat, and put the double-sided photograph into her satchel, which she swung over her shoulder. She glanced at her watch – a quarter to eleven – then looked at the telephone in the hall. *I'd better give Rollo a quick call,* she thought. Checking no one was standing listening at the top of the stairs, she called Rollo's number at *The Globe.* He answered after a couple of rings.

"Rolandson."

"Rollo, it's Poppy."

"Speak up, Miz Denby. I can hardly hear you."

"I can't," Poppy mumbled into the phone.

"What's wrong, Poppy? Are you all right?"

"I am, but I can't talk. I'm at my aunt's and walls have ears."

"Can you tell me what you are doing next?"

"I'd prefer not to. Not here. Do you remember who came to the office today to ask for help? Before you, Daniel and I went to Oscar's?"

Rollo sighed. "I hope there's a good reason for all this subterfuge, Miz Denby. Are you referring to Delilah Marconi?"

"I am. Can you meet me at that person's flat in half an hour?"

"I can," Rollo sounded annoyed. "But this had better be damned well worth it."

"Thank you." She was just about to say goodbye when she decided to ask one more thing. She doubted Miss King would think anything of it if she was eavesdropping. "Has Daniel called?"

"No, he hasn't," said Rollo. "But Marjorie has. And I've spoken to Ivan. I've got a lot to tell you too. I'll see you in half an hour. Goodbye." He hung up the phone.

CHAPTER 34

Adam and Daniel had searched every place they could think of, but still no Delilah. They had visited every club, pub and restaurant she had been known to frequent, called every friend where she might be having dinner at a private residence, and even popped in to see Uncle Elmo – otherwise known as Guglielmo Marconi, the world-famous radio and broadcast pioneer. The latter was tricky, as they did not want to give the impression that they had "lost" his great-niece. Instead they pretended that Delilah had concocted a treasure hunt, where she herself was the treasure to be found. It was a perfectly plausible explanation, because Delilah and her Bright Young friends were always going on highly publicized scavenger hunts in and around London. Uncle Elmo considered it charming, but could not help the young men in their search for his sparkling young relative.

"If we don't find her soon, we may very well have to tell him the truth," whispered Daniel as they got back into Adam's motor. "His contacts could be invaluable. And the police will take us far more seriously with him on our side."

"I'd rather not go to the police just yet," said Adam, firing up the engine.

It was nearly eleven o'clock when Adam and Daniel decided to take a break from their search. As they were in Kensington, Adam suggested they pop into his penthouse apartment for a drink and a snack. He hadn't been home since this morning, when he and Delilah had left to go to the theatre and they were intercepted by the man in the alley. Adam parked the motor in his usual spot, but was careful to scout the area before he and Daniel got out.

"What are you looking for?" Daniel asked.

"I was nearly mugged here this morning," answered Adam.

Daniel looked at him curiously. The photographer had seemed all too happy to accompany Adam on his quest to find Delilah, and the young actor was glad that he seemed to accept his explanation of "we had a tiff and she stormed off" at face value, expressing empathy because apparently he and Poppy had had a tiff too. "Women!" he had declared, and they'd both laughed.

But Adam wasn't sure how long he could keep up that pretence, particularly not after Daniel's next question: "Is this where Delilah thought you had gotten into a sword fight?"

Adam sucked in his breath, then quietly exhaled. So she had told her friends about it. Poppy Denby and Rollo Rolandson were far too savvy to take that at face value. He wasn't sure how long he could string Daniel along. Maybe it was time to get rid of him…

"Perhaps we should call it a night, old man. I'm sure Delilah will turn up sooner or later. We've left instructions all over town to ring me if she does. There's no need for us both to man the phone. Can I drop you somewhere?"

Daniel turned to face him square on. In the diluted light from Kensington Road Adam could see the photographer was looking serious. Adam remembered what Delilah had told him about Daniel's background. He was a soldier and had seen action on the Western Front. Adam himself had been conscripted in 1916, but he had managed to concoct a quick discharge because of a problem with his eyes – the result of reading late at night as a child in the theatre without proper light. It didn't affect his day-to-day life – and he refused to wear spectacles – but by the time he had got through the medical and turned his considerable acting talent to good use, the doctor believed he was practically blind. He didn't care if people thought him a coward. It was a mad war and he wasn't going to sacrifice himself for someone else's insanity.

Adam sized Daniel up, wondering if he could take him. He discounted using the secret rapier – he didn't want to do the man any permanent harm – but he couldn't allow himself to be turned in to the police, if that was Daniel's intention.

Daniel took a step forward; Adam braced himself. Daniel noticed the change in body language and frowned. "What's going on, Lane?"

Adam tried the nonchalant approach one final time. "Not a thing, Rokeby, not a thing. Want that lift?"

Daniel grabbed his arm. Adam winced. It was the stitched wound. Daniel tightened his grip. "Come on, old man; it's time to fess up."

Adam's fist tightened on his cane. Quick as a flash Daniel kicked it aside and had Adam in a half-nelson. "So it's true then. There is a rapier in that cane."

And I should have used it, thought Adam as he threw his weight back against Daniel, trying to knock him off balance. But the photographer just tightened his grip. Adam felt his airway compressing.

"It's not what you think," he croaked.

"I don't know what to think, Lane. Is Delilah really missing, or have you done something to her?"

"What the –" Adam's reply was quenched by Daniel's forearm as he tried to wriggle out of the ex-soldier's grip.

It was no use. Adam could not break free. He raised his hands in defeat; Daniel's arm loosened.

"If you think I could ever hurt that girl, you obviously don't know me," he whispered.

"And that's exactly the problem, Lane. I don't know you. And neither does Poppy. But she does suspect you of stealing that Fabergé egg. The question is, are you simply a thief, or a murderer too? And if you're not a murderer, then someone else is, and both Poppy and Delilah might be in danger. You say you love her – who knows if you do or not? – but I can tell you this: I really love Poppy and I will not let her get hurt; or Delilah. So if there's anything you know that could help, it's time to tell me."

Adam exhaled, sinking back against Daniel's chest. "All right, I'll tell you. But not here. Let's go up to my flat."

Daniel nodded in agreement and let Adam go, but positioned himself between the actor and the cane.

Adam gave a rueful smile. "I could have taken you, Rokeby."

The photographer's demeanour did not change. "You could have tried."

The purple and silver filigree egg was perched on the table between them, its diamond studs catching the light of the gas fire.

"So what are you going to do with it?" asked Daniel, sipping at a cup of tea. Adam had offered him something stronger, but he'd declined.

"Well, now that my fence is dead, I'm not really sure. I could try to flog it on the black market, but that's risky. I could wait until my employer contacts me again…"

"Can't you contact him?"

Adam shrugged. I've sent a telegram to Valetta, telling him there has been a delay in the handover, but that was before Watts was killed. I'll need to send him another. I'll do it in the morning."

Daniel put his cup down on its saucer. "How sure are you that your employer's in Malta?"

"Fairly sure. Why else would he use the Valetta post office?"

Daniel frowned. "You don't seriously think it's Victor Marconi, do you?"

Adam sighed. "No, not really. But it's the only connection I have with Malta. He's the only person I know associated with the place."

"There are hundreds of thousands of people living on the island. It could be any of them."

"Or none of them," agreed Adam. "Malta could simply be a front."

"Or not," said Daniel, trying to puzzle it out. "And it's not true that Victor is your only connection. Didn't the Russian royals just come from there?"

Adam raised an eyebrow. Rokeby was cleverer than he had given him credit for. "Indeed they did," he observed.

Suddenly, the telephone rang. Both men jolted. "Thank God!" said Adam as he went to answer it. "Finally, something about Delilah."

"Kensington 2673. Adam Lane speaking…" He looked expectantly at Daniel, who was perched on the edge of the sofa.

"I have some information on the whereabouts of Delilah Marconi," said a male voice.

Icy fingers clawed at Adam's heart. It was the voice of the man in the alley.

"What have you done with her?" asked Adam.

"Nothing yet. But I will if you do not bring the egg to this address…" The man dictated an address, which Adam wrote down.

"I'll be there in twenty minutes," he said and put down the phone.

Daniel looked alarmed. "Dear God, Lane. I hope they've not…"

Adam's hands quivered as they picked up the egg and wrapped it in the oil cloth.

"If I'm not back with her in an hour, Rokeby, go to the police. Give them this address." He passed the piece of paper to Daniel, who looked at it – his face registering recognition.

"You can give it to them yourself. After you've got Delilah. And whether you like it or not, I'm coming with you – you'll need all the help you can get, where you're going."

Adam weighed this up, realizing that someone as handy as Daniel could be an asset. He nodded his agreement and then went to the sideboard and opened a drawer. He pulled out a revolver and handed it to the ex-soldier. "I assume you know how to use this."

CHAPTER 35

Poppy arrived at Delilah's apartment building and went up to the second floor. Her neighbour across the hall was having a party and Poppy went in to see if Delilah was there. She found the neighbour – Giles – dressed as a Greek god and lying on a chaise longue as an assortment of mythical creatures fed him grapes. The Minotaur greeted her by name. She had no idea who it was. She managed to lure Giles away from his cavorting long enough to gather that he had not seen Delilah since yesterday, and that as far as he knew no one had come to her flat – oh, apart from an old duck earlier in the afternoon. She had apparently made a scathing remark about the crates of champagne Giles was having delivered.

That must have been Miss King, thought Poppy.

"Anyone else?"

"Sorry, old thing; didn't take much notice. Planning a party. And Delilah had said she would come! Tell her she's a party pooper. But she's still welcome if you find her." Then he turned and threw himself head-first onto a pile of cushions already occupied by – *good Lord, could that really be?* – the ballet dancer Vaslav Nijinsky, dressed as a golden fawn.

Poppy closed the door on the high jinks and hullabaloo and put Delilah's key in the lock. The door opened without a problem; no one had put the security chain on the latch from the inside, which suggested no one was home. As she stepped across the threshold and switched on the light, she let out a gasp. Something *had* happened to Delilah. Her fastidiously house-proud friend would never have left the place in this condition.

"Delilah!" she shouted in vain. *Where are you?* Without a second thought about her own safety, she picked up a hefty brass candlestick and started a frantic search of the flat, desperately hoping she would not find Delilah's injured body – or, God forbid, worse – among the mess.

A couple of minutes later, she had discerned that the flat was indeed unoccupied. No Delilah; no intruders. She put down the candlestick, her hands shaking, and sank onto a sofa. Where could her friend be? And who had ransacked her home? To her untrained eye it looked as though someone had been searching for something. But what? The egg?

Then the doorbell rang. *Rollo. At last!* Poppy jumped up and flung open the door. "Thank heavens you're here! Someone's wrecked the place. I've no idea what's happened to Delilah, and –" It wasn't Rollo. It was Andrei Nogovski. Poppy screamed.

Before she could run, his hand slapped over her mouth and he pulled her back into the flat, kicking the door shut behind them. She fought against him with every ounce of her strength, but it was no good.

"Stop fighting and I will let you go," he whispered into her ear.

For that she stomped on his toes and tried biting his hand. He winced, but didn't loosen his grip. Eventually she went limp – not in surrender, but to woo him into thinking she'd given up. He was not to be fooled.

"I don't want to hurt you, Miss Denby. But if I must, I will. However, if you co-operate, both you and your friend Delilah could come out of this unscathed."

At the mention of Delilah's name, Poppy decided to comply. She relaxed against him, and after a few moments he released his hand from her mouth.

"You have Delilah?" asked Poppy.

"I know where she is," answered Nogovski.

"Where?"

"If I get what I need from you, I will tell you."

Poppy could feel his heart pounding against her back. "And what is it you think I have?" asked Poppy.

"Information that will lead me to the missing egg."

"I have no idea where the egg is," she answered truthfully.

"Ah, but I think you do. You just don't realize it. By the way, you dropped something earlier today."

He released her suddenly and she stumbled, taken by surprise. As she steadied herself she noticed Nogovski was twirling something between his thumb and forefinger. It was a red paper poppy.

"You do get around, Miss Denby. You and your little editor. Here, let me put it where it belongs."

He took a step towards her. She took a step back. He raised his hands. "I'm not going to hurt you."

She stood her ground as he threaded the flower stalk through her button hole.

"So, you were the man in the tunnel. How did you manage to stay hidden while we were in it?"

He cocked his head and smiled. "Oh, you give me too much credit, Miss Denby. I wasn't in the tunnel at the same time as you. It was afterwards. The fellow at the paper shop was – how should I say? – very accommodating when I offered to double whatever Oscar paid him to keep the place secret."

Poppy flicked her eyes to the door and then to the window. She could not see an obvious way of escape. She would have to play along. "May I sit?" she asked. "It's been a long day."

Nogovski gestured to a sofa, playing the genial host. She sat and smoothed down her skirt.

"Well, you have been busy, Mr Nogovski. But wasn't it rather silly of you to return to the scene of your crime?"

"And which crime is that, Miss Denby?"

"The murder of Arthur Watts, of course. The reason you went through the tunnel in the first place."

Nogovski laughed. Poppy was surprised at how full of genuine humour it appeared to be. She had expected something colder, more sinister, from a calculated killer like Nogovski.

"Oh Miss Denby, you are way off the mark. I thought more of you. I did not kill Arthur Watts. But I did go through the tunnel to see if there was something the police had overlooked."

"A Fabergé egg, for instance?"

"Exactly. I did not trust the police to do a thorough enough job. They were too busy trying to nail the killing on that poor fool Oscar Reynolds and the theft on Victor Marconi. They could have missed something." He sat down on an armchair, crossing his long legs as if he were about to have a brandy and cigar in a gentlemen's club.

"The police may yet surprise you. DCI Jasper Martin is a thorough investigator. He has an excellent closure record. I believe it's just a matter of time until he cuts through the fluff and finds out what's what." *And discovers that I've been abducted. And launches a rescue,* thought Poppy ruefully.

Nogovski smiled, but this time it did not reach his dark eyes. "You may be right, Miss Denby, which makes it even more imperative that you do not help them in any way."

"How could I help the police?" she asked.

"You have been piecing this whole thing together and it won't be long before it gets splashed all over the morning papers. Let's just say that it is essential that certain information is not made public. And I'm afraid, as a newspaperwoman, I cannot trust you to do the right thing."

"The right thing? You cannot trust *me* to do the right thing? That's rich coming from someone like you."

There was that laugh again. Oh, she wanted to slap him!

"My dear Miss Denby, I think you might have the wrong end of the stick at the moment." His fingers tapped the handle of his cane. She hadn't noticed it before. But now it was all she could see. She swallowed hard and brought her breathing – and her temper – under control. *Despite what he says, this man is still the most likely suspect in the murder of two people. Two people who were killed with a rapier. A rapier that might very well be secreted in that cane.*

He stood up suddenly and loomed over her. She pushed herself back as far as she could on the sofa. He reached out his hand. "Give me your satchel."

Above the sound of the party next door she thought she heard a motor-car engine. Could that be Rollo? Could he actually save her? If she could somehow alert him that she was in danger…

Nogovski slapped her. It was not a hard blow, but it shocked her. Her eyes bored into his, her anger kindled again.

He bent down and leaned both hands on the arm of the sofa. His voice had lost all warmth. "Stop thinking about trying to escape. We don't have much time. Now, give me your satchel."

She swallowed again, her throat tight, and unslung the shoulder strap from across her chest. He took it and sat down with it on his lap.

If he expects to find the egg in there he's going to be disappointed, she thought. And if she weren't so scared she would have laughed at the absurdity of it. Did he really think she'd been carrying a Fabergé egg around on her person?

But that wasn't what he was looking for. He took out the files, quickly discarding his own without opening it, and then placed Adam Lane's on the table. He flicked through it quickly until he came to the coloured pencil sketch of the emerald and ruby necklace. The one stolen from Selena in Paris. He took out a lighter from his pocket and burned the picture, tossing it into an ashtray to smoulder away.

"Now if you and your friend Delilah want to live, you must forget you ever saw that necklace."

Poppy nodded, trying to hide her bemusement. "Have you got what you need now? Can you tell me where Delilah is?"

He flicked some stray ash from his trousers and then stood up. "Better than that, I can take you. He reached out his hand to help her up, but as he did he brushed against the small stack of files on the coffee table, knocking his own file to the ground. It lay open on the floor, the picture of him, Selena and Lenin topmost – and next to it the picture of the Victorian baby.

Nogovski inhaled sharply and snatched at the baby picture. He pushed it towards Poppy's face. "Where did you get this?" he hissed.

"In – in – it was in Selena's room. And there's another picture on the back."

He flicked the picture over and glanced at the old woman and child. He grunted – was that in recognition? – then flicked it over again. After a few moments of studying the infant he picked up the photograph from Paris, looked at it for a moment, then put all the pictures in his inside jacket pocket.

He then turned to her, his face inscrutable, and said: "We are running out of time."

CHAPTER 36

Outside Delilah's apartment building, with the sound of Giles's party spilling onto the street, was the maroon Chrysler, the same motor that had brought Nogovski and Safin to the theatre after Selena's murder. Poppy wracked her brain again, trying to place it in the vicinity of the Old Vic when she first arrived, but she couldn't. Unlike Adam's old Model T Ford the Chrysler started without the aid of a crank. A man in a chauffeur's hat sat in the driving seat. He nodded to Nogovski as the Russian security agent ushered Poppy into the back seat and sat beside her. Without receiving instruction, the chauffeur started the engine and drove off. As he did, another motor pulled up – a cream Jaguar driven by Marjorie Reynolds, with Rollo Rolandson in the passenger seat beside her and the hulking frame of Ivan Molanov in the back. Marjorie's eyes widened as she spotted Poppy being bundled into the Chrysler.

Poppy tried to gesture to her, but Nogovski pinned her arms down and barked something at the chauffeur in Russian. By the way the vehicle lurched forward, Poppy assumed a rough translation to be: "Step on it!"

"Why don't we just stop?" asked Poppy. "If you're really innocent of the murders and haven't hurt Delilah, then Marjorie Reynolds will be able to help us. She can call on the Home Office; she can –"

"If you value your life, Miss Denby, you will shut up," he hissed into her ear.

Poppy opened her mouth to retort, but then closed it again.

Was he serious? Would he really kill her? *Andrei Nogovski is a very dangerous man...* she heard the voices of Marjorie Reynolds, Ivan Molanov and Constantin Stanislavski repeat in chorus. Yes, he was serious.

So, with Marjorie's top-of-the range Jaguar in hot pursuit, the Chrysler roared its way down King's Road, then turned north. The streets of Chelsea and then South Kensington sped past in a blur, with the Chrysler whipping left and right – but the Jaguar remained close to its tail. It was nearing midnight on a Tuesday and the streets of West London were relatively clear. It was only when they passed the Royal Albert Hall and a late-night concert was coming out that they encountered any traffic. A quick exchange in Russian redirected the chauffeur to a series of back streets – but still the Jaguar stayed with them. *Good old Marjorie,* thought Poppy. *Who would have thought she was such a demon driver?*

The motor lurched to left and right, throwing Poppy onto Andrei Nogovski. He helped steady her, but she doubted the firm arm around her shoulder was purely for her safety.

Poppy looked up and saw they were driving parallel to the wall surrounding Kensington Palace Gardens. "Where are we going?"

"The embassy," said Nogovski. "And here it is."

Poppy had no need to ask which embassy as the gates of the Russian diplomatic residence on Kensington Palace Garden Road loomed before them. They slowed down enough for the guards to see who it was and open the gates. As they did, the Jaguar pulled up behind them. Ivan Molanov leapt out and ran at full pelt towards them, screaming something in Russian. But he was blocked by two guards. Ivan fought like a bull and soon other guards piled in to assist their comrades. Through the now-closed gates she saw the archivist being thrown to the ground as

Marjorie and Rollo stood by. Marjorie screamed: "Unhand him! In the name of the British government, unhand him!" But it was to no avail. Rollo caught Poppy's eye – he looked distraught. She reached out her hand to him from behind the Chrysler back window as the vehicle continued up the drive.

"If you're wondering, Miss Denby, your friends – and the police, if they call them – will be unable to get in. This is sovereign Russian territory. And as long as your government recognizes our provisional government – which so far it has – diplomatic rules declare that on this property we are not subject to the law of the land."

"In other words," said Poppy, "you can do whatever you like to me without recrimination."

"As long as we stay in these grounds, yes. But don't worry. I told you I would not hurt you, and I will keep my word. First though, we must find Miss Marconi."

"Find her?" asked Poppy. "I thought you knew where she was."

Nogovski smiled at her, as if indulging a child. "Well, that was a little fib. I guessed as to her whereabouts when I saw the state of her flat. Someone had been there and I have a strong suspicion as to who."

"Oh?" asked Poppy. "And who is that?"

The motor pulled up at the front door. Guards came to escort them. "I shall introduce you to him now. But please, Miss Denby, for your own safety, do not try to question him. I will do my best to get you and your friend out of this alive. But you must trust me."

He got out of the vehicle and offered his hand to assist her. Trust him? How could she trust him? Why should she? He had hardly given her reason, other than his word, that he would not hurt her – or Delilah. And though he had denied involvement in the murders or the theft, without evidence she was none the wiser.

Then she saw a distinctive, top-of-the-range blue Aston Martin parked under a bay window. Suddenly, everything fell into place. She'd seen that car driving up Waterloo Road from the theatre – not a maroon Chrysler, but a blue Aston Martin. She knew exactly who she was going to meet inside: the man who had killed Princess Selena.

Dear God, she prayed, *give me wisdom – and buckets of it.* Then, without any other options available to her, she put her hand – and her life – into Andrei Nogovski's as he led her into the embassy.

Adam jimmied open the window on the first floor at the back of the three-storey embassy. The architecture offered lots of options for an experienced cat burglar, and Adam was certainly that. Daniel followed his lead, scaling the wall, a man confident in his physicality.

They had arrived at the embassy soon after Rollo, Marjorie and another man whom Adam had never met but Daniel had told him was Ivan Molanov, archivist at *The Globe*. The hullabaloo at the front gate confirmed what Adam had already decided: they would not be entering the embassy by the conventional route. Ivan's herculean effort to fight off the embassy guards was a perfect cover for the two men to park the motor in a side street and then scale the outer wall of the embassy behind a line of oak trees. Once in the grounds Adam expertly assessed the façade in front of him and pinpointed its weakest point.

The window opened and Adam silently slipped in. He held back the curtain for Daniel to follow. The room they were in was used as an office, and, at just after midnight, was unsurprisingly vacant.

"Where do you think she's being held?" whispered Daniel.

"Well, I doubt she's here as an official guest," muttered Adam, "so my guess is it will be the basement. It's a good place to start, anyway, then we can work our way up."

Daniel nodded his agreement and the two men slunk out of the room.

Nogovski and Poppy entered the embassy through the front door. He said something to the man who came to greet them, then ushered her into a small waiting room-cum-cloakroom with a hat and coat stand just inside the door. Poppy had passed the room en route to the main hall where the press briefing had been held the previous week. It seemed like a long time since she had first heard the name Andrei Nogovski, and yet it had been barely seven days. He indicated that she should sit.

"I would offer you tea, Miss Denby, but we do not have much time until Comrade Safin arrives, and I must prepare you for that as quickly as I can. I could not speak in the automobile, as I'm not sure where the chauffeur's loyalties lie. So please, listen carefully. I will answer any questions you may have later – if I can – but for now, do not speak."

Poppy nodded her agreement. She had a hundred and one questions, but they would have to wait.

"As you know, Comrade Safin is the Commissar of Trade and also the interim ambassador. The former imperial ambassador vacated the premises in 1917; then we had a temporary one linked to the provisional government. However, as the war back home appears to be swinging towards the Reds, he, a White, has resigned and claimed asylum."

Yes, yes, I know all that; tell me something new, thought Poppy.

"Safin has been appointed by the Reds, but as the Soviet

government has not yet been formally recognized by your government – they are still foolishly holding out for a White counter-revolution – he is here in an interim capacity. His position – and legal standing – is tenuous, and he realizes he could be turfed out at any time. So that has made him reckless."

Reckless? So my suspicions were correct... Poppy's eyes flicked to the door behind Nogovski, expecting Safin to appear at any moment. But for now it remained closed.

"Safin has been trying to get hold of the eggs. I think by now Marjorie Reynolds has told you their content. The one in Moscow held a key; the one in London, a map to a secret location, and at that location – apart from vast treasure – is information that could bring down every royal house in Europe."

Poppy nodded. Yes, she knew.

"Safin wants to get his hands on that information. He wants to overthrow the old world of ruling dynasties once and for all. He is not patient to wait for the worldwide people's revolution that Comrade Marx and Comrade Lenin have predicted; he wants to bring it on from the top down in one fell swoop."

"But isn't that what you want too?" Whoops, she'd spoken. Poppy bit her lip, but her eyes dared him to chastise her.

He raised an eyebrow and said, "Not at any cost, no. Millions have died in the recent war – and in my country, This is not the way it should happen. I want to stop Safin getting that information and using it for his own ends."

So, he's been acting as a sort of double agent, thought Poppy. *At least that's what he claims.* Not for the first time that night Poppy wondered if she could – or should – trust him. From everything she'd seen so far in this investigation, Safin and Nogovski were in cahoots, working together. Now here he was pinning everything on Safin. Really? Poppy wasn't so sure. Again she looked at the door. It was closed, but not for long.

"So, very quickly," Nogovski continued, "when Safin arrives, I am going to tell him that you have information that will cause the British government to withdraw their support for the provisional government and shut the embassy down. With no diplomatic protection, his crimes can be exposed."

Poppy looked at him quizzically.

"A host of murders, two of them in London, committed *outside* the embassy, for which he can be tried and convicted when he is forced to leave here. I am going to tell him that unless you and Miss Marconi leave the embassy safely, your newspaper will splash all of this over your front page first thing in the morning."

"But we haven't –"

He raised his hand. "I know that and you know that, but Safin does not."

What do you really know about what I know? thought Poppy. But what *did* she actually know? She had no firm evidence, as yet, to prove Nogovski was in on it. For now, all she could do was play along. "All right," agreed Poppy out loud and glared at him, daring him to object. All this don't-speak-unless-spoken-to poppycock was becoming tiresome. "Then what?"

"Then we continue with Safin's own plan of using Miss Marconi as bait to get the egg. But unlike Safin, we will not allow the contents of the egg to be exposed. Are we agreed?"

Bait? Delilah? This did not sound like a very good plan at all. But before she could say anything to the contrary, the door to the sitting room opened and the goateed figure of Vasili Safin entered the room.

As Adam and Daniel slipped down the stairs from the first floor, they heard talking in the entrance hall near the front door and made sure they stayed as far away from it as possible. At the back of the house they entered the kitchen and from there found their way to the basement. Outside a closed door was a man dozing in a chair – a strange place to have a nap. Was Delilah behind that door?

Vasili Safin walked into the room and kissed Nogovski on both cheeks. They spoke for a few moments in Russian. Then he turned to Poppy and said in English: "Good evening, Miss Denby. This is a surprise. Comrade Nogovski here has told me you demanded he bring you here lest you print some scurrilous lies about our embassy's involvement in these recent killings. Is that correct?"

Poppy cleared her throat. "That is correct, yes. I believe you have my friend Delilah Marconi here, and unless she and I are allowed to leave, unmolested, then the article will run first thing in the morning." So far to script.

"And what gives you the impression that I have your friend?" asked Safin.

Hmmm, good question.

"You know what these journalist types are like, Vasili. They have snitches and sources everywhere. We inherited half the staff from the old ambassador; who knows where their loyalties lie?"

Safin barked something at him in Russian.

Nogovski opened his hands placatingly and replied in English: "Yes, I know it was my job to check them. But mistakes are sometimes made. As soon as I find out who it is, they will be dealt with."

This seemed to satisfy Safin, who turned back to Poppy and said: "Well, it's no use crying over spilt milk, as you English say, but the thing is, I cannot let Miss Marconi leave yet. I am still waiting for her friend, the Lane boy, to bring something to me."

He paused, feigning affectation, and said in a theatrical voice: "The dastardly scoundrel has stolen our egg!"

Nogovski laughed along with him. Poppy simply sighed.

Then Nogovski said: "Are you sure this is the best way to get it, Vasili? Perhaps Miss Denby here can talk some sense into Lane. Threatening to hurt Miss Marconi might not be the best approach…"

Safin let off a tirade of Russian which, although Poppy didn't understand the detail, seemed to be directed at Nogovski. Whatever camaraderie there had been between the men was now gone. Could Nogovski have been telling her the truth?

Before she could decide one way or the other Nogovski grabbed her by the arm and pulled her up. "Then perhaps it is time Miss Denby left. Don't worry, Vasili, I shall ensure she does not follow through with her threat."

Safin curled back his upper lip, revealing tobacco-stained teeth. "Oh, I do not think so, Andrei. You see, I know you are bluffing. I too have – how did you put it? – sources and snitches. And my inside man at *The Globe* has told me exactly what's going to be in tomorrow's newspaper – an article by Ike Garfield – and none of what you say is in it. So I wonder, my dear Andrei, what it is you are playing at. His hand reached out to the coat and hat stand, and he pulled out a cane. It looked very much like the one Adam carried. Nogovski seemed to be thinking the same thing, because he pushed Poppy behind him and raised his own cane in defence.

"Let the girl go, Vasili; enough blood has been shed."

In answer, Safin unsheathed his rapier and lunged at Nogovski. Poppy waited for Nogovski to unsheathe his own, but nothing happened. He simply countered the older man's blows with the wood of his cane.

So he is telling the truth! Poppy's heart lurched as she watched while the two men thrust and parried. Without a sword, though, Nogovski was at a disadvantage. She had to do something... She skirted the room looking this way and that, trying to find a weapon or something to use. She saw the coat and hat stand. Without giving it too much thought she pushed it over onto the fencing men in an avalanche of outdoor attire. Both men thrashed to break free, but Nogovski, nearest the door, emerged first. Poppy grabbed his hand and pulled him up. Together they ran out of the room.

In the basement, the snoozing man was knocked into a deeper state of sleep. Adam found a key in his pocket and opened the door. And there, huddled in a corner at the back of a pantry, was a tear-stained Delilah.

Nogovski and Poppy ran through the embassy, heading for the kitchen. Nogovski pushed Poppy towards the back door. "Run. There's a back gate. Go through the park. Get to the palace."

"No. I've got to get Delilah!"

"I'll get Delilah," said Nogovski.

"Actually, no one need get Delilah. I'm right here."

Poppy and Nogovski turned to see Delilah, Adam and Daniel coming up the basement stairs. "Poppy!" exclaimed Daniel.

"No time for reunions now," declared Nogovski and pushed them all towards the kitchen door.

Nogovski led them through the grounds to the back gate. They were challenged by a guard, whom he swiftly and silently dispatched. "Put away the gun, Rokeby. They'll hear it," Nogovski ordered. Daniel stared at him for a moment, then complied. The photographer grabbed Poppy's hand and they ran as fast as they could into Kensington Palace Gardens.

A few moments later, the sound of Russian voices behind them told Poppy they were being pursued. Against orders, Daniel withdrew his revolver, but did not discharge it. Poppy trusted that he would only use it as a last resort. *Please God, don't let it come to that.*

They ran full pelt towards the gates of Kensington Palace – the residence of the Queen Mother and the Household Cavalry that protected her. Poppy's chest burned with every breath, but she daren't slow down. Daniel urged her on. And then, as they broke through the treeline, the lights of the palace illuminated their path. The guards at the gate raised their weapons and challenged them with a "who goes there?". The five of them slowed to a breathless halt. Poppy whipped her head round to see what the Russians would do.

Mercifully, the answer was nothing. The shadows of their pursuers retreated back into the park and Poppy fell to her knees.

CHAPTER 37

The captain of the palace guard interrogated them for over an hour. Then they were searched. Delilah gasped when the purple lacquer diamond-studded egg was removed from its oilcloth and placed on the table of the guardhouse.

"So you see, Captain," said Nogovski, "we are not lying. We have come to return the egg to its rightful owner: Empress Maria Federovna, who is a house guest, I believe, of your own Queen Alexandra."

The guard looked down his nose at Nogovski and said: "Wait here." He muttered an instruction to the other guards to the effect of "shoot the first one who moves" and then went off to speak to someone higher up in the household.

Daniel caught Poppy's eye. She smiled at him, relieved that he was there and safe. But he didn't return her smile. He wore the same worried frown he had in the motor when he took her to task for risking her safety with Rollo. Poppy sighed inwardly. *Oh spiffing, we've still got this to sort.* But now was not the time for a lovers' squabble and thankfully Daniel seemed to think the same.

Delilah, surrounded by handsome men, appeared to have recovered from her ordeal and was anxious to fill in as many gaps as she could.

"So exactly how did you get the egg, Adam?" she asked.

Adam cleared his throat and was about to answer when Nogovski chipped in: "He was keeping it safe for me, weren't you, Lane?"

"Ah yes, I was," answered Adam.

Poppy gave Nogovski a curious look. Why was he trying to protect Adam in all this?

Daniel seemed to be wondering the same thing. "And how, pray tell, did you get your hands on it, Comrade Nogovski?" he asked, not trying to hide the scorn in his voice.

"That does not matter. All that does is that a priceless artefact has been recovered."

Delilah arched her eyebrows. "Oh Comrade Nogovski, you don't expect us to believe *that*, do you? And I do wish you'd stop treating me like a silly little girl who has just got herself kidnapped – well, I did get myself kidnapped, but that wasn't my fault, it's –"

"What Delilah is saying, I think," chipped in Poppy, "is that we've had enough of all these secrets, and that it's time the truth was out."

"Ah, but some truths are best unspoken." They all turned around to look at the door. Wearing a dressing gown and slippers, Prince Felix Yusopov stood with the Captain of the Household Cavalry.

"As the empress's aide, I thought it best to fetch the prince," the captain explained.

"Thank you," said Felix. "I think I can take it from here, Captain. Would you mind asking your men to leave? They can of course stand outside the door, but there are a few things I need to ask these people on behalf of the empress and I would prefer it to be in private."

"Well, I don't know…" answered the captain.

"Perhaps we can wake the Queen Mother then, and ask her permission?"

As it was well after one in the morning, Poppy didn't think the Queen Mother would take too well to being awakened. The captain obviously came to the same conclusion.

"All right, but no one is to leave this room without my permission."

Prince Felix Yusopov gave a mock salute and the captain withdrew his men.

Felix shut the door behind them and leaned on it, his arms crossed. "Well, well, what do we have here?" He looked at each of them in turn, starting with Nogovski. "A spy – sorry, a 'security consultant' …"

"That's rich coming from a murderer – sorry, 'assassin'…" retorted Nogovski.

Felix tutted in mock offence and continued his round of the room. "A journalist, a photographer, an actress and a…" he paused, looking Adam up and down, "a jewel thief."

Poppy flashed a quick look at Delilah, expecting her to be shocked, but she wasn't. She'd no doubt by now figured out that Adam was not just a victim in all of this. As had Daniel, obviously.

"I believe Valetta is lovely this time of year," continued the prince. "Have you had any telegrams from there lately?"

"My father should send one today to say he's docked," replied Delilah.

Felix smiled indulgently. "Not you, little kitten, your boyfriend."

"Senor Swart?" asked Adam.

"At your service." Felix took a mock bow and then pulled up a chair, shimmying himself between Delilah and Adam. He turned to the young actress. "Your boyfriend here has been leading a double life, you know? Stealing jewels for his employer."

"Are you his employer?" asked Poppy, trying to figure out exactly how the assassin of Rasputin could be connected to it all. Selena had suggested before she died that Felix and Irina Yusopov were the ones behind it; had she been right?

"No, I am not," answered Felix. "But I represent that person and have been commissioning Mr Lane since 1912."

"The necklace in Paris?"

"Indeed, Miss Denby, indeed. You have unearthed far more in this investigation than I ever thought you would."

Nogovski said something to Felix in Russian. They conversed for a few moments before Adam interjected in the same language. Both the Russians looked surprised; they had forgotten Adam spoke their language.

Adam turned to the other English people at the table. "Well, now that everything is out in the open, I'll tell you what happened. But first I would like to know from Nogovski why he just told Prince Felix that there was no way of tracing the necklace back to the empress."

Poppy turned to Nogovski and demanded: "Well, answer the man! And at the same time you'd better tell me why you burned the picture of the necklace in Delilah's apartment."

Nogovski looked at Felix and then at Poppy. He splayed his hands on the table. "Well, in the interest of full disclosure, I shall tell you that I was trying to protect the empress from all of this."

"Why on earth would you do that?" asked Felix. "You hate the royals."

Nogovski nodded. "I do, but my mother did not. And it was her wish that I stop the truth coming out that Maria Federovna had been behind the jewel thefts all along. Isn't that correct, Yusopov?"

Felix leaned back in his chair and took a gold cigarette case from his pocket. He offered them round. Both Adam and Delilah took one; Daniel, Poppy and Nogovski declined. "Yes, that is correct. But it is not technically theft. My aunt – the empress – simply wanted to retrieve what belonged to our family in the first place. She saw the way Russia was heading and how her foolish daughter-in-law's dalliance with the mad monk was enraging the people. Unlike the tsar and tsarina, she was not the least surprised when the revolution came. Saddened, but not surprised. So she had been gathering a fortune to support us all if we ever needed to go into exile. But she did not want it to be known, so she came up with this elaborate scheme of pretending they were all stolen, when actually she was simply retrieving presents that had only ever been loaned in the first place. She's always had a touch for the theatrical, my aunt, and I was only too pleased to help her."

"What's all this got to do with the key and the map and the top-secret information?" asked Daniel.

Felix raised his eyebrows in mock despair. "An unfortunate by-product of Nogovski's mother not being able to keep her mouth shut about family secrets – once again."

That's the second time his mother's been mentioned, thought Poppy. *Who on earth...* A thought struck the young journalist like a slap in the face. She scrabbled through the contents of bags and pockets that the guards had taken from them and left in the middle of the table. As her friends looked curiously on, she pulled out the photograph of the baby. She slapped it on the table in front of Nogovski. *Circa 1885, said Miss King, and Nogovski is...* "That's you, isn't it? And Selena is – was – your mother."

Delilah gasped. Felix chuckled.

"Your secret's out now, Andrei. A Red commie with blue blood."

Nogovski glared at him and turned to Poppy, his face inscrutable. "Yes, she was my mother. She had me secretly when she was a teenager. Her aunt – the empress – was the only one who knew, and helped her hide it. At least I thought she was the only one..." he said, tossing a sideways glance at Felix.

"The empress arranged for me to be raised by a decent middle-class family who never knew who I really was. I didn't either until years later when Selena came to see me and told me, tearfully, that she was really my mother. She tried to manage my career, arranging for me first to be her bodyguard and then to get a plum position in the tsar's secret police. But it went against everything I believed in. And eventually… eventually… I broke free."

"But you could not stop protecting her," said Felix.

"No, I could not," agreed Nogovski. "She was a silly woman, but she was my mother. It was I who saved her when she was going to be killed at Yekaterinburg with the rest of the Romanovs…"

Yekaterin-what? Poppy flipped over the baby photograph to reveal the image of Anya Andreiovich and Ruth Broadwood.

Adam gasped. "Where did you get that photograph?"

"Do you recognize them?" asked Poppy.

Adam nodded and told them about the job in Moscow and the massacred family. Delilah's hand went to her mouth. "Oh darling! How terrible for you! How terrible for them! But you say the child got away?"

"I think so," said Adam. "I hoped so. But when I saw that man again at the exhibition and then again in the alley, I feared for the worst."

"What did this man look like?" asked Poppy, although she thought she already knew.

"He was in his mid-50s, had a goatee and carried a cane, just like mine. He must have had it made at the same specialist shop in Moscow that I did."

Nogovski and Poppy caught each other's eye over the table. Daniel noticed and frowned.

"You didn't get to meet the man who called you to the embassy this evening, did you?" asked Poppy.

"No," said Adam, drawing on his cigarette. He exhaled slowly and then said: "We didn't announce ourselves when we arrived, did we, Rokeby?" This elicited the slightest twitch of the mouth from Daniel. *Despite himself, he's enjoying this,* thought Poppy.

"Well," said Poppy, "I think the man you saw in Moscow and the man you saw at the exhibition was the same man who killed Selena and Watts. And that man is –"

"Vasili Safin," finished Felix. "Thank you, Miss Denby; that makes sense. I've been trying to figure out why my silly cousin tried to kill him at the exhibition."

"She *what*?" spluttered Poppy.

Felix ignored her and turned to Nogovski. "Am I correct in saying that Safin was there at the execution of Nicky and Alix and the children?"

Nogovski put his fingers to his temples and started rubbing. "You are," he said. "I tried to stop them, but they wouldn't listen. They killed them all. And if it hadn't been for my intervention, they would have killed Selena and –" he picked up the photograph of Anya and Ruth "– these two as well." He rubbed his thumb over Anya's face. "They had the misfortune of arriving on the very same day as the execution. But I intercepted them and hid them, along with my mother. Everyone else was too busy trying to get rid of the Romanov bodies to notice."

"Who is the child?" asked Daniel.

"It's –" Poppy had been about to answer that it was Ivan's daughter, but she realized that secret was not yet out. And she needed to speak to Rollo about it before she revealed it. So instead she said, "It's the child of a Russian aristocrat. But the more important question is: who is the woman with her? The answer is Ruth Broadwood, a British spy, and the person believed to be carrying the key to this Fabergé egg."

Everyone at the table – apart from Nogovski – looked at her in surprise and then at the jewelled egg. "But before we get to that, can we just pick up on something you said, Prince Felix?"

"Of course, Miss Denby. I'm glad to say you are a much better investigator than you are a dancer." He winked at her. Daniel looked as if he were about to deck him.

Poppy put a restraining hand on the photographer's arm and asked Felix: "What did you mean about Selena trying to kill Safin at the exhibition? Is that why she fired the gun? Did it have nothing to do with the theft after all?"

Felix laughed. "Ironically not. Irina, my wife, had smuggled in the weapon with the intention of letting off a round or two in the air to distract everyone while Lane stole the egg."

"Thanks for warning me," muttered Adam.

"But Selena somehow got her hands on it, and when she saw Safin there, she saw red, muttering something about him killing her darlings. At the time it didn't make sense, but now Nogovski's told us that Safin was at the execution…"

"But – but – how did she get the gun out?" asked Daniel. "We were all searched."

"Not everyone," said Poppy, suddenly seeing how everything fit together. In her mind's eye she had been going through all of Daniel's photographs: there was Selena and Irina and Felix and Adam at the bar and – yes, Vasili Safin. Rollo had remarked that he hadn't noticed him when the police were interviewing everyone. Neither had Poppy. He must have snuck out after the shots had been fired. But it could not have been him who removed the gun. The only person it could possibly be was… "Empress Maria Federovna," said Poppy out loud.

Felix clapped. "Give the prize to the little blonde lady. Yes, Poppy; it was my aunt. I retrieved the gun from Selena and slipped it into my aunt's evening bag. She and her sister were the only people who were not searched. Afterwards I told her about it and wisely she has kept it all to herself. Selena had missed Safin and injured a British guard instead. The Brits would not have taken too kindly to that, and our position here as guests of the Queen Mother is tenuous at best."

Felix stood up and stubbed out his cigarette. "And now, Andrei, I would like to have that key." He reached out his hand.

"You have the key?" Poppy asked Nogovski.

Nogovski looked around at the four other people seated at the table. "What assurances do I have that you will return the key to the empress and that the contents of that egg will never see the light of day?"

"You will just have to trust me, dear cousin," Felix purred.

"That's the last thing I will ever do." Quick as a flash, Nogovski was out of his chair and the prince was thrust against a wall with his throat held in a vice-like grip. One false move and Nogovski would crush his windpipe. "Poppy," he said, over his shoulder. "My shoe. Twist the right heel and it will open."

Daniel reached out to hold her back, but she sidestepped him and got down on her knees. Nogovski raised his heel to give her access. She gripped the leather and twisted to left and right, and sure enough the heel turned and out dropped a tiny key on a silver chain.

"Have you got it?" asked Nogovski.

"I have," said Poppy.

"Then get the map and burn it," ordered Nogovski. Felix tried to protest but was silenced.

Poppy knew that it was the right thing to do. Too many people had already died. It was the only thing that would prevent the incendiary information – whatever it was – getting into the wrong hands. So, with her friends huddled round her, she searched the egg until she found a tiny hole. She inserted the key, turned it and a little trapdoor in the purple lacquer clicked open. Her heart pounding, she felt around inside until her fingers found a folded piece of parchment. *This is it*, she thought as she pincered it between middle and forefinger, and withdrew it. It lay on the table before them.

"Shouldn't we look at it first?" asked Delilah.

"No," said Poppy. "The less we know the better." She reached for the lighter and lit the corner of the map. It took just an instant to disintegrate.

"You're a fool, Nogovski, a fool," croaked Felix.

"Let him go now, Andrei," said Poppy. It was the first time she had called him by his first name. "I'm sure the prince will be only too pleased to negotiate our release with the Captain of the Guard, particularly if he doesn't want certain – how should we say? – *compromising* facts getting into the morning edition."

Nogovski chuckled and released his hold. "Of course, Miss Denby. Your wish is my command."

CHAPTER 38

Poppy and Daniel sat in *The Globe*'s Model T Ford outside an address in Battersea. It was Friday, three days since the drama at Kensington Palace had unfolded.

After Felix had arranged their release, in the wee hours of Wednesday morning, they had all returned to Adam's apartment – the closest address – to crash. Fuelled by a few hours' sleep and a hearty breakfast, Poppy and Daniel had gone into the office, leaving Adam and Delilah still asleep in bed.

Andrei Nogovski had set up a meeting with Marjorie Reynolds and DCI Jasper Martin on Wednesday afternoon, and saw them under the protection of the British Secret Service. What went on at that meeting Poppy had no idea, but the net result was the release of Oscar, the temporary closure of the Russian embassy and the arrest of Vasili Safin as he tried to flee the country.

It was also agreed – after discussions with Felix Yusopov and Yasmin Reece-Lansdale – that no charge of theft was to be laid against Adam Lane, because he had returned the egg to its rightful owner. The foreign charges, which Interpol was investigating, were being dealt with by Yasmin, who now represented Adam, as well as the Yusopovs, Oscar and Rollo in their various predicaments. Poppy doubted the solicitor would be on DCI Martin's Christmas card list this year.

After Poppy and Daniel had filled Rollo in on everything that had happened, Rollo told them what he had found out from Ivan. It seems that he was indeed Vasili Safin's mole at *The Globe*, but Ivan claimed he had only done it because the Russian ambassador had said he had information about his family that he would trade for inside tips. And yes, Ivan had sent the chocolates to Selena, but he swore he knew nothing about the poison. However, he thought Safin probably did, because the ambassador had been the one to suggest the switch in the first place. Poppy had asked Marjorie to arrange for the fingerprints of the "unknown person" to be checked against Safin's. And, unsurprisingly, they matched.

After Rollo had taken down Poppy's story, agreeing for now to be vague about Adam's involvement and also the exact nature of the empress's role, he asked whether there would be a kill fee in the offing from the Romanovs. She said she had no idea, but hoped he would simply do the right thing. "I gave them my word," said Poppy.

Rollo looked at her with a twinkle in his eye and said: "Well, that was rather silly, wasn't it? I'll get Yasmin to thrash out the details with them later. I refuse to sit on all of this, Miz Denby; it's far too good a story."

Poppy couldn't deny that at all. However, the best part of it was what Nogovski had told her on the way back from the palace on Wednesday morning: Sergei Andreiovich's daughter and her nanny, Ruth Broadwood, were alive and well, and living at an address south of the river. Nogovski had smuggled them out of Yekaterinburg eighteen months earlier and had been keeping them, under house arrest, in London, until the Fabergé egg containing the map had been found. Now that it had there was no reason not to let them go.

And so here they were on Friday morning. Nogovski and Ivan knocked on the door while Poppy and Daniel waited for them in the motor.

"Do you think she'll recognize her father?" asked Poppy. "It's been what, six years since she saw him?"

"I don't know. But he'll recognize her. A father will never forget his child," said Daniel. He put his arm around Poppy and they waited for the door to be answered. It didn't take long. A man first, whom Nogovski spoke to briefly, then a woman. Poppy sucked in her breath: it was Ruth Broadwood. The elderly woman looked healthy, and happy to see her visitors. She went back into the house and a few moments later returned with a young girl and, at her heels, a little brown dog. The child looked up at the two men inquisitively. Then Ivan reached down and swept his daughter into his arms.

"I think it's time you met my two," said Daniel, and pulled Poppy closer to him.

"Perhaps it is," said Poppy, wiping away a tear.

THE WORLD OF POPPY DENBY:
A HISTORICAL NOTE
ON *THE KILL FEE*

I got the idea for *The Kill Fee* through a confluence of events and coincidences. After finishing book 1 in the series, *The Jazz Files*, I was doing some background reading to see what historical events might form the backdrop for Poppy's next adventure. I considered taking her to Egypt, so she could get caught up in the intrigue surrounding the discovery of King Tutankhamun's tomb; but that took place in 1922, so was too far in the future.

So what was happening in the autumn of 1920? The event that attracted me the most was the end of the Russian Civil War. But how to tie this in to our Poppy in London...? Three things happened: first, I was reading a fantastic book called *The Russian Court at Sea*, by Frances Welch (Short Books, 2011), about the rescue of Empress Maria Federovna and the surviving Romanovs. In 1919 they were picked up in Yalta by the British warship HMS *Marlborough* and taken to Malta. Now Malta, as fans of the *Poppy Denby Investigates* series know, is where Delilah Marconi's father lives. So immediately my ears pricked up. From Malta they were then brought to London. The empress lived for a while with her sister in Kensington Palace, but then, like most of the other exiled Romanovs, she moved on. She died in Denmark in 1928, still in the firm belief that her son Nicholas and his family were alive.

The year 1919 was a bit too early for my timeframe, but I

skirt over this in *The Kill Fee* by having them in the country for "some months" at the start of the story. In reality they landed on British shores in late May 1919.

So I knew I wanted to have the Romanovs in exile as part of my story, but I was not yet sure of the plot. Then, with a phrase from Welch's book – "rolled-up Rembrandts and Fabergé eggs" – on my mind, I came across an article about a man in America who had bought what he thought was a replica Fabergé egg at a junk sale only to discover, ten years later, it was the genuine article and worth twenty million pounds! The day after I read this article I came across my own Fabergé egg in an Oxfam charity shop in Newcastle upon Tyne. This was most definitely a cheap imitation – the silver paint was already peeling off – but the coincidence was remarkable. I bought the egg for ten pounds, brought it home and started plotting my novel.

A few other deliberate tweaks to the historical timeline have taken place. First, the Russian embassy didn't move to Kensington Gardens until 1927 – previously it was in Belgravia. But I needed it there to allow Poppy and her friends to flee to the palace on foot. A second known anachronism is the selling of the paper poppies. These were launched by the British Legion in 1921 – but I have brought it forward a year to allow for the character of Sarge, and to give Poppy an opportunity to remember her brother and remind readers of the shadow of the war, which plays such a big part in the first book in the series, *The Jazz Files*.

Apart from that, as far as I am aware, I have stuck strictly to the historical timeline; from what music was played at the time to the fashion designers who were in vogue. I'm sure you will forgive me for the few deliberate "adjustments" I made for the sake of the story – and for any unintentional errors you may find on the way.

Finally, before I am accused of character assassination, a few words on the Yusopovs. Felix Yusopov was indeed one of the murderers of Gregori Rasputin. The "mad monk" was killed in the hope that, out of his thrall, the tsarina Alexandra would be open to influence her husband towards reform. Sadly, she did not.

Yusopov and his wife did travel with the empress on HMS *Marlborough*, along with their young daughter. The family moved to Paris from London in 1920 and set up a couture house. As far as I know, they had absolutely nothing to do with the theft of Fabergé eggs – or anything else! Neither did the empress. This plotline – as well as the exhibition at the Crystal Palace – is purely a figment of my imagination. This is, after all, a novel, not a history textbook. And I do hope you enjoyed reading it as much as I enjoyed writing it and will be eagerly awaiting Poppy's next adventure.

FOR FURTHER READING:

Visit www.poppydenby.com for more historical information on the period, gorgeous pictures of 1920s fashion and décor, audio and video links to 1920s music and news clips, a link to the author's website, as well as news about upcoming titles in the *Poppy Denby Investigates* series.

Shepherd, Janet and John Shepherd, *1920s Britain*, Oxford: Shire Living Histories, Shire Publications, 2010.

Shrimpton, Jayne, *Fashion in the 1920s*, Oxford: Shire Publications, 2013.

Taylor, D.J., *Bright Young People: The rise and fall of a generation 1918–1940*, London: Vintage, Random House, 2008.

Waugh, Evelyn, *Vile Bodies*, London: Chapman and Hall, 1930.

Waugh, Evelyn, *Scoop*, (1938) London: Penguin Classics, Penguin, 2000.

Welch, Frances, *The Russian Court at Sea*, London: Short Books, 2011.

For more information and fun photos about
Poppy and her world go to:
www.poppydenby.com

THE JAZZ FILES

POPPY DENBY INVESTIGATES

"It stands for Jazz Files," said Rollo. "It's what we call any story that has a whiff of high society scandal but can't yet be proven... you never know when a skeleton in the closet might prove useful."

Set in 1920, *The Jazz Files* introduces aspiring journalist Poppy Denby, who arrives in London to look after her ailing Aunt Dot, an infamous suffragette. Dot encourages Poppy to apply for a job at *The Daily Globe*, but on her first day a senior reporter is killed and Poppy is tasked with finishing his story. It involves the mysterious death of a suffragette seven years earlier, about which some powerful people would prefer that nothing be said...

Through her friend Delilah Marconi, Poppy is introduced to the giddy world of London in the Roaring Twenties, with its flappers, jazz clubs, and romance. Will she make it as an investigative journalist, in this fast-paced new city? And will she be able to unearth the truth before more people die?

ISBN: 978-1-78264-175-9 | e-ISBN: 978-1-78264-176-6

END OF THE ROADIE

A Mystery for D.I. Costello

"Another gem from Elizabeth Flynn!"

- Cindy Kent, Premier Radio

The gig at the Apollo was a triumph.
Apart from the dead body outside the stage door.

Rock-star Brendan Phelan knows how to thrill a crowd – gunshots and cracking whips punctuate the thudding bass and crashing guitar chords.

But after the show has ended, another shot is fired and Oliver Joplin, long-time roadie, is found lifeless, with a shocked Phelan towering over him.

Detective Inspector Costello is called and quickly discovers Joplin was widely disliked and distrusted. His emails reveal the presence of a shadowy figure stalking the dead man. But who would profit from his death?

Little by little Costello unpicks a tangled web of lies. But secrets have left tongues tied and unless someone breaks the silence, the killer may never be found...

ISBN: 978-1-78264-205-3 | e-ISBN: 978-1-78264-206-0

The Name I Call Myself

"Witty, engaging, funny, and poignant...
chick-lit as it should be."

– Anna Thayer

Who will Faith trust with her past and with her real name?

The good news for Faith is that she has met Perry. He's rich, gorgeous, and has vowed to leave his playboy ways behind forever and marry her.

The bad news is that Perry's mother is planning Faith's nightmare wedding, including the dress from hell.

While dreaming about her ideal ceremony, Faith goes to her mother's church – and ends up joining the choir! Here she meets a man who makes her feel safe, perhaps even safe enough to share the dark secrets that are catching up with her.

Secrets she's not even confided in her fiancé, despite the fact that danger is closing in...

ISBN: 978-1-78264-207-7 | e-ISBN: 978-1-78264-208-4